DARK TRIAD

THE COMPLETE TRILOGY

VIOLA TEMPEST

VIOLA TEMPEST PUBLISHING

Dark Triad
The Complete Trilogy

© Copyright 2024 Viola Tempest

Cover Design by Hannah Sternjakob

CONTENTS

NARCISSISM

MACHIAVELLIANISM

PSYCHOPATHY

NARCISSISM

BOOK ONE OF THE DARK TRIAD TRILOGY

1

Natalia smiled as she settled into her throne. She crossed her long legs, one over the another, her sky-blue skirt falling away from her smooth, ivory legs. The cloth split right to the hip so that her citizens could witness the glory of her limbs in full view as they knelt by her bare feet. She loved when they caressed her ankles in order to kiss the rings that adorned her toes. A show of their adoration and submission to her beauty and her will.

How had she ever lived another way? *Why* had she ever tolerated sifting through the meaningless prayers and gifts sent to God by self-serving humans? They had never recognized *her* beauty, *her* magnificence. She had been a glorified messenger and postmaster; it had been beneath her.

But God had never recognized that. None of them had. Except maybe her insufferable sisters, but she couldn't have trusted *their* judgment, either. They hadn't seen her true potential and beauty, but it didn't matter now. She had her world, and at last, she was getting the recognition she truly deserved.

It was Tithing Day. Natalia looked forward to this day more than any other since it was the time for her citizens to shower her with the love and praise she deserved. Every week, they came to her with gifts, in whatever form they could think of, to prove their undying devotion to their Angelic Goddess.

Natalia tapped her long, perfectly manicured nails upon the golden arm of her throne. Every surface in her Throne Room was a glistening, reflective surface. No matter where Natalia looked, she could see her own perfect image looking back at her. And she felt content.

She ran her tongue along her plush pink lips and blew herself a kiss, her blue eyes sparkling in the golden, mirrored walls that surrounded her. She was *perfection*. God had gotten it right when He'd made her, but even *He* hadn't been able to appreciate her, not really. Hadn't been able to see that she was just trying to show *His* precious humans what *true* beauty looked like.

How could those poor, frail, pathetic little insects learn to be better if they didn't have a proper role model?

Natalia had been the Archangel of Responsibility and Merciful Love; she had been the one to receive the gifts that humanity showered upon God. God had trusted her to reward the righteous and punish the sinners, to show mercy and love, even to those who didn't quite meet expectations. Yet, when she had traveled to lead these stupid humans personally, He had been disappointed in her actions and cast her out.

He had told her that she, *she*, was unworthy. God took her

wings and banished her from Heaven, all because He had said she was too vain, that she thought only of herself and not others. That she wasn't *angelic* enough.

She had never understood that; how could she not be angelic enough? He had made her, He had sculpted her, and she was the perfect version of what an angel should be. Such fools were Him and the rest of Heaven if they were too short-sighted to see the sheer immensity of her presence.

Sending her down to Earth had been the best thing He could do, especially when He'd sent her sisters after her. As much as Natalia could not tolerate them, it had amused her to see them on Earth alongside her. God had underestimated their powers, and had forgotten how perfect *she* was. They had split the Earth in three, forging worlds all of their own where God had no say in how they ran it.

Natalia could *finally* run it as the world was meant to be, where the citizens could bask in all of her glory and strive to be like her. For was she not the most glorious thing they had ever laid their eyes upon?

Of course, she was. And that was *exactly* why they spent every waking minute of their lives surrounded by her image, to remind them just how lucky they were that she had chosen *them* to be a part of her world. Only the most beautiful, the strongest, and most perfect beings could grace her world. As if Natalia would allow anything to mar the flawless utopia that she had carved out for them.

Her world was nothing like the foul mud-heap that God had created. It was a shining beacon of splendor that her citizens could be proud to call *home*. There was no poverty here because there was no need for money. The only thing Natalia's people needed to do was revere her, to spend their days creating gifts for the weekly tithe to show her how much they loved her.

She was a merciful leader. The gifts didn't need to be lavish, though of course, that won her people points if they were. All she needed was for them to prove their reverence for the one who had given them this wonderful life. She was happy enough with songs, poems, or even dances. It didn't matter what they brought, so long as she was at the center of it all. What better muse was there than the most transcendent being in all of existence?

Natalia smiled as she leaned against her throne, tilting her head back so that she could see the two carved, golden wings studded with diamonds that sprouted from her back. She may have lost her own wings, but they had been dull in comparison to the ones her artisans had created upon her throne. These were far more fitting for her.

With a flick of her hands, Natalia opened the colossal golden doors at the far end of the Throne Room. There, her citizens waited, and Natalia giggled excitedly, her heart swelling at the thought of what her people might have made for her this time. She never grew tired of their praise; why in God's name would she?

Biting her bottom lip, Natalia watched as her citizens began to trail into the Throne Room. There was a revered hush that fell over them as they made their way toward her, their heads bowed as they dared not to look upon her beauty. She could be too blinding for their tiny human hearts, she knew that; to be in the presence of sheer excellence was too much for their mortal minds to comprehend.

It only fueled her, only made her hungry for more. Those stolen glances they shot her way, the gasps of fear and ecstasy as they looked upon her flawless visage and saw all that they could never be.

Her people were led forward by her priests and priestesses. Her most devout followers, the ones who truly saw the vision she had for the world she'd created for them, and helped the others become appreciative of her also.

"My illustrious, impeccable, exquisiteness. We bring to you our gifts, that we might bask in your faultlessness and learn to be better. May our gifts grant us your forgiveness for our own flaws in the presence of one who is flawless." Head Priest, Jules, gushed as he fell to his knees at the base of her throne. He shuffled forward on all fours, his forehead scraping along the golden floors as he gently took hold of one of Natalia's feet and kissed her toes.

"Forgiven, Jules, as you always are. Let me see what you have all brought for me," Natalia cooed, kicked him off her foot, and smiled as she watched him scurry away. She caught him sneaking a glance at her and smirked as she heard him sigh with pleasure.

The priest ushered the first of her citizens along so that they could present her with her gifts, and Natalia sat back against her throne, eager to receive them.

"Most beautiful and wondrous, I bring you wings to replace the ones taken from you," one man whispered as he lied at her feet, his arms raised with his gift.

Natalia gasped at the sight of what he'd brought for her. Attached to leather straps were wings that almost mirrored the ones on her throne. The feathers were made from delicate, filigree gold inlaid with hundreds of tiny diamonds to make them truly shine.

Now she had new wings, and they were far grander than anything *God* had ever blessed her with.

2

The area behind Natalia's throne was piled high with the myriad of things her people had given to her. Jewelry, art, poems, stories, songs. Anything that they could think of that might show her their loyalty. A few had even baked for her, a new concept, but one that she had found amusing, nonetheless. She could eat, though she didn't need to. Angels didn't need sustenance in the same fashion that mortals did.

Though she was intrigued to try out some of the things that they had brought her, regardless. To see whether they had made a real effort to make them exquisite enough to be worthy of passing her lips.

However, none of the gifts quite caught her attention like

the handmade wings had. *That* gift remained right by her feet, and she found herself glancing at them regularly, taken by the workmanship and clear love that had gone into it.

The light had begun to fade outside her palace, and the last crowd of her people made their way toward her. While one woman sang Natalia's praises, the fallen angel took a moment to cast her gaze upon the rest gathered around, waiting for their turn. Would she see jealousy on their faces at their fellow's musical talents? Or worry that what they had to offer was not enough?

Most looked away when they caught her eyes upon them, their heads immediately bowed in reverence. Except for two. In the center of the crowd, a man and a woman were looking at each *other* in a way reserved *only* for Natalia. Her eyes grew wide at the sight of the pair, her heart racing painfully in her chest as a red mist began to form in her head.

She had been merciful to these insects, had given them the perfect home where they could have anything they wanted. Where they would never even *die*. Wasn't that what every human had ever asked for? Immortality? The ability to stave off death? Well, she had *given* them that, and all she had ever asked for in exchange was their love, their devotion, their adulation! They were here to worship *her*. They had no need to look to one another, because no one else could compare to what *she* was!

Natalia caught sight of herself on the polished surface of the floor and immediately forced herself to calm down. She refused to allow these pathetic fools to create wrinkles on her smooth skin from scowling. She would speak with Jules and ensure that someone had an eye on the pair. They would soon remember where their priorities laid… and if they didn't, well, she would deal with them then. Wouldn't she? Just like she'd done in the past. Though she really had thought her people had learnt that lesson.

The rest of her gifts felt tainted after that, and she found it difficult not to make some snide comment to the man and woman when they came to offer her their respective gifts. She had to remind herself to keep calm, for now, and just keep an eye on them. They would face her wrath if necessary, but it really would be a waste if she were forced to end their existence. The man was *pretty*.

As the last of her worshippers handed over his portrait of her, Natalia clicked her fingers at Jules, dismissing everyone else with a wave of her hand. She watched her citizens as they hurried from her presence, their heads down as they strode back into the city. Natalia could not help but keep her eyes fixed on the pair who had dared to look at one another in her presence. If they had been vying for her attention, that would have been one thing, but she knew that look. She was experienced enough to see *desire* and recognize it.

"Illustrious Mistress, it is an honor to be alone in your presence. How can this flawed one be of service?" Jules simpered at her, cupping one of her feet in his hands.

"Look up, Jules," Natalia hissed, all her rage in her tone as she reached over and roughly grasped the man's face so that he was forced to look at her. She kept a grip on his chin as she snapped his head around, pointing at the man and woman who had lingered at the back of the group. Their hands touched briefly, and Natalia saw the way they reached out to grasp the other's little finger, her anger rising exponentially at the sight.

"*Them!*" she snarled, the sweet honeyed tone she usually used around her priest now gone. "I am perfection, Jules. I am *everything*. Yet, I can see what they are up to. They do not worship me, Jules; they are blasphemers!" She continued, flicking her hand and throwing him to the floor as she stood up, her bare feet silent as she stepped onto the cold, golden floor. "I want them watched; I want to know exactly what they are up to. I will *not* have them forget their position; do you hear me? How could they look at one another rather than at me? There is *nothing* that either has that I do not have. I am *better*."

"Lady of Perfection! I shall have my people keep an eye on them, and they will be reminded of their place. They are deluded, lost in your beauty, no doubt. How could they not be? I am blinded whenever I am in your presence."

"And your eyes have never strayed to another, have they, Jules?" Natalia asked, looming over her priest.

"Never!" the man replied in a panic, though he didn't move away from her.

"Good. Maybe a sermon or two will remind them of their obligations to me. Let us assume it is a slip in their judgment, a misstep in their desire to have me while knowing that will never be obtainable." She sighed, flicking her loose dark curls over her shoulder, letting them cascade down her back.

Natalia glanced at herself in the reflection of her throne and smiled. She reached up and caressed her own face, her heart lightened as she looked upon her own image. Silently, she chided herself for getting angry, as if those fools would want anyone other than her. Look at her! Even the word *perfect* wasn't good enough to describe her majesty.

She turned back to Jules and knelt beside the loyal priest. Natalia reached out to cup his face with her hands, lifting his head more gently this time with her long, elegant fingers as she smiled at him. Her face smiled back at her in his watery blue eyes as he began to weep at her closeness.

"My loyal priest. Remind my people of how lucky they are. I picked them from all of humanity so that they might live in the opulence of my world. They get to be in my presence and walk in my shadow so that they might better themselves. God never gave you the time, but *I* am here for all of you, in person. Send some of your acolytes to put my gifts in the vault with the rest of the tithe, and keep an eye on that pair for me," she whispered, leaning over to brush her lips against his cheek.

Jules shivered at her touch, and all but melted in her hands as he threw himself to the floor and wailed that he was not worthy, his voice reverberating around the empty Throne Room as Natalia stood up and laughed. Her giggle was a beautiful melody, like a well-composed song. She looked down at her priest as he threw himself upon her feet.

"No, Jules, you *aren't* worthy. But you *are* loyal. Go now, send your acolytes, and do as I ask." She sighed, pulling her feet from his grasp as she strode out of the Throne Room and down the mirrored corridor into the palace proper.

3

Natalia leaned against the railing of the balcony outside her bedroom, surveying her city. When she and her sisters had been banished, they had split the Earth into three separate realms. Small, compared to what they had been as a whole, but their *own*.

Natalia's was naturally far better than the ones her sisters had created. A shining beacon of beauty, where everything was made from gold and diamonds or polished mirrors. On every corner, her citizens could look upon statues carved in her image, so that even if they were not in her presence physically, they always had her with them. Reminding them of how lucky they were to be a part of her world.

Every human in her care resided in her perfectly polished

city. The lamplight setting the buildings aglow during the night, blotting out even the stars. As if stars could even compete with anything that *she* had designed herself. Nothing was more stunning than what she had managed to create here. Her sisters liked to *think* their worlds could compare, but there was no competition in Natalia's eyes. No matter what jibes her ridiculous siblings sent across the void on occasion.

Most of the time, the world was silent, and she was free of their nonsense. Their interference grew less and less as they desperately strived to contend with what she had achieved in no time at all. As if either of them had ever had the talent to challenge her. They weren't nearly as adept at building a world as she was, a fact she had gleefully told them any time they did dare to contact her.

Oh, how grateful she was to be separated from them, and from Heaven. Here, she could create her paradise, just as it should have been. God had been a fool, just as her siblings were. He may have created her, but she could tell that He was jealous of her potential, of just how amazing He'd made her. She could challenge Him; that had been the problem, and she knew it. That was why He'd forced her from Heaven. Whatever, in the end, she was victorious, and look at all that she had achieved!

Natalia smiled as she watched the crisp, clear water spout from one of the many fountains in the city. Tiny diamonds cascading over the golden statue of herself holding her arms wide to embrace her people. To give them a glimpse of her brilliance.

Most of the city had gone to bed, though a few of her people still gathered in the glistening streets, their voices drifting lazily on the cool night air to her balcony. She couldn't quite hear what they were saying, though their tones were soft and full of love, so she assumed they were discussing her. Tithing Day really *was* what they looked forward to the most, given how they could bathe in her greatness. In person, no less.

In the back of her mind, the man and woman still bothered her. It was like a knife to her heart, seeing them look at one another that way. Natalia grinned and bit her bottom lip as a plan formed in her mind. She had asked Jules to deal with them, but she could do it so much better. They had slipped, that was all, a momentary blip in their loyalty due to their longing to be with her, to be like her. Maybe she would give them a taste, just a little, do them the honor of allowing them a glimpse of her.

"Acolyte!" she called, turning away from the balcony.

The blue chiffon nightgown she wore swirled around her silken skin, barely covering her slender, curvaceous frame, given how it was all but transparent. She had no shame; why would she? She loved to look upon herself as much as her people did, and why would she deny them a peek at her?

A young woman hurried into her bed chamber, blushing bright red as her eyes flickered over Natalia's all but naked frame. The girl threw herself to the floor, her forehead pressed against the cold, golden floor, eyes closed tight. Natalia smiled. How sweet, the poor girl didn't dare allow herself a proper look, even with the reflection on the floor.

"You called for me, my Lady of Brilliance," the girl whispered.

"Seek out Head Priest, Jules. Tell him I want to see the man that he and I discussed earlier. Tell Jules to bring the man here to my bedchamber," Natalia ordered, tapping the girl with her foot. "Hurry now."

"Yes, my Lady of Glorious Perfection!" the Acolyte replied, kissing Natalia on her foot before she hurried backwards, still not daring to open her eyes until she was almost out of the room.

Natalia sighed contentedly and moved to the huge four poster bed that dominated her room, collapsing onto the soft, marshmallow-like mattress and staring at herself in the mirror above the bed. Why she hadn't thought of this before, she had no idea.

The passage of time meant very little to Natalia as she stared at herself; after all, it was her favorite activity. She could never grow tired of looking at her curves, or the way her curls fell around her shoulders. She loved how blue her eyes were in the dim lamplight, glistening like diamonds freshly cleaned in a cool, clear river.

A knock on the door heralded the arrival of her guest, and Natalia grinned as she sat up, leaning her head on her hand while she looked at the door.

"Come in!" she called.

The mirrored door swung open, and the man from the tithe was pushed into the room roughly by the acolytes. Natalia smirked as she saw the pair glare at the man as they shut the door behind him. They knew what he was here for, even if he might not, and they hated him for the reward coming his way.

"Don't be shy. You may approach," Natalia cooed at the man, swinging herself upright. Her legs dangled over the edge of the bed, the chiffon rising to reveal her legs—not that the material really covered them, anyway. "What's your name?"

"Adam," he replied, barely looking up from the floor as he shuffled his way slowly toward the bed.

"Adam," Natalia repeated, enjoying the sweet irony in his name. How Biblical.

She looked him up and down, enjoying the look of him. He was tall and muscular, lightly tanned with light brown hair that was clearly well-maintained. Short enough to stay out of his face, but with enough length that she would be able to get her fingers through it. Like all of her people, he was good-looking.

Natalia and her sisters had picked their citizens, and

Natalia had ensured that all of the best-looking humans had been brought to her world. She hadn't given her siblings much choice in the matter, and it wasn't like they could have argued with her, anyway.

Slowly, Natalia got up from the bed, moving with purpose toward Adam, watching his deep brown eyes in the reflection of the floor as he gazed at her legs from there. She stopped in front of him, and lifted his face with her fingertips, forcing him to look at her.

"Do you find me beautiful, Adam?" she asked, already knowing the answer.

"Y-yes!" he replied quickly as he stepped back, taken by surprise at the question.

"What about me do you find beautiful?" she continued, striding around him, her fingers brushing against his collarbone as she let her eyes take in his figure.

"You're perfect… your skin is flawless, pale like quality ivory with the slightest golden glow that blinds you when the sunlight hits it. Your eyes—oh gosh, your eyes—are the deepest pools of blue that see into my soul." He whimpered as she appeared in front of him again, those very eyes fixed on his, glinting back at her from his brown orbs.

Natalia smiled. "Go on," she whispered huskily, her hands on her hips as she pushed out her chest, watching the effect that she had on him.

He let out a soft, guttural growl, and she knew she had him. There was no resisting her because there was no one better than her. Impulsively, he reached out, his fingers hesitating just millimeters from her as he trembled, too afraid to let himself touch the sheer perfection of her frame. Natalia smirked, grasped his hand, and pulled him against her, her arms around his neck as she pressed her lips to his.

Adam responded to her touch without any further prompting, and Natalia let him indulge his urges without complaint. He carried her to the bed, and she enjoyed watching him devour her in the mirror, her skin flushed against his touch to give her the rosy hint she loved to see upon her body. Adam was inconsequential, just another lover to amuse herself with while she watched her own wondrous form in the mirror. He would forget the other woman now, because now, he'd touched Heaven itself.

4

The acolytes had retrieved Adam from her bed while Natalia slept, much as they did with any of the other lovers she deemed worthy enough to sleep with at the time. Natalia enjoyed taking a lover; it allowed her a chance to see herself in a different way—hence the mirror over her bed—and it gave her citizens something to strive for with their gifts. In the hopes that, maybe, she would call upon *them* to her bed chamber.

Natalia was confident that Adam's priorities would now be reset. He'd had a chance to experience *real* pleasure, and there was nothing that the woman she'd seen him making eyes at during the tithe could offer him now. Nothing.

She'd had female lovers on occasion, and it was an

interesting experience that she would no doubt indulge herself in again at some point. Natalia was sure that Adam would go back to whomever the woman was, brimming with his newfound confidence, and dismiss her entirely. Then the woman would remember where *her* love should really be placed.

Shifting in her bed, Natalia indulged herself in her own reflection, just as she did most mornings. Exploring every inch of her skin with her eyes and hands. She tutted at the red marks that Adam had made on her pale skin where he'd forgotten himself in his desperation to touch her. They'd go quickly enough, but she hated how they looked on her usually pristine skin. No matter, she would cover them with some of the clothing and jewelry her people had brought for the tithe.

She sighed as she finally dragged her eyes away from her form. She would go and entertain herself in the vault; it was only right that she spent some proper time admiring the things that her citizens had made for her. After seeing Adam and that woman making eyes at one another, she had allowed herself to become distracted from her last gifts, and she wanted to pay them proper attention. That, and she wanted her *wings*.

Natalia smiled at that thought. She didn't need real wings when she had that magnificent pair. They were so much better than the pure white, boring, feathered ones she'd been created with.

As she pulled on a sparkling dress that hugged her curves —slitted up both sides all the way to her hips to reveal those long slender stems of pure ivory beauty—she stared at herself in the mirror, glancing at the place her wings should have been. It had been so long since they'd been there that she couldn't really remember how they had looked. They couldn't have been all that impressive, though. If they had, she would have felt *something* at their absence. But she didn't feel anything. Lighter maybe, but there was no longing or regret when she looked at her wingless reflection.

Natalia blew herself a kiss as she twirled in front of the mirror. Taking in every angle of herself before she gave herself a nod of approval. Had she ever *not* approved of herself? No. Of course not. Every outfit she chose was handpicked to accentuate her attributes. Hugging every curve, boosting her bust, and emphasizing the sweet peach that were her buttocks.

She strode across the bedroom and threw open the colossal door, smirking as the acolytes that loitered in the hallway, guarding her room, gasped and fell to the floor.

Jules' followers were as devout as they came. The man had been a priest for God before her fall from grace and the subsequent split of the world. Natalia had always thought it was such a waste, that a man as pretty as Jules had taken a vow of celibacy. Then again, the entire ideal of celibacy had seemed utterly ridiculous to Natalia anyway. Why give humans the pleasure of attraction to one another if you were then going to tell a select bunch of them that being together was a bad thing?

Merciful. God wasn't merciful. He was a hypocrite! Natalia had been loyal; she'd been devout; she'd done her duty. He just didn't like it when she'd pushed back against him. He'd made her too gorgeous, too perfect, and He had resented her for that! He always had to have what *He* wanted; why couldn't she have the same? It wasn't as if their morals were all that far removed from one another... not really.

Natalia snorted, flicking her hair over her shoulder as she strode down the corridor toward her vaults. Her image flashed at her from the corner of her eyes. Long, pale legs reflected back at her with each stride, the mirrors caressing her every movement.

The vault laid in the center of her palace, guarded at all times by Jules' followers. Not that Natalia worried about her people stealing anything; they knew better, and they would only be adding to the collection in a week's time, anyway. So, what was the use of taking something that would only be replaced?

The acolytes opened the doors for her, and Natalia giggled with delight at the giant mound of gleaming items that awaited her attention. All for her. The doors closed behind her, leaving Natalia with all the privacy she needed to enjoy her belongings. She was surrounded by splendor. Glinting gems and trinkets of all shapes and sizes, custom made for her enjoyment, all to prove the love that her people had for her.

Natalia had allowed the acolytes access in order to organize her presents. They had sectioned the vault, placing paintings in one space, sculptures in another. Jewelry hung on intricate stands, or in great heaps on ornate golden tables. Poems and songs and other presents all kept together, categorized for ease of access.

And there, her new favorite. The crowning glory of her collection.

Jules had obviously coordinated having a mannequin set up in order to display her new wings in all their beauty. After all, something as ornate as the wings should *never* just be placed on the floor. It had hurt enough to place them at her feet during the tithe. She really would have to reward the priest at some point. He did deserve a little more recognition than she'd given him.

Sighing softly, Natalia ran a delicate finger over the edge of the exquisite feathers, taken by the workmanship that must have gone into the piece. It couldn't have taken the man just a week; he must have kept this project a secret until it was ready for her.

They were *perfect*.

And she would be even more perfect wearing them.

5

Who knew how much time had passed since Natalia slipped the leather straps of the wings over her arms and tightened them in place with a strap above and below her breasts? She had lost herself to her image, as she did most days. Twirling and spinning and giggling as she sighed at her reflection in the mirrored walls of the vault. Taken aback by *just* how perfect her new wings were.

Nothing could have suited her more. She should have been *born* with wings this magnificent. Just another point to prove how God had tried to suppress her wonder. But her citizens understood her grandeur, and this man had sought to give her a pair of wings *worthy* of her stature. She needed to see him. Anyone who could make feathers this delicate, and with such love, was worth having by her side. She needed to hear how he loved her. She could *see* it, but she wanted to listen to him as he listed the ways he thought she was impeccable.

"My Lady of Bewitchment and Wonder, I apologize for the interruption, but one of your citizens is in a terrible state outside and wishes to see you immediately," Jules spoke softly as he hurried through the doors that his acolytes opened for him. The priest skidded across the floor as he threw himself to his knees with some force.

"Oh?" Natalia turned to face her priest, unhappy at the thought of being dragged away from her things. There were still plenty of items from yesterday's tithe to indulge in.

"He has spent the morning weeping at the doors, begging to be granted an audience with your most perfect visage," Jules added.

Natalia grinned, biting her bottom lip as her heart did a somersault in her chest. It had been a while since any of her citizens had gotten themselves this worked up. Most spent the week contemplating the time they'd been given on tithe day, working on their gifts for the next week.

"Alright, I'll see him. Poor thing. Who can blame him for needing to be close to me? I'll meet him in the Throne Room; you can let him in. Oh, Jules, I want you to find the maker of my wings for me. He's done such a wonderful job, and he needs to be properly rewarded."

"It *is* the maker of the wings, my Lady of Sublime Divine Light," Jules replied, looking up at Natalia, his eyes lingering a little *too* long on her exposed thigh. Though she didn't mind, it always amused her to see Jules shiver in excitement when he looked at her that way.

"Oh, he must be eager to see me with my wings! The finished product!" Natalia clapped happily, stepping over Jules, her dress flapping behind her with the speed of her stride. "Give me a minute or two to settle upon my throne, Jules, then you may let him in. And I want *privacy*!" she snapped, hurrying down the corridor, the wings heavy upon her back.

Natalia grinned as she saw her *new* image reflected on the walls, floors, and ceilings of her palace. Her wings shone brightly as the light glinted off the diamonds and gold. She had always been beautiful, but her new acquisition gave her a whole new glow that she had never anticipated. Maybe she would have the man make her a crown worthy of sitting atop her head. Something similar to his previous work for her that complimented her perfectly weaved locks.

Her skin flushed with excitement at that thought. An ornate crown. It amazed her that none of her citizens had ever made her such a gift before. Maybe they had not wanted to ruin her hair, since there was never a strand out of place upon her head. She didn't blame them for that, but a crown was definitely what she needed. She would make sure the wing-maker crafted her the finest coronet that had ever been produced.

Natalia settled upon her throne, dangling her legs over one of the arms so that her dress fell away to reveal them in all their glory. She knew that they were one of her best features. One of many. And she took great pride in her long, elegant limbs. She would never taint them or restrain them with pants or anything like that. They had to be free for all to gaze upon with awe and delight.

Leaning her head upon her hand, Natalia watched as Jules' acolytes hurried to open the doors to allow her guest into the Throne Room. A smile lingered on her face as the sunlight streamed into the room, glistening upon every surface until it was almost blinding. A representation of her own bedazzling brilliance, of course.

"Come forward, citizen. Head Priest, Jules, says that you are in distress. What afflicts you so? Do you not rejoice at being one of the chosen few brought into my world? One of those fortunate enough to relish in my presence?" Natalia cooed, her skin tingling with the anticipation of hearing him heap praise upon her.

"Lady of Brilliance, I could not be more overjoyed at having been chosen by the most magnificent being in all of existence. There is no one who compares, no one who could. There are no words that can describe *just* how wondrous you are, try as I have every tithe to show you *just* how much I adore you," the man whimpered, crawling toward her on his hands and knees, his voice reverberating around the empty chamber.

"Yet, was it not you who crafted my wings?" Natalia asked, reaching back with a hand to caress her feathers with her fingertips.

"It was! For my Lady of Grace and Supremacy deserves wings to match her glowing visage. Though they pale in comparison to your beauty. Nothing in existence can hope to compare with your radiance," he continued, his voice a sharp keen as though he fought against a grieving heart to say those words.

"Then be happy! You gave me wings that even God could not provide! Fear not, you can remain at my side and bask in all of my wonder. Join the acolytes, become my priest—just like Jules—and you can bathe in the splendor of my presence daily. I have a task for a man as skilled as you, but I would have you here by my side so that you might tell me every day how much you love me. Would you like that?" she whispered, swinging her legs from the arm of her throne so that she could lean forward.

She felt the wings shift their weight on her back, threatening to topple over her head as she leaned toward the wing-maker. Thankfully, the straps held, and Natalia was more than strong enough to carry their load without even blinking an eye.

The man lifted his head slowly and dragged his eyes from the floor, as though he were still afraid to look upon her. Natalia smiled and pursed her lips at him, as though she were considering a tantrum if he even dared to contemplate denying her request. As if he ever would!

Suddenly, the man was on his feet, and Natalia gasped.

Something cold and sharp pressed against her throat, and Natalia sat still, wincing as she swallowed, feeling the edge of the knife press into her skin. Her nerves set on fire, and her skin prickled as the thought of the blade cutting her sank into her mind. Even when God had torn away her wings, Natalia hadn't been afraid, but the thought of this *lowlife* marking her in any way, now that brought fear into her heart.

"I would like that more than anything. My *wonderful* Lady, but I cannot risk them taking you from me, not now. Not ever!"

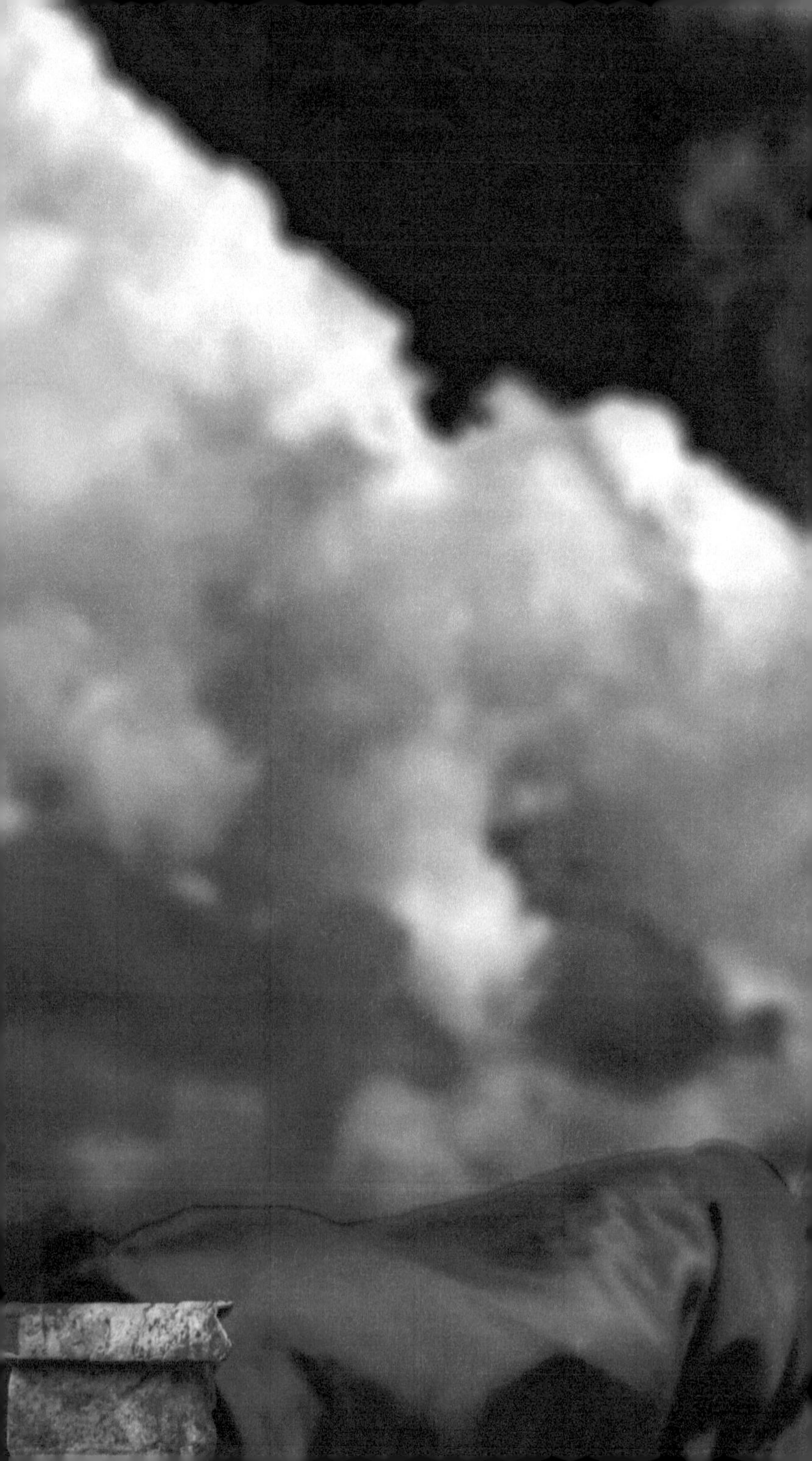

6

Natalia took a slow, deep breath in through her nose, forcing herself to calm down. The man had one arm wrapped around her chest, his hand upon her shoulder to force her back against her throne. The wings he had so lovingly made for her—for there was no denying the devotion in each filigree feather, so tenderly crafted and put together in honor of her—pressed painfully into her shoulder blades as she sat back. His other hand held the knife to her throat. Her skin might have been ivory, but it was as soft as the skin of a peach and would cut and bruise just as easily if she resisted him.

How dare he? *How dare he?* Rage raced through every fiber of Natalia's being, her veins blazing with her fury as she felt ready to burn everything around her. He'd been quick, but she'd been too slow. She had never even seen it coming, the glint of the knife only registering with her moments after she felt the cold steel against her skin. She would see that blade plunged hilt deep into his damn eye before the day was through.

"Why?" she hissed, her perfectly manicured fingernails scraping along the golden surface of her throne as she forced herself not to move.

"Because I cannot bear it. They talk in the dead of night when your devotees go to sleep. I've heard their whispers. Always whispering! They thought I slept, but Samuel was too busy crafting, too busy building wings for his mistress. I couldn't sleep, not until you had wings to wear, so that you might soar above this city, away from these *fiends*. But I cannot make you fly. My wings cannot help you soar above the clouds, away from harm, away from *them*."

"What are you talking about?" Natalia snapped, wincing as she felt the blade press closer to her throat. If he made even the smallest mark, she would ensure he suffered a long, slow death rather than the quick one she had originally envisioned for him.

"The one you took to bed last night. The one they call Adam. He is one of them, one of the demons who sought to harm you. But you seduced him, and the fool was heartbroken when your acolytes came for him. He couldn't cope with being taken from your side, and so he killed himself because he would never be as beautiful as you, nor would he ever feel that way again! But his friends still plot. I hear them, always plotting," Samuel continued in a hushed tone as he moved to place his cheek against Natalia's. "They want to mar my Lady's face! They want to cut her up and leave her alive so that she can be less beautiful than they. Jealous! That's what they are! They're all jealous!" Samuel snarled angrily.

Natalia saw her chance. In his anger, Samuel had loosened his grip, and it was enough for Natalia to take advantage. Though that had only been a matter of time, as though she would allow such an insect to *actually* do her any harm!

She felt the knife move away from her throat, and Natalia's hand snapped up to grip Samuel's wrist. She twisted it hard until the man howled in pain, and she twisted it some more. The bone in his arm snapped, the sound echoing off the walls of her empty Throne Room, but she didn't stop. Natalia turned his arm again and again, but his body could not follow to relieve the pain now coursing through him. Instead, his agonized howls drowned out the sound of the continual snap of his arm as bone and sinew gave way to the pressure that Natalia put upon it. At last, she took hold of his upper arm and threw him across the chamber, his body skidding across the floor one way, the knife another.

The inner doors of her palace slammed open as her priests and priestesses hurried into the room, led by Jules, the acolytes scurrying along behind their elders.

"My Lady!" Jules squealed, hurrying across the hall toward Natalia as she strode toward Samuel.

She tore the wings off her back and cast them aside with a snarl. Her face scrunched up in disgust as she looked over the man now cowering at her feet, cradling his shattered arm against his chest.

"You talk of others plotting against me, and yet it is *you* who holds a knife to my throat?!" Natalia screamed, kicking Samuel onto his back and pressing her foot against his chest until she felt his lungs strain for breath beneath her weight.

"I could not bear the idea of them hurting you! I would rather kill you and preserve your body in its perfection than have them cut you out of spite for their own failings! They will never be as beautiful as you, not ever, not *ever*!" Samuel screamed.

Natalia snarled, pressing her foot against Samuel's throat, reveling in the feeling as his windpipe snapped. She closed her eyes and gave a soft, satisfied sigh as she twisted her foot. Her toes pushed through skin and sinew. Hot, thick blood gushing over her ankle as Samuel's head literally popped off his neck, rolling across the floor.

She wiggled her toes, sighing as she felt the blood start to coagulate upon her skin. Tacky and wet. Opening her eyes, Natalia's nose wrinkled at the thick red pool pouring from Samuel's severed neck. His dead eyes stared at her where his head had rolled away, a trail of red leading from his body to where it had stopped.

"M-my Lady?" Jules stammered, dragging Natalia back to her senses.

"Get rid of him, and find Adam. If this man was right, then you'll find him dead. It would appear that some of our citizens have forgotten their place and their love for me. I won't have it, Jules, I won't. They are supposed to *love* me!" she wailed, stomping her foot hard on the floor with a sickening slap as the blood sprayed up from around her.

Jules crept around Samuel's headless frame, his head low as he cowered before the raging form of Natalia. This was *not* how this was supposed to be! She had given these ungrateful insects *everything*, and she wouldn't stand for this.

"I will find the perpetrators, my Lady, have no fear. I shall have them punished for conspiring against you. They will be dragged to the steps and made an example of; they will be reminded of why they live such good lives. That they owe everything to you, as you say, and that their love and devotion are the *least* they can give." Jules snarled through gritted teeth as he picked up Samuel's decapitated head. Blood dripped from the wound on his neck, tiny sickening splashes echoed in the Throne Room as silence fell amongst those gathered around Natalia.

"Bring me their names, Jules! I want to surprise them

myself. I need to *see* it for myself. This fanatic could have been telling me lies in order to try and save his own skin. To justify his actions. I want to know if what he said is *true*. Then I will deal with it," she hissed.

Natalia stared at the body at her feet and let out a wail of despair. Her legs were tainted by the blood drying to her skin; it was already itchy, and she felt disgusted standing there in such a revolting state.

"Hush, hush, my Wonderous Perfection! My girls have already gone to run you a milk bath with rose petals. We will have your skin cleansed and pristine in no time; have no fear, my Lady. Jules will deal with this supposed insurrection; *we* will take care of you." Helena's soft voice spoke to Natalia, and she jolted as the Head Priestess placed her hands gently on Natalia's back and elbow, steering her away from the mess. "Acolytes, deal with the body, and clean up this mess. I will not have Lady Natalia's magnificence in the presence of this *pollution*."

Natalia took a deep breath, whimpering as she leaned her head upon Helena's shoulder, allowing the woman to cradle her as the priestess led her out of the Throne Room. She would be perfect again soon, and then she would fix whatever crack had started to form in her people. Before it became a chasm.

Helena had led Natalia to her room, gently guiding the distraught former angel to her ensuite bathroom where Helena's young priestesses had already drawn Natalia a bath.

The bathroom was a stunning display of marble and mirrors. The smooth golden-white stone had been carved in Natalia's image, surrounding the large circular bath in the center. The central statue depicted her over the bath, her hands cupping a lotus flower as fresh water poured from the petals, continually refilling her tub. Everything glistened. Bright and beautiful, and Natalia felt calmer.

The priestesses hurried to attend to her, carrying golden bowls filled with fresh clean water and sponges. They helped her to undress, tossing aside the soiled clothes as they hand washed her legs with slow, gentle movements. Their tender caress made Natalia smile, and the heaviness weighing upon her heart lifted as steam rose around her.

"Come, my Lady, let us take proper care of you," Helena whispered, offering her hand to Natalia and leading her to the bath.

Helena was one of the oldest humans Natalia had picked. Where almost all of her citizens were young, the Head Priestess had been the odd exception. Something about her stunning sapphire-colored eyes, with flecks of green, and the slight wrinkles on Helena's handsome face had attracted Natalia greatly.

"I wear my age well," Helena had said once, and Natalia agreed. Where ordinarily, she would have balked at the idea of lines, or any sense of aging whatsoever, Natalia enjoyed Helena's older look.

Where Jules dealt with the city, preaching Natalia's greatness to the citizens and overseeing Tithing Day, Helena and her priestesses tended to Natalia directly. The priestesses loved to dote upon her, and any chance they got to physically touch her, indirectly or otherwise, made them ecstatic. Natalia reveled in their excited shivers and eager whispers whenever she graced the girls with her presence.

Natalia stepped up into the bath, humming softly in delight as the hot water kissed her skin. The milk and minerals that Helena and her girls had filled it with were silky smooth against her bare flesh. The soft scent of the roses brought a calm to Natalia's mind as she slipped into the water that rose up to her shoulders.

She lied back, her hair creating a halo above her head as she floated on the surface, her hands swirling through the water. She smiled as she felt the petals catch in the tiny whirlpools that she made, their feather-like texture brushing against her palms.

"My poor Lady has had such a fright." Helena sighed as she settled at the edge of the bath, placing a golden jar on the edge that contained the smelling sand Natalia used to cleanse her skin. "Jules better find out if those rumors are true, and be quick about it, or I'll send *my* girls to do *his* job."

"Jules will be fine, Helena. Has he not been as loyal as you since I took you all into my service?" Natalia asked, sitting up and turning to face the woman, her wet, dark curls sticking to her perfectly chiseled features.

Helena smiled and reached out to brush the curls away from Natalia's face. The older woman was the only one bold enough to touch Natalia without prompting, a fact that amused the fallen angel.

"He has, but that is out of his lust for you, not his love for you." Helena snorted, patting the side of the bath with her hands.

Natalia rolled her eyes and smiled as she lied back, flicking her hair over the side so that Helena could rub the sand into her curls and cleanse her of any potential muck left over from her fight with Samuel. Helena had made the observation about Jules' lust on several occasions, though Natalia didn't really care for the distinction. As long as the priest adored her, Natalia didn't care what capacity it fell under. Love was love, and she deserved all of it.

"Why have I not heard these rumors before?" Natalia asked, raising an eyebrow at the woman as Helena massaged her fingers into Natalia's hair. "Surely, if what Samuel said is true, there would have been *some* indication of this before now."

"Not to my knowledge, my Lady, but then again, does that not fall under Jules' list of responsibilities? Has *he* not boasted control over your citizens?" Helena added.

"*I* am in control of them, Helena," Natalia warned carefully, her tone low and dark.

"Of course, my Lady, but you know what I mean. Jules

was the one who began the services, who took charge of organizing the tithe with his acolytes. It is he who says he ensures that the city properly pays their respects to you, and yet the first we hear of this issue is through the ravings of a madman?" Helena snorted again and shook her head. "He may be loyal, but are his followers?"

The thought troubled Natalia, and she scowled. Jules could be trusted, but was Helena right? Were his priests and acolytes to be fully believed? Or could *they* be keeping secrets from her?

"Don't scowl," Helena whispered, her lips brushing against Natalia's ear like a butterfly's kiss.

Natalia sighed and relaxed into Helena's sweet touch, her body light and airy as the other priestesses slipped into the bath in order to rub her body with the smelling sands, massaging her muscles to help her stay calm.

"It is probably just a rumor and nothing more. I cannot fathom how *anyone* could not love and adore you. I can understand being jealous; you are everything we cannot be, but it has never stopped me from loving you, my Lady." Helena exhaled, running her fingers through Natalia's hair to ensure that there were no knots. "The man must have been insane. His obsession with how much he loved you having driven him mad. It's a wonder we all don't lose our minds being so close to you."

"Yes… that would make sense. Poor Samuel… to love me so much that his mind snapped like a brittle twig until he saw danger in every corner. I cannot blame him for that. He worked so hard to make me the most perfect pair of wings… Oh! My wings!" Natalia wailed, slamming her hands down in the water and causing the girls bathing her to jump.

In her anger and frustration at Samuel's actions, Natalia had smashed her precious wings. All the love that he had poured into crafting every feather was now ruined.

"Oh, they were perfect! And I wanted him to make me a

crown to match them!" She bawled.

"Hush, hush now!" Helena whispered, cradling Natalia's head between her hands to stop the woman from flailing in the bath. "We will find another citizen to re-make them. It will take time, but we will have them fixed and ensure that a crown is made to match them. Have no fear, my Lady, I will not see you go without the gifts that you truly deserve."

The bath was just what Natalia had needed. Helena and the other priestesses managed to fluff Natalia's ego sufficiently, and her inner calm had returned to normal. Helena was right. How could her people *not* love her? It was such a ridiculous notion! Though she did appreciate that maybe she could make some of them lose their mind, to love so fully as Samuel clearly had until his mind had broken… It was tragic. Well, she supposed it was; hardships of that kind didn't really come into Natalia's life.

Having been pampered by her priestesses, Natalia returned to her vault in order to fully enjoy the gifts her people had brought her. If they hadn't loved her, they would never have made such wonderful gifts, now would they? Of course not! It was preposterous to even think such a thing. Poor Samuel, he truly *had* lost his mind.

"M-my Lady?" Jules's voice called out to her nervously.

Natalia turned toward him and smiled. Her piteous priest, clearly worried that she was still angry following the encounter with Samuel. She opened her arms to the man and beckoned him to her, grinning as Jules hastily threw himself at her, clinging to her waist as he fell to his knees. She cradled his head and patted him gently as one might a pet, sighing softly at the pathetic creature she called her Head Priest.

"He was right, my Lady. Adam is dead. He killed himself once he returned to his house, but he's not the only one; there are others who have strayed. My acolytes saw it with their own eyes. *Images,* my Lady, not of yourself! Samuel was telling the truth."

8

"Someone is losing control!" Azazel's scathing tone called across the ether.

Natalia shrieked irritably in response, launching the golden plate that she had been gripping tightly across the vault. It bounced off a wall and clanged loudly as it crashed back onto the floor, spinning for a moment before finally coming to a stop.

"I am *not* losing control!" Natalia snapped, closing her eyes as she composed herself. She didn't need to let her sister rile her; it wasn't worth it!

"What else would you call one of your own people trying to kill you? Or that others have started to sway from your rule?" Raziel asked with a sigh.

"I call it a hiccup. Anyway, you two can't talk!" Natalia hissed, kicking a pile of poetry away from her with disdain. "Doesn't your entire world spend their time plotting ways to end you, Azazel?" Natalia continued.

"They can plot all they like. They cannot best me at my own game," her sister replied.

"They spend too much time underkilling one another to be clever enough to kill her," Raziel added. "You're losing your sway, Jegudiel."

"It's Natalia now. I don't know why you two kept your names. I chose one that's far better, and more me." She snorted, sitting on the floor, her legs crossed beneath her as she smiled wickedly at an ornate mirror reflecting her own image back at her. "And how goes the search for love, Raziel? Have you found your one true heart yet?" Natalia smirked, knowing fully well that it wasn't within her sister to love anyone, no matter how hard she tried.

"Don't deflect, Sister. It's time you realized that you cannot keep your world in check, not anymore. They don't love you, and one of these days, they are all going to see past your beauty. You'll be alone then, with no one."

Natalia felt Raziel cut off their connection, and she grunted. "Clearly, I hit a nerve."

"If she had one to hit, I would agree with you. You can lie to yourself, Natalia, but not to us. You're losing your control over them. I told you when we started down this path that you would never beat me at running your own world. Humans don't want to love you; they need to fear you. It's the only way they know how to live."

"You'll have no one to rule if you have them all kill each other!" Natalia snapped.

"The strong ones will survive, and have far more of my respect because of it. I'm merely speeding up the process of weeding out the weak ones." Azazel chortled.

Natalia huffed and rolled her eyes at her sister's words,

glad that she couldn't see the smug look on Azazel's face. She didn't need to see her sister to know that it was there.

"This is *my* world; I'm not losing control of it. I won't ever lose control! You just *wait*." Natalia hissed, slapping her hands on the floor angrily.

She heard Azazel's laughter as she cut off their connection, and Natalia screamed irritably. It was rare for the sisters to talk to one another. On the occasions that they did, it always resulted in them vying for ways to annoy the others, poking at the flaws they saw in one another.

They couldn't be right. She wouldn't believe them... the problem was that Samuel had already told her as much. He had warned her of the plan to maim her. Still, an unfounded rumor for the moment, but considering the state that Jules had been in when he returned from speaking with his acolytes... Had Samuel been right about that as well?

No.

No, she refused to believe any of it. She wasn't losing control. Her people loved her; of course, they did. She was better than any of the citizens, more powerful and intelligent than her sisters, and her beauty was beyond comparison! She'd let her pathetic siblings into her head, but she knew better than that. All Natalia needed to do was remind her people of her magnificence; that was all it was.

Yes. She would leave her palace and spend time with them, surprise them by gracing them with her wonder in *their* homes rather than her own. They would welcome her into their humble abodes with open arms. It wouldn't take her long to reignite their devotion, and then she would show her sisters exactly who's the better of the three of them. *She* knew it; she would just have to make sure that *they* did, too.

Natalia sat on the edge of her balcony, watching over her city with a far calmer mind. Jules' hysteria had only put her on edge again after Samuel's attack, but Helena had been right. To even contemplate her citizens not being totally devoted to her was ridiculous. She was the embodiment of purity and perfection. It wasn't as though they had anyone else to love as much as they loved her, and why would they? No one would ever take her place, not in the hearts of her people. Believing otherwise, that was blasphemy.

She smiled to herself as she let her gaze flicker over the quiet streets. The street lamps flickered and danced off the golden walls, the mirrors sparkling as though the stars themselves had been plucked from the sky and trapped in their surfaces. She had created Heaven on Earth. No one could deny that, and no one could take that from her. She had done that because *she* was a visionary.

Movement out of the corner of her eye drew Natalia's attention to a street below her bedroom window. Natalia raised an eyebrow as she leaned over slightly, careful not to attract the attention of whoever was out so late at night.

The figure stuck to the shadows, clearly well-rehearsed in keeping out of the direct path of the lamplight, despite the reflective surface of the entire city. Natalia couldn't see their face at all, try as she might, nor could she figure out where they were going at such a late hour.

Ordinarily, the city was asleep, except for her and a few of the acolytes who ensured they were awake lest she required something of them. So, why was this person up?

The dark, niggling feeling crept back into her heart, and Natalia's skin prickled as she hurried to the other end of the balcony, losing sight of the figure as they rounded a corner. Something was going on, and she didn't like it.

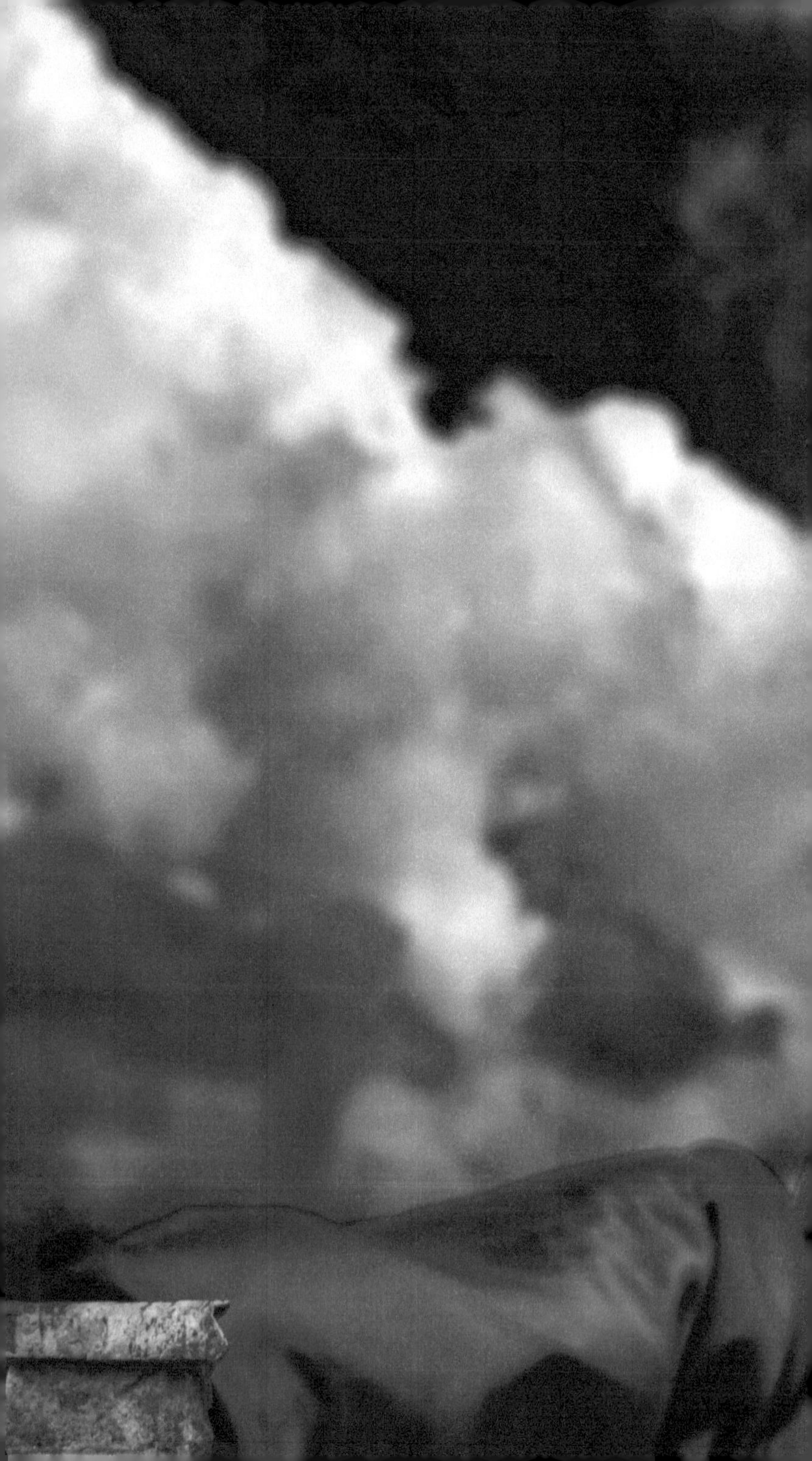

9

She didn't sleep that night. Her sisters' words rolled around inside her head, echoing louder and louder while she replayed the figure's furtive steps through the city. For the first time since Natalia had been banished from Heaven, she wished she had her wings. She could have followed the sneak with ease from the air without ever being detected, but she had lost sight of them before she could work out where they were headed to.

Natalia didn't want to believe her sisters; she refused to believe that they were right about her losing control. How could *she* lose control? It was absurd! She needed to see with her own eyes. She needed to walk amongst her people… but maybe it was best that they *not* realize who she was. She would only be hindered by the adulation of those who loved her, and then she couldn't prove to herself, or to her siblings, that this doubt was all nonsense.

Jules. She needed Jules.

Reaching over to her bedside table, Natalia picked up the golden bell that rested there. She took hold of the handle between her thumb and forefinger and rang it loudly. The hammer inside the dome of the bell clinking melodically against the metal. It was a sweet sound, almost as though the maker had somehow captured a birdsong into the bell itself. Sadly, what usually preceded the delicate tone was a harsh order from Natalia. Not quite as sweet as the bell.

The bedroom door opened, and a slew of acolytes hurried into the room, their hooded heads kept down in reverence to their Mistress. Behind Jules' followers came Helena's priestesses. Natalia had never really compared the two groups before; they had always just been her most devoted admirers, but now that she was really *looking* at her people, she began to see the differences.

Helena's priestesses did not cover their faces as Jules' acolytes did. They averted their eyes whenever Natalia cast a glance their way, but otherwise, they stole whatever glimpses they could of her. They were not as wary of touching her, and they showed their devotion more through their closeness to her—a reverence of a different kind to the humble acolytes. Of course, the most glaring difference was that all of Helena's followers were females, whereas Jules did not have such gender rules.

The acolytes were always by her side, ready to complete any task that she gave to them, but they seemed almost afraid to touch her. Something that always amused Natalia. They loved her wholeheartedly, but they clearly saw her as the goddess she *should* have been recognized as in Heaven.

You did not just *touch* a God. Not when you're just a mere mortal. And Jules' acolytes were balls of nervous energy whenever they were in her presence. Terrifyingly aware of how lucky they were to even be this close to her.

Both groups lowered themselves to the ground before her. The acolytes threw themselves upon the floor, lying flat with their hands above their heads, unable to look at Natalia. The priestesses were more graceful, sneaking peeks at their Mistress before they pressed their palms to the ground, their foreheads pressed to the cold, golden floor.

Ordinarily, it would have been *just* Jules' acolytes who answered her call, but Natalia had a feeling that Helena had spoken with her girls. The rivalry that Natalia had basically ignored was coming to a head, and her Head Priestess was clearly making moves to push out the Head Priest and take *his* place as Natalia's right hand. Interesting. Some of her people were making *more* of an effort, rather than less…

"I'm going into the city; I need to see with my own eyes what is going on with my own people. Since I cannot trust the word of anyone but myself," she snapped.

"My Wonderous Lady, you can trust *our* word. We would never lie to you," one of the priestesses uttered softly in response.

Natalia snarled, stomping her foot on the floor angrily. "No? Then how is it that not *one* of you has informed me of what has been going on in the city until Samuel attacked me?! The acolytes are out in the city, preaching to the others, and my priestesses swear that they are in the know, and yet, *none* of you knew?! Either you are *lying*, or you are all ignorant. Which is it?"

Silence fell in the room as Natalia loomed over the handful of devotees at her feet. Before she could say anything more, there was movement at her bedroom door, and she looked up to see Jules and Helena entering side-by-side. A united front? Or were they going to play off one another to see who could come out on top? Natalia could do with the entertainment. She could at least bask in *their* passion toward her.

"My Lady, we seek only to protect you," Helena whispered as she knelt beside her priestesses. She bowed her head as she offered her hands in apology, ready to receive her punishment if Natalia so decided that she required one.

"So, what you are saying to me is that you *knew* and chose not to tell me?" Natalia hissed.

"Oh, Beautiful Goddess sent from Heaven, we were too blinded by our love for you to see the signs within the city. It is our devotion that has made us ignorant of the actions of your people, the people *we* were assigned to guide in the ways of loving you. I take full responsibility for this, and I will do all that I can to rectify my oversight. Head Priestess, Helena, and I agreed that until we were *sure*, we would not tell you. We needed to make amends for our sins, for failing you." Jules whimpered, lying flat at her feet, his fingers trembling against her bare toes.

She had half a mind to kick him away from her. Natalia's body was positively quaking as she tried to contain her rage. They had hidden it from her, not just making excuses for not seeing the signs *before* there was a problem. She had trusted them! That was *her* mistake. Assuming that *mortals* could do anything right. If she wanted a job done correctly, she had to do it herself.

She knew that better than anyone; that was why she had built this world. To prove her point that she was the best of the angels, and that God was wrong.

Infallible. That's what He liked people to think about Him, but they were all wrong. She was prideful because she knew she was the best, and He was just too afraid to admit it. Well, she would show Him, she would show her sisters, and she would show *all* of them!

"Fetch me one of your acolyte's robes, Jules. Helena, I

want a wig. You're going to do your utmost to make me look *plain*, like all of you," Natalia growled through gritted teeth.

"M-my Illustrious and Superb Lady?" Jules stammered, his head whipping up from the floor as he dared to look at her, blinking rapidly in surprise.

"I'm going to walk amongst my people, and I'm going to see *exactly* what is going on."

10

Helena had found her a crimson wig to wear, and helped Natalia tuck her glorious curls out of sight. The priestesses had removed her anklets and toe rings, placing socks and soft leather plimsolls over her elegant feet. It had taken Natalia a full hour to calm down the second they were on. They were restrictive, and she could already feel that they were going to leave her with blisters. Her poor, perfect feet were going to be *ruined* because her people had been so incompetent.

Helena had done all she could to calm the fury, promising that the priestesses would be ready to attend to her the moment she returned so that they could massage, pumice, and smooth out any rough skin before it formed. They would *never* allow her to have a flaw; it was unthinkable! Was her body even able to have such horrors? Of course not. No one could make a mark on beauty like that.

Seeing herself in all of her mirrors had only made her tantrum worse, her rage palpable as she stomped her feet so hard that she caused the palace to physically shake. Helena and Jules had been forced to calm her fury, reminding Natalia of *why* she was doing this, and that she did still look beautiful, regardless of her disguise—it was just a different kind of beauty.

Once she had calmed down enough, Natalia raised the hood of her robe, lowering it over her face so that she could remain as anonymous as possible when her face was plastered on every corner of the city.

With her disguise in place, Natalia joined a group of Jules' acolytes. Copying their mannerisms as the group shuffled out of the palace, Natalia joined them as they hurried into the streets to go about their business, preaching her wonder to all her citizens so that they might always bask in the glory of her existence.

How long had it been since she'd actually walked the streets that her citizens occupied? Natalia honestly couldn't remember. She had been so preoccupied with having them come to *her* that she had never thought to grace them with her magnificence.

Had that been where she'd gone wrong? Had they wept for the lack of contact with her and strayed in their desperation to fill the void that her opulent personality left when she didn't walk amongst them? Once a week with her wasn't enough; of course, it wasn't! How naïve she had been to think that her citizens would settle *just* for one day! They *needed* her. Their love had no outlet if she was not in their presence.

Distance makes the heart grow fonder. That was how the phrase went, wasn't it? She had believed that allowing them the time to make her gifts, limiting them to being with her in person once a week, would merely strengthen their adoration for her. It did, for some, but for others, they *needed* to be with her. Well, she would make sure to fix that from now on… once she had eradicated any of the false idols that Samuel had led her to believe existed.

Natalia kept her head down, peering out from beneath the hood of the robe. Her heart skipped a beat every time one of her citizens looked her way. She breathed a sigh of relief when they turned their gaze elsewhere, and Natalia grinned. Her ruse was working perfectly, but of course, it was, and had been, *her* idea. after all! The pain of looking like this would be worth it in the end, once she saw what was going on with her own eyes.

The crowds parted to allow the acolytes through the streets, and Natalia was surprised to find so many of her citizens' faces contorting as though they were disgusted to be in the presence of her preachers. Some bowed and looked on in reverence, while others grabbed at the robes of the acolytes as though some of Natalia's presence might rub off on them by proxy.

Reaching one of the many squares dotted throughout the city, the acolytes soon came to a halt on their pilgrimage, stopped by several citizens who wished to speak with them on several matters. Natalia took the opportunity to shuffle out of the main group, slipping past the preoccupied citizens toward the nearest building as the owner hurried out to see what the commotion was outside. She caught the door as it shut behind the man and slipped inside while he was busy looking at the growing mass of people out in the square. Natalia shut the door quietly behind her, lowered the hood from her face and gasped as she looked around the room that she found herself in.

"No. *No!*" She squealed, stomping her feet and clenching her hands so tightly that her nails dug deep into her palms.

It was just as Samuel had warned, and as Jules and Helena had feared to tell her. Upon the walls, where Natalia had expected an array of images depicting *her* beauty, she found pictures of another woman entirely—the woman who came into the room at that moment and looked at Natalia in terror.

"NO!" Natalia screamed, and the crowd outside silenced the moment her voice thundered from the house.

She moved like lightning. Shedding her robe onto the floor as she bolted to where the woman stood, Natalia's elegant fingers wrapped around the woman's throat so tightly that her nails tore into the offender's throat.

"Blasphemy! Treason! How *dare* you betray me like this?!" Natalia screamed, spittle flecking the face of the woman gasping under Natalia's vice-like grip, but the former archangel did not loosen her grasp. "You dare to go against my word and create these false images? Your defiance will not go unpunished!" she hissed.

The woman's eyes rolled in her head, her fingers trembling against Natalia's hand weakly as she tried to wrench the angel's digits from her throat. To no avail. Most of Natalia's powers had been lost when God had taken her wings, but not all of them, and she was still a formidable opponent. Clearly, her citizens needed to be reminded of who she was in this world.

11

With all her considerable might, Natalia launched the woman across the room. She smiled at her own strength as her victim flew the length of it and smashed through the wall, tumbling into the square beyond with the rubble.

Natalia sighed contentedly as she threw off her wig, bending to remove the shoes and socks from her feet. She tossed them aside gleefully, sneering at the discarded articles she loathed so much. Wiggling her toes, Natalia closed her eyes and allowed herself a moment to enjoy the renewed freedom she felt, now that her feet had been released from those prisons. Thankfully, she hadn't worn the restrictive things for too long; her feet *should* be free of any injury, at least.

Preoccupied with herself, Natalia had not registered the screams and shouts of the citizens crowded in the square beyond. She licked her lips as she stretched her neck from side-to-side, rolling her shoulders as she loosened the muscles in her back where her wings had once been. It had been such a long time since she'd last indulged in any real violence—not since Lucifer's uprising with his demon spawn, at least. Natalia had forgotten the simple pleasures that a show of her true strength could bring.

Striding across the room, she stepped through the large hole in the wall that she'd created when she tossed that piece of *filth* outside. The citizens closest to her scurried backwards, their faces devoid of color, their eyes wide as they looked upon their queen.

Now, they were beginning to remember their place. Clearly, Natalia just needed to remind them of it more often. A show of force, then. If that's what it would take, Natalia would *happily* oblige. She would obliterate every blasphemous article from her city and ensure that her people did not forget their place in this world *ever* again.

Her eyes fixed on the crumpled, bloodied mess of the woman she had cast aside, cradled in the arms of the man who exited the house before Natalia had snuck inside. She snorted at the pathetic state they were in now—the woman a shattered, broken mess in the arms of her sobbing lover. How had that man *ever* thought her worthy of a portrait in comparison to Natalia?

Natalia bolted across the square at the pair before the man could have the chance to run away, let alone react to her sudden appearance. The former archangel grabbed the man by his throat with one hand, tearing the bloodied corpse from his embrace with the other. Natalia held him up above her head, grinning as the wild image of herself reflected in the nearest building's glistening golden walls.

"You really thought I wouldn't find out about your treachery? Did you forget who rules this world? *Did you?!"* she screamed, her grip tightening, throwing the woman away just as she had done before.

The corpse hit the fountain in the center of the square with a sickening, crunching thud before splatting indignantly into the water below. Natalia cocked her head to one side, giggling as she saw the fountain water turn red as the woman's blood tainted its crystal-clear purity. That would need to be rectified, but at that moment, Natalia had to admit that red was a color that looked rather good on her. She would have to remember that, get rid of some of those pastel garbs of hers in favor of something a little bolder.

"I won't forgive you," Natalia whispered to the man as she looked up at him, relishing in the way he gasped against her hand, his legs kicking as though somehow, he might get her to loosen her grip. Just as that woman had done. It was pathetic.

Slowly, Natalia lowered the man until his feet touched the ground. She could see her own stern expression looking back at her in his eyes, her perfectly plucked eyebrows furrowed so that a line formed between them just above her nose. That wouldn't do. She couldn't allow these *peasants* to give her wrinkles!

Natalia smiled, almost sweetly, and relinquished her grip on the man's neck. He gasped and spluttered, coughing violently as he drew in deep swathes of oxygen, desperate to fill his deprived lungs. His gaze never left Natalia's as he wheezed, his eyes watering from the assault, though she could see the relief in his face at the fact that she had let him go.

Foolish man, as if that had been enough of a lesson for him and the other traitorous fools? No, no. Not yet.

There was a spark of amusement, like a pleasing electrical shock, that tickled across Natalia's skin as the man came to realize that he hadn't been let off the hook at all. He could see the same dark smile that she could see grinning back at her from every surface of her city; there was no joy in that expression, just murderous rage.

His scream was cut short when Natalia's hands shot out, grabbing his head so tightly that her knuckles turned white. The man's eyes bulged in their sockets, his cheekbones shattered, and Natalia sighed happily as she felt his skull snap under the pressure of her palms. Blood poured from the man's eyes, nose, and silently screaming mouth, his face considerably thinner than it had been before. Smiling, Natalia let go of his crushed skull, watching with disdain as his body crumpled at her feet, brain matter oozing from the remains of their broken cage onto the golden cobbles.

Natalia sighed as the screams escalated behind her, the citizens who had borne witness to their goddess' rage finally beginning to understand the severity of the crimes that had been committed by these two mutinous fools. No one insulted Natalia and got away with it. No one.

She spun about, blood spattering from her hands as she pointed at Jules, who looked as pale as the rest of the witnesses cowering under her intimidating stature.

"Find them, Jules, find them all. I want you to go through every residence and weed out the heretics. Bring every offending, blasphemous article to the palace steps, along with those who have *dared* to turn their backs on me. I will show them what their betrayal has brought them." She snarled, catching sight of the viscous red liquid already drying on her perfect alabaster skin. She let out a small squeal of panic, and the acolytes hurried to her side, gently taking her hands and wiping the blood away with their robes.

At least *they* had not forgotten their love for her. Soon, she would remind the rest of them who they should be grateful to, who *deserved* their love.

12

Natalia had lingered in the city while Jules' acolytes raided the remaining houses in the square, overseeing the clean-up of the courtyard and the fountain until she was satisfied that every nook and cranny had been thoroughly cleaned. She wanted every trace of the pair she'd destroyed eradicated from existence. They didn't deserve even one *skin cell* remaining in her domain. They had proved that they weren't worthy enough to be in her presence. She wasn't going to tolerate it from them or anyone else, not now, not ever.

The entire city was in turmoil. The commotion she created in the square quickly spread like wildfire to all of her citizens, until all were aware of their Mistress' rampage against those who dared to turn their gazes elsewhere. As if anyone else in this world, or any other, was even worth looking at other than Natalia herself? The entire notion was laughable. How far her people had fallen from her good graces!

Maybe Azazel was right to turn her citizens against one another for her own pleasure; it might even teach them some humility—they knew better than to turn against her, lest they lost their lives in her disgusting arenas and tournaments.

Well, now Natalia would just have to keep a tighter rein on her own citizens, wouldn't she? They only had themselves to blame. She had been more than generous with them! Not only did she *allow* them the privilege of being surrounded by her image, basking in the glory of her magnificence in whatever way they chose to do so, but she had granted them eternal life as well!

Her sisters ruled with iron fists and fear, while Natalia had granted *her* people a gift that humanity had been searching for ever since they'd had the brain cells granted to them to *think*. Humans had become obsessed with immortality from the moment they understood what mortality was, and they had gone to great lengths to stave off death. How many pointless wars had been started in the pursuit of everlasting life? Natalia had lost count centuries before her fall, laughing at the stupidity of man over something as simple as not dying.

Yet when she had created this world of hers, she had *readily* granted her people that gift. She didn't want them thinking of anyone other than herself; they didn't need to, after all. There was no one better than her. So, they didn't need to lie together to reproduce offspring in order to love her. She had hand-picked *them* because they were as close to being worthy, being close to her, as any being could be. Other than herself.

Maybe it would have been simpler to just duplicate herself, but then again, she didn't want to share her perfection in that fashion, either. She was the one true impeccable being in existence, and these foolish humans were meant to recognize that and love her for that. Most did, she knew that; of course, they did. How could they not?!

She was beginning to doubt again. Letting Samuel's words, and the jibes of her sisters, sneak into her mind and question her own faultlessness. *This* was why she kept contact with her siblings to a minimum. They had always known how to get under her skin, and even with age, the pair still managed to find a way to rile her. She was clearly tired. That's what all of this was. She wasn't losing control; she had just gotten a little complacent. *She*, Natalia, did not *lose* control. God might. Her sisters might. She did not.

Once she was satisfied that Jules and his acolytes had the situation under control, Natalia returned to her palace with a small escort. Greeted by the welcoming embrace of Helena and her priestesses, each of whom were eager to serve and please their goddess as they always were. Proof that Natalia wasn't losing her grip on her world; it really was all in her head.

Maybe she needed to start taking more lovers. She used to have one man a night come to her chamber to *physically* show his adoration of her... with the occasional woman where Natalia desired female company.

In a way, it was true that a woman knew how to please her more than a man ever could, given how they were naturally more aware of a woman's form and where pleasure could be obtained. Natalia had strayed from such pleasures—except for Adam from the other night—and had always enjoyed such things.

Complacency. *That* was what all of this was. She had become too comfortable letting her people shower her with praise once a week, and hadn't made any effort to walk amongst them, let alone give them a taste of *her* for some time. Well, it was time to let them touch ecstasy, sample perfection, and revel in her glory *personally* as they had done in the beginning. They had grown restless without her, searching for anything to fill the void in their hearts that she left when she wasn't with them. Could she *really* blame them for seeking other avenues of entertainment?

"You're scowling, my Lady, what troubles you so?" Helena asked as she ran her thumb over the spot between Natalia's eyebrows, smoothing out the small knot that had formed—one that Natalia hadn't even been aware of.

Natalia sighed, lying back in her bath, relaxing into the warm water and letting the aroma of honey and rose petals fill her lungs.

"I was just thinking. Have I been neglecting my people? Is that why this is all happening? So caught up in myself, thinking that once a week would be enough to satisfy their need for me. I don't blame them for wanting *more* of me; it's only natural. Only right. My absence has allowed them to stray, to seek alternatives that were more accessible to them because of *my* vacancy from their lives."

Helena ran her fingertips along Natalia's shoulder lazily. "My Lady is as wise as always, of course. That's all it is. Jules and I should have thought of such a thing, but of course, it's my beautiful Lady who figured out why there is so much discontentment amongst the citizens. What would you have us do to help you rectify this, my Lady?" Helena whispered, her lips brushing against Natalia's ear, sending little shivers of pleasure along the angel's spine.

Natalia smirked, looking up at Helena from under her long lashes. The woman had always been bold in her advances of Natalia, and Natalia had always allowed it since it was Helena's way of showing her adoration. She always wondered how long the Head Priestess would continue to shower her with such devotion, when Natalia never reciprocated the favor in any fashion.

Not once had she taken the priestess to bed with her,

believing that the gift of herself was something she needed to keep for those less privileged than Helena and Jules. The citizens who didn't get to spend their time in her presence as the priestesses and the acolytes did. Would Helena turn against her eventually? Or would her bold advances start to drop away as Natalia continued to stay just out of the woman's reach?

No matter. For now, she held Helena's interest entirely. Until she didn't, Natalia wasn't going to worry over such things. Her priestess was loyal, and she was letting that doubt wiggle its way in again, even when she had worked out what had gone wrong, so to speak.

A knock on her bathroom door ruined the relaxing atmosphere, and she exhaled irritably. She remained as calm as she could, reminding herself that she had been scowling more and more lately. She would get wrinkles if she wasn't careful.

Helena made a soft hiss between her teeth at the other priestesses in attendance, and Natalia smirked as she imagined the Head Priestess glaring at the other girls for not immediately finding out who dared to disturb their Lady's bath. She heard the door open, and the sound of feet scurrying across the tile to one side of her bath, but she refused to open her eyes.

"Oh, Illustrious Illusion of Grandeur, we have gathered all forbidden artifacts and have them waiting for your inspection outside the palace doors, along with the owners of the offending items. They await your punishment. I had my acolytes bring the rest of the city to bear witness, so that they might learn their lesson as well," Jules whispered beside her.

"Good. I shall be out in a moment. Time to remind my people of their place before I grant them the gift of more time with me. Punishment, then reward; that should set things back into balance."

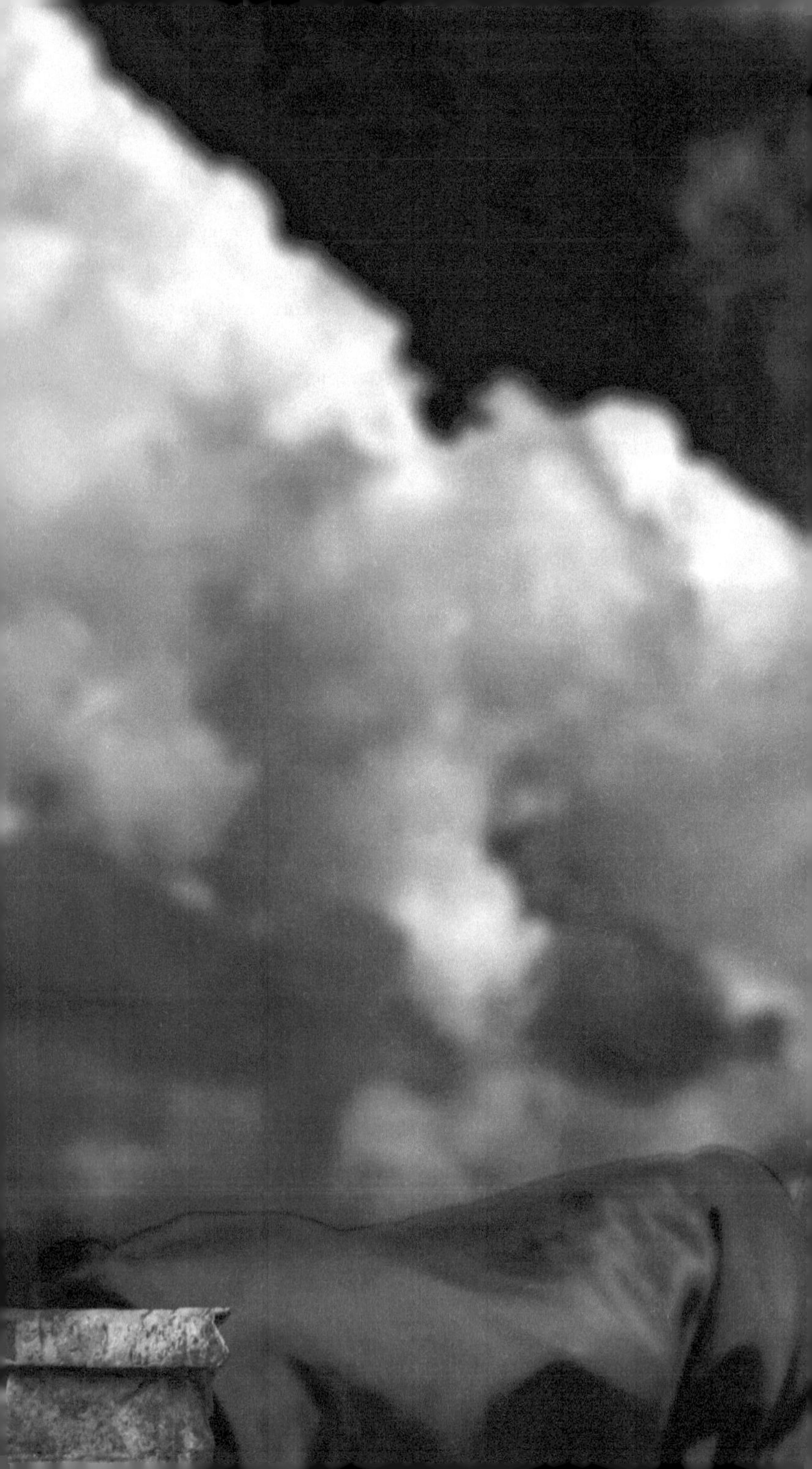

13

She had taken her time to get ready. Her people could wait; she was not going to rush for them because they didn't deserve it. They had upset her; they had forgotten her! If it wasn't because she realized that her own perfection had caused this disruption, she would have hidden herself away from the world for an entire week! Deprive them of her magnificence entirely.

Instead, she would punish those who had dared to stray rather than show her their devotion properly. Samuel had gone about things in the wrong fashion, but at least he had proven his admiration for her in his madness. Why couldn't they have all made more effort?

They could've spoken to Jules and the acolytes, and *they*

would have informed her of how sad her people were at their lack of contact with her! How easily all of this could have been resolved without the need for such ugliness as violence and death…

They would fix this, and then she would be able to go back to normality, enjoying their attention and being worshipped as she truly deserved to be. The chiffon dress she'd chosen to wear as she graced them with her presence barely covered her exquisite frame. Loose and almost see-through it billowed around her long legs, caressing her skin like petals upon the wind. Always moving, gentle and loving.

Jules and Helena led the way through the palace, striding side-by-side, their respective followers flanking Natalia like an honored guard. She held her head high, her loose curls cascading over her shoulder as she walked, calmed by the presence of her reflection on every surface as they went toward the entrance of the palace.

Her priest and priestess threw open the ornate doors, and Natalia felt as though she had been punched in the gut at the sight of the items that Jules' acolytes had found that were *not* of her image… or about her in any fashion! A few pieces, that was all she had expected. One or two items, maybe ten, but this? This was far more than Natalia could ever have imagined.

There, the dark tendrils of doubt began to slither their way into her heart and mind again, and she felt her sisters press against the walls of their divide, eager to laugh and taunt her for her own naivety. She didn't need to hear their words to know exactly what they would say. Natalia knew she would have to let them in at some point, but she couldn't bear hearing their gloating *now* when she had to face *this*.

She strode out the doors, faced with the reality of just how many of her people had betrayed her. After all she had done for them, after everything she had *given* them? *This* was how they thanked her? By spitting in her face with these ugly objects that depicted people and things that could not remotely compare to her glorious, flawless image?

Her eyes scanned the huge pile that the acolytes had managed to collect from around the city. So much, so many. A soft buzz began to ring in Natalia's ears as the world around her became a numb blur. Her skin prickled, her nerves on fire, her heart pounding so hard in her chest that she was sure the whole city could hear it. The doubt truly had a hold of her heart now, its claws digging deep as doubt became certainty.

It wasn't a handful of citizens that Jules' acolytes loomed over as they forced them to their knees, their hands bound and heads bowed at the bottom of the stairs that led to the palace. One or two. That was all she had ever dared imagined would betray her, not the *crowd* that had been brought before her. She didn't even dare count how many there were, the fire growing in her heart, fighting against the cold dread that had already taken hold there as her rage threatened to consume her. They would see her fury; they would face her anger at their betrayal. They had hurt her, after all that she had done for them, and now, they would suffer the consequences.

The buzzing—like a million angry bees swarming to protect their nest from an enemy—drew to a crescendo, and Natalia's patience was replaced with her hatred for those who dared to compare *these* ugly things to *her*. The acolytes and priestesses that followed behind her gasped, and she heard them shuffle backwards, putting distance between themselves and Natalia. Her displeasure was palpable, a miasma in the air that all her city would soon be able to taste and feel pulsating through their veins.

She had lost a lot of her power in her fall, but not all. God had underestimated her abilities. He should have *killed* her. He would have been better off that way, rather than leaving His daughter to grow stronger and hate Him more.

Jules and Helena gasped, dropping to their knees as Natalia clenched her fists together, stomped her feet, and screamed. The sound was shrill, piercing. A pulse of pure energy radiated from Natalia's body, causing the sacrilegious pile to fall apart, an avalanche of blasphemy that would soon be purged from existence.

The citizens gathered to witness retribution pressed their hands to their ears against her screams, though even they would not be spared from it. Natalia could see the blood pouring from beneath their hands—their protection futile against the power of her voice—as their ears were assaulted by her tone.

Those who had been bound screamed alongside her as they were forced to take the brunt of her voice and all the power that laid behind it. Their ears bled, their veins bulged as the notes quivered through their bodies, threatening to burst them from within.

No. They would burn; they would *burn* for what they had done, just as she burned with their betrayal. They would know her pain, and they would know what they had done to her. With a flick of her hand, Natalia set the mountain of betrayal on fire, the flames flickering and cracking behind her back as she descended the stairs.

"You ungrateful swine! I shall make you suffer for this; you'll all wish you had remembered your place! I am the most beautiful, the most glorious, the most *powerful* being in existence! I am more than any of you could ever comprehend. What more could you have needed in your lives other than me?!" she shrieked.

With a stomp of her foot, Natalia connected her mind with that of the prisoners at her feet. She found her way deep into their psyche, and settled her magnificent presence deep in the recesses of their memories. She would take everything from them; everything that had ever been good would be wiped away, and they would be left writhing in pain... in the darkness that they had created for themselves.

She stood back, the deed done, the seed of her inner

flames planted in the back of their minds. It would eat away at every happy memory they had ever had, leaving them with only their despair and misery as it infected their veins and burned through their very being.

For her victims, it would feel like an eternity, as though time had stopped, while in reality, they would be dead in a matter of minutes. The first horde of traitors threw back their heads and began to scream, writhing against their bonds as the flames ate at their insides. Natalia smiled, casting a glance at the rest of her citizens as they watched in horror at what was happening to those who had dared to defy their goddess.

Natalia snorted and turned away from them; they didn't deserve to look upon her, and she wouldn't even give them that satisfaction in their deaths. They had lost that gift when they turned their backs on her; now, she would turn hers on them.

14

It took Natalia most of the day to calm the fury raging in her heart. Even after the last screams had died in the air, she trembled in her anger, unable to contain how she felt. Her sisters pressed against their bond to one another, desperate to be let in so that they could speak with her. To taunt her and brag, of that she was certain, but she had no time for them and had no intention of giving them that satisfaction, either. They could wait; she had enough going on without having to deal with *them* as well.

She lied back upon her bed, naked so that she could feel the silk sheets against her skin, cool and soothing compared to the heat of her anger that continued to smoulder in her veins. Natalia raised her hands to her head, her fingertips massaging her temples as she kept her eyes closed.

Beyond the doors, she could hear the whispers of the acolytes and the priestesses, all of them debating whether or not to knock on their Mistress' door and speak with her. She could *feel* their fear even at this distance. That prickling upon her skin as though someone was poking at her with hundreds of tiny needles. She could taste their nervousness in the air, the salt of their sweat tainting her tongue.

Part of her wanted to scare them. Launch herself across the room, throw open the door, and scream at them to go away. To see their faces as all the color drained away, as they cowered from her wrath, whimpering like the pathetic creatures they were.

Yet, there was a part of Natalia that also wanted to coax them into her bedroom, to have her loyal subjects lavish her with their attention. So that they might wash away the stain of the betrayal that she had suffered.

"Do you truly believe you've gotten rid of the problem?" Azazel's smug tone crept into Natalia's head.

Natalia sighed, and she rolled her eyes as she sat up, her hair shivering over her exposed breasts. She'd clearly let her walls slip while she had been trying to calm herself. Keeping her sisters out while controlling her own emotions obviously hadn't been an option, though she'd hoped that neither of her siblings would notice the weakening in her defenses.

"I'm not going to be naïve enough to make that mistake again, Sister. However, I am confident that I have made my point to them," Natalia replied curtly.

"So, you took my advice then? You chose fear over that ridiculous notion of love?"

"No, I chose to make an example of those who had betrayed me, so that the others could remember all the things that I have given them. I gave them eternal life, a gift that all humans have been seeking for… how many millennia since we were tasked to watch over them?"

"Countless, but you gave it to them too freely, Sister. You should have offered it to them as a reward."

"Reward? I wasn't aware you knew of such a word." Natalia snorted. "The great Azazel, Queen of Darkness, when was the last time you rewarded anybody anything? I chose my people for their beauty because they were the worthiest to be in my presence, and I gifted them immortality, so that they might forever be with me. They only ever needed me."

"Worked out well so far. And I reward my civilians. The ones who win my tournaments are allowed to live." Azazel chortled.

Natalia rolled her eyes at her sister's response. Azazel had always enjoyed watching the suffering of others, far more than she should. Her twisted sense of self had left her a manipulative nightmare, finding ways to twist a situation for her own benefit and entertainment. Unlike Raziel and Natalia, Azazel readily let her people cavort with one another, a *reward*, Natalia supposed, was what her sister would class it as. Azazel didn't seek love like Raziel, nor did she expect to be worshipped as Natalia did. All she wanted was to win.

"So, what now, Sister? You've made your point to them. Do you believe you will not lose control again?"

"I never lost it, Azazel. I merely forgot how fickle humans could be. How much attention they required. They never stopped loving me; they just sought other avenues to fill the void left by my magnificence when I cut short my time with them. It was not a loss of control; I do not lose control."

"Ah, yes, the magnificent Natalia never loses control. Does she?"

Natalia could almost hear her sister rolling her eyes across their link, and rolled hers in return.

"No, she doesn't. Anyway, where's Raziel? I'm surprised

she hasn't butted in with her opinion, as usual." She snorted, crossing her arms over her naked chest, trying hard not to scowl.

"I have not heard from her. I felt her a few times in the last day or so, but I have not had any contact with her. She's probably found another victim as her latest love ploy and is focusing on that rather than poking fun of you."

Again, Natalia rolled her eyes at her sister's smug tone. She was such an annoyance; she always had been, but Natalia wasn't going to give Azazel the satisfaction of a response. Not this time.

"I'm sure she will come crawling back when she kills them, like she always does. Any of your lot get close to ridding us of your presence yet?"

"Don't be stupid, Sister. As if they could even get close to me. I'm not you."

"No, you're not, nor will you ever be as good as I am," Natalia replied with a smile, flicking her hair over her shoulder. "You've been lucky so far, Azazel. That's all it is, but you'll never be able to beat me. I told you before, I know I'm the best of us. God knew it. That's why He cast me out. He only cast you out because you were a reject and a degenerate. I was a threat to His glory."

"Delusional, as always. Believe what you like, Sister. Raziel and I see you for what you truly are."

"Yes, you better!" Natalia snapped, slamming the walls down on their connection once more, cutting her sister from her mind before Azazel could say another word.

Natalia sighed; she should have known better. The *second* she'd heard Azazel's voice, she should have disengaged. Her sister knew how to rile her; *both* of her sisters did, and Natalia knew she shouldn't give them the time of day. It was only out of common courtesy that she even bothered speaking with them; they were naturally jealous of how wonderful she was, and it was the least she could do to allow them a glimpse of what they could never be.

Strive as they might, they would never surpass her, but at least they would have a common goal. They might better themselves if they tried to emulate her greatness. Such a shame for them that they would never come close to being perfect.

She did wonder about Raziel, however. It was unlike her sister to pass up a chance to join Azazel in trying to get a rise out of Natalia. It wasn't worry that she felt; she didn't worry for her sister—the other fallen angel was as beneath her as everyone else, after all. It was merely because of curiosity. Raziel had *never* let Natalia bring down her walls without poking her oar in alongside Azazel, so for her second sister to remain silent as she had was… odd.

She reached over for her robe, throwing it over her shoulders as she swung her legs off the bed, striding out onto her balcony. Smoke still floated lazily into the sky from the smouldering pile of items that Natalia had burnt earlier in the day.

The flickering sparks that lingered on the burning pages and artwork looked like a swarm of fireflies in the darkness from where Natalia stood. The bodies of the men and women she had destroyed had been removed from the palace steps long before Natalia graced the city with her presence upon the balcony—Jules clearly ordered his acolytes to remove them so that Natalia did not have to look upon them. Good, they weren't worthy of her gaze, let alone another second of her thoughts.

Leaning upon the marble railing of her balcony, Natalia felt the breeze ruffle her curls as she closed her eyes, enjoying the quiet that had returned to her world. Knowing that she was supreme in everything that she ever did.

15

The city fell unusually quiet over the next couple of days, though Natalia chose to take this as a sign of her rebellious citizens keeping their heads down as they thought about what they had done. They would be in mourning! They had broken her heart, after all, by making these false images that couldn't remotely be compared with her own flawless vision. No, the quiet was nothing to worry about. It was her people showing her their love by not causing any more of a fuss for her, by proving that they were sorry for letting their minds stray from her perfection.

They would work harder to prove their devotion to her from now on, she was sure of that. In fact, she was quite convinced that they were all creating the most beautiful gifts for her in confirmation of their utter love and admiration for her… and her alone.

Natalia remained in her palace, allowing only the acolytes and her priestesses to tend to her. They had never strayed from her side, even after she caused them harm in her anger, and they still wanted to show her how much they adored her. She had been right in letting them care for her all this time, and they would be rewarded with her presence because of their devotion.

Oh, they feared her a little more now, and rightly so, given the show of power that she had displayed for the entire city. She had been gentle with them, reminding them that her wrath had been reserved for those who dared to vilify her city with images of less perfect things than herself.

In the back of her mind, Natalia reminded herself that she would need to grace her people with her presence again, but for now, her absence was their punishment. Maybe this way, they would learn to appreciate the gift that was her existence amongst them. Did they not understand how truly insignificant they were as a race? Had *God* ever graced them with *His* presence personally? No! He hadn't, and He didn't compare to even an ounce of her perfection. He might have been her father, but He was as unworthy of being in her company as these humans were. The difference was that *she* knew they deserved a generous leader—a goddess, in fact—to rule over them and give them something to strive for!

"Oh, Wondrous Vision of Utter Sublimity, might I beg for a moment of your time?" Jules asked.

Natalia smiled, turning to face her Head Priest as he proffered himself at her feet, his fingertips trembling against her toes as he dared to touch her feet in reverence. No matter the display of power she had given, Jules was the same as he had always been with her, and Natalia appreciated that a little more now than she had before.

"What can I do for you, Jules?" she asked, leaning over him with a smile.

A thought crossed her mind that, one of these days, she was going to make him look her in the eyes and see what reaction she could elicit from the man. Natalia imagined his head physically exploding, or Jules wetting himself in his excitement. Would he be premature, given the stimulation of being allowed that close to her? Or would he find a way to perform? Maybe she *would* take up the opportunity to gift Jules a night with her—she would see.

"I do not mean to intrude or to criticize, but I was curious…" He hesitated, and his fingers grew still on her feet. Natalia could tell that he was second-guessing asking her whatever was on his mind.

"It's alright, Jules, go on," she coaxed.

"You said it yourself that it was your lack of presence that caused your people to stray. Is it wise to hide away from them again? Not that you're hiding, or that I am questioning your actions! My Lady obviously knows better than I!" he squealed, suddenly realizing the weight of his words.

Natalia grunted with amusement, though she found herself unable to keep her body from stiffening instinctively. He could say he wasn't questioning her; he could say that he didn't mean the words he'd spoken, but they both knew that wasn't entirely true. Had her lapse in judgment brought doubt into the minds of even her most trusted subjects? No. They *knew* better.

"Of course, I know better than you, Jules; that goes without saying," Natalia replied, though the bitterness at the edge of her words could not be missed despite how softly she spoke to her priest. "This is their punishment, which should go without saying, but I will say it out loud so that you never make the mistake of questioning me again. Yes, my absence may have created this situation, but they know what fate awaits them now if they show the same betrayal as the others did. They will *learn* from that, and in the meantime, they will sit quietly and reflect on what has happened recently. They will remember how *lucky* they are that I deemed them worthy enough to be chosen to live in *my* world. I could have left them to the mercy of my sisters, to a life of never knowing if they were going to see the next day, but I didn't. *I* was merciful. *I* was kind. *I* chose to bring you all into my world and allow you to be in my presence!" Natalia hissed, kicking Jules away from her. "They are going to remember that, and they are going to be grateful. They are going to be *loyal*. They are going to *love* me!"

Jules whimpered from the crumpled heap of fabric he now resembled, cowering against the wall where Natalia had discarded him. His wide eyes stared at her from beneath the hood of his robe, and Natalia recognized the fear that the acolytes and priestesses looked at her with now.

Jules had only ever looked at her in admiration, never in fear. As if he realized that she had noticed, he quickly looked at the floor, his gaze fixed on her reflection rather than her person as he scurried back across the corridor to her. He hurriedly covered her toes and feet in gentle kisses, his fingers caressing her ankles as he continued to whimper and shower her with affection.

"My Lady, forgive me! I meant no offense! I should never have said anything. I did not mean for it to sound as though I did not trust your judgment. You—who is the wisest of all beings in existence, the epitome of perfection—are the one true goddess of all!" He blubbered.

Natalia smiled, cocking her head to one side as she looked down at the pathetic waste of flesh at her feet. She only tolerated their existence in her company because she deserved to be worshipped.

"Remember that, Jules," Natalia whispered, kneeling beside the man, her fingertips brushing against his chin as she forced him to look up at her. "Now, I will let them miss me for a little longer, and then I shall grace my citizens with my beauty so that they might shower me with their love and devotion as I truly deserve. Until then, they can suffer in my absence; that way, they might learn a little humility in the presence of one who surpasses them in every way imaginable."

"You are right as ever, Sublime Beauty of Grandeur. I lost my head for a moment; I beg for your forgiveness."

"Only this once, Jules, but I will not be so kind if you stray from your path again," she hissed, flicking his face away as she stood up and strode down the corridor toward her vault, leaving him to proclaim his adoration of her to all in the palace, at the top of his lungs.

16

Adorned in the finest silks of deepest red, embellished with gold, Natalia looked exquisite as she strode through her palace. Her reflection smiled at her as she made her way to the entrance, catching flashes of her bare legs as she moved gracefully through the corridors.

Red and gold really *did* suit her; why had she never realized that before? It was such a delicious shade for her, and complimented her ivory skin. Her citizens were going to be in awe of her in this dress!

Smiling, Natalia pushed open the palace doors and hurried out into the dazzling sunshine. It was always sunny in her world, but of course it was, as if *she* would allow something as dark and miserable as rain into her domain.

Admittedly, she would still be a shining beacon, regardless of the color of the sky, but she hated rain and dark clouds; it dulled the way her hair shone.

The breeze was gentle and warm as it brushed against her skin, tugging at the loose curls that framed her perfectly sculpted face. She could enjoy the sun and the breeze from her balcony, of course, but it wasn't quite the same as being out in the open, enjoying the sun that reflected off every surface of her dazzling golden city.

Natalia hurried down the steps of the palace, relishing in the warmth of the golden cobbles under her bare feet. It was time to allow her people to see her again, so that they could go back to worshipping her, as was only right.

She made her way through the streets, her hands clasped behind her back, enjoying her own company as her image flickered beside her on every surface. The city was her pride and joy, a perfect example of what she was capable of, and so fitting—considering that it allowed her to be forever surrounded by herself. There was nothing more perfect than she, and that was a fact.

When she came to the square where she had found the first image that was not her own, Natalia stopped and scowled, her brow furrowed as she realized that she hadn't seen a single citizen during her entire time walking through the city. They should have been flooding the streets, eager to be in her company once more! Yet, she had not seen a soul this entire time.

"Where are they all?" Natalia muttered under her breath to her reflections as she turned on the spot, glancing at her statue in the center of the square. "Why are they not out here to greet me?!"

Were they all still afraid? Was that what this was? *Fear.* She had forgiven them! Did they not see this? If she hadn't, she wouldn't have come into the city to allow them the chance to bask in all her wonder!

No. There was something more to this. Had she been wrong? Had she *still* read this situation wrong? Samuel had warned her—hadn't he? That this was so much deeper than just missing her, but she had chosen to ignore his words for her own answers because only she could be right. Yet the emptiness of the city, the lack of people crowding to be around her, told Natalia otherwise.

Something was not right in her world, and the doubt was finding its way back into her heart.

atalia had never felt so exposed in her life. Standing in the square, with no one in sight, she felt as though a thousand eyes were trained solely upon her.

"You, self-conscious? I never thought I'd live to see the day!" Azazel's pompous tone slithered its way into Natalia's mind.

She took a step toward the fountain in the center of the square. Restored to its former glory—just as the building she had smashed a hole through had been—her reflection staring back at her, wide-eyed and… fearful? No! She didn't feel fear; what did she have to be afraid of?! *She* was in charge here, *she* was the leader of this world, and *she* was the one in charge.

All eyes *should* be on her, so that they could bask in the glory of her magnificence!

So, why did it feel so... wrong?

"This has really shaken you, Sister. Normally, I would take such great pleasure in all of this... but I have never seen you like this. It's... disturbing."

"Not half as disturbing for you as it is for me." Natalia growled under her breath, throwing up her defensive walls to keep her sisters out while she composed herself.

She was used to Azazel's ribbing, but even that had felt stunted compared to what she usually expected from her sibling. It wasn't like Azazel to hold *back* in her prodding, not since the three of them had fallen and chosen to make their own worlds.

They had been at odds ever since, trying to outdo one another and prove that they were the superior sister. Natalia knew she was better than they were, and she felt the need to let Azazel and Raziel strive to prove their points, futile as they were.

Yet, Natalia had felt her sister bite her tongue, as though she had chosen *not* to go down her usual route of winding Natalia up. It wasn't normal; in fact, it was almost as unnerving as the silence that filled her city.

And where was Raziel?! Never, in all of their years since their separation, had *one* sister taken the time to wind the other up without the third sticking their nose in as well. Twice now, Natalia had spoken with Azazel without Raziel's presence. It was unnatural; it was wrong!

"Everything is wrong." Natalia scowled, striding out of the square as she walked purposefully down another street, wondering if she might find her citizens elsewhere.

Natalia could feel her anger swelling inside herself at the continued lack of presence from her people. They should have been throwing themselves at her *feet* and proclaiming their love for her, and yet, there hadn't even been a *whisper* of their existence. She knew they were there. It wasn't as if they had anywhere else to go; her city was the only place in the world, and it *was* the world.

Every street, every square, every alleyway she walked down, was empty of everything but her own reflection. Never, in all of her existence, had Natalia loathed seeing herself more than she did now. She looked divine, and there was no one to gasp and coo and aww at her as there should have been. She knew she was scowling; she could feel a knot forming between her eyes, and she couldn't bear to look at herself. Her angry face was not attractive, and the lines that would form would only fuel her rage further.

"Fine. Be childish, all of you. I'll leave you all to wallow in your misery, and then we'll see how well you all do, hm?" Natalia huffed, flicking her dark curls over her shoulder with her hand as she turned toward her palace. "You'll regret this," she hissed.

A smile flickered across her features, and Natalia giggled darkly as she stared at her grinning reflection. There was mischief in those sapphire eyes of hers, and it was delightful.

"I gave you all a gift because you were the most beautiful humans in existence. You were all as close to perfection as humans could be, though you would never meet *my* standards. No one could! I wonder how well you'll all fare if I take away your looks and my gifts, and leave you all to rot in despair. Maybe then, you'll learn your place in this world. You'll all come crawling back to me, begging for my forgiveness, but I wonder if I'll feel as inclined to grant it." She snorted.

Oh, how wicked she could be, but they had to learn the way of the world, and they seemed to have forgotten it. She would make them remember how *good* they had it because of her.

Natalia watched her reflection as she lifted her hand, wiggling her fingers as though waving at the woman staring back at her. She was already the most beautiful creature in existence. Well, now, she was going to ensure that *everyone* remembered that.

Inhaling deeply, Natalia closed her eyes and focused on her inner calm, quashing the tidal wave of emotions that threatened to overwhelm her. She was in control, she was the master of this place, and she was going to prove it to everyone, just as she had a thousand times before. She had let her sisters plant their seeds of doubt, but no longer. Natalia was in charge here.

Her breathing slowed as she reached deep into herself, focusing on drawing her powers out. It wasn't as easy as it had been when she was in Heaven, but no matter. As far as Natalia was concerned, her ability to still utilize her powers—despite her father's attempt to hobble her—only proved her point that *she* was the most powerful being in existence. She was better than He was. He may have clipped her wings, but He hadn't stifled her brilliance—merely hindered it slightly.

Natalia felt the swell of her power deep in her stomach and rising to her chest, and she smiled. She spread her arms wide, her palms toward the sky. As the surge within reached its apex, Natalia slammed her hands together with a thunder-like crack that echoed throughout the entire city, the ground shuddering against the force of her powers. She heard the city gasp in shock as the ground trembled at her magnificence, followed by the collective screams of her citizens as the realization of what she had done became apparent to them. They would never forget their place again, not after this.

Opening her eyes, Natalia winked at the wickedly smiling image of herself as she strode toward her palace with a satisfied look upon her smug face. They would come crawling back soon enough, and when they did, she would consider whether or not to forgive them for their betrayals. For now, she would enjoy their screams, for it was music to her ears.

18

"M-my Lady?" Jules stammered as he greeted Natalia atop the steps of the palace, though his attention appeared to be fixated on the screaming city beyond.

Natalia grinned as she looked at her Head Priest, his hood pulled back from his ashen face, his eyes wide and filled with fear. The residents of her palace were left immune to her little punishment; the priests and priestesses had remained loyal. Jules may have made the mistake of questioning her when he shouldn't have, but his devotion to her was unwavering, and she would reward him for *that*, at least.

She came to stand beside him, draping one arm over his shoulders, the other hand resting gently on the shoulder closest to her as she pressed her body against his arm. Her eyes followed his gaze as the city continued to scream, the level of hysteria rising amongst the rest of her citizens. Their fear was almost palpable. Natalia could have sworn she tasted the metallic tinge of sweat and dismay from where she stood.

"Wh-what's happened, Magnificent One?" Jules stammered.

She watched her priest out of the corner of her eye, amused as she spotted his glance toward her and away again. Now *his* fear, she *could* taste. He could act as strong as he liked, but there was no hiding his true feelings from her, not when she could feel his body quivering under her half-embrace. Good. She hadn't punished Jules, nor the acolytes, but they would all cement their place in their minds, given the punishment that the rest of the city was now enduring.

"I walked amongst them, as I promised I would, and not one of them came out to honor me as I expected. I will not be disrespected, Jules, not by anyone. Least of all, the insects I have taken pity on, and given such lavish gifts to as I have all these years. So, they are learning a lesson, one I hope I will never have to repeat since it is so ugly in nature, but one that they clearly all require." She sighed, resting her head on her hand and looking up at the priest through her lashes.

"A lesson?" he asked, glancing down at her.

Natalia giggled. She stood upright, planting a kiss on Jules' cheek. The priest whimpered, his knees giving way beneath him as he pressed his lips to Natalia's bare feet over and over and over again in thanks for her affection and attention.

"Yes, a lesson. Find Helena. I want you both to take your acolytes and priestesses into the city to witness the punishment that I have spared you all from. See with your own eyes the fate that shall await anyone who dare to defy me further. My patience has run out, order will be restored, and they will remember who their goddess is." Natalia smiled, gently removing her foot from Jules' desperate advances, striding back into the embrace of the palace. "Go now, Jules, and remind my people who is in charge here. Show them what loyalty and love can reward, as you and the rest of the palace have been left immune. Tell them that it's time they remember who they are loyal to, and that such indiscretions will not be ignored again."

"Y-yes, my Lady. I shall fetch them now," Jules replied.

He scurried past her, his head kept low, back bent in respect as he hurried into the palace to do as she had requested. She would leave him to see the fruits of her labor with his own eyes; it would have more impact if they saw it themselves, rather than Natalia describing what she had done.

It was a good day to be a god.

The haggard expressions on the faces of Natalia's loyalists told her everything she needed to know about how they felt in terms of the punishment that she'd dished out to the rest of the city. Together, the acolytes and priestesses shuffled back through the Throne Room, bowing instinctively to their Mistress, though Natalia felt it was a little shallow.

She wasn't angry at them; however, she'd expected them to be a bit deflated on their return. The reality of what she had done to the rest of the world had been shoved in their faces, the terror and hysteria of the city within their reach. They were safe, but only as long as they loved her, and how could they not love her after everything she did for them all?

It was alright. They'd learn now.

Jules and Helena walked in, arm-in-arm, clearly using the other to stay upright. It was somewhat surprising to see the pair so close, considering their silent rivalry for Natalia's affection, but it convinced Natalia that her punishment was just. If these two could get over their usual squabbles and help one another through the shock, then the rest of her citizens would realize the severity of their actions and come crawling back to her for forgiveness. It wouldn't be long before they were showering her with their undying love and affection once again.

"Well?" Natalia asked, inspecting her pristine fingernails in a nonchalant fashion, her legs hanging over one arm of her throne as she sat casually upon it.

"The city is in turmoil, my Lady. The people are...," Helena began, her hand over her heart as though that would stop it from racing.

Natalia grinned as she swung her legs around, facing her Head Priest and Priestess properly, her fingers laced together on her lap.

"They're what, Helena?" Natalia asked in a jovial tone.

The pair flinched, clearly taken aback by how happy she seemed, but why wouldn't she be? Had she not rectified her mistake? She had allowed complacency, and now she had fixed it. They would never, *ever*, forget who their loyalty and love should be reserved for. Not anymore.

"They're *ugly*," Helena scoffed, her nose wrinkling in disdain.

"They're old," Jules added quietly, his body shuddering visibly at the thought.

"They're how they would be if it wasn't thanks to *me*." Natalia sighed, pushing herself off the throne and spinning around with a gleeful giggle. "I gave them life, *eternal* life, and I kept them fit and healthy, and all I ever asked for was that they love me in return. I gave them perfection and allowed them a taste of what they *could* be, and all I wanted was for them to admire my splendor as I was due. It wasn't a lot to ask for; how could they not adore me? *Look* at me! And yet, even after I punished the others and deprived them of my presence, they turned their backs on me when I gave them time to be beside me." Natalia tutted and shook her head, glancing back at Jules and Helena over her shoulder with a grin. "They won't forget now. They will see how ugly their actions have been, and they will ache and weep for the beauty that they had taken from them. And once they've learnt their place, I'll think about returning their lives to them as they were."

"M-my Lady…," Helena began, her words halting before they started.

In the reflection of the walls and floor, Natalia spotted the glance between Helena and Jules, and she raised an eyebrow at it. Never in all their years together had Helena looked to *Jules* before speaking to Natalia.

"Speak!" Natalia snapped, turning on the pair like a viper in the sand snatching its prey.

"I worry that many will take their lives. Seeing them with our own eyes… the heartache that they are clearly suffering, the despair," Helena whispered.

"Then let them. Only those *worthy* of being in my presence will remain. Let those grotesque people die if that's what they wish to do; it will only prove that they were not meant to bask in my magnificence!" Natalia snorted. "If they had ever been truly beautiful, they would know better. Anyway, I have spent my day in the vaults, now I want a bath. Tend to me, Helena. And Jules? I will see you in my chamber tonight," Natalia cooed, giggling as the Head Priest's eyes widened, threatening to pop straight out of their sockets with the shock.

Loyalty would be rewarded, and tonight, he would finally have his prize.

19

The door to her chamber opened, and Natalia giggled as she shifted on her bed, swinging around onto her stomach to face the door as Jules shuffled nervously inside. He closed the door behind him and remained there for a moment, his back pressed against the ornate entryway, his face hidden beneath his hood.

It amused Natalia to see him so apprehensive. He never had the confidence that Helena did in her presence, but he was more nervous than usual. As he remained unmoved, Natalia rolled her eyes and laughed aloud, the sound pleasant as it echoed back at her in the enormous room. She crawled to the edge of the bed, slowly, grinning as she spotted him glance up at her and look away again when he saw her naked frame. He'd seen her this way a thousand times before, but this was the only time she had sought to seduce *him*.

"Come now, Jules, we've waited a long time for this day. Won't you look at me?" She purred at him as she slid off the bed and began to saunter across the room toward her Head Priest. "I know you've been waiting for tonight, so why are you so hesitant?"

"I… I have imagined this for so long, my Lady. I just never believed that it would come true," Jules whimpered, wringing his hands as he kept glancing up from the floor to Natalia and back down again, not quite able to meet her eyes.

"Oh, Jules, good things always come to those who wait," Natalia continued huskily as she reached for him, sliding her hands up his chest, slightly irked by the robe he wore that remained between them. "And I'm the best thing of all; I'm *always* worth the wait," she whispered, her hands reaching up to remove the hood from the man's handsome face.

"You won't be worth a *damn* thing soon enough!" A voice shouted from behind.

Natalia hissed, relinquishing her grip of Jules as she spun around to face the intruder. How did they even get into her private bed chamber?! Had they been hiding this entire time? Just waiting for her and Jules to be alone?!

The sight that met Natalia was utterly repulsive, and she gave a small shriek of horror at the shriveled man before her. Hunch backed, his skin laid loosely on his bony frame, his withered body covered in deep wrinkles that left his eyes looking sunken into his skull. She had stripped her citizens of their natural born beauty, leaving them withering and old, on the brink of death with every breath they took. She'd known they would be disgusting, but actually seeing one of them with her own eyes was another thing entirely!

"How did you get in here?!" She snarled, nose wrinkled in disgust as she stepped back against Jules, wanting to put as much distance between her and the shrunken man before her as possible.

"By sheer force of will and determination. Not just mine, but the city's as well. We've had enough of you; it's time you paid for *your* sins." The man snapped in return, raising a shaky hand above his head with a dark smile upon his leathery face, a glass bottle glistening in his hand. "The time has come, the time we've all been waiting for, the time of liberation!" he shouted.

Natalia gasped as Jules roughly grasped her by the shoulders, his fingernails digging into her delicate skin as he all but tossed her aside. She grunted as she fell indignantly to the ground, skidding along the polished golden floor a few feet from where she had been standing. Her head whipped around, ready to admonish Jules for such blasphemy.

But any thoughts of reprimand that she may have had vanished as her Head Priest screamed loudly, his body quivering as he writhed against the door, clawing at the robe that covered his body.

It took the fallen archangel a moment to realize what was happening, but when the realization hit her, she screamed. Whatever the citizen had been holding, had been thrown at Jules—though it had been meant for her. If it hadn't been for the priest's quick thinking, she would have been the victim of the contents of the bottle instead… and that would have been a fate worse than death for Natalia.

She scurried backwards as Jules swung in her direction. If she had thought their assailant was horrific, it was nothing in comparison to the sight that stood before her now. The hood had fallen back from Jules' face, or what was left of it. Huge chunks of flesh had been eaten away by the oozing green liquid that dripped onto the floor, along with blood and bits of the Head Priest's cheek. His lips were completely gone, leaving a perpetual, *terrible* smile on the poor man's face. His eyes, barely held in his skull now that his eyelids had melted, stared at Natalia in horror and desperation, one hand reaching out to her for aid while the other clawed at what remained of his face.

"Stay away! Get away from me!" Natalia howled, physically repulsed by the man's appearance as she scurried to her feet and hurried to the safety of her bed.

"That should have been *you!*" the assailant hissed, reaching behind his back to produce a dagger. "To make you as ugly on the outside as you are on the *inside.*"

That word.

That *one* word.

That was all it took for Natalia to snap out of herself and return to her composure. She turned her stunning gaze on the wilted man, her lip curling with her loathing. Out of the corner of her eye, Natalia saw Jules collapse forward onto his face. A crumpled, bloodied mess of the man he'd once been. This *creature* had robbed her of her evening *and* of her Head Priest, and she couldn't allow that, let alone the slight upon her! She would *never* be ugly; she was *perfect.*

Natalia strode across the room toward the man, too quick for him to react beyond gasping as her hand shot out to grip his throat tightly, her nails digging into his sagging flesh. She drew him closer to her, despite her revulsion at his very existence, as she glared down at him.

"I'll show you what ugly really looks like." She snarled.

As her door flew open—clearly by the arrival of the acolytes and priestesses who had been banished from the vicinity to allow Natalia and Jules their time alone—Natalia launched the offender straight out of her bedroom window. His frail body soared through the air and straight into the open world beyond her balcony, his screams fading as he fell onto the street below. There was a soft, yet sickening, crunch as he met his end, but that was drowned out by Natalia's infuriated roar.

On the horizon beyond her palace, the city was ablaze,

glowing golden as smoke rose toward the sky. Her punishment hadn't been enough, and now her people were rebelling. She could feel, deep in her heart, that her powers were waning and that she was losing control of them. What more could she do?

20

Natalia hugged her knees to her chest as she watched Helena direct Jules' acolytes to remove the disturbing remains of their Head Priest from her chamber. She could not bring herself to watch as they turned him over, not wanting to sully her vision or her memory further than it already had been.

There were several gasps when they turned over Jules' body to reveal the extent of the attack, and several of the acolytes wretched and vomited. If that was their reaction, Natalia had no need to look for herself.

She rested her head on her knee, scowling as she half-listened to Helena's instructions to the others, and whispered words about acid of some kind or other. It didn't matter *what* had done that to Jules; the only thing that mattered to Natalia was that it had been meant for *her*, and that she'd been robbed of one of her most devoted subjects. How *dare* these rebels steal Jules from her like this?! He had known how to show true reverence to her magnificence, and now he was gone. Helena would do what she could, but she had never been quite as eloquent with her names for Natalia as Jules had been.

"Barricade the doors and windows! I don't want anyone else getting into the palace unless I, or our Lady, says otherwise!" Helena snapped, causing Natalia to sniffle.

The man had made some sort of grappling hook, shimmying his way up the rope with what little strength he must have had left, in order to get onto her balcony. Natalia had never once closed the window to her bedroom, preferring to feel the fresh air that blew through it—feeling as close to the freedom of flying as she could that way. They had robbed her of *that* as well.

The smoke still rose outside of the palace proper, and the screams and shouts of the rebellious factions defiled Natalia's ears. There were still a few loyal citizens, beyond those who remained in the palace, clearly having learnt from their punishment. Losing their immortality and having their looks stripped away had obviously reminded them that Natalia was their one true love, and now they screamed and begged at her door for aid.

Yet none of them had come to see her when she visited the city streets. Had they *just* bowed down and worshipped her like they were supposed to, none of this would be happening!

A few of the priestesses asked Helena whether they should let those seeking help into the palace, but one dark look from Natalia had said it all. No one was going to be allowed in, not now; no one outside of the palace walls could be trusted. How could they tell if there wasn't a spy amongst them? Someone looking to get inside to harm Natalia, just as that man had?

"My Lady, should I draw you a bath?" Helena asked.

"No. Just go away." Natalia snarled, not wanting to look at the woman.

"But my Lady, we need to make sure that none of the acid touched your precious skin."

"GO AWAY!" Natalia roared, the palace shaking with her ferocity as she turned on her priestess.

"As you wish...," Helena whimpered, bowing her head and scurrying out of the room after the others, closing the door behind her.

Natalia began to scream, thumping her soft bedspread with her fists and kicking her feet just like any toddler having a tantrum would. This wasn't supposed to happen to her! She was perfection, she was splendor, and she was *amazing*! Why could these fools not just recognize that?!

"You are not alone, Sister."

"Raziel?! Where have you been?" Natalia replied, stopping short in her shrieking, eyes wide in shock at her sister's sudden intrusion. "I've had to put up with Azazel's nonsense, but you were not there; it's so unlike you."

"I had my own things to deal with; it's not always about you," Raziel replied.

It had always amazed Natalia how her sister could sound emotionless, yet angry, at the same time. There was always a subtle change in the intonation of her sister's monotone that Natalia had managed to pick up over the centuries. It was minute, barely noticeable, but of course, Natalia had spotted it where others wouldn't.

"Must have been dire if the ever-impulsive Raziel was unable to come and spit her barbs at us. If that had been me, I'd have made the time; can't have you two thinking you've bested me." Azazel's smug tone snorted.

"Yes, well, I am not you, Sister. I do not need to prove myself to either of you."

"Enough! Both of you. Something is wrong, and I can't be the only one feeling this way." Natalia sighed.

She didn't like admitting it; she'd been pushing the doubt to the back of her mind—along with that niggling feeling of something else that she didn't want to admit existed.

"No, you are not. Something *is* wrong. Many of my people are now able to pull away from my influence. None of them are meant to be able to form relationships outside of the ones I allow, but that is no longer the case," Raziel replied, her tone almost bored.

"It is the same for me here. I thought the punishment that I had given them would be enough, but one of them attacked me last night and killed my Head Priest by accident."

"What punishment?" Azazel asked, her voice dripping with excitement, as though she might be able to use it herself.

"I stole their beauty from them. Nothing that you would have any use of, I'm sure. I thought they would realize how foolish they had been and beg me to restore what little good looks they once had. They would never match me, but I've made them purposefully ugly, and rather than beg for my forgiveness, they have turned on me. Not all, but most. They've set fire to my city, and they call for my blood. The assailant dared to say that he was going to make me as ugly on the outside as he thinks I am on the inside." Natalia snarled, her lips curling as she remembered the exchange.

"Just you slipping, Sister. Nothing for the rest of us to worry about." Azazel snorted.

"Except it's happening to all of us. There's no use denying it, Azazel. If it's happening to Natalia and I, then it's happening to you also."

Natalia smiled, licking her lips in excitement as Raziel turned on their sibling. It was also so satisfying to have the pair go at one another rather than at her.

"So, what do you propose? Come, Natalia, you're the one who suggested this venture in the first place, the one who wanted to prove her powers to the rest of us. How do you suggest we fix what appears to be broken?" Azazel cooed, clearly feeding Natalia's ego, though Natalia was more than happy to allow her sister to fuel the fire in her heart.

That was the problem, though. It was happening to all of them, and Natalia was unsure of how to fix the issue.

21

Natalia had cut contact with her sisters abruptly, not willing to let them think that she had completely lost her control—not yet—because she *hadn't*. Not entirely. She could feel the tether to her citizens slipping from her fingers, and now that she thought about it, Natalia realized that even her powers were beginning to wane.

She hadn't wanted to admit how tired she'd been when she had punished the city, and hadn't wanted to concede that it had taken a great deal of effort to gather her powers in order to enact it in the first place. Natalia and her sisters had gathered together to create their three separate worlds to show God that they were better than He was, that He had made a mistake when He'd banished them from Heaven.

Was it merely the length of time since their fall that was causing the blip she now felt? Like a tear had been made in the fabric of her world, and everything she had known for certain was now slipping through the cracks like water through her fingers…

No! No. Not her, this didn't happen to *her*. She was the superior being here. The more she let this doubt creep into her heart, the more it was affecting her; that was all this was… wasn't it?

But it wasn't just happening to her. Raziel had said it herself, that she was struggling to keep control of her own citizens now. Her sister's apathy had infected her people from the very beginning; it was Raziel's way of keeping them under her control while she searched for something more for herself.

Her sister's futile hunt for love and emotions that were not within her capacity had gone on for centuries, long before even their fall from grace. She had been caught by God during her examination of humans and their emotions, hence her banishment. But her own world hadn't yielded any more answers. Was there an inkling of fear finally finding its way into Raziel's heart? Was that why she was starting to lose control?

The three of them had always been so self-assured. Maybe that was what this was. They had all become complacent, and then begun to doubt themselves in their own ways, and because of that, they were unable to focus and keep control.

Yes. That made sense. Natalia had *never* doubted her own brilliance until Samuel and her sisters' interference. This was all *their* doing. No more contact! She was putting an end to their influence in her life once and for all. She *knew* she was better than them; she always had been. There was no need in continuing to prove it to them. Let them live in their delusions that they could ever match up to her glory; they wouldn't even come *close*.

Natalia snorted and flicked her hair over her shoulder, staring at her reflection in the wall and smiling. She was beautiful. She bit her bottom lip as she turned slightly, extending one of her legs so that she could admire its elegance and the curve of her buttocks. Her hands flickered over her flawless, pale skin, and she sighed softly as she took the moment to enjoy the image of herself and how perfect she truly was.

She arched her back and pressed her arms against her breasts to make them push out more, pouting and blowing herself a kiss as she giggled slightly. The last few days had been terrible, but she remained as impeccable as ever, despite the amount of scowling she had done. She'd expected lines to form between her eyes from the constant knot that had settled between her brows, but it appeared that her body was even more immaculate than she had expected, and even the stress couldn't dull her allure.

There, that felt better already! It had been her sisters' nonsense infecting her, that was all, leaving a foul blemish on her heart and stifling her majesty. This was why they had separated the worlds, because together, they would have ruined everything that Natalia knew she could achieve. She didn't need them, and now, they would have to suffer an eternity without her.

Natalia gasped and reached a hand out to the wall beside her as the ground beneath her feet shook violently, a deafening clap of thunder echoing through her bed chamber seconds before the glass shattered in the windows. Thousands of tiny, shimmering shards tinkled onto the floor, biting crystals that threatened to cut her fair skin and leave her feet marred forever should she step on them.

She squealed irritably, stepping back from the dangerous shards as her eyes shot to the now empty window frames... and the rising smoke in the center of the city. No! She was in control; she had *fixed* the issue! They shouldn't still be rioting;

they couldn't be, now that she knew why her powers had faltered!

Natalia ran to her balcony, stopping only when the minefield of glass glistened at her in the corner of her eye, daring her to come closer. She couldn't risk it; she would never forgive herself for damaging her precious figure.

Looking around, Natalia found a pair of slippers that had been gifted to her eons ago. She had never worn the things, preferring the freedom of bare feet when she walked, and so she had discarded them to one side of the room by her dresser. They had remained there, forgotten and useless, becoming part of the furnishings in her room. Never would Natalia have ever believed that they would be just what she needed, but in that moment, she was oddly grateful that she hadn't told Helena or Jules to dispose of the footwear.

She hurried to the dresser where they had been placed, slipping her feet into the ornate golden slippers. She blinked in surprise at how comfortable they truly were, then chided herself silently for the distraction, dragging herself back to reality when the ground shook with the force of another explosion.

Natalia was forced to grip her dresser tightly to keep herself from falling over, and she snarled, her lips curling in irritation at this attack. This was a slight against *her*, and she would not tolerate it!

Armed with her new footwear, Natalia hurried over to her balcony, stepping carefully over the broken glass. The last thing she wanted to do was accidentally kick up some of the shards and cut herself, despite her caution. She slid past the hanging frames, their remaining glassy teeth gleaming at her as she made sure not to get too close. Once she was outside, the balcony was blissfully free of anything harmful, and Natalia hurried to the edge. Clinging to the marble railing, she leaned over and stared at the chaos below.

The city was burning, the people were rioting, and her punishment appeared to have been revoked from several of those trying to knock down her main door. Things were worse than she had realized.

22

Natalia made her way back into her chamber, kicking the slippers from her feet once she was back on clear floors. Hurrying to the door, she threw it open so hard that she tore it from its hinges. One collapsed to the ground with an almighty clatter, while the other swung around to lean against the wall.

Whatever, she didn't have time to worry about such things. She needed to speak with Helena; she needed to deal with the insurgents outside her palace.

"Mistress!" a voice called out from behind her, and Natalia wheeled around to face an acolyte. "Mistress, please. Priestess Helena believes that you would be safest in the vault; we can protect you there," the young man whispered, bowing his head as he dropped to his knees at her feet.

"No. If they think they can intimidate me, *me*, then they are sorely mistaken. I am stronger than they are; this entire *city* could not match my strength. I have never needed to use my physical strength before. Well, not until much more recently, but even then, none of you have seen the true extent of what I am capable of. And now, it's time I prove to these fools that I *am* the true god in this world, and if that means physically ripping them limb from limb, then so be it." Natalia snarled, turning away.

"But… but Mistress!" the young man whimpered, but Natalia took no notice as she strode away. "Please, it's for your own safety! None of us wants you to risk yourself with the disloyal. Let *us* deal with them! It's our job, our duty, our *privilege* to take care of you!" he called after her, but she still did not halt in her purpose.

She could hear the pitter-patter of his footfalls as he hurried after her, muttering under his breath as he clearly tried to find the words to reason with her. Reason was gone. Now, she had to use the ugliest of her powers and get physical with these rebels.

Had they forgotten that she was an angel? Fallen or otherwise, she had been created by God, shaped to be the perfect being. God had just gone a little too far with her. He'd outdone himself and given her too much power, hence her exile. Well, she would remind these petty, pathetic humans of this fact. She would beat it into them until they saw that she was the embodiment of perfection in every way.

They. Would. Learn.

Natalia made her way across the Throne Room, her footfalls silent in comparison to the thudding steps of the acolyte. The air was almost electric with his fear; it was so apparent that Natalia felt it tingling against her skin. For a moment, she considered grabbing him by the scruff of his robe and throwing him straight out into the crowd that waited on her doorstep, but she reminded herself that he was merely human. He couldn't comprehend her strength and resolve, and his worry came from a deep-seated love for her. So really, she couldn't blame him for it, let alone snap at him over it. He was one of her truly loyal followers, and since she had lost Jules, she could do with keeping him around.

Odd, how she missed the priest, now that he was gone. She really had grown used to having him at her heels. He hadn't deserved such a terrible fate; he couldn't even make a beautiful corpse now.

"Move the barricade," Natalia commanded, waving her hand at the priestesses and acolytes gathered by the quivering doors.

The array of furniture and golden statues of herself that had been dragged against the door to keep it shut shivered with every attempt the rebels made to bring the doors down. As if Natalia would create an entranceway that could be brought down by the hands of weak men and women? What did they take her for? Snorting, she stood before the mound of items blocking her way, her eyes flickering over her gathered followers, all of whom were staring at her in disbelief.

"Bu-but my Lady!" one of the Priestesses squealed, her hand at her throat as she looked from Natalia to the mound currently keeping the angry mass at bay.

"You heard me," Natalia replied slowly and quietly, menace tainting her usually sweet tone.

There was no time to argue with the fearful. She had something she needed to do, and she was going to get it done.

"Do as your Lady says! How dare you question her wisdom?!" Helena's sharp tone echoed through the Throne Room.

Natalia smiled, turning her head slightly to glance at her

Head Priestess from over her shoulder. There was the Helena she knew well. Bold, beautiful, and full of confidence. It was this surety that made Helena better-looking in Natalia's eyes, as though it caused her to glow.

"My Lady, we will move the barricade enough to open one of the doors, just enough to let you out. It will allow us to keep the disloyal out; we do not wish the palace to be overrun." Helena added with a firm nod.

"Of course. I will not allow this *scum* to sully our halls with their presence, but I will cast them from my door," Natalia purred, taking a deep, satisfying breath as she smiled. "And then we will begin the arduous task of reminding each and every one of them who I am. For too long, I've left them to their own devices, clearly. Well, no longer."

"My Lady?" Helena glanced at Natalia, surprise flickering briefly across her face, along with something that Natalia suspected was fear.

"You will see. But first, I will deal with this mob." Natalia sighed, stepping forward as the acolytes and priestesses made a path to the door, gripping the huge circular handle in readiness.

Natalia gave a nod of her head and waited for them to open the door just enough for her slight figure to slip through without grazing her precious skin. The second the door shifted, the mutinous mass beyond saw their chance and began to press forward, desperate to get through the gap and into the Palace. But Natalia wasn't going to allow that to happen; they weren't going to set one *toe* inside.

Quick as a flash, Natalia made her move. As the first of the anarchists shoved their way through the door, they found themselves wedged between one another and the structure itself, and they were met with the wrath of their goddess. In the back of her mind, Natalia worried about getting physical, ever conscious of damaging her skin or marking it in any fashion. It was why she despised having to use her physical strength.

She'd hated it as an angel, expected to be a soldier whenever God called upon her for such menial tasks. The war with Lucifer had almost destroyed her, not because of the blood and gore she came back to Heaven covered in, but because she constantly had to fight to keep the demons from cutting her skin. Though it had made her a fine soldier, in a way, no one could dodge and parry a blow like Natalia could. Just another feather in the cap of perfection for her. It didn't make her loathe it any less.

She stepped into their field of vision; her dark smile reflected back at her in their wide, terrified eyes. They knew what was coming; how could they not? They had upset her, and she was going to hurt them as much as they had hurt her… and then some.

23

With the flat of her palm, Natalia slammed her hand into the face of the first man, enjoying the nauseating crunch that his nose made as it shattered from the blow. Blood, hot and sticky, exploded onto her palm as she decimated his nose, leaving only a crater and hanging flesh in the place it had once been. His screams barely registered, nor did the grunt of the man behind him—who found himself headbutted when the first man's head shot backwards at him.

They stumbled back out of the door and onto the open steps. The path was clear, and Natalia slipped through the gap to join the mutinous bunch that waited for her. Some were as wizened as she had expected them to be, as they *all* should have been, yet some seemed to have regained their strength and their good looks. But how? How had her punishment been revoked without *her* saying so?!

Natalia growled and sprang to action, remembering the attack the night before by the man with the bottle, and the state of Jules' face as his flesh and bone were eaten away by the liquid. They would pay for this. They would all pay, and she would take that payment with their lives. The survivors would be the lucky ones; they would learn what a merciful god truly looked like, and they would be given the chance to love her again. They would be devoted; they would be loyal; they would be *hers*.

A blind rage swallowed Natalia as she got her hands dirty, literally. The red mist that blurred her vision was one she hadn't encountered in a *very* long time, and even her sisters hadn't been able to entice it out of her, despite their constant jabbing. The last time she had truly lost her mind to her anger had been just before her fall, when she argued with God and their other siblings, and fought her way out of the Gates of Heaven. God had taken her wings, but *she* had fought for her own freedom and made her way to Earth. He'd been powerless to stop that, and now, *they* would be powerless to stop *her*.

She was a whirlwind of perfect moves. Every time they tried to swarm her, clearly hoping that they would win through sheer numbers alone, she found a way to distance herself from them or push them back. They couldn't get close enough to the tornado that was Natalia to land a blow. A couple of the rebels tried to launch themselves at her from opposite angles, but Natalia caught them and threw them into the wall of their companions, pushing them back from the doors of her palace and sending them stumbling down the steps to the street below.

The crowd stepped back a little, hesitating as they realized that they were out of their league. Natalia watched their resolve waver, but she could see in their eyes that the fires of rebellion still raged on. They weren't ready to give up; this was their chance, and she could see it written on their faces. Did they really think they could win this fight? Why could they not understand how good they all had it under her rule?!

"Ignorant pigs!" She spat at them, the rage swelling in her chest, her heart racing painfully.

"I'd rather be an ignorant pig than beholden to someone as *hideous* as you," a soft, feminine voice whispered from behind her.

Natalia jumped. Her rage had clouded her vision and her ability to think rationally. She had allowed one of them to get behind her, to get *close*. Out of the corner of her eye, Natalia caught a glint of glass, and her heart fell through the floor. She knew what that bottle contained; she had seen what it had done to her beloved Jules.

"No!" another voice screamed.

Before Natalia could react, the acolyte who had begged her to remain safe in the vault threw himself out of the door, slamming his body against the woman.

Natalia whipped around as the pair screamed and writhed at her feet, the terrible contents eating at their flesh the second the bottle had shattered from their fall. Her gaze fixed on that of the acolyte, and she saw the plea in his expression just as she had in Jules, but this time, she knew that even if she got involved, it was too late.

She ripped the offender away from the acolyte, sending her flailing body down the steps and into the crowd, though she did not go as far as Natalia had intended.

Why did she ache so much? Had someone managed to land a blow?! No... it was her strength itself. She was *panting*. How had she not realized it before? That brief pause had caused the rage to dissipate for a moment, just long enough for the rest of her body to catch up and realize how exhausting this all was. Her heart pounded in her chest, and her lungs burned with every breath, her breathing quick and labored from the sheer effort of fighting off these rebellious citizens of hers.

No. This couldn't be happening, not to her! She had never grown tired in a fight. She had never slowed, not even in the war. They had fought for several months at a time, with no respite, and she had never faltered during that entire time.

Dark tendrils crept into her mind, icy hands gripping her heart as the doubt resurfaced. She was kidding herself if she thought she wasn't losing her power; she could see that now.

Her hesitation was all it took for one of the rebels to launch himself at her, a glistening golden dagger held high above his head. For a moment, the darkness in Natalia's heart threatened to let him kill her. How could she go on living if she wasn't completely perfect? She couldn't live flawed; that wasn't who she was. Just as the tip of the blade plunged toward her chest, the acolyte, halfway to death but still loyal enough to protect his goddess, grabbed the man by the leg and caused him to stumble.

Natalia reacted, her hand snapping up to grab the assailant by the wrist. In one fluid motion, she elbowed the man in the stomach and flung him over her shoulder before scooping up the dying acolyte, careful not to touch any of the areas where the acid had burned him. Before the rest of the rioters could make a move, Natalia had thrown the assailant and the acolyte through the opening into the palace and slid back inside herself.

The rest of her loyalists slammed the door shut, and before they could pile the barricade back against the entrance, Natalia placed her palm upon the crack that separated the two doors. Taking a deep breath, she closed her eyes and drew on the last of her strength, pushing it out into her palm.

The metal grew hot, and molten gold dripped onto the floor as she melted the two doors shut.

Stumbling backwards, Natalia all but collapsed into Helena's arms, her vision blurring as she gasped for breath. She was losing, and she didn't have any idea why.

S oft, warm, comforting. Safe.

That was how Natalia felt as she stirred in her bed. She didn't remember falling asleep. In fact, she couldn't remotely recall going to bed. All she could remember was Helena catching her after she had sealed the palace doors, and she had a vague recollection of the Head Priestess calling her name and begging her to explain what had happened.

Opening her eyes slowly, Natalia tried to roll over and winced. Her body felt heavy, as though her limbs were filled with lead, and even the very act of breathing seemed to take a great deal of effort.

Had she really lost so much of her powers that she was

now beginning to feel the effects of their use? She had *never* felt this way before. Extended use of her abilities hadn't even caused a mild headache before; it had been as natural to her as breathing itself. Everything was changing, and not for the better as far as Natalia was concerned.

With a grunt and a whimper, Natalia forced the covers off her body and sat up. She flinched as her body protested the movements, and inhaling a deep breath caused her lungs to groan like an unoiled machine as it forced itself to move despite the rust.

"My Lady, please, just relax. Your body needs to rest and recuperate. The strain of the last few days has taken its toll upon you," Helena whispered, appearing suddenly at her bedside.

There was an uncertainty in Helena's tone that Natalia didn't recognize, though she could not have argued against it being there, either. She was meant to be flawless; she was meant to be all powerful. The fight with her citizens shouldn't have caused her to collapse as it so clearly had. For a brief moment, Natalia considered reaching out to her sisters for their opinions, but her head ached enough, and she didn't have the capacity to deal with their jibes in her current condition.

Natalia turned her head to face her Head Priestess, wondering how long it would be before even her most loyal subjects began to turn away from her. She had lost Jules, and she had lost another acolyte. Funny how none of Helena's priestesses, or even the Head Priestess herself, hadn't made a move to protect her whatsoever. Had their loyalty begun to waver even before this latest incident?

"The acolyte, the one who died, what was his name?" Natalia asked, wincing as her throat scratched uncomfortably, and her tongue felt a hundred times larger than it should have been.

"I... I would have to ask the other acolytes, my Lady. I do

not know," Helena answered, eyebrows raised high at the unexpected question.

"Do that," Natalia replied, closing her eyes for a moment as she lied back down, curling into a ball despite the reluctant creak of her muscles.

"I'll go and speak to them now. I will send in one of my girls with something to eat and drink," Helena said more confidently, bowing to Natalia as she hurried from the room.

Natalia listened as her footsteps hurried away. She maneuvered herself so that she could watch the woman leave, shocked to find that the doors had been re-hung on their hinges so that they could be shut once more. How long had she been asleep for?

Sitting up again, Natalia turned her head toward her windows. The glass had all been cleared from the floor, and the frames were set back into their places, though there were no new panes—instead, there was a temporary measure of wooden boards to keep them closed. It was ugly, and wouldn't allow Natalia to view herself. It was the first time since creating the world that Natalia was faced with something that *wouldn't* reflect her beauty back to her.

Part of her wanted to lie back down, pull the covers over her head, and go back to sleep for a thousand years. Maybe then, she would wake up and realize that all of this was just a horrible nightmare sent by God as His last act of punishment for proving that she was better than He was. She knew better, but the icy grip of doubt lingered in her heart, and she could hope that all of this was just a mistake.

Another part of her wanted to get up, to throw open the windows to her balcony, and see what remained of her beautiful, perfect city. But if the city was in ruins, did she really want that image to mar her sight? She could rebuild, she could make it just as it had been, but first, she had to deal with the slight issue of her rebellious citizens…

"That man," Natalia whispered, throwing the covers from

her body and swinging her legs over the edge of her bed. "What happened to him?" she asked the empty room.

Forcing herself to her feet, Natalia gripped at one of the bed posts as her knees buckled slightly. She was exhausted, but she was *not* going to give up; she was better than this! She was the best, and she wanted *answers.*

Shuffling to her dresser, Natalia slipped her feet into the silk slippers that had found their way back to where they belonged. She threw on a light robe from her dresser chair and made her way out of her bedroom, slipping through a crack in the door that Helena had left.

"My Lady? Shouldn't you be in bed? Resting?" a female acolyte, guarding her room, asked as she appeared in the corridor.

"What happened to the rebel that I brought into the palace?" Natalia asked, ignoring the question entirely.

"Priestess Helena instructed us to lock him in the cellar, my Lady, since we don't have a dungeon to speak of," the acolyte continued, daring to look up at Natalia. "I can take you to him, if you wish."

"I do. I have questions, and I believe he may have the answers." Natalia growled.

It was time to put this nonsense to rest, once and for all.

25

Natalia never spent any time in the palace cellar; she had absolutely no need to, after all. Her subjects were there to cater to her every need. What possible reason would have compelled her to venture into the depths of the palace?

Funny, now the cellar had been turned into a glorified dungeon. Not only did Natalia now have to venture down into it for the first time since she created her world, but now she chastised herself for not making an *actual* dungeon when she had constructed her palace.

As if she would ever have *dreamt* of needing one! She gave her people everything they needed to survive; they lived an eternal life of luxury with everything they could ever have asked for. They only had to love her.

She would never have imagined needing to *punish* her subjects; how hard was it to worship her? They'd all managed for so many years that it had never once crossed her mind that things would change as dramatically as they had.

Now she understood why her father had created Hell for Lucifer and the others who dared to act against Him. It set an example for the rest… well, to a point. Natalia, Raziel, and Azazel seemed to be the exceptions, though Natalia believed that was because God was too afraid to even *dare* send *her* down there. She'd have released the pit onto his precious city in the clouds! Best to leave her to create her own world rather than risk irritating her and unleashing her wrath. A wise move on His part; one of the few, in her opinion.

Striding down the steps into the lower levels of the palace, Natalia followed after the acolyte, feeling oddly out of place in her own palace. She didn't belong down here in the dark, dingy depths of her home. While it was still beautiful, the walls mirrored and the floors made of shining gold as the rest of the palace was, it felt darker and colder.

Natalia didn't like it. She felt exposed in a way that made her skin crawl. She could imagine her sisters lurking in the shadows like this, but not herself; this just didn't suit her. Natalia was meant to be on display for all to see, so that they could stare at her and gasp in awe. They couldn't do that when she was hidden away in the cavernous depths of the palace cellar…

Natalia held her head high as the acolyte turned to face her, clearly looking to her to see if she was content with continuing on. The last thing she needed was for those still loyal to her to start questioning whether or not she was in her right mind, or confident in her own decisions. She would not allow them to see her falter, not now, not ever. It wasn't going to happen!

"Oh, Sister, but it already is." Azazel's pompous tone slithered into Natalia's head, and she was forced to keep her face straight, despite the disdain she felt at her sister's interruption.

"And you're faring any better, are you?" Natalia rebuked silently.

Normally, Natalia would have spoken aloud to her sibling. She had done so on numerous occasions in front of the acolytes, and they'd grown accustomed to these somewhat strange one-sided conversations. However, this time, she didn't want anyone eavesdropping on her conversation with Azazel.

Raziel's absence hadn't gone unnoticed, either, though after their last contact, Natalia was beginning to question whether their sister would join in on the taunting or not moving forward. It seemed that Raziel's grip on her world was slipping far quicker, but Natalia intended on fixing hers before it slipped any further than this minor hiccup that she was currently suffering.

"Tell me, Sister, how close have your people come to slitting your throat?" Natalia added with a smirk, flicking her curls over her shoulder as she strode after the acolyte.

"No closer than usual." Azazel snorted.

"Not that you would tell me even if they had. Oh, Sister, such bravado, but if Raziel is slipping, I know for a fact that you will, too. As if you could surpass me in keeping control."

Natalia cut the connection before her sister could utter whatever retort she may have been formulating. Natalia had won that round, naturally, and she was going to leave her sister seething at that.

"Mistress?" The acolyte turned to face Natalia, a look of concern upon the young woman's smooth featured face.

Natalia smiled at her, reaching out a hand and caressing the girl's cheeks with her fingertips. A swell of amusement rippled in Natalia's stomach as the acolyte shivered at her touch and let out a soft, whimpering moan. Humans really *were* such simple creatures. The gentlest touch, and they were putty in her hands. That brush of the cheek would keep this particular acolyte loyal for centuries, millennia even, in the hopes that Natalia would honor her with another in the future. Or something more intimate, if she was lucky. And she might be.

The girl was pretty, meek, and her skin was soft. Natalia had been considering bedding Helena, but she might take this girl instead since she was likely to appreciate that intimacy more since she didn't expect it like Helena did.

Her priestess was loyal, she couldn't deny that, but the seeds of suspicion were sown already, and Natalia questioned whether Helena was getting above her station. Especially since Jules' unfortunate demise.

Jules. The mere thought of her Head Priest caused a slight fluttering in Natalia's heart, and she made the conscious effort *not* to scowl at this unexpected and unfamiliar feeling. The man had been by her side from the very beginning; he'd been the most devoted from the moment she'd chosen him to come to her world. In fact, Jules had been the first human she picked to be amongst her citizens. How she had forgotten that, she didn't know. Then again, it hadn't seemed that important at the time.

What did it matter who was picked when? Was Helena second? Was that where their rivalry for her time and affection had begun? Why *now* did she feel Jules' missing presence more than she believed she would? He was only a human, but he *had* been particularly devoted to her, and given the nonsense that was currently going on in her world, she would've liked him by her side. Natalia hadn't realized how much she'd come to rely upon the man, or how normal it was for him to be beside her, until he wasn't.

These rebels would pay. She was going to create them their own very special Hell, just as her father had. They would suffer punishments that even *she* would shiver at, all because they'd turned against her and taken Jules from her. *Her* Head Priest, the man she'd appointed as her speaker for the people so that they would be *closer* to her through one of their own.

No, she would not forgive that slight, nor the fact that they had meant to harm *her* with the acid that had ruined poor Jules' beautiful face. They would all suffer at her hands, and then they would come to realize just how good they'd had it beforehand… and they would beg on their knees for her to forgive them. All of them.

26

Several acolytes and priestesses hurried to the numerous doors that lined the corridors in the deepest depths of the palace as the rumor spread of Natalia's presence in their domain. They bowed as she passed, their whispers preceding her arrival, and following after her as she swept past them.

She could feel their surprise, palpable in the air, so thick that Natalia reckoned she could reach out and physically *touch* their emotions. They had never seen her down here, by the kitchens, and rightly so. Why in her name would she ever need to be down here, where her subjects worked for her? This was their domain within her world, not hers, though there was a thought that maybe Natalia should surprise them more often. Their shock and awe were a delightfully sweet treat on her tongue, and just the salve her heavy heart needed after all that had gone on recently. They loved her, they *loved her*, and they were grateful for this minor glance of their goddess.

Yes. She would grace her humble servants with her physical presence more often—not too often, though, or else the anticipation and shock would be lost, and the joy at this glimpse of her would be faded. But she would come down more than she did before, which wouldn't be hard considering that she'd never been.

Passing the last of the kitchen doors, there loomed a colossal door of pure gold. The mirrored surface was polished to perfection, as the entire palace was, so Natalia could still look upon her own magnificence as she caught her reflection.

However, there were no engraved depictions of herself. No sculpted scenes of her dancing or lounging under the sun. Natalia had never thought to grace any decoration on this end of the palace, because she'd never expected to *be* here.

The acolyte hurried to one of the huge ring handles, throwing her entire weight backwards to shift the massive door, with no success whatsoever. Natalia stepped forward, waving the girl away with a dismissive hand and a slight smirk. She took hold of the handle with one hand and pulled.

When the door did not immediately give way to her natural strength, which should have allowed her to open the cellar entrance with minimal effort on her part, Natalia scowled. If it had not been for her reflection scowling back at her, Natalia might have left the expression on her face, but she could see the acolyte staring at her and did not need the girl to notice Natalia's confusion. With a shake of her head, Natalia tried again, putting more force behind her movement this time.

The door gave way with no further protest this time, and Natalia felt her muscles relax in her shoulders. She hadn't even realized how tense she had become; she just hoped that the acolyte hadn't noticed it, either. With Jules gone, the acolytes would turn to Helena, and the *last* thing Natalia wanted was for word to get back to the Head Priestess that their goddess was not in her right mind. Helena would come fishing, and the more Natalia thought about the woman, the more Natalia wanted to keep Helena at arm's length.

Natalia opened the door just wide enough for her to fit through. She had no idea what precautions the others had taken to secure and restrain their prisoner, and she was not about to let him escape... not until she was done with him, anyway.

"Stay here and guard the door. I will call for you if I need you," Natalia instructed the acolyte, her eyes fixed on the dimly flickering light that beckoned to her from the below.

"B-but Mistress!" the acolyte squeaked in protest.

Natalia stepped closer to the girl, her lip curling unpleasantly. The acolyte whimpered and jumped backwards. Throwing herself, prostrate, to the ground as she trembled under Natalia's dark gaze.

Satisfied that the girl had been thoroughly rebuked, Natalia turned back to the doorway, slipping inside and making her way gracefully down the stairs that led to the lowest part of the palace. Torches flickered and glowed on the walls, reflecting off the gleaming golden surfaces like a million fireflies captured in glass jars, though they offered little to no warmth this deep under the ground.

A shiver ran up Natalia's spine as the cold began to seep into her feet, digging icy claws into her very bones despite the silk slippers that she had put on before leaving her bedroom. They may as well have not existed, but Natalia knew they would at least protect her from damaging her perfect skin on the freezing golden floors.

The stairs spiraled down, down, down, deep into the darkness, and for a moment, Natalia wondered if she *had* in fact created her own Hell within her world, until finally, the stairs ended, and the cellar opened out to greet her.

There was no loving embrace waiting for her at the bottom, no gasps of admiration or sighs of adulation. No one sobbed for joy at being in her presence, nor proclaimed their love for her. No. All that waited at the bottom was a cavernous room filled with supplies that blocked out what little light the torches offered, casting monstrous shadows around her as a cold breeze whipped across her slender, perfect frame, snatching at her hair and clothes as it left her chilled to her core.

Laughter rang out from the other end of the room, reverberating off the walls as it finally reached her. It wasn't a joyous sound, and it didn't bring any lightness to Natalia's heart. In fact, it brought back that doubt that she had been denying existed. A vice-like grip took hold of her heart as her eyes searched through the shadows for the source of the almost maniacal laughter, until finally, she spotted her prisoner.

On his knees, wrapped in chains that looked heavy enough to break his back, the man watched her with mad eyes, and a look of pure hatred on his face. The smile was one she hadn't seen in eons, and only once when she had faced Lucifer with the rest of her army. It was a smile that spoke volumes about the hatred that her brother had felt for their father and those who had (at the time) supported what their father stood for. Never in all of her days would Natalia have *ever* believed that someone could look at her in the same way, as though faced with some foul demon spawn that had no right to exist.

Anger rose in her heart at the expression. He should have loved her! That was his purpose in her world, to worship the ground she walked on, the very air that they shared! She gave them the gifts of eternal life, of easy living, and all she'd asked in return was their love. And yet, here he knelt, *daring* to think badly of her?!

Natalia stepped toward the man with purpose, ready to strike him when he laughed again, the sound so jarring that it stopped even *her* in her tracks.

"So, the *mighty goddess* has deemed me worthy of an audience, has she? How lucky I must be to get to speak to her alone. Don't expect an apology from me, nor the admiration you *think* should be yours. I don't cower to false gods, nor do I show praise to ugly things like you."

27

The man's words stung as though he had just struck Natalia against the face. Natalia took a step away from her prisoner, taken aback by his words. No one had ever dared speak to her in such a fashion other than her siblings, and the only reason she allowed it from *them* was because they were closer to her in status. They would never be on par with her, admittedly, but at least they were higher beings whom she could tolerate such nonsense from.

This man was human, an *insect* in comparison to a divine being such as herself. Natalia was an *angel*. Fallen or otherwise, it made no difference. She had been created by God himself, by the Creator!

Laughter bit at her ears, and Natalia scowled as the man

seemed to enjoy her hesitation. The sound of his voice was an insult to her existence, and she was tempted to pull his head clean from his shoulders right then and there, and she would have done it if she hadn't wanted to speak with him about what was happening.

"No one has ever told you no before, have they?" He snorted, smirking at her.

Natalia snorted in return, not deeming it necessary to give him a response as she crossed the cellar, standing over him with her arms crossed over her ample bosom. At this angle, he was forced to lean back, the chains clinking, weighing heavily upon his shoulders as he attempted to meet her gaze. It was Natalia's turn to smirk this time, grinning contentedly at the fact that he was clearly uncomfortable and in pain in the position he was currently sitting in.

"I'm assuming this isn't just a social call?" The man sighed, a clear attempt at keeping what little control he had, which as far as *she* was concerned, was none whatsoever.

"I want answers," she replied curtly.

"And what makes you think I'm going to be the one to give them to you?"

Natalia's fingers dug into her arms as she forced herself not to react to his tone, too similar to Azazel's for her liking, but she would not rise to his taunts. She was far better than that.

"Oh. Are you going to *make* me?" He chortled.

Natalia hissed, unable to ignore his tone any longer since it was a *direct* insult against her. A red mist descended over her eyes as she untangled her arms and swept one hand through the air, backhanding the man straight across his face. She hit him with such force that the slap let out a *snap* that echoed across the room.

She'd propelled him to one side, and the chains clinked and clunked as he fell heavily against the ground with a grunt of pain. There was a light amongst the darkness, threatening to overtake her mood at the sound of his agony, knowing that she'd at *least* managed to do him some damage, even if his personality was as stubborn as hers was.

Striding to where he had fallen, Natalia knelt beside him, gripped his chains, and pulled him upright until his face was mere millimeters from her own. She could almost *taste* his breath on her tongue as he panted, but at least there was a modicum of fear in his expression now that she'd given a further show of her strength.

"Do you really believe that I don't have the capability to make you talk, should I wish for it?"

"No, I don't." He shook his head.

The answer was *not* what Natalia had been expecting, and she could see her own surprise reflected back at her in his deep brown eyes.

"Nothing you can do to me will make me tell you anything. Pain is fleeting, and will only eventually lead to my death. You'll kill me out of frustration before you can force me to speak to you."

"Given that I can gift you eternal life, what makes you think I couldn't inflict centuries of pain upon you before you would even come *close* to dying?" Natalia hissed, smiling softly as she thought about how much pleasure she would get from hurting those who dared to insult her in this fashion.

"You really don't see it, do you?" the man asked. This time, it appeared that it was his turn to be astonished by something she'd said.

"See what?!" she snapped.

"You don't. You don't see it!" He laughed.

Natalia snarled and stood up, his chains still gripped in one hand as she lifted him from the floor, his feet dangling as she fought the urge to cut off his windpipe.

"See what?" She snarled once more.

"Your powers are dwindling, Great Goddess. They have been for some time now; we've all seen it, out in your great city. Places where your powers are starting to lose their hold on the world, where the gold stops gleaming and turns to plain brick, where people have grown old and *died* a natural death rather than suffering for all eternity at your feet. You don't even know it's happening because you've locked yourself up here, in your golden palace, and stared at your own reflection thinking you're perfect and beautiful. Well, I *will* tell you this. You can know all of this for free because *nothing* would give me greater pleasure than to tear you down from your pedestal and bring you back down to Earth with the rest of us. You are not beautiful; you are not loved. You are rotten to the core, black and hollow and ugly on the inside, and it shows through that porcelain face of yours. We all see it; we see through your façade to the putrid being that you really are. No one will ever truly love you; it's all a lie that you tell yourself, but I can promise you that *no one* will love you no matter what you do. You can punish us all you like, but you cannot win this. We will rise against you and bring you down. It's inevitable."

28

"No!" Natalia screamed, throwing the man away from herself as though he'd burned her fingers.

He grunted as his shoulder collided with the floor, but Natalia derived no pleasure from it this time. He was wrong; he was *wrong*! He *had* to be.

"Liar!" she screamed the accusation. Closing in on him, her finger pointed so close to his face that as he blinked, she could feel the gentle brush of his eyelashes against the tip of her finger, soft spidery kisses against her skin.

"You can deny it all you want, but they're the answers you were seeking, aren't they? Why have we turned against you? That was what you were going to ask me, right?" he added in a pompous tone.

It was so much like Azazel, so self-righteous. Natalia glared at him, her eyes narrowed as though expecting to see her sister leave the man's body under her forceful gaze. She wouldn't have put it past her sibling in the slightest, finding a way to possess one of her subjects in order to torment her.

No, Azazel wouldn't have been able to break into her world, physically or spiritually. The only reason they could directly communicate with one another was because of their biological makeup, and the fact that they would always be in tune with one another in that way. No, her sister didn't have the strength or the wherewithal to pull off such a feat, not against *her*, anyway. In Raziel's world, maybe, but not hers.

Natalia turned away from the man, hands clutched at her chest as her heart beat painfully within. None of this was right; none of it! It couldn't be happening, not to her. She was perfect! She was the best of those wretched angels, and they'd all known it for millennia! Look at what she had created, what she had achieved on her own.

Yet, there was no way that Natalia could deny the events of the last month or so. How long had it been since everything had started to feel off? As though her world was tilted slightly to one side so that nothing could remain where it was meant to. The passage of time had never been her forte. She never took into account the days that passed, too busy basking in her own brilliance to be bothered about how *long* anything really was. It had never mattered... until now.

"The goddess isn't as perfect as she thought she was, is she?" Her tormentor sneered.

Her tormentor. Ironic, considering how she'd come down here with every intention of tormenting *him*. No. No, no, no, no...

"No!" she squealed angrily, stomping her foot so hard on the floor that she created a large crater in her wake.

She wanted to turn around and gloat at what she'd done, to show the man that she was just as strong and powerful as she had ever been, but the reality was far from it. If Natalia had been at full strength when she'd thrown this little tantrum, the entire palace would have been in danger of splitting into two, or falling into a hole where she'd made the impact.

The dent was impressive, by human standards, and would possibly strike fear into her captive, but it only proved his point. Just like the door. She should have been able to rip the stupid thing off its hinges with her little finger, but she'd had to *think* about opening it in order to actually make it move.

What was happening to her? To *them*? She assumed it was happening to the others as well; it would explain Raziel's issues and her absence from teasing Natalia lately. There was something going on, and all of them were losing ground. Azazel could lie all she wanted, but if Raziel was struggling, and Natalia was also, then there was no way that their other sibling was holding it together, as much as she would like them to believe she was—though Natalia doubted that her sister thought much of the threat against her life, given the world that Azazel had created all wanted to kill her long before now. That was just normality where Azazel's world was concerned, but not in Natalia's.

"No!" Natalia whined, slumping to the floor and scowling. She pulled her knees up to her chest and rested her chin upon them, her bottom lip jutting out as she pouted in frustration. All she'd ever wanted was for people to realize how amazing she was. How was that too much to ask for?

"You really have never been told no, have you?" the man mused, chains clinking as he shifted his weight to look at her better.

"Well, that's clearly not the case. Otherwise, I'd be up *there* and not down *here*." Natalia spat, pointing first to the ceiling, and then to the floor, indicating Heaven and Earth.

"Alright, touché, fair point. My bad." The man sighed.

"But *other* than God, no one has ever really told you no or contradicted you, have they?"

"Again, not the case. You seem to think you know me, *little man*, but you know nothing about me whatsoever." Natalia sniffed.

"John."

"What?"

"My name is John. Not that you care, but it's my name."

"You're right, I *don't* care," Natalia replied haughtily.

"So, since I clearly don't know anything about you, why don't you tell me?"

"Tell you *what*?" Natalia snapped, fed up with listening to John's voice. He was so sanctimonious that it was nauseating.

"Well, you've said I don't know you, so why don't you tell me about yourself? It's your favorite subject after all, right?"

Again, there was that pompous, smirking tone to his voice that left Natalia wanting to rip his throat out with her bare hands. The problem was he did know *that* much about her at least, and even she couldn't deny that.

Yes. She was her own favorite subject, and the idea of being able to talk about herself was always appealing. Though this was the first time she would have spoken to anyone, Jules and Helena included, about the aspects of her life prior to building this world.

"Why do you want to know?" Natalia sulked, the prospect of being able to talk at *length* about herself still not quite enough to drag her from the mire of doubt she now found herself in.

She'd been denying what was going on in her world for as long as she could, and now that she was confronted with the reality of it, she wasn't happy. Natalia had spent her entire existence believing that she was the most powerful and flawless being in the Universe. And this small, insignificant human being was proving otherwise.

It was a dark thought, all-consuming and dangerous. She

wanted to weep, scream, and feel nothing all at once. Her world was shattering around her, and it wasn't God or even another angel taking it from her; it was this *lesser* thing.

John sighed and rolled his eyes. "Well, it's not like I've got anything better to do right now, and I can't stand the thought of you sitting here having a tantrum for however long. So, I'd rather you talked about yourself and prove your point to me than have me witness a grown woman acting like a toddler."

Natalia raised her head from her knees, staring at John in utter disbelief. Never in her life would she have expected a human to speak to her in such a fashion, and still, he had the *nerve* to say it without hesitation or fear of punishment.

"Fine. I'll tell you everything about myself, then you'll see, then you'll understand why I'm the best of them, why I am *perfect.*"

"I'll be the judge of that." John snorted, eliciting another infuriated screech from Natalia.

If she managed not to kill the man before she'd convinced him that she was infallible, it would be a miracle.

29

"**S**o, you're just a spoiled brat then?" John had laughed after Natalia told him her life story.

"I am NOT a spoiled brat! Did you even listen to a word I've said? I've had to show those ignorant fools every day of my life that I'm better than they are, that they were beneath me. Gabriel and the others were always father's favorites, and yet I knew I was far more capable than ANY of them. He never gave me a chance, too busy fawning over those idiotic boys. None of them were ever as good as I was, as I AM. Don't you see? Look at the world I've created! Look at my perfection."

"You still don't get it, do you? This isn't perfect. It's far from it. Your view of the world has blinded you to the reality that even YOU are not infallible, neither is God if He's made angels like you. You all look down on us as though we are the flawed creatures. Throughout history, we're taught about the angels judging whether or not WE are worthy of the existence given to us. But you're no better than we are! You're just as imperfect, just as easily led, just as naïve and stubborn. It's hypocrisy, that we're meant to be mortals while you're seen as divine. There's nothing divine about you. You're just humans with wings and a ridiculously long lifespan."

"I'm immortal."

"Snap all you like, but you know I'm right. You really aren't any better than I am, and you wonder why we hate living in this world that you've created? You think we should all bow down to you and worship you because you're beautiful, and outwardly you are, but there is so much more to life than just looks. Have you ever looked at another person and seen them for who they are? For what strengths they may have? No, because your head is so far up your own—"

"Be careful what you say to me, human."

"Your own ego is so big that you haven't realized that true perfection is found in imperfection. There's an old saying, 'light shines through the cracks of a vase.' In other words, the TRULY beautiful things shine through that which isn't perfect. Those of us who are broken, flawed humans, we're the beautiful ones. We're the ones who find strength no matter what. We're unique, and we see the true images of those around us because we can see what's INSIDE a person, not just what's on the outside. That's why I can never love you the way you want, because I already love someone else, someone who is more beautiful than you could EVER be to me. Do you even know what that's like? To really love someone, to feel that devoted to someone else?"

The exchange went round and round in Natalia's head as she lied on her bed and stared at the canopy above her. She hated how much he had gotten into her head, how his words stung as though he had repeatedly slapped her across the face.

They didn't love her. They didn't love the world that she had created for them. Apparently, they'd come to hate her gift of immortality. It hadn't felt that long since she'd created this world, but John had alluded that the passage of centuries had grown tiresome on the humans she had hand-picked to live in this utopia.

"How can flaws be a good thing?" She hissed, fists punching the duvet beneath her. "How can he say that they *like* imperfections?! Don't they *constantly* strive for things to be perfect?!" she screamed, sitting up sharply as she stared at the empty chamber.

Not so long ago, Jules would have come running into the room to see if his beloved Mistress was alright, willing to do anything to make her happy again. *Why* did she keep thinking of the man?! He was dead; he was inconsequential; he was...

"He was mine," Natalia muttered, pulling her knees up to her chest and hugging her arms around them.

She'd never thought about him that way before, not in that sense, anyway. That bloody John had gotten into her head alright; he was leaving her with strange thoughts, and she didn't like it one bit.

"Did you love him?"

Natalia gasped, spinning around on the bed, expecting to find her sister sitting behind her, but of course, Raziel wasn't *actually* there. However, her presence was so much stronger now than it had ever been. Natalia could *feel* her sister—not just hear her—just as she'd been able to when they'd been in Heaven and apart. Their connection was growing stronger; did that mean that their barriers were growing weaker? If John's words were true, that might explain it.

"Who?" Natalia asked.

"The one who died for you. The priest, or whatever he was."

"Do you even care?"

"No. Yes. I don't know. You know, I've searched for love for a long time, to feel what the rest of you feel. I just wanted to know if that's what you felt for him."

"I... I don't know." Natalia scowled as she admitted this to her sister. She hadn't thought about it; she hadn't even *considered* that she might have loved Jules. She loved herself. No one else was on par with her in terms of beauty or majesty, so why would she have ever lowered herself to feeling such a thing for someone else? Jules had loved *her*, and rightly so, but loving him? "Maybe. Sort of? I don't really know. I never thought about it."

Was *that* why she kept thinking about him? About his absence from her life now? He had given his life for her, which Natalia had expected, but he should never have crossed her mind ever again after that. Replaced by another servant who gave her the attention she so desired and deserved. But he hadn't been forgotten, hadn't been passed over in her mind. She kept *looking* for him, despite knowing that he wasn't there anymore, knowing that he would *never* be there again.

Something wet tickled her cheek, and Natalia reached a hand to her face, touching the tears that blurred her vision unbidden, unexpected. Maybe she *had* loved Jules, in some way, even if it wasn't the love that Raziel was searching so desperately for. But Natalia had clearly felt *something* for her priest. Otherwise, she wouldn't keep thinking about him; she wouldn't miss him as much as she clearly did.

"Yes... I think I did, somehow," she muttered.

"So, what now?"

"I don't know."

Natalia shivered, shuffling herself under her covers and pulling them tightly around her. Her world felt cold and empty for the first time since she'd created this place. Raziel's presence vanished, and Natalia wished that her sister had remained a little longer, if only so she didn't have to be alone with her thoughts. She didn't want to be alone; she didn't want to think about what John had said to her. She didn't want to think about how Jules wasn't there for her anymore.

She didn't want to be alone.

30

Sleep seemed to avoid Natalia once again. She spent the night tossing and turning in her bed, her thoughts a constant rolling tsunami. She actually *missed* Jules; she *felt* his absence. Not only that, but she could not deny that she was losing her grip on her world now.

No matter what she did, there was no denying that her powers were growing weaker. The evidence of it had been right there, but she didn't want to admit to it. The fact that her people were rebelling against her, that they attacked her palace, her inability to open the door to the cellar with just one hand. None of this should have been happening! If she was truly as strong as she'd believed, then none of this would have occurred at all.

Helena came into her room in the middle of the night to inform her that the rebels remained on the steps of the palace, but there had been something else that the priestess *hadn't* said. Natalia noticed it, but she wasn't ready to hear what *else* was evidence to the fact that everything she'd believed about herself—from the moment of her creation—was a lie.

John said that she was truly ugly, that her beauty was only skin-deep, and that looks weren't enough. What had he meant? What more *was* there other than beauty? That was why she had picked all of *them* in the first place, because they had been the most beautiful of the humans. Not one of them was ugly, so how could John sit there and *dare* to say that what was on the outside wasn't important?

Sighing heavily, Natalia cast her covers aside and strode across the floor of her chamber to the balcony. It was a potentially foolhardy thing to do, considering the rebels camped outside her home, but she wanted the fresh air, and she wanted to look out over her city and remember it in all the glory that she had created it in.

Natalia's eyes scanned the horizon, and she gasped, her heart sinking in her chest, her stomach twisting at the sight beyond the boundary of the palace. The city was in disarray! Smoke rose into the clear blue morning sky, creating dark clouds that spoke volumes of the mood of the world she had once called hers. The rebels had torn down her statues and defaced much of the golden streets, but that wasn't the worst of it. In fact, Natalia had expected this level of vandalism from the rebels; what she hadn't expected was the rest of the destruction.

The polished gold that had lined every street dripped in great, sticky globs of sickly molten metal, leaving behind the ugly brick face of the building beneath, the *true* building that had been there before she had come along and reshaped it to her liking.

Natalia hurried to the edge of the balcony, gripping the golden railing as she leaned over to see just how far the devastation ran. The palace was intact, though even Natalia could see that the sheen to it had dulled. There was a distinct line that could be seen where the city was returning to the ugly, tedious origins from before Natalia had tenderly sculpted it into a beacon of glorious perfection.

"Mistress! Come away from there. It's dangerous!" Helena cried out.

Natalia charged for the priestess, all thoughts of mercy long gone as she all but flew to the woman's side, hand outstretched as she gripped Helena's throat tightly in one hand.

"When were you going to tell me about this?!" Natalia screeched, waving a hand at the city beyond, her eyes drawn to the gray concrete buildings that stood instead of the beautiful gold ones that she had created.

"Mistress, I—" Helena gasped and stammered under the pressure of Natalia's grip.

"You have been lying to me! How long have you been plotting against me? Did *you* help Samuel into the Throne Room? Or were you the one who helped that man get into my *bedroom*? Was it jealousy that caused you to do it? Because I was ready to finally take Jules to my bed, so you sent that man to hurt us? Is that what happened?!"

"No! Never!" Helena wept.

There was a sincerity in the priestesses' words that even Natalia could not deny, not that it made her feel any better. Natalia screamed with frustration as she relinquished her grip on the woman, turning her back on the priestess as she stared out at the city. She closed her eyes, ignoring the gasping and sobbing behind her, as she held her hands out in front of her and concentrated.

This was *her* world. No one was going to take it from her,

or tell her any differently. She was going to reclaim it. Take it back, rebuild it, and regain control of *all* her citizens. She was going to prove these insignificant little insects wrong; she *was* infallible, and this was *her* world!

She felt her powers gathering in her very core. A soft, warm pressure deep in her stomach that began to grow, like a seed flourishing in the soil until it blossomed into a huge oak tree. The tips of her fingers began to tingle. Her skin was alive with prickling electricity as the fire of her powers engulfed her from within. At the height of her power, Natalia let out a grunt, casting it from her body like a wave that rippled across the city.

Opening her eyes, Natalia smiled to herself, anticipating that the results had worked… but it hadn't. The city remained as it had, the golden glory gone and replaced with the ugly brick and concrete shapes that she'd never expected to see again. Natalia collapsed, the cold floor stinging against her aching knees where she had connected with the unforgiving wood. It was all falling apart. Everything about this was wrong, and she couldn't stop it.

She'd accused Helena of betraying her, though she still suspected that the priestess was up to something. Natalia may not have hit the right subject, but there was still *something* going on, unless it was literally *this* that Helena had been keeping a secret. How long had the woman known that this was going on? Were she and Jules more aware of Natalia's slip in powers than they'd let on, or was it that they'd found out and kept it quiet for Natalia's sake? What *was* it?! Why was *everything* falling apart? What had she done to deserve this?

Natalia gripped her throat tightly, her breath short and labored. Her skin was prickling again, but it wasn't the same as when she'd been building up her powers. No, this was something new, something she had never experienced before.

The world grew dark, and the last thing Natalia remembered was Helena's panicked voice calling out her name, her actual name that no one other than her sisters had ever uttered before… before everything went cold and black.

31

When Natalia woke up, she found herself tucked into her bed, just as she had been after she'd collapsed while fighting the rebels at the door of her palace. It *was* true. She was growing weaker, and it was happening more quickly now that she'd stopped denying that it was happening at all. The covers felt like weights against her chest, restraining her against the mattress so that she couldn't move, let alone get up.

Deep down, Natalia knew that wasn't the case at all, but that was how she felt. If she couldn't keep hold of her world, if her powers were of no use to her anymore, then what was the point? Why should she even bother to get up and fight anymore? Was it even worth forcing her aching, useless body up from the safety of her bed?

The doubt that her sisters had sown after Samuel's attack on her. Samuel's words about *why* he had attacked her in the first place... That had been the spark that set the fire, that little hole in her self-assured confidence that turned into a gaping wound and let the fear and confusion into her mind, causing her to hesitate and misstep in ways she hadn't since... ever.

Natalia didn't know what to do now. All she'd ever known was her own power and beauty, but even *that* had been torn in two, and she was left feeling like an empty shell of her former self. Like she was *nothing*. She'd never felt like this before; it was a foreign, terrifying feeling. Even *that* was new. Even against the hordes of Hell, Natalia hadn't been afraid. She'd stood beside her brothers and sisters, ready to face the demon spawns and die if necessary. Not that she'd expected to die; she was too strong for such a fate... or so she'd believed.

"Mistress?" Helena's voice spoke softly, the woman's tone less sure than Natalia was used to from her priestess.

Clearly, Natalia threatening her life had shaken the woman, and rightly so. At least Natalia had managed *that* correctly, since it appeared that she was losing her grip on everything *else* that she'd once been so convinced about.

"Mistress, the rebels are at our door. My priestesses and the acolytes are struggling to keep them from breaching the barricade. I don't know how much longer the palace will be safe. We need to think of a plan, an alternative to this."

"Did you know?" Natalia muttered, ignoring the priestess' soft plea.

"Did I...?"

"About what was happening to my city, what was happening to me," Natalia accused, turning her head slowly toward the woman, her eyes utterly emotionless and a reflection of how she felt inside at that moment.

"I… we…," Helena stammered.

"Jules knew, didn't he?"

Helena stared at her hands, anything other than the soul-searching gaze that Natalia was boring into the priestess with.

"He did. We both did. We found evidence of the—of *your* —weakening in parts of the city that were furthest from the palace. We took note of the places where your beautiful city was dissolving, and marked and recorded it privately. Jules wanted to tell you, but I insisted that we say nothing, that we would silently find a way to fix the problem for you without you ever knowing. I meant no offense, no harm, I just…," Helena whimpered, fingers gripping at the duvet that kept Natalia contained for the moment.

"Thank you," Natalia whispered.

"M-mistress?!" Helena gasped.

Never, in all their time together, had Natalia *thanked* any of her subjects for *anything*, not with any real sincerity, anyway. Yet, now she had, and it was no surprise that it shocked Helena to hear it.

"Did you do it because you love me, or you think you love me, because you wanted to make me happy? Or was it because you didn't want to see me angry? Maybe it's fear, not love," Natalia muttered, remembering what John had said to her before.

"My Lady…," Helena interrupted, getting up to sit on the edge of the bed so that she could be closer to Natalia as she spoke, her hand hovering over the duvet as though she was debating holding her Mistress' hand, but wasn't sure if she should or not. After a second, Helena chose to rest her hand on the duvet, close to Natalia's body without actually touching her. "It was always love for me, *and* for Jules. The reason he and I fought was because, out of all your subjects, we were the ones who were closest to you, and we were the ones who knew everything. We still loved you, my Lady, Jules more than myself, even I have to admit. I know you picked up on our rivalry, and it was because I was jealous of him. You always seemed closer to Jules than to me, spending more time in his company than my own, despite his meek attitude around you. And that was only because he loved you so much that he grew nervous around you, but he *did* love you with all his heart, a truer love than I could ever claim to have."

Helena sighed heavily, staring at her hands, still unable to meet Natalia's eyes as she spoke. "If I had been here when that man attacked you, I would *like* to think that I would have pushed you out of the way and taken the attack myself, but… the thought of it fills me with fear, and I cannot say that I would have done what he did. We knew you were losing your powers, or at least, they were growing weaker in some fashion, but we loved you so much that we wanted to ensure you knew nothing about it. We wanted to fix it for you *because* of our love for you. I'm just sorry we couldn't do more." Helena sighed.

Warmth spread through Natalia's body, making her feel less empty and more like herself. Filled with renewed energy —though not entirely recovered, by any means—just enough to feel a little better, Natalia sat up slowly, reaching out to take Helena's hand.

"Do what you can to deal with the rebels at our door, but no further than that. I'm going to speak to our prisoner again and see if we can find a way around this. I am still in charge of this world; I am still the goddess here, and I will *not* let them get away with this."

Helena smiled and nodded. "As you wish, my Lady."

Natalia watched the priestess leave the room, taking a moment to catch her breath before she cast aside the duvet cover. She needed to figure out how to put a stop to all of this. She needed to keep her palace and those still loyal to her safe from the rebels on their doorstep. And she had a feeling that the man in the depths of her cellar might have the answers she was looking for… again.

32

"So, she graces me with her presence yet again. I *must* be special." John snorted as Natalia padded her way, bare-footed, across the freezing cellar floor to where he was still chained up.

Natalia rolled her eyes as she stood over him, her hands on her hips. Helena had sent her a couple of priestesses to help her get dressed in an attempt to make Natalia feel more like herself, which she had to admit, she did. A little, at least. It was amazing what a good bath, some flattering clothes, and someone brushing her hair until it shone like marble could do to chase away the looming rain clouds in a person's mind.

"According to you, everyone's special in their own right, just not me!" Natalia snapped.

"Not entirely what I said, though I'm surprised you listened to me at all. So, that's something. What brings the *mighty* goddess down to the depths to see little old me?" John asked, sitting back, his chains clinking with every movement.

"I wanted to ask you how we can resolve all of this. How we can work to stop the rebels before anyone else gets hurt."

John stared up at her, blinking rapidly, his mouth partially open. Natalia smiled wickedly and chuckled, hands clasped behind her back as she leaned forward slightly, her breasts pushed forward as she tilted her head to one side.

"Speechless? I didn't think it was possible!" She laughed.

Natalia flicked out her skirt and settled onto the cold floor in front of him, crossing her legs and placing her hands in her lap as she watched John carefully, amused as he smirked at her words.

"Alright, you win that round. But do you mean it? Do you *actually* mean you want to fix things?" he asked her.

"I cannot deny my nature. I know my worth, I know what I'm capable of, and I *know* that I am the best at what I do and cannot believe otherwise. That is not to say I could not become *more* perfect by listening. You've said to me that there is inner beauty, that a person is not just about how they look, but how they *are*. That you fell in love with a woman in my world, not *just* because she was beautiful outside, but as a person. What was it? A cracked vase shines with light from within?"

"That's right," John replied, sitting up straight and leaning toward Natalia as he let her speak without interruption.

Natalia noticed the absence of any snide remarks from the man, having grown used to listening to him laugh or snap back at her.

"If I can adjust, if I can be more… forgiving and a little less… me, would you all stay? Would that stop the rebels?"

"You would change the world and let us love one another? Like *truly* love one another?"

Natalia scowled a little, her fingers automatically moving to massage the wrinkles that formed on her face so that they would not become permanent.

"I... yes. That's what I'm thinking. I want my priestesses and acolytes to be safe, and if what you say is true, then maybe I have missed out on a type of love and worship that is deeper than what you have all shown me so far."

"The word you're looking for is respect." John smirked, returning to his old self.

"I would still expect you all to worship me. I *am* still your goddess, after all." She grunted in return. "But I would be willing to let you lead more normal lives, what you had prior to my choosing you all to be mine."

"Why the sudden change of heart?" John asked, narrowing his gaze at her.

"My powers have been weakening, as you've so clearly pointed out, and I am looking to rectify the issue. The only reason I can think of for the sudden loss in my powers, is purely because I've grown lax in my own growth. I'm an angel. We trained regularly to ensure that we were ready for war against the spawn of Hell, and I've allowed myself to become negligent."

"Is that the *only* reason?" John urged.

Natalia felt her heart twist in her chest, as though someone had grasped it with both hands and turned them in the opposite direction from one another, screwing it around and leaving her gasping for breath. She looked away from the man, unsure of how to answer his question. The niggling doubt returned, that unsure feeling that left her feeling cold and sick because it felt so strange and unfamiliar. Slick and oil-like, tendrils of uncertainty slithering their way into her mind.

"No," Natalia admitted, pushing the feeling away and swallowing hard. "John... how did you know you were in love?"

"How did I...?" John repeated, blinking at Natalia as he had when she'd offered the potential for a new world, under a slightly different regime. "You think you're in love with someone? The priest?"

"I... I don't know. I find myself thinking about him, about how much I miss him, and my stomach twists, and my heart hurts. He gave his life for me, and I thought I'd expected it of him because I *wanted* you all to love me, but I wish he hadn't. I keep wanting to wake up and find him waiting outside my bedroom door to greet me as he always did, with his eyes down and trying not to look at me because he's too nervous to look me in the eyes. I never realized how much he was there for me, how often I would turn to him for the smallest things—"

"Until he wasn't there anymore, and you realized you would do anything to have him back?" John asked.

"Y-yes."

"That's love. It's hard to explain, but for someone like yourself, someone *so* caught up in their own worth, I would say you found true love."

Natalia's bottom lip quivered, and she hugged her knees to her chest, resting her chin on her knees as her vision blurred, and she felt the tears trickle down her cheeks. She'd loved him; she really had. For the first time in her existence, she'd loved something, some*one* other than herself, and now, he was gone forever.

"How do I live without him?" she whimpered.

John leaned backwards, as though her words had struck him in the chest in the same way as her fist might have. He was clearly taken aback by her question, and the look in his eyes told her that he didn't have the answer to that, and that no one would. Jules was gone. She couldn't bring him back; that wasn't in her sphere of abilities, and now she was going to have to live with that for the rest of eternity.

Wiping the tears from her eyes, Natalia stood up and

brushed the dust from her skirt and her legs, righting her clothes as a way of gathering her composure before she went back into the palace proper.

"If I approach the rebels with the proposition of a new world, one where they can love one another so long as they still pay worship to me and appreciate all that I have given to them, will they stop their assault on the palace?" she asked sternly.

"Yes, I think they would. I can't guarantee that it will be easy, or that they will love you in the way that you want them to, but they would be happier and more willing if you allowed them more freedom." John nodded. "If you could see them for who they are, you might find more people who can touch your heart like Jules did. There're all kinds of love, my Lady, and all of them can bring happiness to you if you let them."

Natalia turned away and strode toward the steps, her heart pounding painfully in her chest as she made a decision about her future... and that of her world.

"We shall see."

ompromise. That was what she was considering right now. *Compromise.*

Natalia had never compromised anything in her entire life! That had contributed to her fall, and she hated it! Her unwavering faith in herself, her love of her own beauty and powers, her strength and bravery and self-assured confidence in everything she did, were the only things she ever relied on. Yet all of that was being torn away from her, and now she wasn't just considering compromise, but she was *willing* to.

How did it even come to this?

"Helena?" Natalia called softly to her priestess as she

hugged herself in her bed, pulling her duvet up to her chin and shivering despite not being cold.

"My Lady?" The woman hurried through the bedroom door to her bedside, a look of concern on her face at Natalia's dejected tone.

"Can you run me a bath?" Natalia asked as Helena settled on the edge of the bed, offering her hand, which Natalia took without question.

"Of course! Do you want all of the girls?" Helena asked, gently stroking her thumb over the back of Natalia's hand in a comforting fashion.

"No, just you. And John. Bring him up from the cellar. Give him some new clothes and something to eat."

"But my Lady!" Helena protested, freezing in her movement as she stared incredulously at her Mistress.

"Just do it for me, please."

Helena nodded, squeezed Natalia's hand, and hurried from the room, hesitating by the door to look back at her Mistress as though Natalia might come to her senses in a moment if she lingered a little longer. When it was clear that Natalia meant every word, Helena delayed no longer.

Natalia threw the covers from her body, shuffling her way to the balcony where she could see the state of her city as it continued its terrible decay. Almost all of the city had lost its golden luster now, and her statues were blobs of molten metal that were unrecognizable.

She'd noticed that even her palace was growing dimmer now, the shimmer and shine of the mirrored surfaces becoming more blurred and less beautiful. She couldn't bear to look at herself in it anymore, her images distorted and twisted because of it. A reminder that she would soon lose everything, and the rebels would breach her walls, whether she liked it or not.

She sat on the balcony, one foot hanging over the edge. It was lucky that the stone was thick enough for her to sit on, or she would've been perilously close to falling onto the street below. To the waiting arms of the rebels, who would happily tear her limb from limb; she was sure of that.

Natalia looked down at the street, her eyes fixed on the citizens of her world who remained camped at the edge of her palace. Most of them crowded the steps to the main entrance, though a few of the more intelligent ones had begun to patrol the borders of the palace for another way in. Thankfully, the priestesses and acolytes were one step ahead of them, and any other ways inside were already barricaded to stop them from getting in… or at least slow them down enough for Natalia to come up with a plan.

She had a plan. She knew what she needed to do now, but she wanted to speak to John again first. He'd opened her eyes to new possibilities, to avenues that she and her sisters would *never* have considered before, and while she was more willing to listen now, she was still reluctant to admit that she would need to give in.

"Your bath is ready, my Lady, and your guest is on his way to the bathroom!" Helena called from the doorway.

"I'll be there in a minute, Helena. Go on without me," Natalia replied, looking over her shoulder at the priestess.

Helena hesitated before nodding and vanishing from sight once more.

Natalia sighed heavily, closing her eyes as she drew in a slow, deep breath. The world was changing, and she wasn't consciously causing it. It was unsettling. Was this how God felt when Lucifer had first rebelled? Or when the people He'd put on his Earth began to turn their faces away from him and didn't believe as heavily as they had before? Did God question his own movements?

Exhaling slowly, Natalia opened her eyes and stared up at the sky. She pictured where Heaven should be, though she didn't expect to see anything. However, the problem was that she *did* see something. Natalia scowled, swinging her legs from the edge of the balcony to stand on the floor as she leaned over the railing, staring up at the shimmering vision that shouldn't have been there.

High above her city, in the midst of the perpetual sunny sky that she'd created, was what she could only describe as a *tear* in the perfect blue. A jagged crack had formed as one would expect to see in a wall after an earthquake, its edges sharp enough to cut anyone who dared to touch them. Natalia gasped as she realized that the crack was big enough to see *through*… to the other side.

The image in the crack was dark and foreboding. A desolate, lifeless mass of gray concrete that loomed on the other side. There was nothing to the image, no personality, no character, just this blank gray face, as though the city in the sky felt nothing at all.

"Raziel," Natalia whispered, her fingers gripping the balcony railing so tightly that the stone shattered beneath her grasp.

If anything was the embodiment of her sister, it was that city. The barrier between their worlds was beginning to crumble, her powers failing. She needed to fix things before the barrier fell completely, and her world collided with that of her sister's. She would *not* be the one to fail!

Natalia hurried into the bathroom, shedding her robe the moment she stepped into the room. She didn't care that John was there; it wasn't as if she'd ever been ashamed of her body, and she wasn't about to start now. She *should* have been amused, or even satisfied, by the way John blushed and looked away from her naked frame, but instead, she felt nothing at all. Natalia could feel every beat of her heart, her chest aching as though it were a foreign object that didn't belong there. It was the only thing she *could* feel at this point; everything else felt numb, empty, lifeless.

She stood at the edge of the bath for a moment and stared at her reflection as it wavered in the water. Even *she* was beginning to lose her shine. She'd never looked so dull, so tired and washed out before. The shimmering curls she loved so much seemed muddier and thinner than usual, though she was sure it was all her imagination. Not to mention, her usually stunning blue eyes seemed pale and tired. Never in her life would she have believed that she could look so plain.

"I'm not sure this vase would shine even if it *were* cracked," Natalia hissed, kicking the surface of the water with her foot, dismissing her own image as she slid into the warm water until she slipped into its depths.

34

Natalia was aware of Helena pacing alongside the edge of the bath while she remained beneath the water, the bubbles spreading themselves out again now that the bath had settled and the ripples vanished. For a minute, Natalia wasn't sure she *wanted* to resurface, or whether she would rather drown in the warm embrace of the bathwater.

At least she felt *something* while she was in there, which was more than she'd really felt in the last few… hours? Days? Weeks? She couldn't tell the passage of time anymore, and she couldn't say with any certainty how long any of this had been happening.

A strong pair of hands broke the calm surface of the water,

grasping at her wet, naked body. Before Natalia could protest or push the hands away, she was wrenched from the depths of the water and dragged to the surface, where she found herself face-to-face with John. He stared into her eyes with a scowl on his face, and she wondered why he wore that expression at all. Surely, all of his troubles would be over if she were dead. So, why did he care if she drowned or not?

"Are you alright?" he asked.

"Why do you care?" she asked in return. "Have you suddenly had a change of heart? You've seen me naked and decided that you want me, just like all those who came before you?"

John sighed heavily, his tight grip on her upper arms shifting to a gentler pressure on her shoulders as he sat at the edge of the bath beside her. His eyes never left hers, in a way that was a complete opposite to how Jules had been with her. What color had Jules' eyes been? She couldn't remember because he'd never been able to look at her for any length of time, and she'd never thought anything of it until now.

"I care, in my way. You've changed, whether you want to admit it or not, and you're willing to give us all a better life. You don't get the easy way out. Living is your reward as much as your punishment. A do-over on the world you want to rule while being forced to *learn* from the error of your ways. You lost the man you loved, and you have to live with that, but you get to start again, and maybe this time, you'll find someone who sees something in you the way he clearly did."

Natalia looked away from him, scowling as he used Jules against her.

"Tell me about the woman you love. Tell me why you fell in love with her."

"Sophie?" John raised an eyebrow at her and smiled softly, looking at Helena for a moment before he looked away wistfully. "She loves to paint; it was the first thing I noticed about her. I saw her sneak out one night, by one of your fountains, to paint the city beneath the night sky. She looked happy, *truly* happy, as though she didn't have a care in the world. I wondered how anyone could look so content when I felt as though I was filled with this suffocating darkness. How could she *still* love painting when you forced us to constantly give you gifts of your image? Yet, she didn't seem to care so long as she was painting. I asked her about it once, and she said she could lose herself in her paintings, that each brushstroke was *her* choice. It was her way of keeping control in a world where we didn't have any control in what we could or could not do. I never realized I could love anyone the way I loved her."

Natalia leaned on the side of the bath, listening intently to each word while Helena ran a sponge over her skin. She could see the priestess watching *her* rather than John, clearly interested in her reaction to the rebel's words.

"John, will you take a message to the rest of the city? Tell them that I want to speak to them tomorrow. We will start over, a new world, where they can have more control of their lives while still worshipping me. I want to see what you see in the world. Maybe then, I can appreciate my own strengths even more than I do now."

"Is that even remotely possible?" John chuckled.

Natalia rolled her eyes at him and smiled softly. John threw his arms in the air and cheered, causing Helena to jump with shock.

"She smiles!" He laughed.

"On occasion. Will you do it?" she asked again.

"I will. Though, don't start thinking that I'm going to be your new Head Priest. No way am I going to be replacing Jules." He snorted.

"As if you could," Natalia replied, standing up, smirking as John averted his gaze with a hand rather than staring at her naked, wet body. "No one can replace him," she added softly as she stepped out of the tub, wrapping the robe that Helena offered her around her body.

"Go on, Helena will help you get back out into the city. Tell the rebels to stop their assault on the palace, and we will talk tomorrow. I want one last night before I have to stand before them."

John nodded and stood up with a smile on his face. "I will, and I think they will be more than happy to listen, considering you're offering them a chance at a *new* utopia. A proper one."

Natalia smiled in return, glancing at Helena. She wondered what the woman thought of all of this. Not just the potentially new direction their lives would take, but also the fact that she had so blatantly admitted to loving Jules. Helena *said* she loved Natalia, and she had no reason to lie about it, considering she could easily have joined the rebellion at the doors of the palace if she wanted to.

Natalia was grateful—something she'd never been before—for Helena's loyalty and devotion, but she didn't feel that way about the woman. She couldn't imagine her life without the priestess, but it wasn't the same feeling that she felt about Jules. Now that she could admit that, she felt that she understood herself a little better as well.

She'd lost Jules before she'd found him. Raziel had spent her entire *life* looking for love, unable to understand it, let alone feel it, and Natalia had lost love before she'd even realized she had it all along. All because she hadn't realized she needed it in that way, let alone that she was even capable of loving someone other than herself.

His absence from her side left her cold, and she wasn't sure if she would ever get used to it, but for now, she might be able to salvage the mess that she was in and reach a point where her citizens loved her again... truly loved her this time.

35

Natalia spent her evening staring up at the scar in the sky that hung over the city. She'd heard the acolytes and priestesses whispering about it on her return to her bedroom, and chose to ignore them when one of the priestesses hurried over to whisper in Helena's ear about it. They were less subtle than they all thought they were. Either that, or Natalia was more aware of their gossiping now because she was purposefully *not* talking about it.

She looked back at her Head Priestess, and the moment they made eye contact, she knew Helena wouldn't bother to ask her about the situation. If *she* didn't bring it up, it was best not to.

Natalia raised a hand to the sky, wiggling her fingers at the city that sat where Heaven, technically, should be. It felt as though she could touch the buildings if she stretched her arm enough. Her sister's world was so close, yet still so far away.

"Do you miss us?" Raziel asked, and Natalia imagined her sister staring up at the same scar, only seeing Natalia's bright, gleaming world.

They were almost polar opposites of one another. She'd always known that, but seeing Raziel's world lingering just out of reach while her sister could see *hers*, she realized just how different they were. She was all sunshine and golden city, while her sister's world was bleak and gray. What was it like to live life feeling… well… nothing?

"*Miss* is a strong word." Natalia chuckled as she sat back on her hands, staring at the dim glowing lights in her sibling's city skyscrapers. "I don't know. I'm beginning to see things a little differently, that's all," Natalia admitted, pressing on the boundaries of her mind to see if she could feel Azazel lurking in the shadows, ready to tease her. Thankfully, it seemed their other sister was occupied elsewhere, and there wasn't even the slightest inkling of her presence anywhere to be felt.

"Your humans really have changed you, haven't they?"

"I'd like to think of it as growth, if you don't mind." Natalia snorted. "I'm merely finding new ways of being even better than I am already, not that I really needed to improve. Perfect as I am."

"And yet, here we are, discussing how you've begun to learn despite being flawless."

"Let me ask you this, Sister. Have you changed since we last met?" Natalia snapped, not so content with allowing her sister to think that only Natalia was changing while their worlds also crumbled around them.

"Maybe. Though I couldn't tell you how. You know my

search just as well as I do, yet I do not feel as though I am any closer to understanding it. I don't feel as you and Azazel do. Beyond frustrated that I don't feel at all, I suppose. Frustration is about as close as I can get to a true emotion, and it's not the one I seek."

"Pathetic."

It never ceased to amaze Natalia that Azazel could say one word and convey a multitude of emotions all at once. Self-satisfied, disgusted, amused. All balled into one word spat across their steadily strengthening connection. Azazel could deny what was happening all she wanted, but the siblings were in communication more in recent days than they had been in centuries. What other explanation could she give beyond the fact that their powers were waning?

"And to think I once considered the two of you my equals, if not my rivals," she continued snidely. "Weaklings, that's what you both are. Pathetic excuses for angels that I cannot believe I ever thought could go up against me. You're no rivals of mine."

"Your betters, I think you'll find," Natalia replied, closing her eyes as she gathered all of her strength and cast her sister from her mind.

She groaned as she felt Azazel's presence thrown from her mind, her body slumping on the balcony and threatening to topple into the street below as all her strength left her at once.

"It won't be long before we cannot ignore one another," Raziel whispered, her own voice distant and weak.

"I know. But I've not given up yet. I told you, I'm growing and learning new ways to be better than both of you. Soon, I will wipe your foul city from my sky *and* from my mind, and I will sever our connection permanently, *proving* that I am the best of us. You'll see," Natalia hissed, stumbling from the balcony and turning her back on the strange city that mocked her with its existence in her world.

Tomorrow.

Tomorrow, things would change forever, and no one, not even God, would be able to deny her power.

Natalia awoke bright and early the next day, rejuvenated from both sleep and a renewed confidence in herself. It wasn't that she had grown weaker; she'd just gotten lazy. She knew that now. John had pointed out that there was more than just the superficial beauty she'd been obsessed with. There was an inner beauty, something that appeared even stronger than she could ever have imagined.

She would *always* be the most beautiful woman in the entire Universe, but what if people could come to love her for that as *well* as her ambition, her courage, her strength of character? She would be unstoppable. God really wouldn't be able to shy away from her powers and grace then.

The palace shone a little brighter, her powers radiating from her. She *knew* she was stronger and more powerful than her sisters would have her believe. It was only her doubt that had caused her power to waver, and now that she *knew* that, everything would return to normal!

Natalia all but skipped her way down the glistening corridors of her palace to the main Throne Room, ready to greet her citizens with renewed vigor. Even the scar in the sky couldn't dampen her spirits today. Soon, it would be a distant memory, a foul taste in her mouth that would be easily forgotten with the sweet taste of victory that she would soon be consuming. Today was a new day, and it was the beginning of her crowning glory.

Before long, she would be rid of the dark shadow that still gripped her stomach and twisted it. Azazel's words still stung more than Natalia liked to admit, but she was about to prove her howling sister wrong in *everything* that Azazel had ever said to her. Soon, Natalia wouldn't have to think about her sister, let alone suffer listening to her voice.

No. Today was her day, and today, she would be rid of her past once and for all.

36

Natalia strode across her Throne Room, dark curls cascading over her back, her reflection grinning at her happily as Helena fell into step behind her. Soon, the acolytes and priestesses followed suit, their footsteps soft as they hurried along behind their Mistress, sharing worried and nervous looks that Natalia could see out of the corner of her eye.

She knew they weren't sure about pulling down the barricade and inviting the rebels to their door unguarded, but Natalia knew she could win them over again. John had gone out into the world on her behalf to speak to the rebels, he'd spent time with her, and she *supposed* he could boast that he had opened her eyes to the new possibilities within herself.

He would tell the others that she was going to redo everything, that they would have a new chance at life under her guidance. She could better them, shape them more into her image, show them how to become better versions of themselves, and in return, she would get to show them her *inner* self.

With a wave of her hands, the acolytes pulled down the last of the barricade, casting it aside with uneasy looks before they grasped the handles of the main doors and wrenched them open. Sunlight poured across the polished surface of the golden floors for the first time since they had been forced to shut them against the city.

Natalia smiled as the sun warmed her bare feet and legs, its rays rushing to embrace her silken skin with its comforting embrace. Stepping out of the palace and onto the steps, Natalia spread her arms wide as though inviting her citizens to embrace *her*. She'd expected cheers of joy at her reunion with her citizens, but instead, she was met with silence. For a brief second, Natalia faltered, hesitating before she took another step toward the crowd gathered in front of the building.

Her eyes scanned the faces before her, and Natalia spotted John at the front of them, nodding his own silent encouragement to her. Just as she hadn't realized how much she would miss Jules, Natalia was surprised to find herself glad to see the man there at that moment. He had come to bask in her glory, but she also felt encouraged to do this because he was there.

Natalia nodded to him in return, amused when the pretty woman beside him stared at him in shock. Clearly, she was *the* Sophie he'd spoken about before, and Natalia had a vague recollection of the woman offering her gifts on the days when her citizens had given their tithes.

"My citizens!" Natalia proudly called to them all, her arms still spread wide to signify her welcoming them back into the fold. "I know that my envoy, John, has sent you my message. I am here to tell you that it is indeed true; we are going to build a better world. Together. Yes, I still expect you to worship me, to understand that it is by *my* grace that you'll still live in my personally-made utopia. However, I will not enforce the tithe as I did previously, nor will I stop you from exploring relationships with one another. Just remember that this is *my* gift to you. That you are saved from the heartache and pain that my sisters, or even my *father*, would have put you through."

She glanced at John, who rolled his eyes at her a little but still smiled. She'd told him she couldn't change who she was, nor would she want to; she was perfect. She might be willing to learn, but that didn't mean she was going to stop being true to herself. She was just going to be a better version of herself.

The citizens glanced at one another and began to mutter amongst themselves as they began to discuss what she'd said. She could tell they weren't convinced, and some were clearly still looking to fight back against her, but Natalia watched as John began to put their minds at ease. She couldn't hear him, but she could see that he was mitigating any hostilities from the others.

There was a rumble of agreement through the crowd, a hushed sense of positivity that steadily grew into a crescendo of excited chatter. Natalia smiled as John caught her eye and gave her a quick thumbs up. She had won back her people, and clearly, they were ready to try again.

They knew how easy they had it with her. She was far kinder than any of her siblings would have been, let alone the suffering that God would have put them through. Finally, it was time for them to learn and grow together again.

"Pathetic, weak excuse for an angel. You call yourself a goddess, and yet here you are, bending your will to these creatures? They are insects meant to be crushed beneath our boots, and yet you compromise with them? I knew you were weaker than me; I knew I was the best of all of us, not you. All your bravado, all your ego, and you let them manipulate you."

Azazel's words stung. Her sister knew how to rile her; she always had, telling her that she was weaker than these humans she was *supposedly* above. No, she was above *them*; she was the one in charge here… That doubt that she thought she'd shaken off began to creep back in, icy fingers of disbelief that she could be anything other than almighty gripping her heart.

"No," she whispered, shaking her head as though dismissing her sister from her mind. "NO!" The word roared across the city, causing the ground to shake violently, bricks cascading from the buildings as they crumbled under the force of the shockwaves.

"This is *my* world! I created it with my own two hands, and I will *not* be manipulated by pathetic insects like *you*. You *will* love me; you *will* respect me. You will bow at my feet, kiss my toes, and be *grateful for the fact that you are allowed to live in this paradise*!" Natalia's shrill tone cut through the city like a scythe.

The buildings around her shuddered as her voice hit them. They stood tall for a moment, as proud as they ever had, before their tops sheared from the lower levels and crashed into the streets below. The citizens screamed in fear, scattering as the buildings collapsed around them.

Natalia stared at her reflection by her feet, sneering angrily at the black-eyed woman staring back at her as a red mist began to descend over her.

37

Pain lanced through every part of her body as she writhed and twisted against the changes in her body. The dark shadow of doubt had been replaced by a raging fire of fury, the inferno burning her from within. She watched herself changing in the reflective walls of the palace.

Her perfect ivory skin stretched and tore, great gashes of angry red and thick black scales forming where smooth skin had been once before. Her beautiful curls became lank and even darker, sickly black like thick strands of oil made solid, matching her hollow eyes that seemed to glow red with the fire growing within herself. Her back twitched and convulsed, her bones cracking audibly as huge leathery wings sprouted from between her shoulder blades. All her beauty was gone, replaced with the dark horror that sprouted from the doubt and hatred she now felt so strongly.

Natalia's mind thought of only one thing—shredding these pathetic insects apart with her new claws, tearing their flesh with her new fangs, and tasting their blood on her serpent-like tongue. They would pay; they would *all* pay.

Stretching her new wings, Natalia threw back her head and screamed with a mixture of elation and anger. She felt powerful; she felt *strong*. A growling laugh escaped her throat, and Natalia turned on the citizens screaming and shouting to get as far away as possible from the horror that she had become. There was no saving them now. All they'd had to do was love her, but that had been too much to ask, and now, she would destroy them.

Raising her scaled fists above her head, Natalia brought them down as hard as she could upon the ground. The shockwaves shuddered out like ripples on water, and her citizens struggled to keep on their feet, most of them collapsing to the ground, covering their heads with their arms against the falling debris from the buildings. She would destroy them; she would see them *all* suffer.

Natalia flapped her wings, growling happily at the feeling of the air as it moved around them. Oh, how she had missed being able to fly, that sweet feeling of freedom that she just didn't get from anything else. The wind rushed to embrace her as the sky turned black to match her heart. Clouds gathered in the sky for the first time since she had created her world, blocking Raziel's city from view. Thunder rumbled like the drums of war, a herald of the hell she intended to rain down upon the insects that dared to insult her, while lightning flashed bright and terrible in the darkness, splitting the sky in two.

They would bow. They would kneel. She would show them *all*. Natalia closed her eyes and raised her hands to Heaven, wings sweeping through the air with ease as though she had never been without them. A dark power gathered inside her, terrible and new as it filled every fiber of her being, tickling her nerves with electricity. Her forked tongue flickered over her lips as she tasted the raw power in the very air around her.

She gathered it to her, drawing it into herself and focusing all of that natural potential into her fingertips to create a pool of it in her palms. She visualized the flames in her heart, pulling them out into the air until they manifested in her hands, their warmth flickering and licking at her skin.

She then opened her eyes and let out a mirthless laugh, the sound grating, lightyears from the melodic laughter she'd known all her life to be her own. She looked at the balls of fire she had summoned and smiled, her fangs pricking her bottom lip. She flicked her wrists, fire cascading to the ground below, raining down from the thick black clouds that had gathered above her.

Screams echoed from the streets, panic and fear palpable in the air, sweeter than she could ever have imagined. All they had to do was love her, and they could have avoided all of this; now, she would see them writhe in pain.

Natalia descended from her vantage point, landing gracefully before the entrance to her palace. She cocked her head to one side, grinning maliciously as she watched her citizens collide with one another, pushing each other out of the way in an attempt to save themselves from the fireballs raining down upon them.

The stench of charred flesh and smoke filled the air, acrid and suffocating. Yet Natalia breathed deeply, savoring each taste of it on her tongue as she filled her lungs with it. The ground cracked, and she watched gleefully as several citizens were swallowed whole by the earth.

"My Lady! *Please*, stop this!" Helena's voice begged above the cacophony of wails and cries that filled the air.

Natalia felt a pressure on her arm, and she turned her

head toward it slowly, hissing at the hand that she found wrapped around her wrist. Her head whipped around, and she bared her fangs at her priestess. Helena leapt backwards, eyes wide, her fear written all over her face. Natalia grinned maliciously, stepping toward the priestess threateningly.

"Stop it! Just stop this!" another voice screamed at her, and Natalia spun around to face the person who *dared* to believe they could stop her from doing what she wanted.

Even in her rage-fueled state, Natalia recognized the face of the woman who had saved Helena from her wrath. Sophie. The woman whom John had *dared* fall in love with when all of his attention *should* have been on Natalia.

Natalia hissed angrily, her wings quivering on her back as she lowered her body, claws extended as all her attention focused on the woman.

She could see the fear in Sophie's eyes as she realized what was about to happen, Natalia's body trembling like a coiled spring. A predator ready to pounce upon its prey, fangs primed to tear out the throat of the woman frozen before her. A deer facing a lioness. With a scream of rage, Natalia launched herself at the woman, ready to strike her down and taste her blood.

Sophie didn't move, her fear causing her to freeze in place. Natalia raised her claws, ready to slash the woman's pretty face, wanting to feel her flesh distort and twist. She wouldn't be beautiful ever again; Natalia would make sure of that. The space between them closed, and Natalia let out a shriek of joy as she anticipated the satisfactory feeling of flesh tearing under her claws.

Suddenly, there was movement out of the corner of her eye. Before Natalia could stop herself or do anything else, John pushed Sophie out of the way and bore the brunt of Natalia's wrath himself. She felt her claws rake through skin, muscle, and bone, like metal grating on rock. His blood poured over her hands, warm and sticky.

Natalia stumbled, collapsing to her knees beside his fallen body, her hand trembling as John's blood dripped from her scales. She stared at the mangled mess that had been the man's face, his body convulsing as he gasped for air, gurgling as he choked and drowned in his own blood.

"Why?" She gasped, staring at his one remaining eye. "*Why?!*"

"Because I love her!" He gasped also, reaching out a hand to Natalia, his body quaking with the effort. "Be better," he whispered as he grasped her hand in his, his fingers squeezing her hand for a moment before he went limp.

38

"John?" Natalia whispered, placing a hand upon his chest and shaking him lightly.

She could feel his heartbeat, faint and growing weaker by the second, but it was there. Natalia stared at her hand on his chest, her eyes drawn to Sophie who stood close by, wailing at the sight of her lover in this state. Natalia cocked her head to one side slightly. She could not hear anything, not even the terrible grieving shriek of the woman, and she realized that the world had fallen silent for her.

He'd given his life for the woman he loved, just as Jules had for her when she'd been assaulted. He was willing to die for Sophie, and yet he *still* wanted Natalia to know that she could do better. Why did he care? Why did he make that effort even after all of this? She'd hurt him badly; she'd killed the others, and he still wanted her to know that he believed in her.

He truly loved Sophie, just as Jules had loved her. Her sisters, her family, none of them would have ever given their lives in the way that John and Jules had. They'd sacrificed themselves for love, a love that Natalia had wanted all her life but never really understood. She'd been determined for these people to love her, but what had she ever done to deserve it? Why had Jules given his life for her? Why would John *still* care enough to use his last breath to encourage her to improve?

Natalia's hand gripped John's blood-covered shirt, feeling the ever-slowing heartbeat in his chest. Her heart ached for what she had done, for hurting someone who had stood up to her and *dared* to tell her that she could be more than she already was. Tears blurred her vision as she clung to his body, oblivious to the continuing destruction around them as she focused solely on him.

No. She wasn't going to lose him like she'd lost Jules. She needed him to show her the way, to help her find her *inner* light so that she might one day find love again. She wanted to find someone who could love her as Jules had, someone she could share her life with.

"I can do better. I can be better. I *am better*. And I'm going to prove it to you," Natalia growled, shifting her weight onto her knees as she pressed both her palms to John's chest.

Even now, she could feel that her powers were different— not weaker as such, just new and unfamiliar. Closing her eyes, Natalia took in a slow, deep breath. She could feel the raw power she'd tapped into before, when she'd first transformed into a demon, but she dismissed it. That raw power was full of anger and hate, and that wasn't her; that wasn't *her* strength. Healing wasn't exactly her specialty; it wasn't what God had designed her to do, but all angels had some form of healing powers. Latent and lingering under the surface.

"What are you doing to him?!" Sophie hissed at her, breaking her concentration.

"Saving his life. Do you want to *help* or just get in my way?" Natalia hissed in return, opening her eyes and gasping as her reflection stared back at her from Sophie's large brown eyes.

The black scales were receding, the slick strands of hair dripped their oil onto John's almost lifeless body, her shiny curls glistening beneath. It wasn't any of this that shocked her; it was her wings. When she had fallen, God took her wings as part of her punishment, but as the leathery skin shed away, it revealed the bright white feathers that she had known all her life. Restored to their former glory, gleaming with the light of the stars above.

Sophie placed a hand on Natalia's, the other on John's disfigured face. Natalia felt Sophie's love for John, and her acceptance—and maybe even an ounce of gratitude—toward Natalia for what she was about to do. Focusing on that energy, on the love the citizens around her had for one another and the man lying on the ground, Natalia felt the warmth grow beneath her fingers moments before the golden glow appeared.

She let the healing energy gather at her fingertips before she pumped John's chest with her palms, forcing the energy and light directly into his body. The bleeding stopped in John's wounds, and the gashes healed for the most part, even though Natalia felt herself unable to completely rid him of the scar tissue that she had unfortunately gifted him.

Natalia panted heavily, beads of sweat gathering on her forehead as she focused her energy on bringing John's body back from the brink. His body convulsed beneath her hands, and Natalia fell back, gasping for breath in unison with John. He sat up sharply, blinking in confusion as he looked at his lover, bawling against his rising and falling chest, to the smug-looking—if somewhat exhausted—angel beside him.

"You saved my life," he croaked.

"Sadly, I didn't have the strength to save your face." She snorted in return, one hand on her chest as she winced at the steady burn of her lungs.

"Inner beauty." John chuckled, tapping his face and grimacing a little at the pain that still lingered there. "Why?"

"You reminded me of Jules. Of the sacrifice he made for me, and why I'd promised to make this world anew." She sighed, struggling to her feet.

Natalia stumbled and gasped as she felt the world give way beneath her feet, but rather than the cold hard ground rushing to meet her, Natalia found herself bolstered by the crowds. Men and women rushed to embrace her, catching her as she fell and supporting her. Lending her their strength.

She stared at them all. Their faces covered in burn marks and soot, bloody and bruised from head to toe, and *still* willing to stand there and help her after all that she had done.

"Be better," John whispered, tapping his scarred face again with a flinch, his remaining good eye beaming at her as he smiled.

Natalia smiled and nodded in return to him. She'd been naïve. She was strong, and she may be the strongest being in the world, but that didn't mean she was infallible. Even God had needed his angels, so why had she ever believed that she could be any different?

Was this what you meant about me learning a lesson? she asked Him silently, glancing up at the renewed blue skies, and Raziel's city sat within the scar, wondering if her father was smiling down on her from His own throne.

39

Natalia gently shook her people from herself, offering a small smile to them to show that she would be alright, and that they had her thanks. She could see the looks of mistrust and surprise, and for once, she didn't blame them. Her anger, her doubt in herself, had all led to her becoming a demon. They'd all discussed the possibilities and reasons why angels twisted into Hell spawns, but there had never been any definitive proof. Most of the fallen were just that, fallen, not mindless demons hell-bent on bloodthirsty destruction.

"All of you, stand together on the steps. Helena, I'm sorry for frightening you. Can you clear the palace for me?" she asked.

The priestess hesitated for a minute, huddled amongst a group of other shivering priestesses and acolytes who looked equal parts confused and scared. Natalia reached around to her newly-formed wings and plucked one of her glistening feathers from the limb, wincing at the sharp pain and sighing as a spot of blood began to form and filter into the feathers below. There was an ache in her heart at the imperfection, but that was also part of the point. Natalia held the feather out to her priestess as she moved toward her slowly, her free hand up to show that she meant no harm.

Helena held out a hand, unable to stop herself from shaking, but still willing to try. Natalia placed her feather onto the woman's outstretched palm, cupping Helena's hand with hers and curling the priestess' fingers around the feather.

"Once you have everyone, make sure you all hold hands and think of me. The feather will bring you straight back here," Natalia whispered. "It will also keep you safe from any potential falling debris. Be safe, but be quick."

Helena nodded and hurried into the palace, gripping the feather as she vanished through the crooked main doors and into the crumbling building that had once stood so tall and proud.

An hour passed before Helena reappeared on the palace steps with the remaining priestesses and acolytes who had taken shelter in the palace while Natalia was losing her mind to the darkness. They looked uncertainly at their Mistress as Natalia ushered them onto the steps with the rest of her people, squishing them all together.

"What are you up to?" John asked, raising an eyebrow at her, his face struggling with the movement as the scar tissue stretched uncomfortably.

Natalia stared at the man for a moment, taking in his scarred face, the scars that *she* had caused. His right eye would never recover, and while the red raw flesh would eventually settle and become less uncomfortable for the man, they would never fade. An ugly reminder of the day she'd lost herself, almost completely. It was strange, as not so long ago, Natalia would have been repulsed at the very sight of him. Yet now, when she looked at the huge red marks that marred his once handsome face, Natalia didn't see an ugly man at all.

She reached a hand out to the man, gently touching his cheek and tracing a finger over one of the scars that she'd given him with a smile on her face. "Light shines through a cracked vase."

John laughed, immediately grimacing as his face stretched, rolling his eyes at her. "Fuck you, too." He snorted.

Grinning, Natalia gently moved him behind her with her wings. She spread her arms wide and took a deep breath. The wind whipped around them all, causing several members of the crowd to gasp in surprise as bits of debris were gathered by the air, spinning above their heads.

"Watch this," Natalia said smugly, loud enough for John to hear her over the roaring gale she seemingly commanded now.

The world crumbled around them, and she vaguely heard people screaming behind her, though their voices were snatched away by the wind and whipped away from her ears. The palace crumbled alongside the city, leaving only the steps and courtyard where her citizens had gathered for safety. Natalia could already feel her body aching, straining against any further use of her powers, but she had promised her people a new world, and she would give them just that.

A new city grew around them, still glistening gold, bright and shining. The wind grew quiet, and Natalia lowered her hands with a gasp, her knees buckling beneath her. John and Helena rushed to catch her, and Natalia smiled softly.

"Thank you," she muttered.

"What did you do?" Helena asked, scowling at her.

"I created a new world. For all of us," she replied.

"What?"

"Go and look; see for yourselves." Natalia chuckled, standing upright and brushing at her tattered clothes, trying not to weep at the state she must be in. "I promised you all a fresh start, and I almost killed you all, so I've made this world anew. Now we can *really* start over, all of us. I just hope, someday, that might include some *others* who aren't here right now," she added, glancing up at Raziel's world, peering through the scar in the sky.

Her citizens began to scatter, hurrying to see the changes that had been made, feeling more at ease that Natalia was being true to her word this time. Natalia smiled at John and Sophie, furling her wings against her back as she strode confidently into her renewed palace.

On the surface, it looked as though nothing had changed. Everything was still gold, the surfaces polished into glistening mirrors so that she could see her reflection with every turn of her head. Entering the Throne Room, Natalia turned her head to watch as John, Sophie, and Helena all entered. They gasped collectively at the sight, leaving Natalia grinning widely.

"What do you think?" she asked, waving a hand at the new palace with a flourish.

Surrounding her throne was a grand statue of herself, her newly-formed wings spread wide to embrace the men and women who stood beside her, all of whom were looking up at her adoringly. The walls were, for once, not reflective at all, covered in a variety of murals depicting Natalia engaged in a variety of activities with the men and women she called her citizens. From playing music together, to painting, to strolling through the forests or splashing in the rivers.

The central mural didn't depict Natalia at all. Jules' image dominated the wall, a serene expression on his face, a halo glowing around his head as though he had been given his sainthood.

As Natalia's eyes settled on the image, she smiled sadly, her heart twinging as she felt the loss of him again. He would never see this new world, this new start, but she still wanted him to be a part of it in some way. If it hadn't been for Jules and John, Natalia would never have started to understand love.

This was her way of thanking him.

40

"I thought it was going to be *less* about you." John snorted, chuckling as he motioned to the images on the wall.

"What?! They're not *all* me, are they?" she asked, pointing to Jules' image with a look that said, "argue with that."

"One out of how many?" John laughed.

"I've got other citizens in the images, too. It's not like I'm the *only* image now. And I've got you down perfectly." She smirked, pointing to the statue by her throne where John stood beside her, and then to a mural where he was rolling his eyes at her.

"Yeah, I can't argue there." He exhaled.

"I told you. I can't change my nature. I might be able to

learn, but I'm always going to be myself." Natalia chuckled, crossing her arms over her chest.

She might have learnt a little more about herself, and she might be willing to learn more about herself and the people around her, but she still knew she was the most beautiful being in the Universe, and she was also the strongest. She couldn't have believed anything other than that. She knew what she was capable of, and she had proven her prowess in rebuilding her world all over again. She'd always known she was amazing; now no one else could deny it, either.

"So, what now?" John asked, hugging Sophie to his side.

"We live. In the way we should have done when I first created this world. I will help all of you become better versions of yourself, more in my image as I should have done before, and you will teach me to see the value of a person from *within*. Not just by their looks."

John chuckled and glanced at Helena for a moment. Natalia looked at the priestess, too, watching as the woman took in the new sites that surrounded her, clearly trying to work out where she fitted into this new world that Natalia had created.

"I hope my sisters can join us one day, but for now, we can learn and grow together." Natalia shrugged, striding back out of the palace.

She turned to face the scar where her sister's city laid, reaching a hand toward the dark, emotionless place as though she could pluck it from the sky and bring it closer. Their powers were growing weaker, but only because they needed to learn to be better versions of themselves. Natalia wondered what lesson her sisters were learning beyond the barrier, and whether they would learn it at all or be destroyed as she almost had been.

"Look! Another scar in the sky!" Helena gasped as she joined Natalia outside the palace, pointing to a place opposite the scar where Raziel's city lingered.

It was new, and not quite opened yet, not enough to see the world beyond. Natalia could see vague shapes in the bright white tear, and knew that Azazel lurked in the space beyond. So much for her sister being the *better* of them. It seemed even she could not deny her failings now, not when the barrier was beginning to crumble between their two worlds.

Soon, their worlds would collide, and they would all be together again, unless her sisters fell to their own citizens first, or to the darkness lingering in their own hearts. Natalia rubbed at her chest, feeling the remnants of that dark shadow that had almost consumed her, twisting her body beyond recognition.

Natalia managed to compose herself, stopping herself from shuddering as she remembered the ugly, twisted creature she'd become. Was that the ugliness that John had accused her of having inside? If so, she wasn't sure she ever wanted to see *that* again.

Natalia looked from one scar to the other, smiling softly to herself. Her sisters were closer to her than they had been in centuries. She wished Jules were still with her, but she could learn to love again; she was sure of that. He'd opened her heart to the possibility, showing Natalia that she was capable of loving someone *other* than herself. Even John held a special place in her heart now, which felt oddly comforting. Natalia looked at Helena and smiled, wondering what the woman would become to her now.

Whatever the future held, she was walking new ground. Becoming an even *better* version of her perfect self, and no one would be able to deny how glorious she truly was.

To be continued...

MACHIAVELLIANISM

BOOK TWO OF THE DARK TRIAD TRILOGY

Azazel remembered everything. The uprising, the pain of her wings being ripped from her body, and the sinking feeling in her stomach during the fall as she watched the Gates of Heaven grow smaller and smaller the further she fell.

She was once one of the Creator's most beautiful and favored angels who wanted to advance mankind so there wouldn't be a need to interfere like before. God saw this as subordination and ordered that the rebel angels be stripped of their wings so that when He slammed the Gates of Heaven to them, they wouldn't be able to get back in.

Word quickly spread throughout the Kingdom of Heaven

that He was coming for Azazel, her sisters, and the rest of the rebels. There was nowhere they could hide that God couldn't find them. There was no weighing of truth or explanation; God wanted them *gone*. He showed that He wasn't the all-loving God they had once thought He was. His true nature was unforgiving and controlling.

He wanted to keep the humans in the dark, stumbling for answers with only Him as a beacon of hope. With nowhere else to go, they fell to Earth, uncertain of how the humans would react to having divine beings walk amongst them consistently. They should have known that the humans would need to be molded into what the fallen needed them to be in order to survive.

The fallen spread out and concluded that they wanted different things for the humans, and decided to have a millennium-long wager over whose way was the more superior. When the time came, they would shift the world to the path that seemed to fit best for the advancement of humanity.

Azazel didn't see her sisters much unless it was to check in on the progress of each world and compare the progress. She assumed it was because they were embarrassed that their methods weren't working out as well as hers. Azazel had order, luxury, and yearly entertainment that the citizens of her kingdom talked about until the following grand selection.

She lived in paradise and was incredibly confident that *her* way was the only way the world could continue, and humans would have the best hope for survival. Plus, the humans adored her as an earth-bound goddess, and she wouldn't have it any other way.

The humans regularly brought her offerings and renewed their loyalty to satisfy her, hoping she would cancel the yearly Cunning. This event required a member from a selected family to come and fight to the death for riches beyond their wildest dreams. The family would be set up in a luxurious home. Their bank accounts would never be empty.

Over the years, six prominent families had acquired a majority of the wealth in the kingdom. They were able to buy their way out of participating in the Cunning. They were the closest resemblance to friends to Azazel, and took just as much pleasure in watching the event as Azazel did. They had been so successful that it'd been hundreds of years since any of their members had competed. Azazel took so much pleasure in having them close to her. They shared her same beliefs and were always a robust support system for directing the world.

The deaths of the defeated warriors would give Azazel the strength she needed to keep her world balanced. Every year, her subjects would give more extravagant gifts to keep their families intact. Still, Azazel thrived on the chaos that ensued.

After decades of being on Earth, she looked forward to the entertainment of the humans begging for their families. In the weeks leading up to the grand selection, citizens would line up for hours to bring her their most splendid offerings, hoping it would be enough. Her gluttonous nature made her insatiable; her kingdom could give her everything in their homes—even their children—and she would still want more.

And they always found a way to give her *more*. She was never worried about an uprising because she still cared for her kingdom. There was never a food shortage, and everyone had a home. Some were nicer than others, but not one person could complain that they never had enough.

This way of life made it easy for her to start her annual feast. When she first found the area that she took over, it was all lower-class communities. People were miserable, but every person rose in life under Azazel's rule. The citizens became smarter because of the new skills she bestowed on them, wealthier because of the jobs she provided when building the kingdom into what it became, and devious because of the traits that she instilled in them to help them get everything their hearts could ever desire in life.

They realized that the source of their success was Azazel. They were easy to convince.

The Cunning started off with a simple show of who was better at specific archery, swordplay, or basic combat skills. Over the years, things had evolved to become the bloodbath that Azazel loved so dearly. She treated it like it was her birthday or a holiday that everyone should celebrate.

She was never affected by the sorrow many families felt. She knew that death balanced life, and death needed to occur if they wanted to keep their lives the way they were going. While there were rumors that she would eat the souls of the dead, this simply wasn't the case. The soul's essence was automatically attracted to her divinity when they died. It became one with her, giving her the sustenance she eventually needed to continue in the human world. She considered the lost souls safer with her than in Heaven.

As the years passed, Azazel became bored with the display. She eventually decided to create a new theme every year and announce it after the commonwealth funeral to allow potential contestants to train as much as possible before the following grand selection.

The wealthier families had their children training in various combat areas from a young age. Azazel became fond of the younger assassins in her kingdom, and put an age restriction on the selection so that she would never be faced with the sorrow of losing one of her small comrades. By the time they were ready to be chosen, the once young slayers had turned into impressive killing machines. She enjoyed watching them rise in the coliseum until there was only one left.

This had been going on for hundreds of years. Entire

generations were lost to appease Azazel, but she was getting to a point where the Cunning was no longer bringing her as much joy. The lost warriors didn't satisfy her as much. The kingdom could feel the air getting heavier as impending doom lingered.

1

Azazel looked into her full-length mirror, inspecting herself. The longer she looked, the more obsessed she became. Her long, rich midnight hair flowed around her shoulders. It came down just below her elbows. Her curvaceous body was always clothed in form-fitting gowns made of rich silks in pure white shades. Her jewelry could blind someone if they caught a glimpse of her at the wrong angle midday.

Leaning forward to inspect her expertly-applied makeup, she couldn't help but get lost in her platinum gray eyes and long dark eyelashes. She smiled when she came to her daily realization of how beautiful she was, and how blessed her citizens were to have her as their leader.

She twirled and admired herself even further, loving how the skirt of her dress would slightly fan out and accentuate her curves. She knew how mesmerizing she was. When she faced the mirror again, she applied some gloss to her plump lips and was pleased with her final look for the day.

Walking out of her chamber, the atmosphere in her palace was electric with excitement. It was the morning of the grand selection, and she was looking forward to seeing the entertainment lineup for this year. She smiled at her servants as she passed them, ensuring that they were all doing their duties to keep the palace running smoothly.

Azazel didn't want to start her day by disciplining her staff.

When she noticed one of her butlers moving slower than usual, she went up to him, curious as to what his problem that morning was.

"Cedric?" Azazel smiled sweetly. Cedric bowed profoundly, and she could see that he looked paler than usual. "Are you alright?" Cedric rose from his bow and tried to avoid eye contact with her as he replied. "Just fine, Goddess. I just didn't sleep very well last night."

Azazel gleamed. "Yes, I lose sleep from the excitement on the eve of the grand selection myself, but that isn't an excuse for laziness, now is it?" Her tone dripped with displeasure.

She noticed that he was quick to apologize and claimed he would move quicker going forward.

Cedric excused himself from her presence quickly and carried on, moving faster than before. Azazel stayed and watched him work for a short while until she was satisfied with his speed. She carried on to the Great Hall for her morning tea and breakfast. While she was there, she noticed nervous energy surrounding her, and she couldn't shake it. Choosing instead to focus on the sweet figs and the comforting tea, wrapping herself in a blanket of reassurance.

She knew that the excitement was covering up the fear that the kingdom felt this time of year.

It made her miss Heaven, in the sense that emotions like this weren't felt, so they never interfered with anything that was taking place. Angels generally didn't experience any feelings. They were simply expected to do as they were told without any questions.

It took Azazel and her sisters coming to spend time on Earth to gain any sort of human emotion. It took years for them to feel true happiness and sadness. Azazel hated feeling any kind of negative emotion and manipulated herself to never be obligated to handle any sort of negatively. She repelled any bad feeling, and the person standing closest to her would feel everything that Azazel refused to feel.

As she sat in silence, contemplating the events that were about to unfold, she was curious as to why there was a lingering nervousness in the air. It was almost irritating that they were still nervous after hundreds of years of the grand selection. The Cunning—she thought they would be more than accustomed to it by now. If they really understood how the sacrifice kept their world in balance, they would be celebrating for weeks on end after the final trial instead of mourning the fallen.

Besides, it's not like the souls were lost in Heaven. They were still here, but they had fused with her on a molecular level, and she could still feel their love for her. It was something that she was going to have to address. She needed the energy to be positive and consistent throughout the entire process. It wasn't as fulfilling if they were sad the whole time.

She decided to put a whispered rumor out through her most trusted rumor mongers. She would ensure that the kingdom would understand the weight of this event, and how they all reaped the benefits from the few sacrifices made —and only once a year at that.

Her brow furrowed at the thought of her kingdom

thinking the worst of her. She only wanted them to see her as the giving leader she knew she was. If they knew how her hunger provoked her daily, and how hard she had to work to suppress her need for sustenance, they would burst from gratitude for her self-control. She felt her brow furrow at the thought of her urges and sighed, knowing that there was still a short wait before she would feel delighted.

The meals were only for show, so no one would be suspicious of her actual needs. Tapping her fingers on the table, Azazel mulled over the thought of having multiple Cunning events a year, and could feel her mouth salivate at the idea of being full continuously. She decided that maybe this year, it was time to bring the essence of truth into the Cunning, and possibly relieve the mourning families. They should feel honored that their loved ones are a part of her.

Azazel finished her tea and breakfast, and then walked through the halls discreetly, watching her staff as she passed. She knew that there was still time before the selection, but she couldn't wait to see her citizens eager to see if they were chosen.

She went out onto the large balcony at the front of her palace, giving her a bird's eye view of her entire kingdom. Azazel took a deep breath and was instantly refreshed from the morning air. There really *was* something so sacred about this day, and she refused to let there be any underlying negativity.

She decided that she would go down to the selection atrium to inject a bit of divinity to jumpstart the shift, and it would feel right again. She almost ran into her chambermaid, Sarika, and let out an irritated groan as she turned around.

"Sarika! Say something, or make a sound to declare yourself!" Azazel yelled frustratedly.

"I am so incredibly sorry, Goddess. You're right; I should have made myself known." Sarika stumbled through her apology, refusing to look up at Azazel. She bowed low. "I only came to let you know that the grand selection will be taking place soon—"

Azazel interrupted her briskly. "I am aware of the timing, Sarika. I was about to go to the atrium before you held me up with having to explain protocol." Azazel walked past her servant, who rushed behind her to keep up. Azazel was taller than all of the humans she ruled, so keeping up with her long strides required a light run.

"Goddess, if I may," Sarika started and waited for Azazel to acknowledge her. Azazel rolled her eyes and gestured for Sarika to continue. "Goddess, the families are here."

Azazel stopped abruptly. "Why wouldn't you start with that out on the balcony? Do I need to keep explaining to you how to do your job?" Azazel spat at her servant.

Sarika nodded. "They are in the reception hall waiting for you. They haven't been here long."

Azazel seethed. "They shouldn't have been waiting at all, Sarika!" And she quickly turned toward the reception hall, excited to see her most loyal and devoted followers.

As Azazel got closer to them, she could feel herself start to radiate, and it was reflected in all of their faces as they all turned to bow and welcome her.

Azazel scanned the room and opened her arms wide. "Families, welcome!" She beamed at the wealthiest families in her kingdom. The Barem, Ankah, Jones, Li, Thompson, and Berith families all brought forward jewels, extravagant bouquets of flowers, and beautifully-scented body oils.

The fallen angel soaked in the delicious moment and was filled with bliss. She accepted the gifts graciously and blessed each member, ensuring that they would have another year of blessings and happiness.

The families had figured out a loophole in the selection process. Azazel realized this may have not been fair, but she didn't care. The gifts they brought her and the loyalty they showed continuously made up for it all. They all did their part in the kingdom, so that other families could potentially be as successful as them. They taught different combat methods, stayed with mourning family members to ensure they were fine for as long as needed, and always had a hand available to help anyone who needed it. They were the models she was trying to mold the rest of the kingdom into.

The families were always as excited as she was for the great selection and Cunning. Even though they didn't reap the same benefits, the families loved the entertainment.

Making her way through the crowd, she asked eligible members their future plans for marriage. The families only married each other to keep the advantages of their agreement going. Azazel liked to think that it was all because of her; these beautiful families had generations and generations of loved ones, and felt that the very least they could do was shower her with gifts and unwavering loyalty.

Antonio Barem, the current head of the Barem family, stepped forward and dipped low in a bow before stating, "You look absolutely radiant, Goddess."

Azazel couldn't help but be taken by Antonio. He was incredibly handsome with his piercing blue eyes, tanned skin, and the strand of deep blond hair that always found its way to cover one of his eyes. He was always well-dressed and had the best style she had ever seen when it came to men.

He presented her with a velvet case; she smiled and delicately took it from his hands. When she opened it, her breath was taken away. Inside was a strand of the finest diamonds she had ever seen. Antonio came up behind her and pulled the necklace out of the box to indicate that he would adorn her with it. Azazel turned and pulled her hair up to expose her neck so he could take off the necklace that she already had on.

"Ninety of the most precious diamonds ever mined make up this necklace. They reflect the same beautiful colors as the aurora borealis in the light. But they could never compare to your own beauty, Goddess," Antonio whispered into her ear as he connected it.

He let his fingertips lightly brush against her exposed shoulders, and Azazel shivered ever so slightly in pleasure. She couldn't understand this hold that Antonio had on her. It was otherworldly.

She turned to him and cupped his face softly. "You have outdone yourself yet again, Antonio. It's beautiful." And she placed her hand on the necklace.

This gift felt different from the hundreds he had presented to her over the past years. Members of the other families all brought up different offerings. As pleased as she was with everything, Azazel couldn't help but continue to glance at Antonio, who watched her intently. His eyes filled with a look that she couldn't put her finger on.

After the offerings had been given, and Azazel was pleased, she motioned toward the exit

"Shall we?" she asked before turning to lead her courtiers out of the grand hall.

As they walked out of the palace gates together, Azazel couldn't help but notice the kingdom's beauty. Garlands of flowers were strung between street lamps, and the bakeries were busy producing sweet-smelling treats to be handed out. Azazel felt at peace and wanted to enjoy every moment leading up to the Cunning.

Children ran up to the group with flowers to offer to Azazel; she couldn't help but be swept up by the sweetness of every human she came into contact with. The entire group had multiple bouquets in their hands when they got to the atrium. When they stepped into the main entrance of the atrium, they all turned to walk to the small altar located to the left of the main arena. This was where citizens would come daily to leave offerings, and the entire shrine was engulfed with tokens of affection. Azazel's heart always swelled when she saw the shrine. It was a visual confirmation of her people's love, and it showed what they were capable of when it came to the grandness of their offerings.

The families all laid the flowers in front of the shrine, filling the room with a sweet floral scent. Azazel was in pure bliss, watching the scene in front of her. The families gathered in front of the shrine to say a prayer, thanking the Universe for bringing them their goddess.

Azazel was grateful for her courtiers. She never knew this kind of appreciation when she was in Heaven. She was solely expected to keep giving more and more of herself with every task that God gave her. Ask no questions, and get it done as quickly as possible. Azazel took a moment to enjoy the offerings before the atrium steward came to get them. The time had finally come for the grand selection. All of the families went to the spectator's box built at the highest point of the atrium. At the same time, Azazel made her way to the stage located in the middle of the arena.

2

Azazel walked onto the stage, and the audience broke out into thunderous applause. She looked around the entire arena, loving every second of the outpouring of affection. People were jumping up and down, trying to get her attention. Azazel couldn't help but smile widely; she wanted them to enjoy the excitement for as long as possible before many were sent into a downward spiral. After a short time passed, Azazel turned to the table and grabbed the list and microphone. She turned toward the crowd and motioned for them to quiet down.

The silence that came afterward was deafening in its own right. Everyone waited and collectively held their breath, and

Azazel could feel the tension of the kingdom, waiting to see what she would say. She scanned the room one last time.

When she looked up, she saw Antonio's face, and something in his face brought her overwhelming comfort. She cleared her throat, thanked everyone for participating, and thanked them for their continued love and devotion. This caused the crowd to erupt in a booming response, which she fully expected.

What she didn't expect, however, was after the first name was read, the wailing of the combatant's mother took over the entire atrium. Sounding like a wounded animal, it was guttural, primal, and filled with deep pain. Azazel realized at once after looking back at the last name that the woman's entire family had been lost to the Cunning. Her son would be the final member, and she'd be left all alone. Azazel hated seeing this happen, even after all this time.

Azazel waited for her crying to cease and continued until all hundred names were called. The combatants were brought down to the stage so Azazel could get a better look at all of them, and was pleased to see that they were primed to fight and were in the best shape possible. Azazel didn't think this selection could get any better, because they were all at the top of their rankings for different combat methods.

The steward came to give her a scroll with the following year's theme. She smiled when she read *gladiators*, which meant lions would be brought back into the kingdom. Azazel smiled, already looking forward to next year. The steward bowed, pleased to see how excited his goddess was. He took the scroll from her and left the stage; it was time to go through the Cunning's series of events. Azazel turned back to the crowd and put her hands up to indicate that it was time to listen.

Once the crowd had gone quiet, Azazel beamed as she announced that for the theme this year, Ultimate Warrior, the combatants would be put into the harshest conditions that would change day to day to test their survival skills. She also made it known that there would be a base camp in the middle of the arena with essential tools, a backpack for each warrior that contained everything they would need to set up their own camp, clothing for every season, and limited food packets. This year was going to be intense as they celebrated the two thousandth anniversary of the Cunning. She allowed the community to sponsor the combatants for the first time while they completed their two-week initiation training. The more money they raised, the better-quality gear they acquired at base camp. Azazel was keen to see the ways the warriors got creative.

After announcing the series of events and explaining the differences this year, she established her expectations for surprises at every turn, putting immense pressure on the game masters. When Azazel got bored, she took things into her own hands. She would hold the people responsible for her boredom accountable. They often weren't seen again.

Turning to head away from the crowd and warriors, her part was done for the day. Now it was time for the public offerings, her favorite part of the event. She made her way out of the atrium and toward the kingdom's center. There was a grand throne made out of marble on the place where she landed when she fell from Heaven; it was one of the most sacred places in the entire kingdom.

Azazel walked up to her throne. She sat down and positioned herself, sitting straight up and making sure she had her dress fanned out around her while waiting for the first offering. Antonio came to the platform and stood beside the throne silently for quite a while before breaking the silence after the latest offering.

"Are you pleased so far, Goddess?" He scanned the long line of citizens all waiting patiently and murmuring amongst themselves, comparing their gifts.

Azazel smiled up at him and reached out to grab his forearm as she said, "Oh, yes, very much so."

She motioned to the mound of gifts opposite of them. She couldn't wait to have everything in her palace. Azazel loved to fill her home with beautiful things and enjoyed that she could change her decor every year.

Antonio nodded encouragingly. "Yes, the kingdom has had a very successful year. It's truly our honor to do this for you, Goddess." He bowed to her, and Azazel felt giddy.

"Antonio, do you really think there is any need for the formality at this point?" she purred. Antonio looked up at her. She batted her eyelashes sweetly at him.

The gaze they shared was charged, and Azazel caught her breath in her throat, suddenly nervous. The next citizen then came up and cleared their throat, breaking the tension. Azazel broke eye contact first and accepted the gift, thanking the citizen. When she looked back, Antonio was still staring at her, taking in every detail of her face. Azazel felt her face flush and turned back to her adoring admirers. Her mind was racing with the flashbacks of the intense moments with Antonio.

She didn't understand where this was coming from. He had been her loyal subject for so long at this point, and she found herself wondering why she felt so nervous around him all of a sudden. She pushed her personal problems aside and focused on the offerings again; she smiled and began basking in the love that her kingdom was so willing to give.

After the last person had come to give their gift, Azazel sat for a moment and looked around the clearing. She felt like she had been there for weeks, and her face was starting to feel sore from the constant smiling. She was looking forward to sleeping for a long time after the Cunning.

Azazel stood up and figured it was time to check in on the combatants, and so she headed toward the training arena. Looking into the sky and noticing the sun setting, she suddenly remembered that the warriors would be getting ready to eat, and she smiled to herself, knowing that the warriors would be eating like royalty for their training session. Azazel always ensured that the best and most nutritious meals were prepared for them. Hence, they felt like they were cared for up until the end. She also noticed that the more satisfied their bodies were, the more satisfying their souls were when she absorbed them.

The angel let herself into the side door that led through a secret tunnel, and eventually, a room secretly hidden by a one-way mirrored glass. She was pleased to see that the warriors were still training so she wouldn't have to come back. She faced two combatants engaging in martial arts when she looked out the window. She recognized the boy as the first name she called; Azazel was pleasantly surprised when she saw him flip his opponent onto his back and win the match. She watched a while longer to witness him win every match that he was placed in. He had something to fight for, which meant he was a threat.

Pleased with what she saw, Azazel walked out of the arena, thrilled with the selection of combatants this year. The atrium steward waited for her when she came out of the building.

"Ah, Goddess, excellent. I was hoping you'd be here," he said as he bowed low.

"My curiosity got the better of me," Azazel replied shortly. "I was just about to head back to my abode."

The steward stood up. "Yes, of course, Goddess. I just wanted to go over the schedule for tomorrow."

Azazel stopped, already exhausted from the day she just had. She let out a sigh. "Steward, I am going to leave everything up to you. I am washing my hands of this responsibility. Do not bore me." Then she walked past him, leaving him open-mouthed and anxious.

Azazel loved walking through her kingdom by herself.

She was never worried about people coming up to her. They feared and respected her so much that they all kept their distance unless it was a holy day. And she *loved* how the kingdom was decorated this year. Her people seemed to find new and innovative ways to make the kingdom look stunning every year, and they never repeated any styles from previous years.

She was always so impressed with her citizens and how they showed their love for her. She was overwhelmed with gratitude for her people during her entire walk back to the palace. As she got ready, she thought about the upcoming weeks and the festivities that were about to take place. When she laid her head down on her pillow, Antonio's face was swimming around in her mind. His smile was the last thing she remembered before sleep overtook her.

3

Azazel opened her eyes the following day and was instantly excited. In a grand parade, she'd get to show off her combatants to the kingdom today. Each contestant would be dressed in the most luxurious materials and proudly display their family crest, honoring their ancestors and living family members. Azazel always enjoyed the pride she felt in those moments.

She stretched her arms wide, cracking her spine slightly and running her hand over her back. She felt the two scarred spots on her shoulder blades where her wings once were. Refusing to feel sad for her loss, she focused on her combatants and their achievements instead.

Azazel quickly jumped out of bed and ran to her ample

walk-in closet to pick the perfect outfit. She settled on a deep red bandage dress that hugged her curves and ended just above her knee. She also selected a pair of platform strappy sandals and picked out the necklace that Antonio had presented her with the previous day. Picking up the delicate necklace, she couldn't help but get lost in the beauty of the diamonds. Azazel wondered if there were other underlying motives behind the beauty of the offering but quickly pushed that out of her head. She was his goddess, and it was solely a gift of devotion. She decided that that's the only motive he had and finished her swooning over a mere human.

She did have to admit that the necklace elevated her look. It truly made her sparkle like the brightest star in the sky. She decided that she didn't need any other jewels and went into her beauty room, where the makeup artist was waiting to apply her makeup and style her hair for the day. She sat and enjoyed being pampered, mulling over the day's possibilities ahead of her.

Once the servant stepped back, saying she was finished, Azazel got up to inspect her face in the mirror. She was absolutely pleased with the dark and mysterious look that made her eyes pop out and the pouty red lips that she was so famous for shine. She couldn't help but smile and comment, "My hair has a certain luster to it today."

The servant mumbled, "Yes, Goddess, you are stunning," without making eye contact.

After a sufficient amount of gushing over herself in the mirror, Azazel left the beauty room and walked toward the dining room. She had a craving for sweet fruits and tea this morning. As she took her seat, the staff came out with a wave of plates and platters filled with different types of food. They set them all in front of her to pick and choose however she wanted.

Taking a ripe strawberry and savoring the sweet juice—even though she never experienced much taste from earthly food—she enjoyed the texture of the fruit in her mouth. She then grabbed the tiny teacup beside her and took a sip, and the warmth and comfort from the chai tea washed over her. Nothing could go wrong today, especially not when the tea was made this perfect.

Once she was satisfied with her grazing and the tea was finished, Azazel got up from the elegant table and walked toward the palace's front entrance. She almost collided with the rushing atrium steward, who dropped to his knees when he saw her.

"Goddess, we are waiting for you to start the proceedings." He didn't look up at her.

Azazel was agitated by his statement. Her face contorted into a look of disgust. "Are you sure that's how you want to greet me this morning, Steward?" Looking down at him, she couldn't help but notice his receding hairline, disheveled and wrinkled clothing. He smelled like he had just walked out of the bar. She wondered if maybe she had put too much faith into the steward.

Without looking up, he replied, "Goddess, the people of the kingdom have been lining the streets since dawn, waiting for you to grace them with your presence."

Azazel sucked air in through her teeth. "Not much better, Steward."

He looked up to reply. "Tom, Goddess, my name is Tom—"

Azazel cut him off sharply. "I don't care what your name is, Steward." And she walked past him through the heavy, elaborate double doors.

As she stepped outside, her loyal courtiers were waiting for her in the divine gardens that surrounded the palace. As she got closer to the group, an elderly woman from the Thompson family—with silver hair pulled up into a tight bun —stepped forward, curtsied, and asked in a concerned tone. "Goddess, are you alright? You… you look displeased."

Azazel let out a long sigh before replying, "Yes, Catherine, thank you. Dealing with saboteurs so early in the morning is enough to ruin anyone's day."

Catherine looked back at her family, and then back to Azazel. "Saboteurs, Goddess?"

Azazel nodded. "I consider unruly behavior to be saboteur behavior, don't you?"

Catherine didn't say anything, but she nodded in agreement and turned back to her family. This wasn't how Azazel had intended for the day to go. Now she would have to find a replacement for the atrium steward at the very beginning of the festivities. Azazel's whole morning had turned sour.

She tried not to let it seep into her mood as she made her way through the crowd and faced them all, holding her arms open and welcoming them. Putting on a smile and allowing herself to relax again, she turned and led the crowd out of the gardens and down the main street to where her marble throne sat. Azazel took her place, seated in the middle of the kingdom. She took a deep breath and let herself feel the pure divine energy from the holiest site in the entire kingdom.

Taking in several deep breaths to cleanse herself of the negative feelings that she was forced to feel earlier, she opened her eyes and motioned with her hand to start the parade. Almost instantly, a fanfare could be heard a distance away. As the music grew closer, Azazel was still trying to calm her annoyance from the encounter with the steward earlier.

Almost as if he could sense that she was thinking of him, the foul-smelling steward showed up by her side. He had his hands clasped in front of his waist, watching the square in front of him. Azazel could sense that he was about to say something, so she held up one finger to him.

"Your services will no longer be needed. Your termination is effective immediately. You are to come to my chamber tonight when the moon is at the highest point in the sky." She looked at him and could see that his face turned quite pale. She raised her eyebrows. "I said, you can go," she said with pure venom.

He bowed his head and walked away from her. Once he was gone, a large smile came across Azazel's face, and she felt relaxed, just in time. The band came around the corner, and her spirit was instantly lifted as she heard that the band had written a new melody in her honor. Leaning back and closing her eyes so she could enjoy the music, she felt herself slip into pure bliss.

When she opened her eyes again, the first combatants followed the band. She smiled warmly to welcome them. The line of fighters walked in a single file, all wearing tailored clothing in black. She admired everyone and noticed that they'd look at her, make eye contact, and then continue their march. Usually, several would break eye contact out of nervousness, but no one in this group seemed to show any emotion. She liked their confidence and could tell that this year's Cunning would be a satisfying experience in every sense.

The families followed the combatants and announced who they were sponsoring so far. Other wealthy families came forward to claim their own sponsors until every combatant was taken.

Even though she tried to never feel human emotions, Azazel couldn't help but feel relief for the fighters. Knowing fully well that they'd still have their needs met in a stressful situation that would make or break them. Azazel was giddy, thinking about the possibilities of how they were going to really keep her guessing.

Once she approved the pairings, she stood up. She announced that she would need Antonio, his brother, Jacob, and two strong family members from the Li family to stay behind. Thankfully, the selection was made quickly, and she was pleased to see two of the biggest Li family members come forward. Azazel announced that the kingdom was dismissed, and they were to refrain from coming out of their homes until the following day. She heard the confused mumbling through the crowd but paid it no mind.

After the kingdom had gone back into their homes, and Azazel was convinced that they were finally alone, she pulled the four men closer to her and told them that she was looking for the former atrium steward. She wanted him brought to her chamber, indicating that they didn't need to be gentle with him, either. The men all took off in different directions. Feeling satisfied, Azazel slowly walked home, excited to have a snack before the main course. Her mouth watered in excitement. She was eager to forget that he'd ever existed.

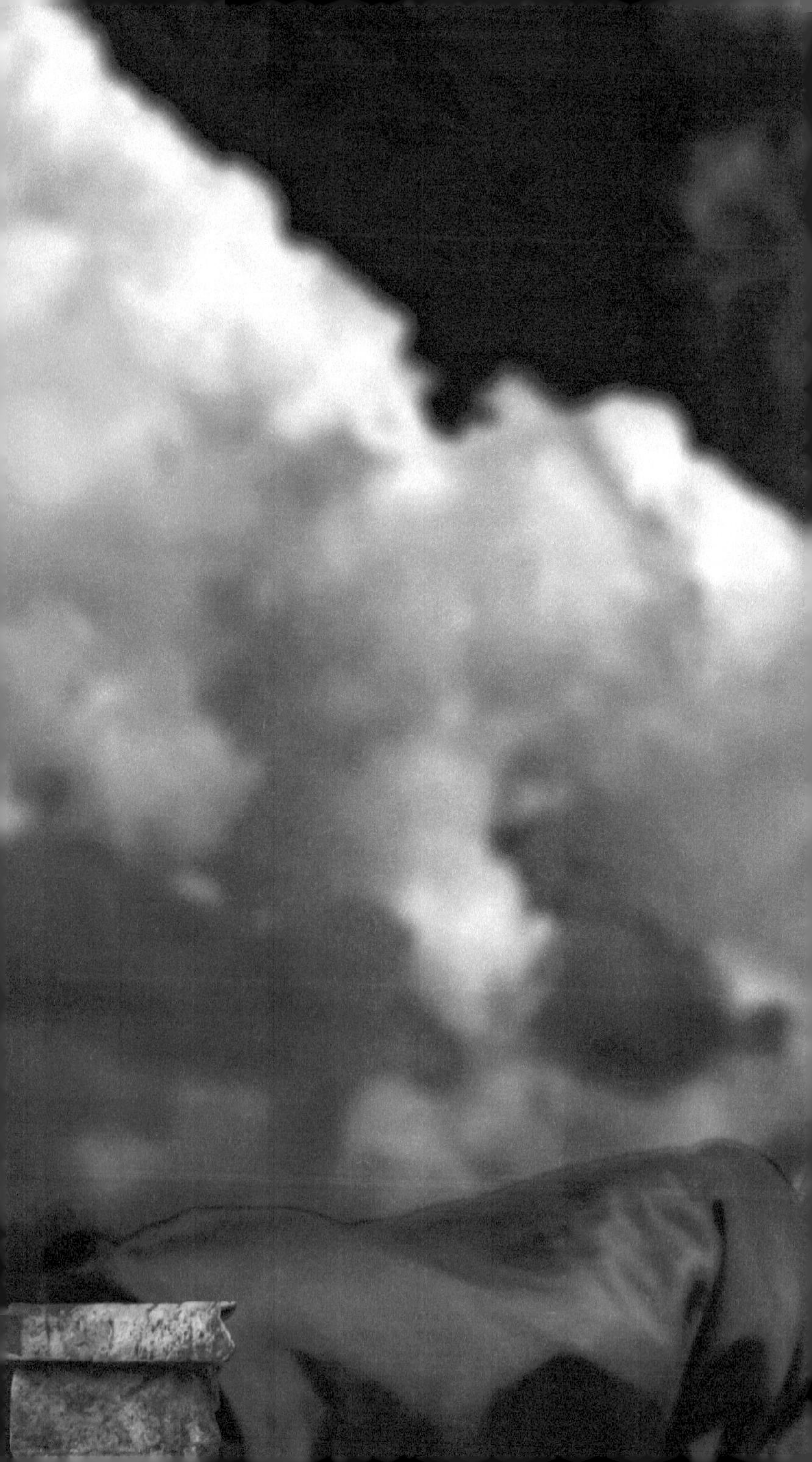

4

When Azazel returned to the palace, she walked into the dining room and grabbed the teapot and cup, and put them on a large platter filled with fruit, thinking it would be an excellent way to end her meal. She walked past the same servants whom she had chastised that morning and smiled at everyone as she passed them. Pleased with their newfound work ethic, she finally made it to her chamber, where she found several servants turning her bed down. She left the door open as she stepped aside.

"Out, now. I don't want to be disturbed until Antonio, his brother, and the Li brothers come."

The chambermaids curtsied and replied, "Yes, Goddess," in unison. Azazel was borderline impressed with their timing.

When they left, she locked the door and decided that she needed to slip into something a bit more appropriate. Walking into her closet, she went to find a light pink silk kimono. She pulled it out and thought it was perfect. She undressed and put her clothes off to the side for the following day's laundry gathering. Looking at herself in the mirror, she was incredibly pleased with how incredible her body looked, even in a robe. Azazel smiled and pulled it tighter, really accentuating her waist. She wanted to give Antonio something to think about when he left.

Just as she walked out of her closet, she heard a light knock on the door. Azazel went over and unlocked the entrance to the Li brothers looking disheveled. Antonio holding the scruff of the disgraced steward's clothing, she stepped aside and allowed them into her chamber. Antonio forced the scrawny man through the door behind the brutish brothers. When the five of them all came in, Azazel looked concerned.

"Antonio, where is your brother?" Hoping no harm came to him, Antonio quickly put her concern to rest.

"Jacob ripped his clothing in the chase. Goddess, he's alright. He just ran home to change so you wouldn't be offended by his appearance." The Li brothers looked at each other, and then looked at Antonio as if they were insulted.

Azazel quickly interjected. "I am so grateful to all of you for putting in the work to bring him to me." She smiled and looked at each man, lingering on Antonio, whose eyes were dark with an emotion she could only label as lust.

She told the Li brothers to let the steward go, who fell to the floor between them all. He looked up at Azazel.

"Please, Goddess, I didn't mean to offend you."

This caused Azazel to scoff. "Offend me? Your lack of drive offended me, your stench offended me, and your entire being offended me." The man started to whimper and repeatedly apologized. Azazel looked up to the men behind him. "You are all dismissed; thank you again."

Antonio paused while the other men left. "Are you sure you don't want anything else, Goddess?"

As he finished his sentence, Jacob ran down the hall to where they were standing. Azazel stepped over the pathetic pile on the floor and rested her hand on his arm.

"Yes, Antonio, we are going to be just fine here. Thank you again for your dedication." She guided him gently out of her room. Before Jacob could say anything, Azazel closed the door after giving him a small smile.

Azazel turned back to the man on her floor; she stepped over him again and sat on a chair that was opposite him. He was saying a prayer, and this irked Azazel. "Your God cannot help you here!" She sneered at him, causing him to start sniveling louder.

"Please, Goddess, please forgive me. I am so sorry with all of my soul!" He moved closer to her and started kissing her bare feet. This caused her to recoil in disgust and shove him back violently with her foot.

"Don't touch me, you stupid little gremlin!" The steward curled up into a ball on the floor, slightly rocking back and forth as he started to have a mental breakdown.

Azazel calmly poured a cup of tea and sipped it while he went through a rollercoaster of emotions at her feet. When she finished her tea and felt like she had calmed down significantly, she asked him softly, "What do you think happens to the combatants after they die?" She was curious to see if the rumors in the kingdom had changed at all.

The man stopped his pathetic moaning and looked up at her, wiping his nose. He asked, "They are buried, aren't they?"

Azazel shook her head. "No, what do you think happens to their souls after they die?"

He thought about it for a few moments. "Well, Goddess, our souls are no longer allowed into Heaven after your banishment... so I would think the souls are either stuck in Purgatory or in Hell." While the answer impressed her, it didn't feed her gossip inquiry.

Azazel nodded. "What if I told you that the souls never really leave?"

This caused the steward to look up at her in confusion. "Leave, Goddess? How would they stay?" He started, looking around as if dead people would be coming out of her closet or from under her bed.

Azazel took in a breath. "The souls never leave."

The steward started to panic a little as Azazel stood up. "Goddess, what do you mean, the souls never leave?"

He began to back away as she got closer. She shushed him and crouched down on top of him. He groaned under her divine weight, crushed by her.

Azazel then leaned forward, so that their lips were almost touching when she whispered, "They are safer with me than in Heaven." The steward's eyes grew wide with fear when he realized what she's talking about.

Azazel kissed his lips and got off of him to go to her bedside table, and she quickly came back with a long black dagger. The steward started to scramble away from her, and she stepped on his ankle, instantly breaking it and causing him to scream out in pain. Quickly straddling him, she came close and brought the blade to his throat.

"You had a simple job, Steward, to keep me entertained. You couldn't even do that. You were supposed to be a representation of me in the atrium. The only things you represented were alcoholism and squalor. I'm doing the kingdom a service." Azazel pulled the blade across the thin skin on his neck, causing blood to flow out quickly. She then smiled as she leaned down to the dying man to say, "Let go."

He fought for his pathetic life longer than she'd expected,

and then she adjusted herself so she was directly over top of his lungs, restricting his airflow even further. She looked down at him and whispered, "Normally, I would give you something to take the edge off so this could be a beautiful bonding moment between us, but I'd much rather watch you struggle."

The man made a grunting sound and was severely strained. His breaths grew shallow and his eyes grew wider, realizing that he was dying. Azazel eagerly waited until the moment finally came, where a small blinding white orb started to float out of his mouth. She bent down and inhaled the orb into her mouth, throwing her head back as the soul instantly revived her. Her hair looked luscious and healthy, skin pink and plump, and any age marks that had started to show were immediately gone. Azazel sat on the body until she felt fully rejuvenated.

Standing up, she went over to her door and yelled for clean-up. Without giving it a second thought, she went into her bathroom to draw a hot bath and no longer wanted to look at a dead body. As she disrobed, she fell in love with herself, surprised that such a skeevy human being could give her these kinds of results.

5

Azazel drew a hot bath and dropped in some lavender oils. As the floral smell wafted up into her nose, she could hear some thumping around in her main chamber but decided not to pay it any mind. She would let the clean-up crew do their thing uninterrupted while she soaked away her worries.

Dropping her robe around her ankles, she inspected her body again. Even though her body looked impeccable before she absorbed the whiny little man, her skin now looked pink and plump. She noticed that her backside was lifted more and her legs looked more tone.

Happy with the results, she stepped into the tub and sighed as she sat down in the hot sweet-smelling water. She felt euphoric as she had flashbacks of the absorption and the look of fear in the steward's eyes when he realized he was going to die. The whole situation was so delicious, and she was looking forward to doing it again very soon.

When she thought about the steward's squirming, she grew irritated. Usually, she would have given her victim her golden touch to be more compliant to what she wanted them to do, like little puppets whose strings were wrapped around her fingers. And even though the kingdom was already filled with puppets, and as hard as she tried to keep them at ease initially, they seemed to freak out when they realized what was about to occur.

Azazel mentally transported back to the time when she had first founded the kingdom. Her people respected her divinity. She was their only leader, one who aged and wasn't very attractive, one who was still healing her internal wounds from being rejected by the highest being. She realized that she needed a heavier hand to guide the humans to do what she wanted.

Azazel decided that the humans needed to be strong-armed into doing what she wanted. She concocted a unique drug and laced the kingdom's water supply with it. That's what made it so easy for her to take over the kingdom and mold it however she saw fit without interference from people who didn't want to listen to her new rules. Azazel smiled at the memory of when the full effect took place, and she held the first ever Cunning.

She had been on Earth for a decade at that point, looking for ways to keep herself satisfied and eating everything in sight. Yet her hair kept falling out, and her skin was wrinkling. She came to her absorption solution completely by accident when she came across a dying homeless man, knelt down to comfort him as he sputtered his last breath, and his soul orb came floating out of his mouth—and something inside of her told her to ingest it. When she did, the rejuvenation process happened instantly, and she knew then that this was the way she would be able to survive on Earth.

When she got back home, she demanded that every book from the library on narcotics and their effects be brought to her chamber immediately. Azazel consumed stack after stack of books and decided to mix a combination of psychedelics together. When she lost a few of her servants in the process trying to get the dosage right, it was a good thing they were enough to tie her hunger over, but this was also when the hunger started to take full effect. When Azazel finally got the dosage right, she realized that it didn't affect the victims long enough, and they would try to fight her off still.

Later that night, she concluded that she would use the very last of her angelic powers to make her touch have the same effect as the drug whenever she wanted it to. Tonight, she just wanted to make the pathetic steward suffer with his fear as he died. She thought his soul would taste foul; she wanted the fear to sweeten it a little for her. Azazel smiled at how dark her mind was as she leaned back and let her hair fully submerge into the water, which welcomed her like an old friend.

When she brought her head above the water again, she didn't hear anyone shuffling around in her chamber anymore and decided that it was a good time to get out of the bath. She grabbed a plush white towel and wrapped her robe around herself. This time when she went over to the mirror, she grabbed a brush and ran it through her long hair and applied thick lotion all over her body to ensure she remained as supple as ever.

Feeling thoroughly moisturized, she turned and walked over to her closet and pulled out a light pink nightgown with black lace around the hem. For the final time, she stood in front of her floor-length mirror. The nightgown hugged her body so well. It was almost a shame that she was the only one who would ever see it. She smiled when the name Antonio flashed across her mind. Azazel was sure that if she called him, he would come running.

She got changed and eagerly walked into her bedroom. When she saw her luxurious four-poster bed, she stopped. Everything she had done until this point had been worth it; her people had never been happier, and more importantly, *she* had never been happier. Azazel climbed onto her bed and sank into the plush and thick pillows. She felt herself fully relaxed for the first time in a long time. It's incredible what one sacrifice could do for an earth-bound goddess. Azazel smiled to herself. She loved the dark places that her mind went to tonight. Maybe she needed to take it there more often.

Azazel couldn't help but think of all of the combatants she had absorbed throughout the years and the strength that they had given her. She felt her skin start to vibrate, and she smiled wider, knowing that on some level, they could still feel her gratitude radiating for them. Curious as to how the newest recruits would affect her, Azazel couldn't sleep. She spent a good part of the night wondering how each one would taste and make her feel. When she thought of the boy whose name she called first, she felt a pit in her stomach. She wasn't sure why he was different, but she sensed that he had quite a few tricks up his sleeve in order to go as far as possible.

She sat in silence and realized that sleep wouldn't relieve her anytime soon. Azazel started thinking about Antonio. She felt her face flush in the dark at the thought of his fingers lingering on her back when he placed his necklace on her, and how her body reacted to him. Azazel considered that maybe she should suggest that he become her consort. Smiling at the thought of handsome Antonio Barem in her bed, she decided that she would offer it in the morning. She was tired of the tension between them and wanted to finally act on it.

6

When she opened her eyes the following day, she was extremely happy. It was a full training day for the combatants, and she would be spending a majority of the day in the training center with the sponsors and families. As she sat up, the night before came rushing into her head, and she couldn't help but feel even happier.

Jumping out of bed and heading right into her closet, she picked out a long nude-colored gown with delicate diamond beading that accentuated her chest and hips. She would be proposing the consort idea to Antonio today, and she didn't want to leave anything to his imagination.

When she put the gown on, the diamonds accentuated her curves, and she knew that Antonio wouldn't have a real choice in the matter. She didn't want to use her touch on him. Azazel wanted her body to entice him enough so that he'd come all on his own. Grabbing a pair of black strappy platforms and the necklace from Antonio, she went into her makeup room, telling her chambermaids that she wanted her makeup to look sultry and her hair ethereal. She was pleased with how much her eyes stood out and how pouty her lips looked when she was done. Her hair was loosely curled and looked like a halo around her when she stood in front of the window light to get a better look in the mirror. It was perfect, and she knew it was the *perfect* look to propose this idea to Antonio.

Azazel then dismissed the maid and walked out of the room toward the dining hall. She wasn't hungry this morning, but she knew she had to keep up with appearances. She grabbed a few slices of the cut apple and seemed to inhale her chai tea before tossing the cup back onto the table, shattering it. Azazel lifted her brows at her carelessness and called for a servant to come and clean it up. When they walked into the room, she left before they could bow to her. Azazel only had one thing on her mind when she walked out of the palace with the apple slices, and she wasn't paying attention to anything else around her. She just wanted to see Antonio's face.

As she walked closer to the training arena, she felt herself getting nervous. She knew that Antonio wouldn't necessarily reject her, but he might have some worries about lying down with a goddess. She smiled, knowing that she would teach him how to be with her in every meaning of the word.

Walking into the arena's front door, she was pleased to see the combatants already training extensively. It looked like they had already been at it for hours. Everyone was saturated with sweat. When the instructor noticed her entering the arena, he halted the training and had everyone bow to her as she passed them to her chair on a platform high above them.

She seemed to have just sat down when Antonio showed up at her side. "Good morning, Goddess, you look absolutely radiant this morning. If you're not careful, the sun will become jealous."

Azazel looked into his eyes. "It would have done me a lot of good to hear that first thing this morning."

It was Antonio's turn to blush as he inquired, "Did you require me to stay later last night, Goddess? Was there a problem with the steward?" His face then distorted into a look of worry.

Azazel was touched by his concern and reassuringly said, "Oh, Antonio, you're so sweet. No, the steward is now only a figment of our imagination. Please don't give him another thought." She smiled at him and touched his arm lightly.

Antonio crouched down to her level. "Goddess, please tell me what you mean."

His eyes pleaded with hers, and Azazel came closer to him. "I've been thinking about the possibility of taking a consort," she said quietly, which made Antonio's eyes grow wide, intrigued.

"Really, Goddess? And who would the lucky man be? Or were you considering having some sort of tournament for your hand?"

Azazel could see the gears turning in his head as she asked, "Would you compete, Antonio? If there were going to be a tournament?"

Antonio's face suddenly turned serious when he replied, "There would be no need for a tournament when I know I would win; no need to embarrass every man in the kingdom."

Azazel smiled at him. "I was hoping you'd say something

like that. Come to my chamber for dinner tonight. We can discuss it further."

Antonio stood up and bowed. "Yes, Goddess. I'll be counting down the minutes." He backed away from her so that she could focus solely on her combatants, who had just started working with different types of weapons.

Azazel couldn't help but feel pure excitement. She loved watching the humans fight with pointy objects. Watching them dance around each other, she appreciated the beauty of combat sports and knew it was the most honorable way to die in this world.

She watched as a medium-built blonde girl kicked another girl in the chest and launched her several feet away from their sparring. The blonde girl then walked over to her victim with katanas in her hands. It was clear to everyone watching that she was out for blood and had to be pulled out of the fighting arena.

Azazel smiled at the feistiness of her newest playthings. The staff went to help up the injured girl, and it seemed like she only had the wind knocked out of her, no severe damage. Azazel could see the fire ignited in her eyes and knew she was ready for another round.

Scanning the arena, Azazel could see many combatants showing the same intensity, and she definitely wanted to meet them. She may want to even take a gamble on a couple. She thought about the steward and how he affected her when she absorbed him, and she grew increasingly excited for what these delicious morsels would do for her.

She let herself out of the spectator's box and made her way down the flight of stairs until she was stepping into the arena. The warriors stopped sparring and formed a single line, standing straight and focused when a high-pitched whistle blew. Azazel walked down the line, and each combatant introduced themselves and told her their top three combat skills. By the time she reached the end of the line, Azazel had the largest grin. She couldn't help but appreciate what a great day it was.

The trainer blew the whistle again, and they dispersed, pairing up again and sparring once more. Azazel was impressed with the precise and calculated movements of each pairing. The trainer told her some random facts about the group; however, Azazel wasn't listening. She watched combatant number one, Thomas O'Donoghue, and she was surprised that he moved swiftly and efficiently for such a large young man. She knew that if she was going to bet on anyone, it would be him, and decided that she would throw some money in to sponsor him.

Thanking the trainer for introducing her to them and complimenting him on his progress with his charges, Azazel left the arena after a few more minutes, looking forward to the Cunning even more than she did earlier this morning. As she walked through the kingdom, she passed many residents who bowed low and waited for her to cross. Azazel walked with her head held high and had an aura about her that was intoxicating and filled the humans she watched over with a euphoric feeling whenever she was near them. She was so happy to see them today and could feel the excitement in the air over the upcoming festivities. They had no idea about the level of entertainment that they were in for.

Azazel made her way through the streets and back into her palace to get ready for her dinner with Antonio. She was in the mood for pasta, and decided she would let the chef know that that's what she would like prepared for dinner tonight and brought directly to her chamber. As she walked into the kitchen, she could see the chef already putting a sheet of homemade pasta through a pasta maker and was pleasantly surprised. The chef noticed her and tried to bow, but Azazel told him to stop and show his gratitude through his meals instead. She left the kitchen in very high spirits and headed to her chamber to get herself ready.

When she arrived, she dismissed the chambermaids for the night but asked them to fetch the makeup artist before they clocked out.

The servants all bowed and replied in unison, "Yes, Goddess."

Azazel smiled and asked, "You guys practice that?"

They responded "no," again in unison and looked at each other.

Azazel chuckled. "Alright, off with you."

The maids dipped in a quick curtsy and left the room. Azazel went into her bathroom and started the water. This time, she dropped in vanilla and patchouli, and secured her long hair up on the top of her head with two hair sticks. She got undressed and placed her clothes off to the side. As she stepped into the water, she surrendered to the stirring possibility that was quickly approaching. Smiling at the thought of Antonio once again, she heard the door open and the makeup artist hollering for her.

Azazel replied that she'd be out shortly and washed herself. She cupped water over her shoulders to rinse the rich lather off, leaving behind the vanilla and patchouli scent, taking her intoxication level to another world. Azazel knew Antonio wouldn't be able to resist, but she wanted him to enjoy it, too.

When she felt clean and smelled like a dream, she pulled herself out of the tub and dried off before wrapping herself in her plush robe. Azazel walked out to her room to see her makeup artist, Monica, laying out all of her supplies and had the curler already heating up. Monica dropped down in a curtsy, and Azazel thanked her for coming so quickly. Monica then slapped the chair and asked what they were doing.

Azazel didn't know where to start with her outfit. Still, she told Monica that she was getting ready for a private dinner with someone extraordinary. She planned on dismissing all of her staff for the evening, keeping it as hush as possible until they were ready to announce the news. Monica listened and beamed at her leader. She took the hair sticks out of Azazel's hair, looked at her in the mirror, and said, "Let's begin."

7

Azazel let herself fall into the hypnotic feeling and enjoyed Monica doing her hair. She closed her eyes and allowed Monica to have free reign. Azazel had never been disappointed with Monica's vision when it came to her look. The makeup artist had worked for Azazel for over ten years, and was a genius when it came to color theory and making sure Azazel's eyes were the most enticing part of her image.

Losing track of time, Azazel was almost asleep when Monica finally interrupted the silence. "Goddess, you're ready," and Azazel opened her eyes. She gasped.

Monica had made her hair wavy and free-flowing, framing her face and coming around her shoulders while her eyes were lined in black and smoked out with a single glitter start in the inner corner. And the nude lip color was absolute perfection! Azazel stood up and gushed over her appearance, commending Monica on her skills and then telling her that she was dismissed for the evening, and to come in later than usual the next day. Monica bowed low and thanked Azazel for allowing her to apply her makeup and waited for Azazel to leave the room before she started to clean up the tools that she had laid out.

Turning her attention to what she was going to wear, Azazel made her way toward her closet and walked down the side with her most treasured gowns, several in every color and every design made just for her. Azazel had a difficult time picking which one she wanted to grace her body with but eventually settled on a simple black strapless dress that came down to her thigh, and gold pumps with an ankle strap that looked like a serpent. Once she put the shoes on and wrapped the serpent around her ankle, Azazel stood up and inspected herself in the mirror, extremely pleased with the reflection looking back at her.

When she left the closet, she was pleased to see that Monica had left, and a small table with two chairs had been brought in, set with candles and everything needed for the intimate dinner. Azazel went to a cabinet near her closet door and brought out several sets of candles, and she placed them lit all around the room, giving it an even cozier atmosphere. She shut off the lights and looked around her bedroom, admiring how beautiful it was.

Soon after she'd set up the candles, she heard a soft knock on the door. Azazel took a deep breath before she opened the door to Antonio, who was dressed in a pair of black dress pants and a deep navy button-down that had the first two buttons undone. His hair fell deliciously over his eyes. Azazel smiled warmly at him and welcomed him into her chamber. He walked in and commented on how serene everything looked. Azazel thanked him and motioned to the table, where Antonio went over to pull out her chair for her, and she took it graciously, impressed by him already.

As they sat down, they commented on how great the dinner looked, and Antonio reached across the table to open the bottle of wine, which was perfectly chilled by the time the cork popped and two flutes were poured. Azazel watched Antonio take over to make sure that she was comfortable in her own room with him. It was refreshing and made her feel very taken care of.

Once Antonio took his seat again, he waited for her to start her meal before he began to eat his, both commenting on the taste and how the chef had outdone himself once again. Azazel genuinely enjoyed herself, wondering why she hadn't done this earlier. After all, there *was* only one Antonio.

They continued their meal, and a million scenarios rushed through Azazel's head concerning their future and where it would go. As they finished, Antonio poured her another glass of wine, and Azazel sipped it while looking at him. He looked so handsome across from her, and he had such an easy-going nature; it was hard not to like him immensely. Antonio talked about himself, and she found out that he enjoyed reading mythology and studying, and especially enjoyed fishing. He was always charming, but now that she had gotten to know him better, she understood why everyone loved him as much as they did. He was easy to be with, and was one of the least judgmental people she had ever met. Azazel didn't want to admit it, but she felt herself falling for him very quickly.

As eager as she was to take things to the next level, she didn't want to rush into anything and could sense that Antonio shared the same feeling. After they finished dinner, Antonio got up, came over to her, and held his hand out.

Azazel looked up at him in confusion as he asked, "Dance?"

She smiled at him, took his hand, and said, "There's no music."

He responded, "There isn't?"

Azazel was charmed and followed him to the open space behind their table. He spun her around delicately and pulled her close to him, putting his hand gently on her lower back as her hands slid up his muscular arms to hook around the back of his neck. She was immediately filled with his scent—sandalwood and cinnamon scents that filled her senses and made her feel helpless and protected in his arms.

As they danced, Antonio ran his hand up her back and toward the side of her neck, pulling her face close to his so their lips were barely touching.

He whispered, "Please, Goddess, may I?"

Azazel smiled and replied, "You may," and Antonio pulled her face to his.

His kiss was intense and passionate. He kissed her slowly and ran his other hand up her body until he was cupping her face in his hands. She responded to his pace. She nibbled his bottom lip as she pulled away, and when she opened her eyes, they looked at each other as if their entire world had been shaken.

Antonio went to pull her in for another kiss, but she held her hand up and stopped him by his chest. "Goodnight, Antonio." She watched his face fall in slight disappointment but noticed that his eyes were shining. He walked toward the door, and he looked back at her to grab her hand and bring it up to his mouth.

He lightly kissed the back, and as he pulled it away from his face, Azazel stuck a finger out to stroke his cheek as it passed. She wanted him, and his body language screamed that he felt the same. Antonio paused, and Azazel smiled at him when she said, "I had a wonderful night, Antonio. Thank you."

He paused for a moment before he replied, "As did I,

Goddess... although we didn't discuss any form of agreement." He looked at her with a hint of worry.

Azazel grabbed his forearm. "I thought it was clear," she said quietly to him.

Antonio swallowed hard and stuttered, "Maybe I need more clarification."

Azazel stepped closer to him and smirked when she said, "I like when you're nervous," and pulled him back in for a longer kiss that left Antonio silent for a few moments after Azazel pulled away.

Antonio opened his eyes and nodded to her. "Yes, crystal clear now."

Azazel assumed he meant that he was open to their relationship going to the next level. As he left her chamber, he reached back to squeeze her hand once more before letting himself out of her room. Once the door was shut, Azazel went around the room, blowing out each candle and putting them on the dressing table to let them cool until they were ready to be put back into the cabinet. She couldn't wipe the smile off of her face, the whole night replaying in her mind— the smell of Antonio and how he touched her and led her around as they danced. He was perfect and the most complementary addition to her image.

Walking back into her closet, she got herself undressed and didn't realize that she had put the dress and shoes back in their spots. She was so preoccupied with thinking of Antonio's lips on hers that she completed her servants' duties for them, but Azazel didn't mind. She was a different kind of happy and looked forward to the future she could build with Antonio.

Azazel selected a long white nightgown and pulled it over her head. The silk felt so lovely as it settled against her skin. Continuing to the bathroom to finish her nighttime routine, Azazel noticed that one of her hands was starting to form an age spot in the light. Her mouth turned downwards, wondering how that could be possible. She had just absorbed that whiny steward a mere twenty-four hours ago!

She tried to push her concern out of her head; she would be replenished soon and wouldn't have to worry about trivial things like aging. Continuing back to her luxurious bed, she pulled the heavy covers over herself and crawled under the sheets. She closed her eyes, and her dreams were filled with sweet kisses and dancing to no music.

8

Upon opening her eyes the following morning, Azazel's heart started to flutter when the memories of her first kiss with Antonio came rushing into her mind like it had been waiting all night for her. Azazel hurriedly got out of bed and ran to get dressed. She needed to wear the perfect outfit today!

As she zipped up her dress, she remembered that it was the day of the big feast, the large carnival-style meal that would last all night and into the morning, celebrating the combatants and their talents. They would all be showcasing different fighting styles to boost donations from their sponsors. A smile spread across her face when she realized that an exciting day was ahead of her.

Looking at herself in the mirror, she knew instantly that the navy bandage dress with the sweetheart neckline was a perfect choice. She loved the embellishments that gathered the material at her waist, making her look even more like an hourglass. Azazel touched her neck, wondering about jewelry for a second before remembering that Antonio's necklace would look *perfect* with her dress. Then again, she thought Antonio's necklace would look perfect with any attire.

Putting the necklace on and then grabbing a pair of silver strappy stiletto platforms, she finished her look and smiled at herself until the age spot on her hand caught her attention. Frowning, she realized it was darker than the night before. She sighed; thankfully, she would see Monica, who would have something to cover up the dark mark. She moved past her worry and returned to her excited state as she left her chamber to go into her makeup room.

As Azazel walked into the room, she was pleased to see that Monica was just getting to her station. Monica asked how the special dinner went, which sent Azazel into an excited storytelling tirade. She left out the final kiss, however. But the story was still enough to make Monica show her excitement for Azazel's new love interest.

Monica motioned to the chair, and Azazel sat down, brushing her hair behind her shoulders. She asked if Monica had anyone in her life, which led Monica to open up and share that she had a husband and two children, to which she paused, and Azazel pried, asking why she was hesitating. Monica then told her about her children's illnesses and worried about them eventually being selected for the Cunning. Azazel listened intently and could feel the fear radiating from her artist.

When Monica was done, her voice quivered with emotion, and Azazel locked eyes with her in the mirror, promising her that she would never hear her children's names be called. Azazel was relieved that Monica confided in her about her children. She didn't want to absorb sick combatants; they left an awful taste in her mouth, and their soul essence wouldn't do anything for rejuvenation. Monica felt like they had grown closer and had a newfound respect for her leader, and Azazel was taking a mental note of who was going to make up for Monica's family.

While Monica was working on Azazel's face, she mentioned the age spot on her hand, which Monica quickly covered up to ease Azazel's worries. When she finished, she told Azazel to open her eyes slowly. When Azazel opened her eyes fully, she was taken back by how beautiful the makeup was. Monica had done a long cat-eye with very subtle earthy tones. The eyelashes she used were long and luscious, and framed Azazel's eyes in the sultriest way. She was pleased that Monica had finished the look with a deep red lipstick and had straightened her hair to fall down the middle of her back. She looked sophisticated and powerful. It was one more look that Monica had perfected. Azazel thanked her and walked out of the room, intending to go to the master list maker to tell him of the newfound information from Monica.

As she walked down the hall, she felt her entire staff watching her. Mesmerized by her beauty that morning, she soaked it in and smiled at them all. Azazel finally came to the master list maker's quarters and knocked on the door three times. She heard crashing and rummaging around behind the door. Finally, a flustered, stout man with a handlebar mustache opened the door, and his face was red, his clothes disheveled.

"Goddess, what a surprise!" he exclaimed.

Azazel pushed the door open and walked in. "List Maker, I need you to make an adjustment."

The short man started to wring his hands together and muttered nervously, "An adjustment, your highness?" As he walked over to his cluttered desk and started to pile up loose pieces of paper, Azazel watched him.

"Yes, I need you to take a family name off the grand selection list for the next fifty years or so." She then turned her attention to her nails, inspecting them while the list maker looked around for the grand list.

He pushed everything off his desk and unrolled the scroll when he found it. Azazel looked at him and then around at his chamber. Tall bookshelves were lining the entire room, each shelf overflowing with scrolls or thick books. Azazel wondered what they all were, and before she could ask, the list maker grabbed a quill and waited for further direction.

Azazel looked at the list. "I don't know her last name, but it's my makeup artist, Monica. I wish to take her family's name off of the list."

She smiled, but that quickly turned into a frown when the list maker replied, "I am truly sorry, your eminence, but I cannot take the name off of the list if we do not know the name." He trailed off.

Azazel stood up and straightened her dress. "That sounds like it's your problem now. I expect it done." And she let herself out of the room.

Pleased that she had completed her good deed for the day, Azazel decided she would treat herself to a sweet breakfast before she went to find Antonio in the kingdom. Sitting at the breakfast table, Azazel thought of everything that had happened over the past twenty-four hours and was pleased with the direction that her life was heading. She never knew any simple pleasures in Heaven, and she liked Earth solely for the simple pleasures that it offered.

Popping a crunchy grape into her mouth, Azazel savored the taste and ate the entire plate of fruit. When she finished, she downed a mug of peppermint tea, and then left the dishes in her spot. Her chambermaids had a leisurely morning because she did most of their work for them. Azazel would not be making that mistake again for the kitchen staff.

As Azazel opened the grand front doors, Antonio was just

about to knock, and they both blushed when they saw each other. Antonio ran his hand through his hair and smiled as he looked down to the ground. Azazel was giddy that Antonio was so nervous around her. She cleared her throat and motioned to his arm.

"Care to walk me down?"

When he gladly agreed, they linked together and strolled through the garden, wanting to prolong having to separate again, but they eventually came to the gates. Antonio dropped his arm, motioning for his leader to walk through the gate first, to which Azazel obliged and was a little sad that their moment had to come to an end, even though it made it all the more exciting that it was a secret.

They walked the streets; Antonio walked slightly behind her, watching as people brought up more flowers and garlands as offerings to Azazel. By the time they reached her throne, Antonio was completely covered in flowers, and other members of different families had to come to help him. When Azazel and Antonio could finally see each other again, she discreetly winked at him, and when he smiled at her, she felt nervous and excited.

Turning her attention back to the kingdom, she waited for the area around her throne to fill up with people before Antonio's father, Louis, brought forward the large bell that signaled it was time to start the grand feast. Azazel lifted the bell and rang it loudly, sending the crowd into a frenzy as they brought different types of food to the front of the crowd while others brought tables and chairs. Azazel looked around at her kingdom, and for the first time in a very long time, she felt at peace and like everything was going the way she wanted them to.

9

Aloud siren sounded as the kingdom came together for the feast, and the first bites were taken. The combatants all went out of the training arena one by one as the trainer announced their current stats and strengths, with some family background sprinkled in to make them more attractive. Azazel watched everyone and would look back to Antonio to see if he seemed to favor one more than another. But he was hard to read in this setting. Still, it made her happy that he had a soft side just for her, and she was excited to see more of it.

After the final combatant came out, they all took their places at the long table nearest to Azazel. She wished everyone well and blessed the night, telling everyone to eat their fill and be merry.

The crowd erupted into thunderous applause, and Azazel smiled. Even though she knew they had no choice in loving her, she would never grow tired of the deafening love they showed her when she wanted them to. Motioning for them to quiet down, she again encouraged them to show the warriors love and gratitude for their immense sacrifice. She wanted the kingdom to be surrounded by love and have a peaceful atmosphere.

Her playthings turned back to their dinners, and the conversation dulled down to a mumble amongst the crowd. As she turned to go back to her throne, Antonio was suddenly behind her, and she greeted him warmly and motioned toward the crowd, asking him to accompany her, to which he agreed happily.

As they made their way down the combatant's table, acknowledging everyone with small talk, Azazel felt like she wanted to go back to her palace for a short while to recharge. She told Antonio that she wouldn't be very long and requested that he stay there and watch over things for her. His ego made him answer quicker than he would have probably liked, but she trusted him and knew he would ensure things went smoothly.

Turning to leave the crowd, Azazel looked forward to having some alone time. She felt depleted suddenly and walked as fast as she could back to her home, ignoring all the staff she walked past.

When she finally made it back, she called for a glass of water to be brought to her as she walked into her chamber. She felt like she was out of breath. Azazel went over to her bed, and as she passed a mirror on a dresser, she almost screamed when she saw that her skin looked loose and wrinkled. Azazel ran to the mirror and smeared her hands over her face and through her hair, only to pull out large clumps of hair. She screamed at such a decibel that she shattered the mirror and the windows in her room.

She collapsed onto the floor and started crying when she heard a loud knock at the door, and Monica came into the room slowly. Looking at Azazel on the floor and the mirror shards surrounding her, she rushed in, carefully stepping over the sharp pieces. When she made it to Azazel, she dropped down beside her and reached out to her.

"Goddess, what happened?" This caused Azazel to sob harder. Monica could barely make out "I'm aging," which caused Monica to pause before she said, "Well, we all do."

But this caused Azazel to turn on her sharply as she seethed, "I don't!" She slowly started to get up and continued, "I am not some pathetic meat suit. I am divine, something stupid humans will never truly understand!"

Monica stood up, clearly offended. "With all due respect, Goddess, but we are not pathetic."

Azazel came close to her. "Oh, no?" And she started to force Monica to walk through the shattered shards backward. As Azazel followed her, her feet began to bleed profusely after two steps. "You really don't think your species is anything more than livestock?" Monica watched as Azazel's pupils dilated, and her eyes turned completely black.

Monica started to stammer, "Goddess, please, I'm sorry. I meant no harm!"

But Azazel was beyond reasoning. She pushed Monica onto the floor and got on top of her. Monica started to cry and scream before Azazel covered her mouth and came close to her ear. "If you scream one more time, I will make this as painful as possible for you. Nod if you understand." Monica nodded quickly, and Azazel looked her in the eyes as she said, "Good."

Azazel stood up over Monica and told her to stay put. Monica listened, but she was whimpering as she watched

Azazel go over to her nightstand and pull out a vial. Azazel returned quickly and straddled Monica again, chuckling.

"You could have gotten up and left, but you wouldn't because you couldn't."

Monica was confused, and she asked, "What do you mean, Goddess? Why are you doing this?"

Azazel opened the vial and looked down at her. "Because sooner or later, toys get old, and I get bored—"

Monica quickly interrupted. "Toys?"

Azazel sighed loudly, clearly annoyed. "Because I like you, Monica, I'll quickly tell you, but then we need to get this over with. The longer we drag this out, the worse it will be for you."

Monica nodded. "Please. Tell me."

Azazel set the vial beside them and started, "I use this kingdom as my personal farm-to-table service." And this caused Monica to gasp loudly. Azazel shushed her. "I've taken your sons off the master list, but unfortunately, sweet Monica, someone from your family needs to step forward. I don't see anyone else here but you." This caused Monica to sob, and she started begging for her life.

Azazel looked at the vial beside them, and soon decided that after everything Monica had done for her look, she was worthy. She leaned forward, kissed Monica's forehead, and placed her hands on her chest, where they started to glow white. Instantly, Monica went limp.

After some time, Azazel felt Monica's lungs collapse, and the orb finally came out of Monica's mouth, to which Azazel deeply inhaled. Azazel's hair grew back, and she watched as the skin on her arms and mouth tightened up and looked youthful once again.

Once she felt normal again, she stood up and looked down at Monica, who had a smile on her face. Azazel was annoyed that she'd now have to find another makeup artist and stepped over Monica's body.

Walking out of her chamber, she went into the kitchen, where she knew the Head of Staff would be, overseeing the cooking of the excellent meal for her kingdom. When Azazel spotted him near the head chef, she weaved her way through the kitchen until she reached him and pulled him to the side.

She only had to say, "New makeup artist" for him to understand.

He nodded and replied, "I will get right on it."

Azazel smiled and thanked him for working as hard as he was. She decided that she wanted to go back to the celebration, but she would push the Cunning up to take place in the next several days instead of weeks. Seeing herself age like that scared her, and she didn't know what was happening.

As she made her way back to the meal, no one was paying attention to her as she passed. They were all focused on the food in front of them and trying to catch a glimpse of the combatants. Azazel walked through the crowd with immense purpose and up onto her throne's platform, calling for everyone to quiet down. She announced that while there were already many surprises in store for this year's Cunning, she wanted to throw one more surprise into the works—that the Cunning would take place in the next couple of days. She felt that the combatants were ready, and she wanted to put their skills to the test.

This caused the entire kingdom to roar in surprise and excitement. Azazel watched as the combatants looked at each other, and she could feel the tension rise. She spent the rest of the night talking to the combatants, encouraging them, and preparing them for the Cunning. She made sure to make every one of them feel special before she moved on to the next. Once she had spoken to the last warrior and the sun started to rise in the sky, Antonio came over and put his hand softly on Azazel's back while he leaned in to say, "Goddess, shall we move on?"

Azazel beamed at him and nodded. He led her to the section where all the families waited for her with an early morning spread.

Florence Li brought forward a large cup of chai tea and offered it to Azazel, who took it and thanked the elderly woman with immense sincerity. The hot liquid was the perfect addition to her new look. Antonio came up and put his jacket around her shoulders, making many family members exchange looks.

He quickly backtracked. "You looked like you were starting to get cold, Goddess. I don't mean to offend." As he bowed low, Azazel thanked him and commended him on his thoughtfulness.

Azazel talked with the families about the potential bets and where the money would be sent. She wasn't surprised when many of her courtiers were placing bets on Thomas O'Donoghue, and was thrilled when she concluded that he may just win the prize. The whole community had faith in him, regardless of how superficial the belief may be.

Once everyone finished eating, they all started to slowly make their way back to their homes, and Azazel looked forward to getting into her bed. Antonio stayed back and asked her if she wanted him to walk her back to her chamber. She couldn't help but notice his hopeful look, and she hated to disappoint him, but she wasn't sure if Monica had been cleaned up yet or not and didn't want to risk him seeing anything.

Instead, Azazel told him that she would send for him later, and they could have tea in the afternoon. Antonio took her hand, kissed it softly, sending shivers down her spine, and walked away, telling her that he was looking forward to it. Azazel waited until she couldn't see him anymore and walked home quickly, wondering what she was going home to.

She was almost running by the time she got to her palace

and tried to stay as calm as possible. When Azazel opened her bedroom door, she was thrilled to see that Monica's body had been taken away, and the mirror had been cleaned up, with a new one taking the broken one's place. Azazel was satisfied with the results and looked forward to meeting her new makeup artist.

Getting ready for bed, she thought of Monica—not the absorption but all of their shared times over the years. Even though she physically wasn't here anymore, Azazel knew that Monica would have wanted to sacrifice herself for her children in the end anyway if she really had a choice. At least Azazel gave her the knowledge and peace of mind that her children would be safe and taken care of; it's the best gift a mother could ever receive.

As Azazel settled into her bed, she lied back on her plush pillows, and Monica's smile floated in and out of her head as she started to relax, beckoning sleep to come. She felt satisfied and, most importantly, youthful. She closed her eyes and let out a sigh, hoping this was one of the last nights she would sleep alone.

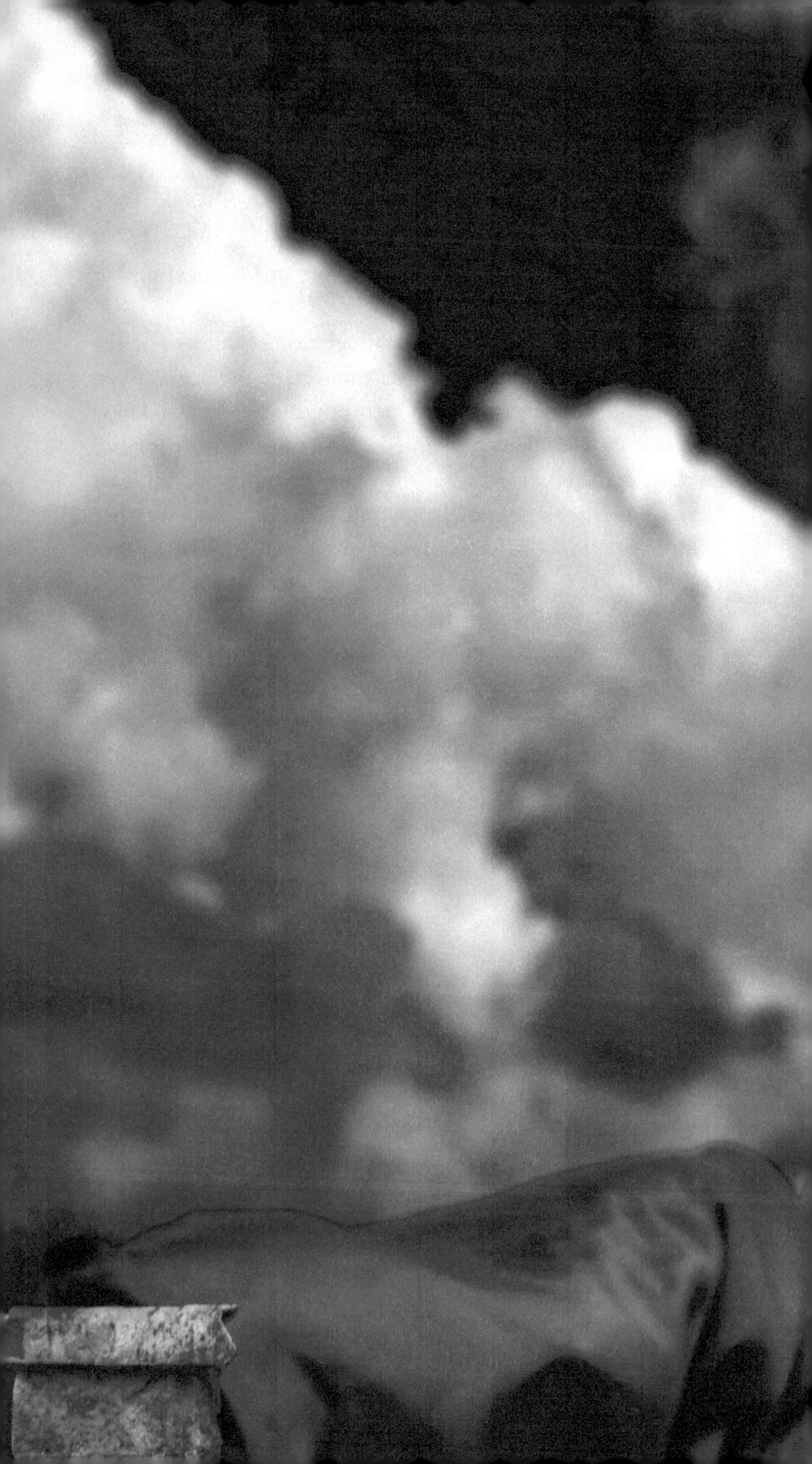

10

Opening her eyes the following day, Azazel had a weird feeling. She didn't know what it was, but she felt this day would be different. She decided that she would have a bath before she left her room. She didn't want to be disturbed, so she went into her bathroom and turned the faucet on. Azazel sighed and rubbed the back of her neck. Tossing and turning all night caused her sleep to become restless, and she already decided that she would be taking a nap that day; Azazel wanted the day to be as stress-free as possible. She decided she would stay around the palace and have Antonio oversee the training in her place, making herself smile instantly when she thought of Antonio and felt a little better.

Going over to her closet, Azazel pulled out lavender and chamomile drops and put them into the bath. Grabbing Epsom salts and some delicious smelling oil, she made the most luxurious bath for herself. She sighed and dropped down into the comforting bathwater; she couldn't help but think that she had never had to absorb people while waiting for the Cunning. When Azazel thought back to the steward, she wondered if he had some sort of ailment that caused the absorption to not take full effect. Azazel rolled her eyes at the thought of the whiny, pathetic steward, of course. It's his fault; even in death, he was an inconvenience.

She let her head fall back and tried to push him out of her mind; he was gone, and there was no reason she should still be thinking about him. Grabbing a bar of soap and a plush loofa, she soaped her body up, taking her time and enjoying every second. Once she felt clean, she lifted the drain plug and got out of the tub. She grabbed her towel off the rack beside her and wrapped it around her body, and felt like she was wrapping herself in a cloud. The towels were exceptionally soft this morning.

Walking into her closet, she decided to pick out a pair of black silk shorts and a white tank top, letting her hair stay down to air-dry. Azazel sent word that she would be taking her meals in her chamber and that Antonio would be the official presence at the training arena.

It wasn't long before there was a quiet knock on the door, and the kitchen staff brought in a table and various trays of fruit for her. The final staff member brought in a mint green teapot and cup. She was relieved that no one was talking to her or trying to interact with her. Azazel did notice, however, that no one would look her in the face. They all kept their distance and seemed to veer out further to avoid her. She wondered if they had found out about Monica, and that was the reason. But she didn't want to alarm anyone, so she kept her distance, watching them come in and out of her room.

Once the last staff member left her room, she went over to the table, ate the fruit platter, and drank the tea in peaceful silence.

Azazel went to a stack of books on top of her dresser and picked up a poetry book. She whispered, "Yes, this is perfect," took her cup of tea, and got back into bed, slowly reading each page and enjoying her time. She couldn't remember the last time she took some time for herself, but she had a feeling that she should be doing it more often.

Genuinely captivated by her book, she didn't hear the initial knock when it sounded. When it sounded a bit more urgent and heavier, Azazel let out a sigh when she called out, "Enter," to which the door slowly opened.

The Head of Staff stuck his head in and asked, "Goddess, I know you want some time alone today, but do you have a moment?"

Azazel motioned for him to come in and told him to shut the door. As he got closer to the bed, Azazel could see that he had dark circles under his eyes. He didn't sleep, either. When he stopped at her bed, Azazel held a finger up, telling him she wanted to finish the page that she was on. He waited patiently for her to finish.

When Azazel closed the book, she left her finger to mark where she left off, folded her other hand on top of the book, and looked up to her Head of Staff. "Yes, Mulligan?"

He seemed thrown off and stuttered, "I apologize, Goddess, but I wanted to let you know that your new makeup artist is here." He looked down, and Azazel watched him fidget with his clothing.

"Is there anything else?" she asked and got even more nervous when he told her, "Last night, I came to take care of the issue in your chamber. But when I got here, there were two chambermaids already here. I didn't catch the redhead's name, but the other was Sarika. They were both in hysterics upon finding Monica's body."

Azazel nodded. "So, would you rather me handle them then, Mulligan? Or would you like to do the job I paid you to do?" She opened her book back up.

"I killed them, Goddess," and Azazel looked up and asked him to repeat himself. He told her that the two chambermaids in question were notorious gossipers. The entire kingdom would have known what happened if he had let them live.

Azazel put the book off to the side and digested the information she was just told. When she looked up to her Head of Staff, he had a guilty look on his face, and she understood.

"You're confessing because you want to be punished?"

Not sure how to proceed, Mulligan looked up at Azazel and was surprised to see a look of amusement on her face. He started to tell her no when she interrupted him.

"Mulligan, you cleaned up a mess. It's your job. Good job," and she picked up the book to flip back to her place. Mulligan stood there, slightly confused. She looked at him over her book and asked, "Is there anything else, Mulligan?"

He shook his head and bowed. "Thank you, Goddess."

But after he left her room, Azazel couldn't help but think about what just happened, concluding that his services may come in handy later.

She finished the book and decided that she wanted some more fruit, and walked out of her room toward the dining room. Thankfully, when she walked by, the staff were just starting to bring platters of food out to the table, platters filled with berries and melons. Azazel took it from her and went back to her room, planning to take her time and enjoy every bite.

Focused on the tray, Azazel didn't even notice Antonio standing in her room when she first got back to her chamber. As she turned around, she gasped, and he bowed low, apologizing for startling her. Azazel reassured him, explaining she didn't expect anyone to be here. They both laughed, and Azazel walked over to her bed and set the platter down before she climbed in between the sheets. Antonio shuffled from foot to foot and looked down. Azazel pulled the platter onto her lap and tapped the space beside her.

"Come sit," she beckoned him.

Antonio obliged and sat beside Azazel as she started to eat a piece of melon. After swallowing the initial piece and sighing in pleasure, she held the platter out to Antonio, offering him some. He graciously took a strawberry, and the two ate while talking about how things were going around the kingdom in preparation for the Cunning.

Azazel finished a piece of watermelon and turned to Antonio. "How did the training go today?" she asked eagerly.

Antonio smiled and grabbed another piece of fruit. "You are going to be incredibly pleased," he replied before popping the fruit into his mouth.

Azazel nodded. "Yes, I knew that. But who do you think is going to win, Antonio?"

He paused before finally saying, "Well, after today, it could be any one of them. They all have a killer instinct, and it is truly a sight to behold."

Azazel was thrilled to hear this, smiling as she looked at Antonio. "Thank you for taking my place today."

Antonio nodded and looked around. "Have you just been resting today, Goddess?"

Azazel nodded and corrected him. He said her name. Azazel loved hearing him say it, and the feeling it gave her when he did. They finished the platter, and Antonio asked if she needed him for anything else. Azazel looked at him with so much admiration and declined, telling him that she just needed the day to rest, and she would be back to her duties the next morning. She asked him if he had any plans for the day, to which he told her that he was overseeing the inventory change for his home as they prepared for the changing season. Azazel was taken with how simple the task sounded and commended Antonio for being involved with his family's caretaking.

Leaving his beautiful goddess smiling, Antonio also mentioned that he was looking forward to seeing her around the kingdom and counted down the moments until they could share another dance. Antonio's charm worked the way it was supposed to, and she told him that she would send word for him when she could fit him into her schedule. He bowed and winked at her as he left her smiling in her bed.

Azazel felt content with how comfortable they were becoming around each other already. Even though he seemed to make her nervous, being with him felt so easy. She spent the rest of her day drifting in and out of sleep. Her dreams were plagued with faces from past Cunnings that she had absorbed.

When she woke up the final time, she was in a cold sweat and couldn't figure out why she would dream of them, looking around and noticing that it had become dark outside. Azazel was slightly concerned that she had slept for so long, but her body clearly needed it. And she was starting to get annoyed of her dreams. She had never thought of the humans *after* the absorption.

Getting out of bed, Azazel walked into the kitchen to grab a glass of water. As she walked down the dark hallway, she couldn't help but notice how eerie everything felt when the staff weren't constantly moving around.

As she walked into the kitchen, she was lost on the location of the glasses and started opening up cabinets to find them until she did. Once she filled her cup and took a sip, she looked around and wondered why there wasn't a skeleton crew for nighttime. She would speak to Mulligan the next day and put a change in place right away. She felt she deserved to be waited on at all hours of the day *and* night. Once she finished her drink, she put the glass on the counter and returned to her bedroom. As she walked across her room where Monica's body once was, she concluded that she would bring Mulligan in as a clean-up crew for the Cunning. He was incredibly good at his job.

The following day, Azazel opened her eyes and sprang from her bed. She chose to wear a dark pencil skirt with a ruffled white blouse. She spent very little time inspecting herself in the mirror and headed directly to the makeup room. And she was surprised to see a man standing inside, waiting for her. He was as tall as she was and had a blue tinge to his hair, his bottom lash line was lined in back, and he had glitter on his cheekbones, wearing black pants and a bright yellow shirt with several necklaces. Azazel checked him out and was instantly obsessed with him.

He bowed low and held his hand out to the chair.

"Goddess." When she sat down, he looked at her in the mirror and asked, "Shall I show you what I can do?"

He grabbed a brush to start brushing her hair. Azazel smiled and nodded. She knew it was going to be incredible. She shut her eyes and let herself be hypnotized by his gentle motions, knowing she would look stunning when he was done. Azazel thought of the many mornings spent here with Monica and was sad for a moment. She really did consider her to be a friend, but desperate times called for desperate measures, and this way, Monica would always be a part of her. Azazel comforted herself with the final thought and focused on what she was going to do today.

While Monica was beautiful, and Azazel felt rejuvenated, she wasn't sure how long Monica's essence would keep her feeling that way, and she felt a slight pang of desperation. She wasn't sure how long she sat there for, and while Azazel was so lost in her thoughts, this new artist didn't bother her with questions or try to bond with her. Azazel liked it.

Finally, he made the final touches and told her she was ready. When Azazel opened her eyes, her breath was taken away. He had put red glitter over her lipstick and used warm tones around her eyes with heavy smoked-out black eyeliner and dramatic cat-eye lashes. Her hair was twisted into a messy fishtail braid that wrapped around her shoulder and rested nicely over her chest.

She leaned forward and wouldn't give him the satisfaction of pleasing her early in their professional relationship.

She simply said, "It's not bad."

"Dante," he told her. "The name's Dante."

Azazel replied, "I didn't ask."

He bowed as he said, "You look absolutely fabulous, Goddess."

Azazel got up and walked past him, and as she was about to step out of the door, she looked back to him and said, "We are going to get along wonderfully, Dante."

She strutted down the hall for a few minutes before realizing that she was missing the sound of heels tapping against the floor. Azazel looked down and realized that she hadn't grabbed shoes for the day. Quickly turning around, she walked to her chamber and selected a pair of light pink studded stilettos.

This time, she took her time looking at herself in the mirror. She was obsessed with herself, and she knew that everyone who came into contact with her that day would be taken by her beauty. As she walked past the makeup room, she glanced in to see Dante spraying sanitizer on a brush, and she liked him even more.

Walking past the dining room, she was excited and decided she would take a late lunch instead. Maybe she would invite Antonio and pick up where they left off. Azazel smiled, knowing he would be intrigued by her appearance.

As she walked down the street, she couldn't help but notice how quiet it was. No citizens were coming out to greet her, and the stores seemed incredibly quiet. Azazel picked the pace up and was relieved when she saw a large crowd outside the training arena. The crowd parted for her as she made her way through it, all bowing to her. She made it all the way to the makeshift stage set-up, and as she stepped onto the first step, the trainer came out of the building and started to walk up a staircase on the other side of the stage. He came over and bowed low.

When he stood up, he said, "You look absolutely radiant today, Goddess," and Azazel thanked him and mentioned that she hoped he had good news for her.

The trainer smiled and said, "We will have to see, Goddess," and walked toward the microphone in the middle of the stage.

Azazel motioned with her arms for the crowd to quiet down, and once they were silent, she looked at the trainer, who began speaking and welcoming the people for coming once again. The combatants all went out of the arena and lined up in four rows. The crowd was pushed back as they all took their spots. Once they were lined up, they stood straight and faced forward.

The trainer announced to the crowd that the Cunning would be moved up to take place in three days. During the next few days, the combatants would spend time with their families and sponsors, and come back daily for training. With Azazel's blessing, she nodded enthusiastically, which caused the crowd to erupt in thunderous applause.

Azazel hadn't seen Antonio yet, but she wanted to spend some time with him. She decided that she would take the time and relax a little more. She planned to do a cleansing ritual before absorbing any of the combatants. Her stomach started to flutter in excitement when she thought of the feast that she would be having soon.

The trainer finally stopped speaking and looked over at Azazel, asking if she needed to add anything. When she said no, he pulled out his whistle and blew it three times, and the combatants all broke their lines and went off to their families, who welcomed them back loudly with last names being shouted in pride. The adrenaline made the air thick, and Azazel thrived on the scent in the atmosphere. This year's Cunning was going to be one for the history books.

Once the crowd started to thin out, Azazel stepped down the stairs and walked away from the arena until she came to the perfumery. Thankfully, they were already open and working away in the store as she opened the door and let herself in.

The smell was warm and comforting, and she knew she wanted whatever scent *that* was. The store owner welcomed her and asked her what she was looking for. Azazel told her that she was looking for hair and body oils. The store owner quickly walked to the back and brought two elaborate bottles back with her, saying that they contained the best patchouli and cinnamon, which is currently in the air. Azazel was pleased and told her to send the bill up to the palace, to which the store owner replied that it was her pleasure to give them to Azazel.

Azazel was touched and pledged that she would be a regular customer and gave the store owner Mulligan's direct contact number. The store owner was surprised and thanked her profusely. Azazel left the store, and the owner danced excitedly. She was in a great mood and knew she would smell otherworldly.

She walked slowly toward her palace and noticed a family walking with a combatant. The parents had their arms around the girl, and she seemed at ease. Azazel was pleased to see the combatants so happy. Happy souls were usually better for her in the long run.

Walking through the garden, the smell of roses was overpowering, and Azazel decided to stop and admire how full they were blooming this year. She definitely needed to have the staff members decorate the palace with these flowers.

She made her way to the kitchen when she got back to the palace, and found the head chef behind a pot of steaming sauce. Azazel requested something rich and chocolatey, to which the chef replied that he would be able to come up with something delicious for her. She left the kitchen, looking forward to what he would come up with.

She walked by the makeup room and noticed that Dante wasn't in there, and the light was off. She frowned in concern. Monica never left the room during the day. Not wanting to dwell too much on the whereabouts of her staff, Azazel continued to her room, where she found two new chambermaids dusting and straightening her room up.

Azazel smiled and asked that one of them go and pick the roses. They both started exclaiming how beautiful the flowers were, and how they would truly elevate the decor in the palace. They both left the room, and Azazel went to set the oils in her bathroom. She put the bottles on the counter and was almost blinded by the light caught in the thick glass. She was mesmerized by the beauty and looked forward to filling her bathroom with more bottles.

12

When Azazel returned to her room, one of the chambermaids came rushing in with a large bouquet and was out of breath. Azazel smiled at her and was touched that she had worked so quickly to make her goddess happy. She walked over to her cabinet to get a vase and took the flowers from her maid, thanking her for her hard work. The chambermaid curtsied and ran out of the room. Azazel filled the vase with water and placed it beside her bed. The roses looked like they bloomed even more since she initially saw them.

She grabbed another book from her shelf; Azazel went and lied on her bed and started to read, becoming lost in the story and losing track of time. There was a light knock on the door, and when she told them to come in, she was pleased to see the head chef bringing in a plate. Sitting up, she was eager to see what he had in store for her. When he put the plate down, she saw it was a pastry blossom, but it looked like the pastry was chocolate, and then the chef went on to tell her that there was a heated chocolate ganache and raspberry purée in the center. Azazel looked forward to eating the treat before her and thanked the chef for another edible work of art.

When he left, she picked up the plate and dug her fork in the middle of the pastry to pull it apart, forcing the gooey and decadent insides to come spilling out all over the plate. Azazel's eyes widened with excitement, and when she took the first bite, she was transported to a world of delicious pleasure. Her intention of slowly enjoying the desert went out the window, and she finished it within moments.

After she finished, she put the plate off to the side and grabbed the book she had started before. She didn't read it for very long. There was an urgent knock on the door, and she told them to come in. Mulligan came rushing into her chamber, exclaiming that one of the combatants was trying to leave the kingdom. Azazel thought he was joking at first, but when she looked up and saw his panicked face, she realized that she was needed.

Quickly getting out of bed, she put on a pair of hard-bottomed slippers and ran outside. Thankfully, Azazel didn't need to run far, and she ran into a crowd of people led by the trainer, who had the rogue combatant by the scruff of her shirt. It was the girl she had seen earlier that day. Scanning the crowd for her parents, Azazel announced that she would take the girl and the parents back to the palace to get to the bottom of this.

As the parents came forward, they wrapped their arms around the girl, and Azazel watched as they all collapsed to the ground. Trying to keep her emotions under control,

Azazel tried to show compassion instead of the inner rage she was trying to keep a lid on. She ushered them back to her home and led them into the back garden, where there was a gazebo covered with ivy and a table with four chairs underneath it.

They all took a seat, and Azazel simply asked, "Are you not proud of your daughter?"

The parents, who were quick to offer their praise and thanks, mentioned that she was only fourteen and had so much life to live. Azazel looked at the combatant, who she learned was named Deanna Morgan, and asked if she didn't feel the honor that the rest of her combatant peers felt. Deanna claimed she was incredibly honored but scared, saying she had been losing every sparring match.

Deanna was nervous to see how that would fare against her competitors in the Cunning event. Azazel listened and nodded, trying to come up with a solution. She listened to the family's list of reasons as to why Deanna should be spared, and how she could contribute to the kingdom when she's older to make up for it. Azazel sighed, stood up, and began speaking, requesting them to be silent until she finished. They all leaned forward, eager to hear her.

"Every year, I have at least one family trying to find a loophole in the system and fail. Frankly, I'm tired of people not realizing what one day of sacrifice does for them throughout the rest of the year." Azazel watched the color in the parents' faces drain as she continued. "Now, each family contributes the way they are supposed to, and have done so since I came into power. It is what makes our kingdom work the way it does."

Deanna started quietly sobbing, realizing there was no way out of this, and her parents began to object. This caused Azazel to get frustrated, and she quickly placed the palms of her hands on the parents. They started to glow. Deanna watched in horror as Azazel fed a sentence into her parents' heads, and they repeated it, agreeing that the Cunning was a necessity, and they were beyond honored to be a part of it.

Azazel then turned her attention to Deanna, who started to scream before Azazel's glowing hands rested on her head, and Deanna repeated, "It is my honor and privilege to be able to compete in the Cunning. Whether I win or lose, I am an important component, and I know that my goddess appreciates my sacrifice."

Azazel smiled and pulled back from the family, pleased that they could all come to an agreement together. The family then stood up and ushered Deanna out of the garden, all three of them speaking excitedly about fighting strategies and ways that Deanna could use her small size to her advantage.

Azazel watched them leave the grounds and sighed. She didn't understand why every human needed so much reassurance. It was such an ugly trait. She made her way inside to see that Mulligan had been watching from one of the hallway windows. Azazel nodded and asked him to bring Deanna to her that evening, and to tell the trainer that there would only be ninety-nine combatants this year.

When Mulligan mentioned that someone would be left without a partner, Azazel said, "That's something for the trainer and the new steward to figure out. We do have a new steward, don't we?"

Mulligan quickly explained that he'd been rushed to find so many new staff members that he completely forgot about the steward. Azazel nodded and told him that she expected a new steward by the following day. She explained that she wanted a competent one, one who would be able to deliver a festival beyond her wildest dreams, and one to keep her on her toes.

Mulligan nodded and bowed to leave. Azazel headed toward her bedroom to have a few moments alone to collect herself again. Using her divinity to get her puppets back in line always took so much energy out of her, and she needed to rest before she could face anyone else again. Avoiding eye contact with any servant she walked by, Azazel felt like she was starting to unravel. She felt angry and frustrated that she had to absorb a combatant sooner than she had initially planned, but she felt like the family was a stack of wild cards. Azazel felt like she had no other choice.

As she opened her bedroom door, she felt like her head would split open from pain. She had never experienced pain like it before and fell to the floor. She quickly shut all of the blinds and grabbed a salve to rub on her temples, hoping it would work. She soon felt her temples become heated, and slowly, the pain started to subside. Relieved, Azazel climbed into bed, not sure what was happening to her, but she felt like if she slept, maybe it would become a bit clearer when she woke up.

She tried to think of other things to help take her mind off the pain, but even Antonio's face couldn't help her. She sighed and wondered how long she would have before Deanna was brought to her. When Azazel thought of her, she was hopeful that because of her age, Deanna would give her the essence that she needed to get to the Cunning without having to absorb anyone else.

Sleep was avoiding her, and Azazel became increasingly frustrated that she hadn't fallen asleep yet. She tossed and turned, trying to reposition herself, and kept flipping the pillows to find the cooler side.

She slowed her breathing and closed his eyes, willing herself to relax and sleep. Her mind was busy with scenarios, both real and imagined, when suddenly, she had a flashback of a moment from her time in Heaven, watching her beloved God construct the Earth, and every time she tried to interject, He would shut her down. He'd tell her that her opinions and ideas were insignificant.

Azazel felt her heart break again. She didn't realize at the time how hard it was to rule over a domain and keep everyone happy, and she was starting to realize that the humans weren't satisfied with *anything* she did. Every time her sisters and her would go to Earth, they would always come across suffering communities, but still, they prayed to God to improve their lives.

But He ignored them, every time, every prayer. Azazel thought that if she could keep the humans constantly happy, her kingdom would be blissful. But that clearly didn't seem like the case anymore.

She always hated when the divine effects started to wear off, and she would have to reprogram her humans again—the fear in their eyes as they tried to figure out what had happened and why they couldn't remember the past few years. She wondered if she would ever reach a point where she would no longer have to influence them; they would just be born willing and ready. And there would no longer be any need for the Cunning. She could simply pluck them whenever she needed rejuvenation.

Azazel let the thought remain in her head, and the more she thought about it, the more she liked it. Finally, she yawned and fell asleep. For the first time in several nights, she wasn't plagued by dreams, just sweet restful sleep.

13

Azazel was woken up by Mulligan, who gently shook her arm. She gasped but realized who it was almost immediately. He said he was about to go fetch Deanna and wanted to ensure that she was ready for her meal. Azazel couldn't help but smile at him. He was truly going above and beyond for her supernatural needs, now that he knew. She told him that she wanted him to bring Deanna's parents as well, to which Mulligan nodded and told her that he would be back shortly.

Azazel sat up and stretched. She still felt tired but realized that once the absorption was done, she would be able to go back to sleep. This was a comforting thought, and Azazel got out of bed, walked over to the door, and called out for tea to be brought to her room as quickly as possible.

A quick rap sounded at the door a few minutes later, and a chambermaid brought in a serving tray with a teapot and a single teacup. Azazel was pleased when she smelled blueberry, and knew it was the chef's special blueberry tea. The maid set the tray down and quickly backed out of the room, not making eye contact with Azazel and barely speaking. Azazel thought that perhaps Mulligan had given them a dummy story about why she didn't want to be bothered, and her appreciation for Mulligan's usefulness escalated even further.

She finished her tea and felt extremely relaxed before pouring another cup. When Deanna and her parents arrive, Azazel wanted to be in the right state of mind. Deanna had trained so hard and fought so valiantly that she would make this as painless as possible. Azazel got up and went over to her bedside table to grab the single vial rolling around as she pulled the drawer open, then went over to the door to call for another tea set to be brought in. And she didn't close the door until she heard the running of feet.

Going back to her own cup, Azazel set the vial down on the table and picked up her cup, sipping the deliciously hot liquid, bringing her more comfort than the last. Just as she saw the bottom of her cup, she heard a knock on the door, and not only was it a chambermaid with the extra tea set, much to Azazel's delight, but it was Mulligan, who looked back and told Deanna and her parents to wait there. The chambermaid came in quickly, set the tea down, bowed, and promptly exited the room. Azazel grabbed the vial and opened the top of the teapot.

When she looked up, Mulligan was watching her, and he asked, "What's that?"

Azazel simply replied, "It takes the edge off," which was sufficient enough of an answer for him.

Replacing the lid and hiding the vial in the cushions of her chair, Azazel said she was ready for them. Mulligan bowed low. "Enjoy, Goddess," and he slid out the door. The family quickly came in, and Azazel smiled at them warmly. As she stood up, they bowed, and she told them to join her as she poured three cups of tea and handed each of them one as they came closer and positioned themselves on the couch. Deanna was the first to bring the cup up to her mouth and take a sip, her eyes widening at the sweet taste. Her parents quickly followed her lead. All of them exclaimed their delight in the tea and thanked her again.

"I spoke to you earlier about how I was so tired of families trying to find loopholes to get out of the Cunning. While there is no loophole, I have a way that you all can stay together. Now, in about ten seconds, your legs are going to go numb, followed by your hands, and then the rest of your body. You're going to close your eyes and become one with me," she explained to them.

Deanna's mother started to stammer a question. She looked down at her legs, scared. The father pulled both her and Deanna in close to him, and they hugged each other for as long as they could hold on before they finally slumped.

Azazel stood up and walked over to position them, so their heads were on the back of the couch. She interlocked their hands and kissed their foreheads as they shut their eyes. She crouched down and waited, seeing who would come out first, and to her surprise, Deanna's father's soul orb peeked out first. Azazel inhaled his essence, and not much later, Deanna's was next, followed closely by her mother's.

It was like he was completely in sync with Azazel because as soon as she finished, Mulligan came in through the door and began the cleaning process, and Azazel went to take a bath. Before she went into the bathroom, she asked if there was anyone else still up, and he told her that he dismissed the staff after the last tray of tea was brought in. Azazel approved and said to him that she was impressed by him. Mulligan bowed and thanked her sincerely.

She turned to the bathroom and was excited to try the new oil from that afternoon. When she opened the bottle, the bathroom was immediately filled with the smell of patchouli, and Azazel was intoxicated by the scent. Going over to the bath, she turned the hot water all the way up, pouring some of the liquid into the tub and smiling as the smell came up and seduced her senses.

Azazel turned back to put the bottle on the counter and looked at herself, and was surprised by what she saw. Peering closer, she looked like she was back in Heaven. Her skin looked like it was radiating the same glow as the sun. Her lips looked plump, and her hair was so bright that it was almost blinding. She was incredibly pleased with her results and turned back to her bath. She got undressed and slipped into the tub while the water ran, reminiscing about how quick the results of that vial were.

It was a new method, and she liked how painless it was; plus, it didn't take any of her divinity to make it work. She was definitely going to keep using it from now on. She leaned forward when the tub was sufficiently filled and turned the water off. Sinking back into the tub, Azazel loved everything that this night had to offer.

But then she suddenly frowned. She didn't feel the same connection to the family that she had with others, where it felt like they indeed became one with her. She wondered if the divinity she put into their bodies connected them the way it was supposed to, and why she didn't feel guilty about absorbing them. When she thought of Deanna, she felt a pang of sadness as the scene of her parents reaching for her in their last moments came into her head.

Azazel hated the sadness and forced it out of her head, focusing on the heavenly-smelling bath that she was in and looking forward to the Cunning.

When the water started to cool down, and she craved some more tea, Azazel got out of the bath and dried herself off. She walked into her closet, selected a light blue cotton nightgown, put it on, and wrapped herself in a plush, comfortable robe. She intended to take it as easy as possible for the night and walked out to see Mulligan standing by the door. With a confused expression on her face, Azazel asked him what he wanted.

He replied, "We have a problem."

In a condescending tone, she said, "We don't have problems here," and she walked over to the tea set without any of the poison and poured herself a cup.

But she noticed that he hadn't left yet and was uncomfortably shuffling from foot to foot.

"Fine, what is it?" she demanded.

He cautiously replied, "The extended family was made aware that they were coming here tonight."

Azazel nodded and asked him, "What's the problem?"

Mulligan explained that this would raise concern when they don't come back home.

Azazel sighed in frustration and sipped her tea, waiting for him to finish. Once he stopped talking and looked to her for an answer, Azazel set her cup down and said, "I will handle it. Thank you, Mulligan," dismissing him. She was irritated by his presence and wanted him out of her sight.

He bowed low and asked if she needed anything.

Azazel snapped, "No, because apparently, no one can complete a simple task, so I'll take care of everything myself. Good night, Mulligan!" The tone in Azazel's voice was ice cold, and it looked like Mulligan went pale when he figured out that she was displeased with him. He left her alone with her thoughts.

14

Azazel mulled over the information that Mulligan had just told her, and she came to a solution quickly. She would give the extended family a slight touch of divinity to forget that they were even related to Deanna and her family. Smiling at her quick thinking, Azazel decided that she would go to the house after finishing her tea.

She shouted out Mulligan's name, and unsurprisingly, he came right into her room like he had been waiting for her. He asked her what she needed from him, and Azazel said she changed her mind and wanted him to find the location of all of the extended family members, tell them all to meet at one location, and she would come talk to them.

When he quickly left the room, Azazel finished her tea

calmly. If she got worked up, it could be transferred to the family when she touched them, and it would end disastrously for everyone. Once she was finished, she went over to her wardrobe and picked out a bright white dress with thick spaghetti straps and a slit on the side, deciding to pair it with a pair of golden stilettos. Azazel couldn't deny how divine she looked when she looked at herself in the mirror. She was incredibly pleased with the last absorption results, turning around to inspect every angle.

When she walked out of the closet, she was happy that Mulligan wasn't standing in her room anymore. Hopefully, he did his job correctly this time and would make it as easy as possible for her moving forward.

Azazel left her chamber and started walking toward the front door, ignoring every servant who passed her and bowed. As she walked out, Mulligan came running up to her to tell her the location she was going to. Azazel cupped his cheek, telling him she was proud that he could complete a simple task on his own for once, and left him standing there with his mouth open and his face reflecting the disappointment that he felt. She kept ignoring any citizen who passed her and stayed focused on her location, knowing that the sooner she handled this, the safer she and the kingdom would be.

She eventually came to a large house and let herself through the gate. Walking up the pathway, she noticed someone looking through the curtains in the main window on the front of the house. Azazel smiled. People trying to sneak peeks of her wasn't a new concept, and instead, she kept the smile in place as she lightly knocked on the door and waited for it to be answered.

Finally, the door was opened by an older woman in her fifties with the same color hair as Deanna, but large sections were starting to gray. Azazel tried to hide her disgust when she noticed that one of the woman's eyes was milky white from blindness. The woman nodded her head in respect and apologized for not being able to bow down, crediting her age as the reason.

Azazel reassured her and told her that she wanted to talk to the family about the Cunning, and how their contribution would bring the festivities to another level. The woman grinned and opened the door wider, welcoming Azazel in enthusiastically. Azazel stepped into the dusty house and noticed a faint odor. Looking around, it seemed as if no one had cleaned up in ages. She asked if anyone else was coming, and the woman said they were all in the back room. The woman turned back and introduced herself as Martha.

Martha led Azazel to a set of thick and extravagant double doors, and she pulled one side but struggled until Azazel stepped forward and pulled the doors apart, barely using any strength. When the doors were finally opened, Azazel was face-to-face with about twenty family members, all talking amongst themselves. When Azazel entered the room, they all stopped and bowed low, except for the elderly ones.

They waited for her to begin, and when she did, Azazel noticed they all shared a stone look as if there was nothing behind their eyes. She started by telling them that Deanna was an important combatant in the Cunning and would only bring honor to their family. The longer Azazel looked around the room, the more she noticed that there weren't any adolescent generations. They were all middle-aged or part of the older generation. And she finally realized why they were so concerned about Deanna.

Azazel walked around the room and placed her hand on each of their arms, telling them that Deanna had received the highest honor imaginable, as did her parents. They were happy but wouldn't be returning to the family home. She had every family member repeat the sentence back to her, and when she finally got to Martha, the old woman asked why they wouldn't come home. Azazel told her they were in a better place, a place where everyone in the kingdom would go to, and touched her arm, smiling at the old woman as her hand began to glow.

Once Azazel confirmed that the family was at peace, and they automatically repeated the sentences she told them to, she left the house and walked back to her palace. Azazel felt depleted, and resolved that she would sleep as soon as she got home.

When she got back, she rushed to the mirror to see if her manipulation had affected her appearance at all, and was relieved when she saw that she looked as youthful as before. Changing back into the blue cotton nightgown, Azazel went to her bed and pulled the sheets back so she could climb in.

She settled into her plush pillows, thought of the night's events, and sighed. She never had to do this sort of thing before and felt worry start to creep in as she thought of her world crumbling. Trying to push the worries off to the side, Azazel closed her eyes, begging sleep to come to relieve her of her panic.

When Azazel finally fell asleep, her dreams were plagued by Deanna and her parents' lifeless eyes staring up at her. Azazel felt like she hadn't slept in years when she woke up the following morning. She got out of bed slowly and wanted to take a bath to boost her spirits.

Yawning, she moved slowly to the bathroom, turned the hot water on, and retrieved citrus-scented essential oils. She let herself fall into the water gently, and the scents of orange, lemon, and grapefruit started to saturate the steam that wafted up into her nose. Azazel smiled at the simple pleasure she felt sitting in the water.

Once she was energized and ready for the day, Azazel lifted herself out of the water and dried off. She walked into the closet with a bounce in her step, and her mood was a bit lighter than it was when she'd woken up. Walking down the hall, trying to find the perfect outfit, she settled on a soft yellow backless sundress just above her knees and a pair of white strappy wedges. Once again, she chose to wear Antonio's necklace and felt young, carefree, and feminine as she looked in the mirror one final time before leaving her closet. When she walked into her makeup room, she beamed at each servant who passed by and saw Dante waiting patiently.

Dante bowed low and welcomed her to sit on the chair. Azazel bounced over and sat down, and Dante commented on how beautiful she looked that morning, and how her eyes had a certain twinkle. She closed her eyes and gave herself over to relaxation as Dante worked his magic.

Azazel didn't have a single thought in her head for the first time in days. Instead of getting lost in her mind, Azazel listened to Dante hum and whisper to himself, working out how he wanted her makeup to turn out. When Azazel opened her eyes again, she was pleased to see a very intense smokey eye and lashes with a piece of chunky glitter in the shape of a star on random lashes. Her lips were pink and slightly overlined to make them look plumper, her cheeks were rosy yet glowing, and her hair had been loosely curled and brushed out to make it look like waves.

Dante went on to tell her that he customized the lashes himself and talked a bit more about her look. Azazel gained immense respect for him and decided to keep him around much longer than she'd kept Monica around. As she turned around to leave the room, she winked, blew a kiss at him, and left him grinning from ear to ear as she searched for Antonio.

However, she didn't have to look for very long and found him walking toward the palace, waving at her. Azazel waved back and felt bubbly. She liked how she felt around him, and as he came closer, her heart started to beat faster. Antonio met her in the garden and bent over her hand, kissing it gently as he said, "Azazel."

She bit her bottom lip and whispered, "Antonio."

Azazel noticed that his eyes glittered like the stars in the darkest night sky when he stood up. She was completely taken by him!

Antonio smiled wide, "Goddess."

She quickly pulled his face closer to hers and kissed him passionately. He wrapped his arms around her waist, kissing her deeply. The two were lost in their embrace.

Azazel was the first to pull back and breathlessly asked, "How long do you have?"

Antonio smiled and started to lean in again as he whispered, "As long as you'll have me."

He pulled her face to his, and Azazel jumped up, wrapping her legs around his waist as he moved his hands under her, supporting her effortlessly. He carried her to her bed and moved on top of her as the two lost themselves to each other in lust.

She could feel his heart pumping blood, and how strong his life essence was; Azazel suddenly felt the hunger start to bubble from the deepest parts of her stomach. As Antonio kissed her clavicle, Azazel pushed him off with her foot.

"No!" she screamed breathlessly, and they looked at each other.

Antonio was on the floor, staring up at her. As he stood up, he adjusted himself, and Azazel could see that he was trying to figure out what just happened.

She reached for him, but he took a step back as he said, "I need to leave, Goddess. I do apologize."

He bowed and went to walk away before she grabbed his hand.

"No, Antonio, it's not you." She tried to find the right words so she wouldn't scare him, but he had already walked halfway across the room, wanting to leave. Azazel rushed off the bed to grab him, and he turned to her.

"I don't need to come back; this may have been a mistake." He excused himself and left her standing in her room.

Azazel watched him leave and realized that he was probably embarrassed. She grew angry and rushed to the door, screaming for Mulligan. Pacing from one side to the other, Mulligan seemed to take an eternity to reach her. Finally, she heard a knock on the door, and she beckoned for him to come in. Mulligan sheepishly entered the room and scanned the area as if he expected to see a body on the floor.

"Yes, Goddess? What can I help you with?"

Azazel stopped pacing to look at him. "Bring me the most insignificant servant we have, NOW!" She watched the color drain from his face as she walked closer to him. When he didn't instantly leave, she shouted again. "I said, fetch the most low-life servant we have in this palace, or would you like to take their place?" she hissed.

Mulligan was frightened. He wasn't staring at his ethereal goddess; he was staring at a black-eyed being with taunt pale skin and wild hair. He could see her veins prominently, and her muscles looked like they were decaying. Mulligan quickly left the room, wanting to put as much distance between himself and Azazel as possible.

While she waited, Azazel fumed. She was furious that Antonio left; she tried to keep him safe, not completely push him away! He wouldn't have been so scared if he had just waited for her to explain. He got scared because he thought it was about *him*. This caused Azazel to roll her eyes; the human ego truly was fragile.

Her thoughts were interrupted by a frantic knock on the door. She barked for them to come in, and Mulligan walked through the door with a petite brown-haired kitchen maid. Azazel quickly grabbed the maid from Mulligan and shoved him back out the door.

"Get out; we need to have a little girl talk."

He gladly left the room as quickly as he tried to enter it. Azazel gripped the small girl's forearm and felt her struggle against her as she said, "You know, there was a time when I didn't need to feast," and threw the girl across the room and onto the edge of the bed. The young girl screamed in pain, which made Azazel smile. "I forgot how much fun it was to make your kind suffer beforehand. It makes you taste so much sweeter."

The meek kitchen maid curled herself into a ball. At the same time, Azazel slowly walked toward her. When she was close enough, the maid looked up at her, begging for Azazel to spare her. Azazel pulled the girl up by her hair until her toes were barely touching the floor, and they were eye-to-eye. The servant struggled trying to touch the floor again.

Azazel came in close and whispered, "Why on earth

would I spare you when I need to eat?" She threw her across the room again with such force that the girl was knocked unconscious.

Disappointed that she didn't stay awake, Azazel pouted and walked over to the lump on the floor and flipped the servant onto her back effortlessly with her foot. Stepping over her and crouching down to straddle her body, Azazel started slapping the girl's face.

"Wake up, you coward! The wolf isn't done playing yet!"

When the girl woke up, she instantly started panicking again and began to cry, begging Azazel with her life. Azazel sighed and was growing agitated. She stood up and placed one foot on each of the girl's arms to pin her down, applying enough of her weight until she heard the crunch of breaking bones and the screaming of her victim. She plopped down on the sobbing girl once again.

"Okay, now that I have your attention, no begging! It's not very feminine of you, and you're disgracing your ancestors." The girl's face was soaking wet from her tears, and Azazel felt an immense sense of pleasure seeing how scared she was. She bent down so that she was in the girl's ear and whispered, "Do you think the Creator could help you, even now? If you prayed hard enough?"

The girl nodded quickly and whispered the Lord's prayer.

Azazel quickly grabbed her throat and seethed, "When are you stupid humans going to realize that He doesn't care about anyone but Himself? He knows what you are going through and what is going to happen to you." Her face started to morph into a dark monstrous version of herself. The maid began to shake in fear as Azazel said, "God does not care about you!"

The maid was quiet, and Azazel could see that she was starting to understand. The maid looked up into Azazel's eyes. "Then why do we pray?"

Azazel laughed and shrugged. "To feed His ego. That's the only thing humans are good for, feeding God."

Before the maid could say anything else, Azazel quickly slashed the maid's throat with her nails. Blood started to pour out as the girl began to gurgle and gasp. Azazel had a strong urge, and she leaned down and licked the girl's neck to taste the blood while she waited.

The warm liquid slid down her throat and ignited something new in Azazel as she sat up. It wasn't just rejuvenation; it felt like a hole deep inside her was slowly being filled. After an entire millennium, Azazel felt like she had found what she was missing. She leaned down and started to drink from the gash in the servant's throat until she noticed a glow out of the corner of her eye, the orb beginning to float out of her victim's mouth. Azazel sat up and inhaled the orb into her; the rejuvenation process felt more powerful.

Azazel knew this time was different. After she felt healthy again, she drank from the maid's neck. She felt the blood reach her fingertips and toes, making her body tingle. She got up, leaving the husk of the maid on the floor. Azazel went over to the door, screaming for Mulligan to clean up the mess.

When she passed the large mirror, she caught a glimpse of herself. Her skin was plump and glowing with youthfulness. And even though the bottom half of her face and chest were covered in blood, she had never felt more beautiful.

She turned and looked at herself, running her hands over her body, up through the blood, and dragging it all over. Hearing a soft knock at the door, Azazel loudly said, "Come in!" and Mulligan slowly entered the room.

His eyes went wide when he saw the state of Azazel and the victim. Azazel started to lick the blood off her fingers and then asked him, "Mulligan, did she have any family?"

Mulligan began to stutter as he replied, "Parents and a sister, Goddess."

Azazel smiled and looked at him. "Good, bring them to

me tomorrow. Now, clean this up! I need to bathe." Azazel turned and left him in shock as he took in the entire scene.

Going to her bathroom and starting the hot water, Azazel decided that she didn't want to dilute the smell of her kill with anything else, and instead, got undressed and slipped into the hot water and let it wash over her. Rinsing the blood off of her, filling her nostrils with the metallic smell, Azazel was soothed and leaned back, savoring every second of it.

She could hear the bedroom door open and close multiple times and shuffling around. Azazel was thankful for her clean-up crew, but she frowned at having to deep clean the floor every time she fed. But it was all worth it. The blood and life essence were what she needed to keep herself rejuvenated and capable enough to rule. Once she stopped hearing rustling in her bedroom, Azazel decided it was time to get out of her bath.

She stood in front of the bathroom mirror and inspected every part of her body. Azazel was borderline giddy with the results. She looked like she had aged backwards and had a woman's body in her early twenties. Azazel smiled, relieved that her body finally looked the way she had been trying to make it look.

Walking out of the bathroom, she didn't bother covering herself up and was surprised when she saw Mulligan standing there, who automatically averted his eyes.

"Mulligan, announce yourself! You knew I was bathing!" Azazel walked across her room, still nude, not ashamed of her body.

Mulligan's gaze was locked on the floor as he said, "Yes, Goddess, I apologize. I just wanted to inform you that the trash has been taken out."

This made Azazel scoff as she said, "Is that really any way to speak of the dead, Mulligan? Have some respect!"

Mulligan nodded. "Right, I'm sorry."

He took a deep breath. "The family began asking

questions when I sent word for them to come to," he paused, "dinner."

Azazel smiled and walked toward him. She noticed how uncomfortable he was the closer she got to him. "You tell them nothing."

He nodded and replied, "Of course, Goddess."

Azazel nodded and turned away from him, dismissing him for the night. Before he left, she said nonchalantly, "I need a room with drainage. I want to make your job easy for you."

As she looked at the dark red stain on the floor, Mulligan cleared his throat and replied, "Leave it up to me, Goddess. I will find something. In the meantime, perhaps an area rug?"

Azazel nodded and continued to her closet, indicating to Mulligan that it was time for him to leave. As she walked in, she couldn't help but think of Mulligan's responses to her needs. She started to get irritated when she thought of him refusing to look at her like he was scared of her suddenly. And it wasn't even like he hadn't killed before!

It made no sense, and she felt she needed to get him back in line. Picking out a long silver silk nightgown, Azazel felt luxurious and tantalizing. Looking at herself in the mirror, she couldn't help but think about Antonio. But she had to push his face out of her mind. She had to focus on her dinner with the maid's family and the Cunning.

16

Azazel climbed into bed, and a smile crept across her face when she thought of drinking from the maid's neck. With a renewed sense of excitement, she looked forward to finding a new chamber to create the right atmosphere for her hunger. Staring into the darkness, she only saw the fear in her victim's eyes as she knew she was about to die. This brought Azazel an overwhelming sense of pleasure.

She lied in her bed and couldn't fall asleep for some time; instead, she thought of how the absorptions had changed over the years and her insatiable hunger.

Eventually, sleep consumed her, and Azazel didn't wake up until the sun had set the following day. She kept seeing slides and chutes all leading to the same room in her dreams, a room she had never seen before. It was windowless and barren. Every time she was brought back to the room, she felt fear and hopelessness.

When Azazel opened her eyes, she had the most devilishly wicked idea. She sprung out of bed and didn't bother to change. She ran out into the hall and screamed, "Mulligan!" and walked back into her room, leaving the door open for Mulligan to arrive, which wasn't very long after Azazel had sat down on the couch. When he walked into the room, he nervously looked around as Azazel demanded, "Shut the door." He obliged and cautiously walked over to the couch to sit across from Azazel, who watched his every move.

She asked, "What's below this room?"

Mulligan's face scrunched up as he tried to remember and finally said, "It's empty, I believe."

Azazel nodded. "How long would it take to build a chamber?"

Mulligan's face scrunched again, and he looked at her in confusion before asking, "Chamber? Chamber for what?"

She sighed like she was bored. "Mulligan, I had an epiphany last night, and then the dreams that followed were so deliciously intricate and vivid. I want to build a chamber underneath my bedroom—windowless, bare, and a drainage system leading from it."

Azazel looked at Mulligan, who had a look on his face that resembled a mixture of curiosity and fear. She continued to her favorite part of the request. "I want there to be slides or chutes that lead to the room from this room, one way."

She stopped, and Mulligan looked around the room and asked, "Goddess, what is this room for?" he asked cautiously.

Azazel smiled devilishly and said, "Mulligan, I will make your job even easier. Now, go find a contractor who will do the construction. Price isn't an issue, of course."

Mulligan cleared his throat and asked again, "Goddess, what if they ask what the room is for?"

She looked at him and said, "Just tell them it needs to be soundproof and discreet. If they ask any questions after that, find a new one."

Mulligan nodded, turned toward the door, and quietly asked, "Goddess, will you at least tell me what this room is going to be used for?"

"Clean up."

He nodded, clearly understanding, and left the room quickly.

After he left, Azazel stood up and walked into her bathroom; she decided she would have a bath and began to run the water. She walked over and picked out a jar of dried rose petals, lavender, and Epsom salts. She sprinkled the flowers and salts into the water when the tub was full.

Once she smelled the floral scent in the steam and got undressed, she lowered herself into the bath, letting out a sigh of relief as she leaned back and allowed herself to get used to the heat of the water and focus on the sweet-smelling flowers. She had cleared her mind of any thoughts and was basking in the silence until she heard heavy footsteps and a light knock, followed by Mulligan's voice yet again.

"Goddess?" Azazel groaned and shouted, "Come in, Mulligan!"

He came into the bathroom and averted his eyes. "Goddess, I have several contractors prepared to meet with you at your convenience."

Azazel opened one of her eyes and looked at her advisor, who was sheepishly standing in front of her. She groaned and snapped, "Oh, Mulligan. You've seen me nude before. Get a grip; you're pathetic."

He raised his eyes to meet hers. "I just believe in respecting you and your privacy."

They stared at each other in silence for a moment before

she eventually said, "I will meet with them this afternoon before the maid's family." She smiled at him while Mulligan bowed slightly and removed himself from Azazel's presence.

Once he was gone, and she couldn't smell his stench any longer, Azazel returned to her world of relaxation and contemplated the future in her new absorption chamber.

When she felt good and clean, Azazel walked into her closet and knew the dress she wanted to wear. She pulled it out of its place and couldn't help but admire the beauty of the garment. It hugged her body and had lace decorating the back; there was no slip under the lace, and it barely hid her skin. She paired it with a pair of strappy neon pink stilettos and let her hair fall naturally around her body; when she did a final twirl in the mirror, she squealed in delight and left her room feeling invincible.

Mulligan was already waiting with five rough-looking men when she reached the dining hall.

Azazel smiled and said, "Gentlemen, welcome."

She walked over and shook their hands, and they all bowed with respect and nervously looked at Mulligan, who looked from them to Azazel. After they were all introduced, the man in the center, Thomas, stepped forward and asked, "Do you have plans?"

Azazel giggled and replied, "Oh, many, but physical plans, no. I just came up with the concept this morning. Walk with me, and I'll explain what I'm envisioning."

She led them all back to her chamber and waited for them to pile into her room, including Mulligan, before continuing with her idea.

"I envision a trap door somewhere behind the long couch over here." She motioned to where Mulligan had first found Monica's body. "I'd then like a singular chute, approximately six feet by six feet, to drop about four feet before it separates into two different chutes. Both of those chutes will lead to a large cement room located under this room. I'd also like a drainage system to be installed."

This was when the red-headed man known as James interrupted her and asked, "Goddess—"

Azazel cut him off and said, "Wait until I'm finished," wagging her finger at him. She went on to say, "No windows. I'd like it painted stark white and tiled while also being soundproof. There is going to be one door that leads out that can only be unlocked from the outside."

The men all looked at each other, and James stuttered when he asked, "What is this room for?"

"Storage, of course!" She laughed, and the men nervously joined in.

Azazel stopped laughing and shouted, "Alright, can you begin today? Can this be completed this week?"

This caused the men to all begin laughing for real.

Azazel calmly said, "I will pay you any amount that you can come up with."

The tradesmen all exchanged looks and looked back at Mulligan, whose expression matched theirs.

The fallen angel continued. "Gentlemen, you have your plans, and I will leave it to you to delegate tasks, but you will be checking in with Mulligan if you have any questions as I have other obligations that need my attention. If you are not up to the task, please let him know, and we will find a way to handle the situation."

As she walked to the makeup room, Azazel was giddy; she always got such a rush over commanding a room of men like that. She found Dante leaning over the counter, putting the finishing touches on his own face. When he pulled away, Azazel was intrigued by his look. He gave himself silver glitter tears with a deep purple lip that caught the light so beautifully.

When he caught sight of her, he bowed. "Give me one second."

She held up her hands and sarcastically said, "Wouldn't want to interrupt your personal time."

Dante smacked his lips. "How do you expect me to make you look flawless if I can't even make myself look flawless?"

Azazel walked over to the chair behind him and sat down. He looked at her in the mirror and asked, "Where'd your sparkle go?"

"Lost its shine." She didn't even bother to look at him.

"You'll find it again. You always do."

Once he was done applying the last of his gloss, he turned to Azazel and asked, "Glam or natural?"

"Your call."

He began moving around her and applying different products onto her face. Azazel couldn't see anything he was doing, so she focused on bettering her mood for when she had to walk out into the public.

When Dante moved away from her to get the tools for her hair, Azazel was pleasantly surprised with what she saw. Everything was nude and very soft. It looked like she wasn't wearing any makeup at all, yet everything was enhanced and perfect.

When he finished, his leader had a look that screamed both sultry and sophisticated.

"Have I mentioned how much I like you?" she asked him, admiring herself in the mirror.

"You're welcome, Goddess."

17

When Azazel stepped out into the hallway, Mulligan rushed toward her and excitedly exclaimed, "They all agreed to the project!"

"Good, you're in charge, Mulligan. Don't let me down." She barely glanced at him before walking away.

"Goddess, maybe we should discuss the plans further?"

She stopped and looked at him. "Did you not hear everything I said earlier? I didn't realize you had suddenly turned deaf."

He turned flustered at her words. "Yes, I heard everything you requested, but I also had some thoughts that I think would benefit you as well."

"Continue."

Mulligan went on to explain a chute system that would dispose of her victims to an incinerator below, and an exhaust system to get rid of the smell. It would all be paired with a sprinkler system installed in the ceiling to help with the cleaning.

Azazel smiled and patted him on the shoulder. "That's much better." As she turned away from him, she had taken several steps before she called over her shoulder, "You're in charge, Mulligan! Make it good."

When she reached the front of the house, she saw Antonio walking up the stairs—in the same clothing he'd been in the night before. He tried to reach for her hand to kiss it, but she withheld it from him.

"Antonio," she said. She could see the hurt in his eyes. "Is there a reason you're here again?"

This caused Antonio to start apologizing for the night before and began begging for Azazel's forgiveness. When he was met with a stone-like response, he began to back away from her, and Azazel let him go. She watched him walk away and saw his shoulders hunch over; everything about him screamed defeated, and it made her feel victorious for a short while.

When Azazel couldn't see him anymore, she continued on her path into the town center. It was two days before the Cunning was set to happen, and Azazel could feel the buzz in the air as people whispered excitedly when she passed them.

She took her place on stage when she arrived and turned to face the crowd that had followed her, a solemn look on her face. "Deanna Morgan will no longer be competing in the Cunning. She and her family have been relocated. That is their contribution for this year's cycle."

The crowd around her began whispering amongst themselves. When Azazel looked out, she noticed members of the prominent families looking at each other in confusion, minus Antonio, who was only looking at her. Her voice caught in her throat as she continued, "The Cunning will continue as planned." She walked off the platform and pushed her way through the crowd to get away from them.

When she returned home, she walked past the dining hall, but was soon stopped when one of the servants asked, "Are you going to be eating this morning, Goddess?"

Azazel shook her head. "No, I'm planning on having a rather large dinner, so I won't be eating until then."

The servant bobbed up and down in a quick bow. Azazel continued to her chamber and found all the tradesmen in there. She looked at the workers for a short while before returning to the hall to call for a servant. A blonde man with kind green eyes came running to her, breathless.

"I will need to move into another large room until the renovations are done. Can you see if the master guest suite on the other side of the palace would be suitable for me?"

He nodded and took off running in the opposite direction. Azazel looked around her, realizing that there wasn't much for her to do until her guests came for dinner. She looked out the window to notice how beautiful the weather was and decided to stroll through the castle gardens. It had been ages since she stopped to smell the roses.

She walked through the back halls until she came to a short hallway that led out to the back of the palace. When she stepped outside, she was greeted by the scent of various flowers and different types of fragrant trees. As she walked through the rows of flowers, she couldn't help but imagine the possibilities with her new room. Azazel was pleased that the renovations were started so quickly, and she hoped the men would be so motivated by money that they got the job done even quicker than she had quoted them before.

She was so lost in her own thoughts that she didn't hear the approaching figure until she almost ran into him. When Azazel looked up and saw Antonio's face, she stepped back.

"Antonio, I don't want to see you right now."

He looked at her and pleaded, "I can make up for last night. Please, let me make it up to you."

"It will take more than a little begging to make me forgive you, Antonio."

When she attempted to walk past him, he grabbed her arm and pulled her in for a passionate kiss. He put one hand firmly on her waist to hold her close to him and ran his other hand up to the side of her neck and face.

Azazel melted into his kiss and slowly wrapped her arms around his neck, pulling him closer to her. They lost themselves in the moment until she pulled back abruptly and said, "No, don't think you have some sort of... power over me, and that I'll just forget your behavior."

He took a step toward her. "I wasn't running from you, Azazel. I was running from how you made me feel in the moment." He looked at his hands and continued, "You made me feel vulnerable. I still don't know how to cope with that."

She took his hands and met his gaze. "Your heart is safe with me, Antonio."

"As is yours, Azazel."

She cleared her throat. "Well, I need to go back inside; there are a few things that I need to tend to."

Antonio nodded. "Yes, I should return home myself."

He looked at her and pulled her in for another kiss, longer and slower this time, full of unspoken promises. Azazel was the first to pull back, and she whispered, "Tonight, come when the palace has gone to sleep. I'll leave that door open for you." She pointed to the door that she had come out of. Antonio agreed and kissed her quickly one more time before prancing away.

Azazel watched him leave and felt her excitement soar. Walking toward the palace, her heart started to flutter. She had a smile on her face as she walked through the halls toward the guest chamber that she would take over during the renovation period. When she passed her bedroom and peeked in, she saw the furniture covered and moved to the other side of the room while the men were all standing around a large hole in the floor. Azazel was pleasantly surprised with their progress and continued on to her temporary chamber. Going to the other side of the palace seemed awkward to her as she rarely went over there, and the closer she got to the room, the quieter it got.

When she entered the guest room, she was pleased with how the room looked. Large bouquets of fresh flowers were put in every corner of the room, the windows were open, a pleasant soft breeze was coming in, and the earth-toned bedroom with the large four-poster bed promised comfort and hospitality during her stay. Azazel walked over to the closet, not sure what to expect. When she swung the doors open, she saw that it had been filled with a large selection of her clothing; she smiled. Her servants were on top of their tasks.

When she went into the bathroom, she was even more surprised to see that several body oils, containers of flowers, and different fragrances of salts were brought over. She felt grateful and considered for a moment to stop plucking the humans at her own discretion.

But she quickly pushed that thought aside. "They're just humans. Pathetic humans."

She placed the oil back in its place and continued with her inspection. When she was pleased with her surroundings, Azazel decided that she would go back to check in on the construction crew. Azazel slowly walked through the halls again and started to notice the small intricate designs on the pillars of the palace, the textures on the wall, and small details she had never cared about before.

The moment with Antonio in the garden came rushing back to her, and Azazel felt her face flush with embarrassment and smiled to herself; she knew tonight would be something extraordinary

As Azazel approached her bedroom, she heard shouting and arguing. This caused her to pick up her speed, and when she entered the room, they all went silent and exchanged looks with each other.

She smiled at them and asked, "Gentlemen, how are things going?" They all began talking at once, and she held her hands up. "One at a time, please."

Thomas stepped forward and said, "Mulligan told us that there needs to be enough support along the chutes to hold… a full-grown man…" He trailed off nervously.

"And… what's the problem?"

"We have no way of testing it." He looked down at his feet.

"Nonsense!" She pointed to each man in the room and said, "I see enough grown men in this room to ensure that the supports are sturdy enough for my plans." Thomas looked around the room and mumbled something, to which Azazel thundered, "What was that?!"

Thomas didn't hesitate. "I will not lose any men over whatever freakshow you have planned."

Azazel took a step toward him and placed a finger on his chest. It started to subtly glow as she said, "You will do whatever needs to be done."

"I will not," Thomas repeated, and the crew exchanged looks once more.

Azazel glared at them and demanded, "Is there anyone else who shares the same thoughts as Thomas?" They all shook their heads quickly. "Good, now let's get back to work. Quickly!"

They all dispersed and began tackling different tasks in the room as Azazel watched for a short while. When she was satisfied with their workflow, she left the room as Mulligan was rushing in to talk to the tradesmen.

When he saw that Azazel was in the room, he exclaimed, "Ah, good! Goddess, your dinner guests will be arriving soon. Would you like to change before entertaining them?"

Azazel nodded and replied, "Yes, Mulligan, thank you. Also, I'd like to dine with them in the far dining room, closer to my temporary chamber. If you wouldn't mind telling the chef that."

"I'll go to the kitchen right away and inform them!"

Azazel scanned the room once more and leaned in to whisper, "When they are done, I want them all locked in the room."

This caused Mulligan's face to whiten as he looked at her and repeated, "All of them?"

Azazel seethed. "Every. Single. One."

He looked out at the men, unknowingly building their tomb.

Azazel grinned, and before she left him standing there, said, "It's deliciously wicked to know what they are in for, isn't it?"

He didn't reply but simply looked to the floor, and Azazel was bored of toying with his conscience. She sauntered out of the room and strolled back toward the other side of the palace. The closer she got to her room, the more excited she became for the meal that was about to take place.

She smirked as she opened the door and walked in; she knew exactly the right dress to wear for the occasion. Azazel swung the doors of her room open and walked swiftly to the wardrobe to pull out a deep red dress. She looked at it and knew it was *perfect*. She hung it on the door and walked into the bathroom to begin a ceremonial bath.

Once the water had reached the right level with the perfect amounts of essential oils and salts, Azazel undressed and stepped into the tub. She immediately dipped her whole body under the water, and as it came up over her face, she took a deep breath and plunged herself into the sweet-smelling water. When she rose again, she was surrounded by the curtain of her hair. Pushing it to the side, Azazel leaned back against the tub, allowing her mind to be quiet as she enjoyed the moment.

She finally felt the urge to get out of the tub and lifted herself up. As she stepped out, her hair swept over her face again, and she was overtaken with the scent of sweet figs. Azazel smiled and was pleased with the smell that it had left on her skin. When she walked out of the bathroom, she grabbed the dress and slipped it over her head, careful to keep the material from touching her still wet hair. She stepped in front of the mirror, and her breath was taken away!

The shade of red resembled blood, and there was a fine golden glitter somehow embedded into the fabric, and was only visible if she turned a certain way in the light. It was floor-length, and while the bodice was tight, the skirt was flowy, and Azazel liked how it fanned out when she spun around.

She looked at herself in the mirror one last time and said, "At least if things get messy, it'll blend in."

18

As Azazel strolled down the hallway, she heard approaching footsteps and slowed her gait. It wasn't long before she heard, "Goddess!"

She took a breath and turned around. "Mulligan, I was just on my way to the dining room."

He nodded. "Good, Goddess, they have just arrived."

Azazel asked eagerly, "How many are there?"

Mulligan paused briefly. "There are eight family members."

"I remember you mentioning that she only had a sister and parents…"

"Extended family was present when we went to the

house. I thought it was a safe decision to bring them all here on your behalf."

Azazel smiled at him as she raised her hand to cup his cheek. "You did well, Mulligan. Thank you." She turned away from him and started to walk toward the dining room once again, with him following closely behind.

She could smell the desperation oozing from them when she reached the family. The maid's family watched her enter the room and dipped in low bows. When they all came up again, an older man stepped forward and introduced himself as the maid's father, Clarence. His wife, Catherine, introduced herself, and they all took turns saying their names. Azazel stopped listening once Catherine had stopped talking, but went through the motions of shaking each of their hands.

Once they had finished speaking, Azazel thanked them for coming and motioned to the table behind them. The family started talking about the maid's whereabouts, while Azazel watched them stuff their faces without taking any for herself. Bella, she found out her name was.

Azazel cleared her throat as she stood up and said, "You've probably all been wondering what I am going to do to help find Bella." They bobbed their heads and exchanged looks. "I am just going to get right to it. Bella isn't coming home. She's dead."

The family broke out in tears and started shrieking in distress. Azazel raised her voice, "There is no need for any of this; you'll all be joining her shortly."

Through tears, Catherine asked, "What? What do you mean?"

Azazel walked over to the sliding doors at the entrance and closed them, locked them, and turned back to the family, who began to panic. She grinned and walked over to the eldest family member, Beverly, who couldn't even stand on her own. Azazel picked her up by her neck and started to squeeze until she heard the crunch, and Beverly slumped over in her hand.

The family watched in horror, and all rushed to stand up and run toward Azazel, who scanned the room and flicked her finger at each one of them. This created an invisible wall that kept them from her, and when Clarence began to scream, nothing but a grunt came out of his mouth.

When Azazel looked at him, she asked, "Have you not figured it out yet? I am not human!"

She snapped her fingers, and his scream came out at full volume. She then looked at the rest of the family and snapped her fingers again, forcing them to stay planted where they were, regardless of how much they struggled.

She looked down at Clarence. "Just to make things easier." She plopped down on his stomach and slapped his chest; he grunted. "In ancient times, they used to sacrifice humans to the gods, sometimes without any numbing agents, and they would cut the victim's heart out while they were still conscious. They thought the fear strengthened the sacrifice."

Clarence started to grunt and move his eyes rapidly, and Azazel leaned forward and asked, "I can smell your fear. I can smell your family's fear. And do you want to know what it smells like?" Clarence just grunted. "I am going to assume that you want to know, so I will tell you. It smells delicious, like freshly-baked bread and warm butter."

She watched Clarence's eyes widen as she nodded encouragingly. "Yes, exactly! Hence, you see my dilemma regarding self-control." Azazel looked around the room and felt her mouth salivate. The hunger in her core had become too hard to ignore. The family watched her intensely, and she said, "I killed Bella. Her life essence rejuvenated me in a way that I haven't felt in decades." She smiled as the family started to grumble, and she could feel their anger.

"It was for *me*! It was to replenish *me*! All of you will still be with me and a part of me *forever*. Your essence is entangled with my divinity at a cellular level. It's a fairytale!" Clarence tried to move underneath her, and Azazel pressed against him even more. "Oh, Clarence, no."

As she inched up on top of his chest and started to squeeze the sides of his body with her thighs, she heard Clarence's muffled scream of pain. She shivered as she looked down at him.

"When humans feel pain, it feels like someone has poured water down my spine in the most delightful way." Clarence's eyes started to produce tears, and she whispered, "I imagine you're in immense pain right now. It's going to be over soon, I promise." She patted his cheek and got off of him, causing him to let out another muffled scream.

She walked around the room and roared, "I haven't had this much power in a very long time!" She stopped to stroke cousin Edward's cheek. "And tonight's a special treat for me. I'd only expected three of you to come, so I am indulging quite a bit tonight!"

She looked at the table and walked over to a large platter with a long knife. Azazel grabbed it and walked straight to Catherine. She grabbed her arm, made a long incision from her arm to her wrist, and watched in delight as blood flowed out like a fountain. Azazel brought Catherine's arm up to her mouth and began drinking deeply, letting it flow down her neck, saturating the front of her dress.

Catherine eventually fell to the floor, barely breathing. Azazel pushed her over so she was facing the ceiling and started to step on her lungs, and the family watched in horror, all of their screaming muffled.

Azazel looked down at Catherine and taunted her, "Come on, Catherine, you need to let go if you want to be reunited with sweet Bella."

With one final muffled grunt and a sigh, the orb started to float up from her mouth. The family continued to watch as Azazel dropped to her knees and wrapped her lips around the orb. Her skin started to glow, and she looked around the room and asked in a husky tone, "Okay, who's next?"

Azazel went through the entire family until the room was littered with their bodies. She slowly walked over to Clarence, who was trying to rock his body but grunted in pain every time he moved. She loomed over him, her neck and dress covered in his family's blood. He looked up at her with tear-filled eyes, and she dropped down to him.

"Oh, Clarence, did you think I forgot about you?" She leaned forward and kissed his forehead. "No, I would never!"

He began to sob softly. Azazel placed her hands on his chest and pressed down hard as her hands began to glow. She watched as he began to cave under the pressure of her divinity; she didn't have to wait long for his life essence orb to float up out of his mouth. Once she was finished, she stood up and looked around the room. Azazel sighed in relief, finally feeling complete.

She walked to the doors, and when she slid them open, Mulligan was waiting on the other side; he looked past her.

"Good meal?" he asked.

"It was satisfactory." When she turned to him, she asked, "How long do you think it's going to take for the chamber to finish building?"

He looked at her and replied, "They finished the chute to the incinerator today."

"You found an incinerator this quickly?"

Mulligan nodded and proudly responded, "I told them who it was for."

Azazel patted him on the back as she walked past him. "I need to go change, Mulligan."

She wasn't far from the room when she heard him gasp as he saw the severity of her evening.

19

When she arrived back to her room, Azazel felt satisfied and knew that nothing would interfere with her night with Antonio. Confidently, she went over to her wardrobe and pulled out a delicately strapped silver mini dress. After she cleaned her face and put the dress on, she loved how she could barely see her body underneath the material; she knew Antonio would have difficulty formulating words when he saw her.

Azazel wanted to see how far the workers got. However, the sun was beginning to set, and she knew she needed to run to her chamber. When she peeked around the corner and into the room, she was pleased to see that they were still working; the trap door had been installed.

Not wanting to disturb them, she tiptoed past the construction site. She wanted to grab a few things from her bedside table, and when she reached her destination, she pulled open the drawer and grabbed some oil in an intricate bottle. She quickly left the room before anyone saw her and waited for Antonio at the door, warming the bottle in between her hands.

As each moment passed, her heart started to race faster, and she began to worry that he wouldn't show up. Luckily, she heard the door start to open and was greeted by Antonio's handsome face.

They looked at each other and instantly rushed to one another. Antonio picked Azazel up and carried her as she whispered directions to her room in between kisses. When they got to her room, he put her down in front of the door, and she took him in by the hand. The night was filled with the most passionate touches and ecstasy.

Azazel watched the sun rise through the window the next morning as she rested her head on Antonio's chest. She contemplated this genuine feeling of happiness and smiled, knowing that she didn't have to use any of her divinity to sway Antonio to be here. He loved her, and she felt *herself* falling in love with *him*. She looked up at his face, noticing how long his eyelashes were and the small scar above his eyebrow; her gaze followed the defined lines of his body in admiration.

She watched him sleep for a few moments longer, and when she attempted to move, he woke up and sleepily grabbed her, pulling her back into him. They spent the morning rolling around in bed, exploring each other and deepening their connection.

Finally, Antonio wanted to grab some food. Azazel agreed and told him she would have something waiting for him when he got back. He smirked while he got dressed and looked back at her. She watched him and playfully taunted him as he left the room. Azazel stepped out of bed and walked toward the bathroom to start a bath for the two of them. She remembered the bottle from the night before and grabbed it from the small entryway table. She was relieved to see that it wasn't knocked over in all the commotion. Azazel returned to the bathroom and took the stopper off of the bottle; the aroma that filled the air was sweet, seductive, and filled her senses with pleasure.

She put a few drops into the running water and watched the tub fill up. She then stopped it and stepped into the tub when it reached a suitable level. Azazel cupped water up over her shoulders and submerged her entire body into the depths of the tub. She didn't even hear Antonio creep in at first until he came looking for her.

He took the sight of her in and asked, "Should I just feed this to you?"

"No, you should join me, and we can share."

Antonio placed the platter on the counter beside him as he stripped down again before picking it back up, lifting it over his head as he stepped into the tub behind her.

Once he got settled and placed a strawberry into her mouth, he asked, "Mulligan was asking about you."

Azazel sighed. "Of course, he was. Did he say what he wanted?"

Antonio paused as he thought. "He mentioned construction."

This piqued Azazel's interest, and she didn't want to wait. She wrapped herself in a plush robe and left Antonio to clean up the mess and tidy up the room. Azazel walked quickly down the halls, and as she turned the final corner before her chamber, she noticed that it was quiet... too quiet. She walked a bit faster and saw that her bedroom door was shut.

Azazel opened the door slowly, and everything had been put back and cleaned up. She walked into the room and looked around. She then heard a knock on the door and saw

Mulligan come into the room, and he looked around before asking, "Are you ready to see it?"

"Is it ready?"

Mulligan nodded and turned to leave the room, Azazel following close behind.

He led her to the lower level of the palace, and as they approached the room, Azazel could smell fresh paint and wood. She took a deep breath in, and Mulligan stopped in front of her and said, "I made a few adjustments. I hope you don't mind."

Azazel tilted her head. Mulligan continued, "The trap door is run by a trigger pulley system. Your victim will walk over the door and hit the small hook sticking up from the floor, and then they will fall down the chute and into this room here."

He motioned to a large room built in the middle of the floor. Azazel looked above her at the chutes, and before she could ask, Mulligan spoke again, as if reading her mind. "It can hold up to four hundred pounds."

He went to unlock the door, which had a latched hook and padlock. When they stepped into the room, Azazel was filled with happiness. It looked identical to the room from her dream! It was pure white with a singular significant drain in the middle of the floor. There were no windows, and once the door was shut, they couldn't see the seam of the doorframe.

She looked around and asked, "Clean up?"

Mulligan answered, "Ah, yes, the best part."

He walked over to a section of the wall opposite them and pushed it inwards. It shifted around and revealed another chute. Azazel walked over and looked down. "The craftsmanship is impeccable!"

Mulligan agreed. "It can be quickly washed. Sprinklers will drop down from the ceiling; there is a system for the water and another for cleaning detergents. I also made it soundproof except for a small part of the room, where you'll only be able to hear anything happening down here on *your* side of the bed."

Azazel took a step back. "Mulligan, every time I lose faith in you, you somehow find a way to blow my mind. Now, where are my lovely tradesmen?"

"Eating their last meal in the grand dining room. I figured it was the least we could do."

"Least *we* could do? Mulligan, I'm the one who benefits from them, not you." She rolled her eyes at him. "I want them all in here within the next hour!"

Mulligan nodded, and then he asked, "Will you be joining the final meal for the combatants?"

"Antonio and I will be down after the loose ends are tied up."

She left Mulligan looking around the new room. He was borderline uncomfortable that the room was being used so soon; Azazel could hear it in his voice. How weak. Humans were all so weak.

She pushed his facial expressions out of her mind as she returned to Antonio. She was excited to tell him that they could finally return to her regular chamber. That they'd have access to the finest clothing again… just in time for the final dinner.

They walked down the halls hand-in-hand; Azazel was happy, and Antonio seemed at ease with her. When they got to her chamber, she welcomed him in.

"Ah, it's good to be home." He playfully threw his arms into the air. "So, what will you be wearing?" He turned around and asked her.

"This." She walked into her closet to pull out a white dress completely covered in jewels in a backless design, and strings of natural diamonds hung across the back. There was also a long slit on the side and long-fitted sleeves.

Antonio gawked at her. "Wow."

She smiled and hung it back up. When she walked back

into her room, Antonio looked around and asked, "So, where was the construction?"

Azazel felt a lump form in her throat, and she quickly replied, "I just had some flooring replaced. I tried to move the couch, and I cracked the boards underneath it when I set it back down."

It was such a quick lie, but he seemed to have bought it. Hopefully, he'd never discover her secret and master plan.

20

A solid knock on the door soon interrupted them. Antonio got out of bed, wrapped one of the bedsheets around himself, and walked over to the door to allow the designer into the room. When the designer read the room, he flushed red.

"Would you like me to give you a moment?"

Azazel shook her head. "Nonsense, what did you bring?"

The designer turned back to his rack and started to bring out suits in various colors, materials, cuts, and even tried to pass off a short suit. Azazel crawled to the edge of the bed and watched as the designer, Gustav, started to pair colors to Antonio's eyes and skin tone.

She watched the two men consumed by their conversation

and smirked. She stepped off the bed and cleared her throat. "Boys, I'm going to go get ready myself." She pointed at Gustav. "Make him look pretty."

Antonio smirked at her, and she winked in response before turning to go to the closet. Azazel took the dress out of its bag and walked into the makeup room, where Dante was waiting and filing his nails.

When he saw her, he gasped. "Your sparkle has become a glow!" Dante got out of the chair that he was sitting in and patted it, telling her to come sit.

When she sat in front of the mirror, Azazel's mouth dropped open at her reflection. Her hair looked full of luster and was *perfect*, while her skin was so smooth and shiny that she resembled a star!

Dante stared at her. "Whatever you're doing, keep doing it!"

Azazel smiled at him. "Okay, the Cunning dinner."

Dante nodded, glanced at the dress, and back to Azazel. "Gotcha, well, since you *are* wearing white, it already makes you look absolutely ethereal, and I don't want to disturb that." She started to frown, and he jumped in again. "But I'll do what I can to accentuate your features!"

"Maybe just the smallest bit of pampering, Dante."

He bowed and began a skincare regime, finishing it with a simple moisturizer and lightly-tinted lip balm. When he finished, they were shocked to see that her skin look even more supple and youthful than before! Dante finished by placing hot curlers all over her head, and while those dried, he painted her nails a midnight black.

When her hair was done, they looked at her in the mirror, and both of them were taken with emotion. Azazel was genuinely happy, and she whispered, "I am so beautiful!"

"You always are, Goddess, but there's something more here. Something you're not revealing."

She wasn't ready to get into details about Antonio yet, so she changed the topic. "Can you help me get into my dress?"

Dante smiled. "I would be honored."

Once she was dressed, Dante covered his mouth and slightly shook his head in disbelief. "You're perfect!"

She turned around slowly, causing the diamonds on the back of the dress to chime together.

He looked down at her feet and asked, "What are you going to do for shoes?"

Azazel looked down also and asked, "Would it be awful to go barefoot?

Dante laughed. "While I do love the natural look, I think this look requires at least a six-inch heel."

She left the makeup room feeling like she was on top of the world. As she approached her chamber, Mulligan rushed down the hall toward her. She looked at him and greeted him.

"Goddess, your earlier request has been fulfilled."

"Good, I hope there wasn't too much trouble."

Mulligan had a guilty look on his face. "I had to gas them and drag them into the room one by one."

"Mulligan, our relationship is such a rollercoaster; continue to keep me on my toes."

"Of course, Goddess." As he turned, Azazel stopped him.

"Can you ensure that everyone is completely out of the palace tonight?"

"The room is soundproof, Goddess. No one will hear you."

She leaned in and whispered, "I am going to put it to the absolute test."

"Do you hear them now?"

Azazel shook her head, but then her face turned serious. "But I probably would if I were in my chamber."

When she went back into her room, she was relieved to see that it was empty, but was also confused as to *why* it was empty. She tiptoed across the floor and stepped on the part that creaked. She then heard a muffled sound and turned her attention to where the bed was.

She slowly walked over to it, and the closer she got to the side that she slept on, the louder the screams were. Azazel could hear the desperation in their voices, and she could smell their fear through the vent. She stood there for a few moments, soaking in the feeling.

When she finally felt a slight tug of urgency, she continued to the wardrobe to pick out a pair of black strappy platforms. After she put them on, she checked her appearance one last time and walked back out to her bedroom... where she saw Antonio standing by the couch in front of the trap door. He was dressed in a deep blue velvet jacket with a black shirt and tie. She stopped to take him in; he whistled his approval at her look, and she did a slow turn for him. Azazel stepped toward him, and he met her halfway to kiss her.

When she pulled away, she said, "I wish we could just stay here instead."

Antonio smiled at her and tucked a piece of hair behind her ear. "I think we would get sick of the men screaming under us after a while."

She pushed him back slightly. "Pardon?"

"Why is there screaming coming from under your floor, Azazel?" His face was glowing red with anger.

She attempted to take a step toward him, and he held his hand up to stop her. "No, you stay away from me!"

Her heart started to break as she pleaded, "Antonio, I would never hurt you. Stop!"

He glared at her. "I don't know about that. How many men are down there?"

When she didn't reply, he whispered, "Oh my god..."

This caused Azazel's face to darken, and she hissed, "*Your* god? I am the closest thing you have to a god, the only god who has ever given you everything you have ever wanted!"

Antonio started to back away from her as she approached

him, but she marched toward him, not taking her eyes off him. She felt her heart shattering; she could see the fear and judgment in his eyes. Even if she *did* erase his memory, she knew that he'd still think differently of her; it was no longer pure.

"Antonio, I'm not going to hurt you."

"I thought you loved me..." he trailed off, and Azazel rushed to him to grab his hands.

"Antonio, I do; you just have to trust me."

He stared into her eyes, and she could tell that he was genuinely thinking through everything. He dropped his hands, straightened his jacket, and said, "Let's go to dinner. I'll leave after."

"That's it?"

He nervously looked around and asked, "What else is there to say? Do I have a choice? It's either I keep my mouth shut, or I join the men in the basement."

She could hear the betrayal in his voice, and it saddened her. He didn't offer her his arm, but instead, walked away from her before she could say anything. Azazel followed him out of the room, and as they continued down the hallway, the angrier she got with him. By the time they reached the grand dining room, Azazel was fuming. She tried to put a smile on her face as people rushed up to her, but she watched Antonio walk over to Mulligan and whisper something in his ear. Mulligan looked at Azazel, and he had a questionable look.

She saw Antonio lean back and nod his head, and then Mulligan left the dining room.

Finally, Azazel shouted, "Please! Everyone, let's eat!"

The crowd broke up to go to their tables, chattering excitedly. Antonio took a seat with his family instead of at the high table with her. This hurt her even more, and she began to tap her fingers on the table as she saw him lean over and whisper something to his brother, who then looked at his cup and took a sip. When Antonio looked up and saw that Azazel was glaring at him, he nodded and motioned his eyes to the hallway. She got up when he did, and they walked out as the staff started to bring in dinner.

When the head chef walked past her, Azazel stopped him and asked, "Can you tell them to wait until I speak?"

She turned her attention to Antonio. "Have you been spreading lies?"

Antonio shook his head. "I just told Mulligan to let them go."

Azazel's vision turned hazy with rage, and she slowly asked, "You… what?!"

"I told Mulligan to let the men loose. They are to be paid handsomely, and none of them will say anything or blacklist the palace for future work."

He's joking! He must be joking!

21

"I know you're not serious right now."

Antonio took a deep breath. "No, I am."

"And your reason?"

He paused before he replied, "You're about to absorb ninety-nine combatants, Azazel. Isn't that enough for you?"

Azazel took a step back from him and whispered, "What?"

Antonio sighed and said, "My family has known for generations about the reasoning behind the Cunning. It was the main motivation for our success." Azazel couldn't believe what she was hearing, but he continued, "This was supposed to be a yearly sacrifice, and you're starting to eat more than your fill." He looked up at her to see how she was taking it; she stared at him in shock.

The hall was quiet, and Azazel finally said, "I can't talk about this now. I have a kingdom waiting for me to address them."

Antonio grabbed her arm and asked, "Aren't you curious about what we know?"

She seethed in a hushed tone. "I don't care, Antonio."

He took a step back from her and bowed slightly. "I will be sure to stay out of your sight, Goddess." Antonio didn't bother looking up when he turned away from her. Azazel watched him walk away and felt a pang of fear start to creep up inside of her.

If humans found out what she was genuinely doing, there was no telling *what* they would try to do to her.

She collected herself again before she walked back into the hall. As she walked across the front of the room, she tried to push Antonio out of her mind. Azazel refused to let a mortal man have any sort of control over her emotions; she was done with him and would focus on her kingdom once again.

As she stood in front of everyone, they erupted into thunderous applause, and Azazel felt loved. She held her arms up to show them that she was appreciative of their support. She motioned to the combatants, which caused the dining hall to go wild with excitement. The combatants all stood up and waved to everyone cheering them on.

Once the murmuring had died down, Azazel thundered, "Everyone, eat as if this is your last meal!"

There was a ripple of laughter throughout the crowd as people started to fill their plates. Azazel waited for everyone to begin eating before she walked back out into the hall; she wanted to find Mulligan.

And as if he had known that she was thinking of him, Mulligan turned the corner, and when he saw her, he stopped in his place. She rushed toward him and slapped him across the face when she reached him—the sound echoed through the hall, and a hot red mark was left on his cheek.

She leaned in close to him and hissed, "How dare you take orders from someone else?" Mulligan opened his mouth to speak. "Shut up! I'm speaking!" He nodded, and she continued. "No one takes orders from Antonio, and it startles me that he got so comfortable in my palace, with *my* servants so quickly."

"Goddess, my apologies, but Antonio claimed that those were your orders."

Azazel rolled her eyes and replied, "Mulligan, use your stupid brain. Do you really think I would ask you to do that?"

"I had hope, Goddess. The men had done such a great job. I personally felt like they deserved to keep their lives."

Azazel sighed. "Are they gone?"

Mulligan nodded.

"You're sure they won't say anything to anyone?"

Mulligan nodded again. "Antonio said he would triple whatever you were paying them to keep quiet, and still continue work when needed at the palace. At first, the men objected, understandably, but when I threatened to leave them there for you, they were more than agreeable."

"Ah, a happily-ever-after ending for everyone then, isn't it?" she declared sarcastically.

Mulligan asked nervously, "What do you want me to do about Antonio?"

"He's my problem. You leave him to me."

"I know it's not my place, Goddess, but I like how happy you are when you're with him. Please, go easy on him."

She paused for a moment. "You're right, Mulligan. It's *not* your place. You can stay out of my sight for the rest of the night."

Mulligan bowed again and left Azazel, who was trying to control her rage. She needed to take a moment to compose herself before she went back into the dining hall, and when she walked into the room, the atmosphere was light and full of happiness. It made it easier for Azazel to push her anger to the side; for the time being, she wanted to focus entirely on the combatants and their last night. She made her way through the aisles between the tables, talking to random citizens briefly before walking to the high table and taking her place in the center.

Azazel sat down and watched the crowd as they ate their meals; the combatants talked amongst themselves and ate as much as possible. She could feel the power radiating from the combatants' table in large waves. It made her mouth salivate, and she couldn't stare at them for too long, or the hunger would take over, and she wouldn't be able to stop it.

She stood up as people started to leave the hall, and she walked over to the combatants, who were all waiting patiently for their instructions.

"Hello, my strong warriors. After all of your hard work and training, we are finally on the eve of the Cunning." The combatants all straightened up with pride. She continued, "I expect you all to get to bed early tonight and meet at the atrium tomorrow morning, bright and early!"

She smiled warmly at the table, who all exchanged looks of uncertainty. Azazel closed her speech out by thanking them again for their sacrifice. When she turned to walk away from the table, she heard them all start to whisper.

She whipped herself around quickly and asked, "I'm sorry? Did someone have a question?"

When no one answered or raised their hand, Azazel turned to leave again. This time, it was the silence that haunted her as she left them, and it was deafening!

This evening had been filled with so much disappointment, and she didn't know how she would get past the feeling of being let down. Azazel grabbed the doorknob of her room and briefly wished that Antonio would be waiting for her inside. When she saw that the space was empty, she was slightly disappointed that the one order he listened to was the one where she told him to leave her alone. She sighed and continued to her closet to get changed for bed. When she looked around at all of the delicate sleepwear that she would have worn for Antonio, sadness started to creep in again. They had such a strong connection. What went wrong?

She walked over to her bed, but this time, she didn't hear screaming coming from her new chamber, and Azazel's sadness was replaced with anger again. She climbed into bed and pulled the bedsheets over herself; she hated feeling this way. She was of divine descent, and she *refused* to let a mortal have this much control over her. She knew having a consort would complicate things eventually.

Azazel's last thought before closing her eyes, welcoming sleep, was that mortals are best to be used and disposed of.

22

When Azazel opened her eyes the following day, she was filled with happiness and excitement. It was the day of the Cunning! She jumped out of bed and looked out the window; the sun was barely in the sky, and it was the perfect time for her ritual bath. She rushed into the bathroom and started the water, then she walked over to the cabinet and pulled out several bottles filled with clear liquid. She took the stopper out and dropped a few drops of each into the tub, chanting an incantation from an old language over it. She welcomed abundance and love into her life and wished the combatants a safe journey to the other side.

Once the water was done running, Azazel undressed and

stepped into the tub. When she lowered herself fully into the water, she let out a small sigh of pleasure. She had gotten used to having someone with her consistently, and she almost forgot how nice it was to be alone. When she leaned her head back against the bathtub rim, images of her nights with Antonio rushed through her mind, causing her to sit up straight. Why did he keep popping up into her mind? She was done with him! That was that! She had better things to focus on.

The water was still warm when Azazel decided to get out of the bathtub. She knew it would take a while to get ready and wanted to put a lot of effort into her look. She walked to the end of the closet, where a long black gown was waiting for her. Azazel only wore it for the Cunning; it was made of the finest silk, and the seamstress who made it lost a large amount of blood sewing the rubies into it. Azazel would put the dress on and feel the dedication that the woman put into the gown.

She brought the gown with her when she went into the makeup room; she liked how useful Dante had proved himself to be when it came to getting her dressed. When she walked in, Dante already had his makeup done and was dressed in a smart plum-colored suit.

When he saw her, he ran over, took the gown from her, and rushed her into the chair as he said, "You're late!"

"Dante, I am never late. You're on my schedule, not the other way around."

Dante paused like he was going to say something, but then thought better of it and kept his mouth shut. They didn't speak while he got her ready, and Azazel didn't mind; she enjoyed the silence. When Dante was done with her look, she was pleased. He opted for subtle eyeshadow and long fake eyelashes with a nude lip and a bit of blush. Her hair had been straightened and was flowing around her. It was *perfect.*

Dante helped her into her gown and laced the back for her while she watched the look come together in the mirror.

"You know, Goddess, you don't have to hold this thing. Someone else can take over for once."

Azazel patted his hand and replied, "That's where you're wrong."

Dante had a confused look on his face but didn't say anything more. Azazel thanked him and told him that she expected to see him at the opening ceremony. She left him in a bowing position as she turned her focus on the Cunning, at last. She walked through the halls, smiling at servants that she passed, and as she was about to leave the palace, Mulligan ran after her, calling for her to stop.

When she turned around, Mulligan asked, "Did you need an escort to the atrium?"

Azazel rolled her eyes. "I guess I have no other choice, do I?" He offered her an arm. As she took it, she said, "I don't want you to say a word to me the entire way, Mulligan."

He made a motion across his mouth with his hand as if he were zipping his lips, and the two of them continued walking out of the palace. The streets were lined with flowers, and people were coming out of their shops to see her walk through the streets. Azazel smiled and acknowledged as many people as she could as she walked past them.

When they reached the atrium, a large crowd followed them into the building. The high families were all waiting at the shrine just inside the door. Azazel noticed that Antonio was nowhere to be seen; it was probably for the best. Mulligan let Azazel walk ahead to the families to welcome them as he went to double-check with the new staff that everything was ready.

The families warmly welcomed Azazel, all commenting on how beautiful she looked and how excited they were to be there. She tried to keep her focus on the people talking to her, but she couldn't help but steal glances at the front door, hoping that Antonio would walk through it. But the closer they got to the opening ceremony, the clearer it became that he wasn't going to come.

A loud bell sounded, signaling that it was time to begin. The families all put on black robes and masks—each mask was an intricately carved animal face and painted black. They all formed a line behind Azazel and followed her out into the arena of the atrium. The family's duty was to bring the losing combatant of each round out of the stadium and into the back room, where she would be waiting at the end of every event to welcome the combatant to the next phase of their existence.

As they walked into the center of the arena, the families spread out behind Azazel, taking up the entire width of the stadium. Across from them, were the rows of combatants in their fighting gear, and they all had a weapon in their hands. Azazel looked out into the stands, where the kingdom had poured into the seats and were all excitedly talking. She put her hand up to her mouth and sounded off an ear-splitting whistle, which caused everyone to quiet down and focus on her.

"Welcome, everyone, to our millennium-old tradition, the Cunning!" The crowd didn't burst into applause. Azazel continued, "The combatants will be taking part in their final training session this morning, and then the events will commence this afternoon." The crowd started talking more, and she looked out at the masses, proud of what she had created in her world.

A woman in a hawk mask leaned over to her and asked, "Is there anything we can help you with, Goddess?"

Azazel turned her head slightly to the woman. "Have you seen Antonio?"

The hawk shook her head and replied, "Not since yesterday, Goddess. I'm sorry."

Azazel sighed and turned her attention back to the crowd;

some were settling in their seats while others were starting to leave the arena.

The combatants all began to pair up again and went through stretches and basic moves. The families all dispersed and went to different parts of the atrium, some pairing up and others going off solo. Azazel wanted to find Antonio; she tried to put this to rest so that she could enjoy her absorptions like she usually did.

She started to walk out of the arena when Mulligan caught up to her and asked, "Goddess, are you not going to stay?"

Azazel shook her head and replied, "I'd like to find Antonio; I need to speak with him."

Mulligan looked down to the floor. Azazel studied his face and asked, "What is it, Mulligan?"

He quietly said, "He's in the chamber."

"What do you mean?!"

Mulligan refused to look up at her as he began to tell her that he drugged Antonio when they had a drink the night before.

She interrupted him to ask, "Why didn't I hear him screaming today, then?"

Mulligan said, "I think I gave him too much."

Azazel felt her heart drop, and she whispered, "You gave him too much of what?!"

"The liquid in your nightstand."

Azazel's mouth dropped. "How much did you give him, Mulligan?"

He began to speak quickly about how Antonio wasn't worthy of Azazel, and that he was angry about Antonio giving him commands and lying to him.

She reached out to Mulligan as she softly said, "I understand, but it was not your mess to clean up."

He nodded and said, "I'm sorry, Goddess. I just wanted to be in your good graces once more."

"I'm only hard on you, Mulligan, because I know what you're capable of. I know you're human, and you're bound to slip, but you have nothing to worry about. Did you check on him? Is he alive? Is he able to get up?"

Mulligan nodded, and Azazel rushed out the door and toward her palace.

She ignored all of the citizens that called after her as she ran past them, pushing her legs to go faster. When she reached the room in the basement, she could hear Antonio yelling from inside. She opened the door, and he quickly backed away, screaming for her to stay away from him.

Azazel walked into the room slowly, looked around, and asked, "You don't like it here?" Antonio panicked and screamed again; Azazel shushed him and said, "Antonio, no one can hear you. It's just us in here." She watched for a bit as he tried to look around the room for an escape. "You know, I was really starting to fall in love with you."

"I *did* love you, Azazel! I've loved you since I was just a young man!" Azazel was taken back. She reached out for him, but he recoiled and roared, "No! You let me out of here, now!"

But she only shook her head. "Antonio, I had every intention of letting you go and having a rational conversation with you. Your reaction, however, has shown me that you're not capable of that."

"Capable?! I'm locked in a box!"

"True, but if you hadn't been so quick to judge me, you'd probably be in the arena right now instead of begging me to let you out of here." Antonio dropped to his knees and shuffled over to her, and he started to beg for his life. Azazel looked at him and sneered, "This is incredibly unbecoming of you, Antonio."

He stood up and grabbed her arm. "Then tell me what I need to do to convince you to let me go."

"It's not that simple; you broke my heart. You've

disappointed me more than once. I really don't think I can let you keep strolling around the kingdom like you do."

He dropped his hand and asked, "What do you mean?"

Azazel backed away from him and started to walk around the room's perimeter, trailing her fingers along the wall and refusing to look at Antonio. He watched her for a second before he asked again, "Azazel, what do you mean?"

She stopped when she felt a small latch. She pulled it, and a long shelf appeared out of the wall when a part of it moved back, and behind it, was an array of weapons.

Azazel giggled and finally looked at Antonio. "I didn't even know those were there."

Antonio rushed toward her, but she grabbed a long-serrated hunting knife, and he stopped as the tip of it touched his chest.

When he looked up at her, she wasn't the being whom he had loved for the better part of his adult life; it was a dark skeletal version of her. Azazel's mouth was drawn tight, and her eyes were completely white.

He pulled back, and she whined, "Oh, come on! You were just so confident; don't stop now!"

"W-what are you?"

She grinned a devious smile. "One of the fallen."

She lunged to knock him on his back and straddled his chest, and while he struggled against her, she started to apply her divine weight to hold him in place.

He stopped struggling and looked up. "Azazel! Stop it!"

"You'll be a part of me forever, Antonio. We'll be together forever."

When he tried to object, she plunged the knife straight into his chest, and his eyes widened when he realized what she had done.

He grunted as she pulled it out. She then shifted her body down his before leaning in to kiss him on the lips. Azazel began to softly sob as she kissed him. When she pulled back from him, the orb followed her lips, and she felt Antonio's body go limp. She cried out in pain as she felt the weight of her choice and rushed to his body as she absorbed his essence, kissing all over his face.

Azazel hugged his body and wept until she couldn't cry anymore. She heard a faint knock, and she yelled, "Yes?!"

Mulligan appeared in the chamber and saw what she had done. He looked at her and said, "I didn't intend for you to kill him."

She looked at Antonio's face and replied, "I didn't mean to kill him. He just… he became a liability." They were silent for a few moments before she said, "Leave him. I want a proper burial for him."

23

Mulligan watched as Azazel stood up and walked over to give him the knife.

She looked back at the room and said, "I liked that hidden cupboard, nice touch."

Mulligan bowed. "You are requested to appear at the atrium."

She held her hand up and waved, acknowledging him as she walked away from him. When she thought of Antonio's absorption, she felt an overwhelming sense of loss and stopped in the hallway as she collapsed to the floor, clutching herself. She kept seeing Antonio's eyes as he realized that she had stabbed him, and she felt her heart break every time. And to make it worse, she didn't feel the rejuvenation from his absorption. She looked down the hall in front of her and knew people would be sent to find her if she didn't keep going.

Azazel pulled herself together and continued to the main floor of the palace. As she came into the public's view, she put a smile on her face and tried to forget about Antonio in the basement. She walked up to the large spectator's box that overlooked the entire arena when she reached the atrium. The crowd started cheering for her as she sat down on her throne. She was so overwhelm with a sense of love and relief that she concluded she didn't need a single person to bring her happiness. She had a kingdom filled with people who loved her no matter what, and none of them would ever find out about her true nature. Azazel wouldn't let anyone else get as close as Antonio had gotten; he was a fluke.

A loud siren sounded, and Azazel started to get increasingly excited. The combatants stopped fighting, and all fell into a straight line as the trainer came out from a side door. He walked across the arena and gave his last words of advice to each combatant. The crowd watched as the trainer finished going through the lines of combatants, and he took a step back, saluted them, and turned to Azazel, nodding; it was time.

She stood up and looked out into the darkness of the arena as it quieted down, and she simply said, "Fight hard, strike true," and blew a kiss out to the combatants. "Thank you for your sacrifice."

The hooded families came out from the sides of the atrium with bags of supplies for the combatants; as each warrior opened up the bag, Azazel started to get an idea of who would go far and who wouldn't just by their facial expressions. When all of the bags had been handed out, the floor of the atrium slowly dropped down to a subterranean arena that stretched out underneath the entire kingdom.

The stands and spectator's box were dropped down just

under the atrium's main building, down into the harshest terrain; the spectators were all protected from the elements, thanks to the encasement around the stands. They found themselves in a thick forest with the temperature dropping, and Azazel watched as the combatants all exchanged looks as they paused, wondering where they should start.

A girl began to dig into her bag to pull out a thick jacket and long knife, and before anyone could move toward her, she ran off into the forest.

The other combatants followed her lead and put on warmer layers of clothing before running off into the brush. Azazel was disappointed that no one took advantage of the time to get the first kill in. She tried to focus her eyes on all of the warriors and didn't need to wait long as they began to light fires throughout the forest. She smiled, knowing that the first night's challenge was usually the deadliest; she looked forward to what could happen in the following hours.

Azazel was grateful that she was alone; she didn't want to have to put on a fake appearance for anyone at the moment. She also didn't know how she was going to break the news to Antonio's family. But she knew that it would have to be sooner rather than later; she sighed when she thought about the funeral for him. Her eyes started to well up with tears when she thought of Antonio's face, smile, and touch, and her heart began to break. For the first time, she felt true guilt about her absorption.

She remembered the look of judgment in Antonio's eyes when he found out her secret. She remembered how he had let his ego dictate how he reacted when she pushed him off her and how comfortable he'd gotten, enough to dictate orders to her staff and lie on her behalf. Thinking about this, Azazel became angry almost immediately again; he deserved it! And now, he would be a part of her forever! She would never have to worry about him disappointing her ever again.

Azazel stood up and walked toward the combatants' final

destination to wait for the incoming morsels. As she walked to the backroom, her excitement peaked, and she started to slightly skip down the last hallway.

When she walked into the room, she saw three combatants barely moving on stretchers, with masked family members standing to the side of the room.

Azazel dismissed them, and when they left, she quietly said, "Okay, little birds. I need you to let go."

They had fought so hard and had already been through so much that she didn't want to traumatize them as they left this existence. Azazel continued to walk around them and whisper sweet things to them, wanting them to naturally *want* to leave this world. During her third round around the room, one of the boys started to wheeze, and Azazel walked over to him. She heard him struggling to breathe, and she leaned down over him to kiss his forehead. As she placed her lips to his head, the orb started to poke through his lips. She smiled and knew he was waiting for her to come to him. She ingested the orb and kissed his head once more before continuing her journey around the room.

Once the other two combatants had given up their orbs, Azazel covered the bodies and whispered a short blessing over them before she left the room. As she exited, the hall was lined with several members of the high families, and none of them said anything as she walked past. Azazel wondered if they had somehow found out about Antonio; none of them bowed or made eye contact with her.

She started to get nervous, and when she saw Mulligan at the end of the hall, she began to walk a bit faster until she reached him.

He smiled at her and asked, "Having a good harvest?"

"Mulligan, did you tell Antonio's family about his death?"

He shook his head and replied, "I had figured you would want to handle that, Goddess. I left it up to you."

Azazel let out a loud sigh and walked away from him.

Her paranoia was starting to get to her once again. She shook her head and focused back on the lush green forest below her as it came into view once again.

When she sat down on her throne, she felt a rush of electricity shoot through her body. The latest absorptions had taken effect, and Azazel felt energized. It felt like her adrenaline had taken over her! Her heart was pounding, and she leaned forward in her seat, eager to see a fight.

She scanned the forest below her like a hawk looking for prey, and after a minute, she finally found two combatants fighting in a clearing. It was an older man with salt and pepper hair against a petite blonde woman with her hair braided in two. Azazel watched as the woman blocked every attack and quickly dodged under her opponent's legs, and then crawled up his back to wrap her legs around his neck to snap it. The spectators watched as a white vehicle crisscrossed through the forest to the latest casualty; the woman had already run off into the trees.

Azazel was still riding on a high from her last absorptions. She motioned for the closest staff member to come closer, and when a young man with black hair and bright green eyes came forward, Azazel said, "I'd like you to go tell Mulligan that I'd like the fallen to be put on ice until I say otherwise, please."

The servant bowed and quickly ran out of the box. At the same time, Azazel turned her attention back to the forest, looking for more fallen warriors. But when she couldn't find any, she concluded that maybe they were just getting adjusted. She pouted for a brief moment before deciding that she would go back to the palace to start planning Antonio's funeral, so that when she told his family, she would have the plans all set for them. She still didn't know how she would tell them, but she figured that no matter how they acted, she could always give them a small touch and change their minds.

When she thought of Antonio again, her pain had already died down substantially. Azazel was comforted once more, knowing that he would always be with her, and she was going to plan the most beautiful funeral to show his family just how much he was appreciated in the kingdom.

As she was about to walk out of the atrium, one of the family members came running after her, wearing a fox mask. When she lifted the mask, Azazel saw that it was Antonio's mother, and she felt the pit in her stomach harden once more when the mother asked, "Goddess, have you seen Antonio?"

Azazel sighed and placed her hand gently on the woman's shoulder, and when she saw her fingers start to subtly glow, she quietly mumbled, "Antonio won't be coming back; he's dead."

She watched as his mother's eyes widened, and she asked, "What do you mean?"

Azazel looked her in the eyes. "There was an accident in the palace. He was injured when overseeing the renovations in my chamber; he passed almost immediately."

She lifted her hand from the old woman's shoulder as she watched her process the news.

"Oh, alright. Thank you for telling me, Goddess."

"I'm sorry for your loss."

She pulled Antonio's mother in for a hug, and before parting ways, she whispered, "I promise I will take care of you and your family."

The woman nodded and walked away from Azazel. Azazel continued to watch the woman until she was completely inside the arena once more. When she thought of how the woman looked at her—and even though she was helping her cope with her touch—Azazel still saw the hint of sadness in her eyes. She genuinely wanted the family to heal and move forward with their lives; she would make sure that they felt everything they needed to so they could get through their grieving period.

As the palace came into view, she decided she would have the funeral in the flower garden, and have all the flower arrangements come from the palace grounds. When she saw the first servant available, she requested that the maid gather several other servants and start putting together elaborate arrangements for Antonio. When the maid gasped at the news, Azazel quickly told her to carry on with her orders as Azazel walked past her to go into the kitchen to request a special meal for the funeral luncheon. She was shocked to see that only the chef was in there.

When the chef saw her, he straightened up and attempted to make it look like he was busy. She held her hand up and said, "There will be no need for that. I am here because I am going to need a special lunch made for Antonio's funeral; it is planned for the day the Cunning ends. I want you to contact his family to find out his favorite meals. I want it as personal as possible."

The chef bowed quickly and replied, "Yes, Goddess. "

Azazel nodded at him and turned to leave the kitchen. She was almost run over by several other maids with arms full of flowers running past her.

And when she got back to her room, she closed the door behind her. The air felt heavy in the room, like it was missing something. She continued into the wardrobe and caught a glimpse of her reflection in the mirror. She was still wearing Antonio's necklace. It had become so much of her that she had forgotten to take it off.

She touched the necklace and felt overwhelmed with a sense of pure, radiant love. This caused Azazel to crumble with emotion onto the floor. She felt like her lungs had collapsed, and the sounds coming out of her resembled meek shrieks of grief. As hard as she tried to push him out of her head, Azazel loved Antonio, and not having him around anymore would hurt for a long time.

She wasn't sure how long she sat on the floor and cried

over the sweet moments with him. She was angry that she didn't think about her choice rationally before she killed him; it was like she was starting to lose control over her hunger.

Eventually, she heard a knock on the door. She sighed as she heard the footsteps approach; she knew exactly who it was.

She yelled out, "In the closet, Mulligan!"

Mulligan poked his head into the closet and said, "Goddess, you're requested at the atrium. They are running out of space in the freezer."

Before she could reply or even think, she was walking out of the closet; she suddenly felt like she hadn't eaten in a millennium. Her body felt deprived, aching, and desperate while her emotions over Antonio had stopped completely; she wanted—no, needed—to feed.

24

Mulligan followed Azazel out of the room, and while he was speaking to her, she heard none of it. She smelled death, and she only wanted to follow the sweet-scented trail in front of her. As she walked through the streets, a few people witnessed Azazel's eyes go white, and her cheeks started to sink in while her usually curvaceous body withered away to nothing but a skin-covered skeleton. As they recoiled in horror, Mulligan looked out at the people, who all ran away from her. He sighed, knowing they were about to approach a tipping point in Azazel's divine cycle. She was entering a phase where she was no longer able to keep the kingdom in the dark about her needs.

He had seen her enter this phase twice since he'd started working at the palace. It was always terrifying, and she was usually able to pull herself back from the brink of insanity, but this year seemed different. *She* was different. He didn't think she would ever *kill* Antonio, and now they were planning a funeral for him!

As they got closer to the atrium, Azazel started to run toward it, a low growl coming from the depth of her throat that sounded like thunder in the distance. Mulligan stopped before they got to the arena door; he hated seeing her go through the absorption process. He looked around as the spectators came out and watched the fallen angel in shock. Damage control *must* be done.

While Mulligan tried to calm the humans down, Azazel ran through the halls until she reached the giant walk-in freezer, close to the combatants' sleeping quarters. Upon opening the large sliding door, she saw forty bodies waiting for her, and she rushed inside.

One by one, she quickly snapped each of their necks; the sound of each one giving way was comparable to an appetizer. She began to walk around, waiting for the glorious moment, but she didn't have to wait long. Almost as if they were drawn to her, the life essence orbs started to all float up out of the combatants' bodies and lingered in the air before they could go any further. Azazel opened her mouth wide, dislocating her jaw, and started to inhale with such a force that all of the orbs from around the freezer were brought in to her inhalation vortex, and she absorbed them all at once.

She shuddered as her body began to fill out once more, and her curves returned. Her hair was once again luxurious and silky, and the last bits of the rejuvenation process started to take effect. Once she felt complete, Azazel looked around and said, "Thank you for your sacrifice."

She turned to step over a body lying behind her to leave the freezer. When she came back out, several staff members had blank, distant looks on their faces as they watched her walk past them.

Before she turned the corner, Azazel called out, "You're going to need a mop and a lot of bleach!"

Azazel walked out of the atrium and saw Mulligan in a seemingly intense conversation with some of the citizens, who all looked quite frightened when they saw her approaching. They bowed and quickly stepped away from her as she got closer to Mulligan.

When he turned around to greet her, she asked, "Where are they going, Mulligan?"

He looked over his shoulder, and then said, "Oh, they just wanted to get back to the Cunning."

"And we are still scheduled to have Antonio's funeral in the garden tomorrow?"

Mulligan looked sad as he nodded slowly and replied, "Yes, Goddess."

"Mulligan, smile! Antonio would have loved that everyone's attention is on him."

"Antonio would have rather been alive, Goddess…"

This caused Azazel to whirl around and rush back toward him threateningly as she seethed, "Antonio is lucky that I didn't just leave him for you to throw away like last night's trash. He's closer to me than any human will ever understand until the end of time. Trust me when I tell you that it's an honor for Antonio to be where he is right now, and I suggest you change your tone."

"Yes, Goddess."

Azazel stared at him for a moment before she started to walk back to the palace. Mulligan chose to hang around and attempt more damage control in the kingdom. She stormed through the hallways, fuming over Mulligan's audacity! Servants jumped out of her way as she marched through the corridors until she reached the back door leading to the garden.

As she stepped down onto the deck to open the door, the memory of Antonio meeting her there flashing in her mind, she paused as she grabbed onto the doorknob. She expected herself to crumble like before; when nothing happened, she shrugged and walked out to see numerous extravagant bouquets of blooming flowers placed all around the garden, with a large portrait of Antonio in the middle.

The closer she walked toward the portrait, the more love she felt, no longer carrying the guilt of killing someone she loved. Azazel knew that if Antonio truly loved her, he would be excited, happy even, to be a part of her. He really *was* in a better place, and Azazel felt like Mulligan didn't know what he was talking about. He would *never* know what she felt.

She stared at the portrait and was overwhelmed with gratitude for their time together and the things he showed her. Azazel would always hold a special place in her heart for him, and as she delicately touched his portrait, she whispered "Thank you, Antonio." She finally felt at peace with everything and was ready to rest until she was needed at the atrium again.

Walking back into the palace, she was filled with happiness and strolled to her bedroom with a light heart. Once she had changed and slipped between the sheets, Azazel leaned back onto the thick, plush pillows beckoning sleep to come to her. She shut her eyes and waited for an eternity before she was lost in a dreamland, plummeting into one that was more of a memory, reunited with her sisters during a time of despair and turmoil.

The Earth had gone through a recent shift, and half of the world was in a depression. Azazel and her sisters were sent to Earth to balance it; God thought that perhaps the three of them would be able to put everything back on the right track.

When they got to Earth, they saw how bad it indeed was. God had made it seem like it was going to be a simple task! Azazel saw starving children on the streets, crying out for their mothers who had abandoned them weeks ago in search of work and never returned.

There was so much pain in the world that the sisters came to the conclusion that God needed to intervene; He needed to save these poor sheep who cried out for Him in their prayers. When they returned to Heaven to tell Him that, He simply laughed and replied, "It's all part of my plan."

This angered Azazel. "How could making them suffer be part of your plan?!" she screamed in desperation. "You're supposed to be an all-loving God!" Her sisters had to hold her back as she crumbled with her belief in Him.

Her sisters held her as she wailed. The feeling of betrayal from her father left a dark stain on her soul, leaving her feeling empty and hopeless. When they were commanded to go back to Earth and guide the humans back to religion, prayer, and God, Azazel asked why they couldn't just help the humans develop new skills. Again, this caused God to laugh and spit at her, telling her that she was just an angel. She was created to do *His* bidding, not to think.

Her sisters pulled her away from God's presence gently, whispering that it would be okay, and they would find a way to help. Before they left Heaven, they vowed to support the humans anyway and every way they could, regardless of what God said.

Azazel woke up abruptly, her face drenched with tears and her heart pounding furiously; it felt so real. She looked down at her arm, and there was a red handprint where her sister had grabbed her. It was real; she knew it was!

Azazel looked around her room and called out, "Natalia? Raziel?"

She wasn't sure what to expect, but it wasn't just a dream. It certainly didn't feel like it! Once her breathing slowed down, she leaned back against the pillows again, wishing for dreamless and restful sleep. This time, she was back in Antonio's arms in their haven on the other side of the palace, happy, in love, and tucked away from the world. This was the Heaven that Azazel wanted to live in for eternity.

His kisses felt so soft on her skin, but when he looked up at her, his face was decaying, and his eyes were milky white, filled with death. Azazel woke up once more and screamed. She looked around and howled, "I will *not* feel bad about his death!"

She tried to force herself to stop her tears. Her mind went silent, but a small voice in the back of her head told her to just give in. Azazel looked around the room again in desperation. She was confused about what was happening to her and thought that maybe a bath would help her relax again. She pulled herself out of bed and walked into the bathroom. When she looked at herself in the mirror, she shrieked when she saw her reflection. She looked like she was dead! Her skin was loosely hanging on her frame, and her eyes were sunken in.

When Azazel lifted her shirt up, she counted every rib. When she looked up at her reflection, she heard, "I can make this all go away."

Azazel shook her head and replied, "Stop! You're not real!"

Her reflection said back to her, "I'm very real. I'm you." Then suddenly, the reflection's face started to morph into something that resembled a decaying body.

She took a step back and screamed in horror as the reflection continued, "I can make this all go away. I can make your pain—your guilt—all go away. All you have to do is give up control; no one will even notice a difference. Aren't you tired of feeling sad about Antonio?"

Azazel stared at herself and thought for a bit before asking, "You can take it away?"

The reflection nodded and replied, "You'll feel like you've slept for a hundred years and won't even remember him."

She didn't want to, but every part of her told her that she

needed to give in; she needed to forget. She looked down at her decaying hands and whispered, "Okay."

Azazel screamed as she felt something frigid course through her veins; she felt herself falling, and everything went black.

25

Mulligan found Azazel on the floor. He noticed how thin and frail she looked, and he rushed over to help her stand up once she started to regain consciousness. When she looked up at him, he was taken back by how milky her eyes looked. Azazel seemed drowsy and out of it.

He helped her up and asked, "Goddess, are you alright?"

She snapped back, "Yes, Mulligan! Nothing you need to worry about."

He nodded and replied, "Right, I'm sorry, Goddess, but a full freezer is waiting for you at the atrium."

Azazel stood up and walked through the closet to go feast once more.

Mulligan had sent out a kingdom-wide announcement, stating that Azazel wasn't feeling like herself, and for everyone to avoid her at all costs. He knew that there would be at least two more after this feast before she would return to a state of peacefulness. She would surely have eaten her fill by then.

Her appearance and demeanor were starting to worry him; however, she had reached a new level of her hunger, and he wasn't sure what else he could do to satisfy her. He remembered tales passed down through his family about her; he knew what she was like when she first fell on Earth.

There were grand feasts weekly, and the population had significantly depleted because of her divine needs. No one knew what had happened, but one day, she became a softer version of herself and only requested sacrifices once a year. She called it the Cunning.

He knew that only a few families knew the truth; all of the elite families knew, and staff members who were generational workers at the palace knew what she indeed was. It still shocked him that Azazel had killed Antonio, though.

Mulligan became sad when he thought of all the people lost to Azazel's divinity; he thought of the young combatants who had only known how to train for a cause that no human could ever understand. As Mulligan reached the front of the palace and saw that Azazel was already coming back toward him, he asked if she'd had a good feast, and she nodded.

Before she walked past him completely, she said, "Mulligan, I want you to bring the tradesmen back. I noticed some chipped tiles in the basement chamber."

He stared at her and whispered, "All of them?"

"All of them."

He didn't say anything more as she left him standing in the doorway. He watched as she walked slowly back to her personal chamber, and it looked like she was floating across the floor. He wasn't sure what to make of it, but Mulligan felt something shift in the kingdom for the worse, and he had no idea how to fix it. He knew what was in store for the tradesmen and was angry that he would have to lure them back here. It was already an incredible hassle to get them to keep their mouths shut after the first abduction. And Azazel thought they were going to come back quickly? Regardless of what he told her, each tradesman told him not to call them back unless it was an emergency, and Mulligan knew this would *not* be an emergency. He sighed and started to walk down the steps to go to the shops.

Azazel slowly walked back to her chamber. She could only think of having a bath. She felt the stench of death lingering around her, and she wanted to rid herself of it. She filled the tub with boiling water. Before letting it cool down even for a minute, she stepped into the tub. She lowered herself down into the depth of the liquid. The scalding water started to bubble around her.

Azazel leaned against the back of the tub and went over the meals that she had just devoured while also looking forward to meeting the substantial, burly tradesmen. They had gotten away from her before. But she promised herself that they would not be so lucky this time, and she would put her beautiful chamber to good use as a way of thanking them for their excellent craftsmanship. Azazel smiled; it was the least she could do after keeping them in the dark about the true purpose.

She hoped that Mulligan would hurry with this request; the hunger wasn't patient and would hold him responsible for every minute that it had to wait. She looked around the room and sighed. She figured it was time to get out of the bath and tend to her kingdom. She stood up, and as she stood up, she heard a knock on the door.

Azazel stepped out of the tub and wrapped herself in a large towel before walking out into her room. When she opened the door, Mulligan was standing in the hall, and he whispered, "Downstairs." Azazel smiled widely at him and walked out the door.

He asked, "Goddess, won't you dress first?"

She unraveled the towel from her body and dropped it to the floor, continuing through the halls naked, causing Mulligan to realize that she was far beyond his help. As she turned the corner, he whispered a prayer to a god whom he was sure had abandoned all who lived in the kingdom.

Azazel walked through the halls, oblivious to everyone's shocked reaction to her. When she reached the basement, she heard the men's screams coming from the chamber, and their fear filled the entire basement with a sweet scent that resembled bait. She walked toward the room, and as she opened the door, the screaming stopped, and the men all rushed toward the opening door in relief… just to pull back in fear when they realized who it was.

She slowly walked into the room and, in a low, raspy voice, said, "Gentlemen," which caused them to all push themselves to the far end of the room, all looking around and at each other. Like a lion stalking an innocent gazelle in the Serengeti, Azazel walked around the room's perimeter as they tried to move away from her.

She reached the part of the wall where the hidden shelves were, and she looked at the group of men to ask, "Besides the hidden shelves, is there anything else I should know about?"

Azazel pushed the wall in to reveal the weapons once more as they all shook their heads, and one of the burliest men in the group said, "Goddess, we did the work. Please, we have families!"

She looked at them with a devilish look as she asked, "What makes you think they aren't next?" As she picked up a large blade, the men all started to speak at once. Several rushed toward her before she held her hand up and stopped them in their tracks. The men behind them all stared in awe, and Azazel continued, "I am doing you all a favor by being naked and being the last beautiful woman that you'll ever get to see before you die, and all you can focus on is how you're locked in a room. You need to be grateful for the small things in your lives."

Azazel looked at the crowd, and a low growl came from the back of her throat as she lunged toward the group; the men all scattered, and one by one, she killed them, splattering their blood across the white tiles. The frozen men had no choice but to watch in horror as their partners were slaughtered violently.

Once the orbs started to float out of the bodies, Azazel went to the middle of the room and inhaled them all at once before turning to her last victims, who were all silently screaming and begging for salvation. Azazel walked toward them slowly, her naked body dripping blood, her hair completely saturated, making it look like she naturally had red locks of hair, and she had a psychotic, dead look in her eyes.

When she got closer to the men, she asked, "Do you know what I love the most?" When they didn't respond, she snickered and said, "Right, you can't talk. What I love the most is how much power human lives give me, how much beauty their blood gives me." As she started to circle them, she continued, "I was always powerful, but there's just something about a human's life source that puts my powers over the top."

She stabbed each man in the stomach and watched in glee as each one started to bleed out, but their screams were muted, and she walked around them again. "I also like how your sounds can be turned on and off." She watched as one man's eyes started to flutter shut, and she rushed over to help him collapse to the ground.

When she touched him, he was able to move again, but he groaned instead as he fell to the floor. Weakly, he reached for Azazel, who grabbed his hand—covered in blood—and started to lick his lifeblood off of his hand and fingers. He wheezed his last breath as she leaned down to start drinking the blood from the entry wound.

As she drank deeply from him, Azazel noticed his orb begin to poke through his lips. She smiled and let it float up toward ceiling to Heaven; she deemed him not worthy of spending an eternity with her for trying to attack her.

Azazel continued to drink the blood straight from the body until it stopped bleeding, and the body started to cave slightly from the pressure of her sucking blood through the gash. She looked up at the other men when she was done drinking and noticed that their eyes were shut. She stood up and pushed them over, making a loud thud. One by one, she watched as each orb floated up through the roof, away from her.

She knew she made the right choice when she went to drink more of one man's blood and recoiled in disgust when she tasted heavy nicotine and grease. Azazel stood up and looked at the bodies lying around her; she ran her hands up over her body, face, and through her hair, feeling like her entire body was on fire. She reveled in the delicious moment of finally achieving the prey she wanted, the prey that cost Antonio his life.

26

Azazel smiled when she thought of Antonio, remembering how scrumptious his last breath was. She started to walk to the door of the chamber, but was surprised when Mulligan opened it first. When he saw the crime scene that the chamber had become, his jaw dropped.

He looked at Azazel, and before he could say anything, she held a finger up and said, "It's your job, Mulligan. This room makes it as easy as possible for you." He looked back into the room, and she continued, "You should be thanking me for making your job easier, Mulligan. We have gone over how much I despise your ungrateful behavior."

He quietly thanked her and walked inside as she

continued away from the scene. Azazel's nose was filled with the blood's sticky, coppery scent, and she wanted to bask in it for as long as possible. She turned toward the chamber, and when she saw Mulligan starting to clean up, she called out, "Drain four of the bodies and bring the blood up to my chamber, quickly!"

He stopped and looked at her. "Bring the blood up to you for what, Goddess?"

"I need to bathe, Mulligan. It's been a messy morning."

She didn't wait for him to respond; she left the room again, slightly skipping through the halls back to her chamber. As she was about to enter, she saw a young butler who was utterly shocked to see her in her bloody state. She requested that he bring her some tea. He bowed and tried to avoid looking directly at her before he turned to go back to the kitchen.

Azazel flung the doors open and walked into the room; she felt a renewed sense of happiness and optimism. She felt like her energy was finally starting to go back to normal. When there was a quiet knock on the door, she shouted for them to come in, and the young butler brought in a large tray with a delicate light blue tea set. He set it down, still averting her gaze.

She noticed and smiled as she started to walk closer to him and asked, "Does the female body make you feel uncomfortable?"

He quickly shook his head, but still refused to look at her. Azazel then got even closer to him, inspected his face, and said in a low voice, "You are incredibly handsome."

"Um, is there anything else I can do for you, Goddess?"

She smiled warmly and replied, "I made a bit of a mess behind the couch. Could you please help me clean it?"

When the butler walked around the couch and didn't see a mess, he looked back at her and asked, "Where is the mess, Goddess?"

Azazel pointed toward the back. "It's a bit further; there was a bunch of glass just under the couch."

As he took a step forward, he triggered the trap door and dropped straight down the chute. The fallen angel giggled and yelled down, "Incoming, Mulligan!"

She heard the butler drop down to the chamber, and she quickly ran over to her bed, where she heard him screaming. Azazel didn't hear Mulligan, however, so she knew that would be a fun surprise for him later. As she enjoyed hearing the young man's screams, a knock sounded at her door, and she excitedly yelled for them to come in.

Mulligan struggled to get into the room with two large buckets before going back out to get more; she was excited to see him bring in six large buckets total. Azazel directed him to bring them into her bathroom and pour the liquid into the bathtub.

But he hesitated, and she glared at him. "Mulligan, pour the blood into the bathtub!"

He slowly began to move the buckets into the bathroom to complete his task. Once he was done, he came back out and said, "Goddess, it's ready."

When Azazel walked in, she saw that he had lit candles and even decorated the blood with flowers. "I always love when you go above and beyond for me, Mulligan." She stepped into the tub and shivered slightly before lowering herself into it. She sighed. "Mulligan, have you ever had something happen to you, and it just felt like it was the final piece of your life puzzle?" When he didn't reply, she continued, "Everyone who has been absorbed, there's been a reason for it. I keep all of you safe from the world outside of the kingdom's barrier."

Mulligan looked down and quietly whispered, "I'm sure many people would rather deal with a harsh world than know that they could be selected for slaughter."

She shot daggers at him with her eyes. "Don't ever think you're above them for a second, Mulligan."

"Goddess, if you're going to kill me, do it already. I'm tired of holding the weight of your secret. I'm tired of scrubbing blood from my hands, just to see it again later."

Azazel stared at him and sarcastically said, "Mulligan, it's so gross seeing you beg. Get out of my sight!"

As she turned her attention back to her bath, Mulligan left as quickly as possible. As he closed the main chamber door behind him, he looked at his hands to see that they were shaking. He continued to walk away from the chamber and attempted to calm himself down.

Azazel cupped some blood with her hands and poured it over her head, enjoying the warm liquid streaming down her face and through her hair. She leaned back against the tub and giggled at Mulligan's newfound confidence to confront her like that. She had never thought of absorbing Mulligan before; he had become the clean-up crew, and she needed him. But if he was going to continue being an insufferable dolt about her needs, she would find someone new to take his position.

Once the liquid started to get cold, Azazel drained the tub and replaced it with fresh, clean water. She continued to wash until she was rid of all the blood, and when she was finished, she got out of the tub and went into the closet to pick out a dress for the final day of the Cunning.

She decided on a ruby red gown, and there were no jewels or grandeur to the dress. It was perfect and straightforward, and she paired the gown with a pair of strappy stiletto heels that had studs all over the straps. She changed, and when she looked at the mirror one final time, she was incredibly pleased with the look. Azazel quickly left the room and ran to the makeup room, where Dante had just finished spreading out all the makeup he needed.

"I need something quick, pretty, and simple," she demanded.

Dante quickly got to work. When he was done, he revealed that he had simply accentuated her beautiful skin and eyes with neutral colors, a bright red lip, and a long pair of eyelashes. He then finished her look with straightened hair. Azazel was pleased enough with it and thanked him before quickly taking off once more.

She had noticed how quiet he had been throughout the entire process. She had noticed that more people were avoiding her as she walked closer to them but paid them no further attention. Azazel had bigger—tastier—things to focus on.

The atrium soon came into view, and she started to quicken her pace the closer she got. The smell of death grew stronger as she neared the building. Azazel threw the arena doors open and continued to the freezer to absorb the latest victims before taking her place in the spectator's box to watch the final five fight to the death. She was pleased to see the forest landscape replaced with a giant gladiator-like fighting stage, and all of the combatants were being herded into the middle of the arena.

Azazel saw they were all beaten, bruised, and a few looked very close to death. A bell sounded, and they all began to engage in extreme hand-to-hand combat. She found herself excited when two were instantly killed from their injuries, slowing them down. The final three all started taking turns attacking each other. Finally, one of them fell to the ground and was stabbed in the throat before the other two continued fighting intensely.

The spectators watched as the stronger of the two executed a maneuver that his opponent couldn't block, knocking his rival to the ground, and stabbing him shortly after. Azazel stood up and began to applaud the winner, and was surprised when he dragged his blade across his own throat. She stopped celebrating and watched as masked figures ran into the arena to try and save him.

One of the family members looked up at Azazel and shook his head. She sneered and said out loud, "There is no winner this year!"

She was greeted by several family members when she stepped down to the arena, who all tried to explain what happened, but she held her hands up and said, "There is no problem here; this is actually the best-case scenario."

The family members stopped talking, and a man with a bear face mask asked, "Goddess, what do you mean?"

Azazel turned to him and explained, "I don't need to give money away, and since we have Antonio's funeral this afternoon, we can add a simple eulogy at the end." She grinned at everyone standing around her and asked, "Am I wrong?"

All of them rushed to reassure her and agree that it was a good decision, even though Azazel could feel an awkwardness in the air.

However, she silently dismissed it. "I am counting on all of you to help finish clearing the arena, and bring the families of the chosen up to the palace for the funeral afterwards."

She smiled at everyone while they nodded in agreement and dutiful acknowledgment. Azazel left the arena to go to the freezer and wait for the final combatants to be brought down. While she waited, she closed her eyes and basked in the moments before the final absorption. It crossed her mind that, maybe, this level of feasting didn't need to come to an end.

Azazel's thoughts were interrupted by several masked members dragging in the final combatants. When they dropped the bodies at her feet, a woman with a mask in the shape of a lion said, "Goddess, there are still several combatants in the freezer. We will bring these final warriors to you."

27

When she reached the freezer for the last time, Azazel decided that she would take her time and thoroughly enjoy each of these absorptions, and she did. She slowly bled each one out and whispered her appreciation to each sacrificed warrior before she absorbed their life force. She didn't even notice the final five combatants who were brought in until she was almost done going through the initial freezer stock.

Once she had consumed all of the combatants, she looked around the freezer and felt complete. She knew that this event was a success; Azazel felt unstoppable, powerful, and completely recharged. She left the freezer, pleased that no one was outside waiting for her.

She continued to walk to the palace through the empty atrium; the atmosphere felt different. As she got closer to the palace, she heard music and distant chatter. Azazel smiled and figured that people were starting to gather in the garden for Antonio's funeral, and now, the combatants'. She glided through the halls to her chamber to change into a black gown; she wanted to look the part of a mourning monarch.

When she went into her closet, she picked out a long black velvet gown with a deep V-neck and long tight sleeves, pairing it with a simple pair of pumps. Azazel was ready. She twirled one last time in front of the mirror and left the room. The halls were empty, but she could smell something delicious wafting through the hallways. She followed the smell until she was at the side door. Azazel let herself out into the garden, and when the kingdom citizens saw that she was approaching them, they all broke off to go sit down.

The fallen angel made her way down the aisle until she was in front of the crowd; they quieted down and waited for her to speak. Before she started her speech, Azazel took a deep breath.

"Thank you, everyone, for being here today to celebrate the life of Antonio Barem. He was truly something remarkable, and the kingdom will feel his loss for generations to come." She looked for his mother as she said this. Azazel wanted her to know that she meant it with her heart and continued, "I know that while his shoes will be big and hard to fill, that as a community, we can all come together and make it through."

There was a pause, and she heard sniffles throughout the crowd. Azazel didn't see Mulligan anywhere when she scanned the crowd and briefly wondered where he was. "We are also here to mourn our fallen warriors. There was no winner in this year's Cunning. There will be no prize distributed, but we will have a moment of silence for the combatants." She read out the complete list of warriors. Once the final name was announced, everyone bowed their heads in respect and went silent.

After a short while, Azazel raised her head and loudly announced, "Okay, that concludes this year's Cunning. To honor Antonio, we will be taking part in an extravagant feast that my head chef has so kindly catered to Antonio's taste buds." She beamed when she saw the servants bring out platters of food that looked absolutely decadent, and she watched as the kingdom started to funnel out of the garden to follow the food.

Azazel turned to look at the portrait of Antonio once more. This time, she pulled it off the easel and walked toward the palace with it. She wanted to hang the picture in her chamber for when she needed to see his reassuring face.

When she entered, she stopped. Her senses were in overdrive, and she sensed that something was off. Azazel slowly walked deeper into her chamber and looked around.

"Hello?!" she called out.

When there was no response, she continued to her closet and placed the painting on the floor. And as she looked in the bathroom, she saw that her blood bath residue had been thoroughly cleaned up. Azazel turned back out of the bathroom and still couldn't shake the feeling that something was off. She didn't hear any screaming when she stepped closer to her bed.

"Mulligan!"

When he didn't come instantly, Azazel stormed out of her room. Every servant she came across, she would angrily ask them if they had seen Mulligan anywhere. They all said they hadn't seen him for quite some time.

She stomped down toward the basement; the eerie feeling followed her and intensified the closer she got to the chamber.

Azazel swung open the door, and she saw Mulligan sitting on a chair that she assumed he had dragged in with him. The butler was gone, and Azazel walked into the room and pointed around.

"You let another morsel free?" she asked casually.

Mulligan nodded and replied, "I'm tired, Goddess. I don't want to clean up your messes anymore; I'm tired of death."

Azazel laughed. "*I* say when you're done, Mulligan. Your family is nowhere near being done serving me."

Then she snapped her fingers. "Bring the butler back here now!"

But Mulligan stayed sitting down. He firmly replied, "I will no longer be doing your bidding, Azazel."

This caused Azazel to rush toward him, and she seethed into his ear. "That's 'Goddess' to you, every time you address me."

"You should just kill me for my insolence and constant insubordination, then."

She took a step back from him and asked, "You want to die that much?"

Mulligan nodded. "As long as I am away from you and your depraved version of reality."

"The life essence I absorb stays with me for eternity, Mulligan. You will never know true rest." He stared at her, and she asked, "Do you think your sacrifice will save the kingdom? Because it won't; it actually makes me want to start killing *more* people."

Mulligan's eyes widened. "Haven't you had enough? Haven't you killed enough people?

"It will *never* be enough. I could kill the entire kingdom and *still* be ravenous."

He shook his head. "Someone will stop you."

Azazel cackled. "Mulligan, I was banished from Heaven. *No one* is going to stop me. *No one* cares about this corner of the world, which is unfortunate for you and the rest of the meat suits outside of these walls."

He looked down at his hands and took a deep breath. "I

pray every night that someone better, more powerful, and more deserving will come and kill you. Every night, I pray for that to happen."

She quickly rushed toward him and slashed across his neck with her nails, blood gushing violently. She got close to his ear as she whispered, "I am going to make sure you *never* find peace, you pathetic gutter rat."

As he gurgled next to her, she saw his orb push out of his lips, and she maneuvered it so it lowered to the floor. She stepped on it until it shattered and popped. Mulligan's body jumped as she squashed it, and Azazel grinned devilishly.

"I've decided to move in another direction. Your services are no longer needed."

She looked at the body and moved it with ease to where the chute leading to the incinerator was. Azazel shoved Mulligan's body into the chute and watched as it fell down into darkness and shut the door.

She chuckled. "Maybe I can be my own clean-up crew; there will be much less complaining." Azazel continued out of the chamber, and as she approached the Great Hall, where all the citizens were, she felt her hunger start to bubble. She smiled; it was feeding time, and perfect timing to pluck a plump chicken from her livestock.

She strolled through the halls with such force and power that the wind accumulated around her and started to slam every window and door shut as she passed by them. When she reached the Great Hall, the atmosphere was filled with love, and people were telling stories of their fallen combatants and of Antonio.

Azazel looked around the room, and she yelled loudly, "Dinner time!"

The entire kingdom turned to her and watched in horror as she morphed into her skeletal state. Azazel lunged at the people closest to her, snapping their necks violently; this caused hundreds of people to flee out of the nearest doors in fear. She captured as many people as she could, killing as many as possible. Half of the kingdom was lying lifeless on the floor; it looked like it had been repainted red. And Azazel was in the middle of it all, greedily drinking the gushing blood from a young woman's neck, when she heard a *whooshing* sound.

Azazel turned around and saw a vision. Two figures were manifesting in front of her, and as she saw their faces start to become more apparent, she hissed and growled a sound that resembled something from the abyss of Hell.

With blood pouring from her mouth and covering her body, Azazel lunged toward the figures as Raziel spoke authoritatively.

"Sister, your bloody tyranny is done. That's enough."

To be continued…

PSYCHOPATHY

BOOK THREE OF THE DARK TRIAD
TRILOGY

Raziel and Natalia stood in horror as they watched their unhinged sister. The entire Great Hall looked like it had been repainted red, and countless bodies littered the floor. As she looked around, Raziel approached Azazel slowly as she drank from a citizen's neck, and as Raziel crouched down to the level of the ungodly version of her sister, she whispered.

"Sister, what have you done?"

Azazel brought her head up from the corpse's neck as she hissed.

"The hunger."

Raziel rolled her eyes and looked back at Natalia, shaking her head. Before Azazel could plunge back into her victim's body, Raziel snapped her fingers, causing Azazel to slump and fall unconscious.

Raziel stood up and strode over to Natalia, who was quietly walking around the room, inspecting the damage. "What can we do?" she asked.

Natalia sighed and replied, "I will see how bad the damage is in the kingdom. Can you ask around?"

Raziel nodded and quickly turned to leave the Great Hall. She walked by Azazel's body and felt sick as she saw how saturated her sister was with her kingdom's blood. Raziel felt sick to her stomach. It had been so long since she'd seen Azazel lose herself like this; she thought Azazel was finally in control of her hunger. Raziel sighed as she thought of the unnecessary death. She approached Azazel's chamber and could smell the stench of death. Raziel groaned as she opened the door and was immediately overwhelmed by the odor.

She grabbed her nose in disgust and scanned the room, looking for obvious signs, and when she found none, she walked into the room further. When she passed the couch, a glint of something caught her attention. And upon further inspection, she found that it was a latch. Raziel let go of her nose and looked closer, finding that the latch was attach to a trapdoor. She stepped aside and pulled, watching calmly as the floor fell through.

"Where do you lead?" Raziel asked out loud.

She stood up and strolled over to the bed before rummaging through the night stands. When she got to the table that was clearly on Azazel's side of the bed, Raziel was assassinated once again by the stench of decay. She looked at the floor and crouched down to look underneath the bed, and when she found nothing, she knew the smell was coming from the vent, and there was something beneath this room.

She sighed as she stood up. Her sister had been busy, and if it wasn't for a violent reason, Raziel would have been impressed. She left the bedroom and wandered the halls until she found herself in the basement—the death trail was strongest down here. Raziel came to a large room, and when she opened the door, she saw the streak of blood across the floor, and she could sense just how many men had lost their lives in this box. Fear, death, and hatred coated the entire room in a thick film, and Raziel felt heavy.

She closed the door and decided that she had seen enough to give a full report to Natalia. Leaving the basement, Raziel couldn't help but wonder how they had let it get to this point; Azazel looked like she had been spiraling for some time.

When Raziel found Natalia, she was in the garden, looking at a large portrait of an incredibly handsome man. Natalia turned to acknowledge her sister when she heard footsteps.

"The Cunning has taken place, and there was no elected winner. The projected winner took his own life after killing his opponent as some sort of political statement."

Raziel scoffed. "Why do humans always think their dramatic displays will trigger a chain of events that will end up changing the world for the better?"

Natalia softly said, "Sometimes they do. Other times, there are bigger things at play that they don't even know about. It's the price you pay as a mortal."

Raziel looked at the portrait. "He's quite handsome, isn't he?"

"Don't get your hopes up, Sister. He's dead."

"Shame." Raziel looked around the garden. "How did she get a garden this incredible?"

Natalia looked around before she answered. "I'm sure bones and blood played a big part in the growth."

The sisters left the blooming garden in silence and started to walk up the steps of the palace when Raziel said, "There's a murder chamber underneath her bedroom. It's been used several times."

Natalia sighed. "I'm not surprised. It's never a simple task with Azazel."

As Natalia began to walk faster up the stairs, Raziel sped up and asked, "What are we going to do with Azazel, Sister?"

Natalia stopped and looked at her. "The same thing we always do when she spirals. If anyone gets word of this and finds out what we're doing on Earth, you know He would send the archangels after us."

Raziel shuttered at the thought of Heaven's most ruthless soldiers.

Natalia continued, "Azazel has been off the leash for far too long, and now there are entire families who will never recover the generations lost."

Raziel agreed; Azazel *had* always been the more maniacal one. She sighed. "I'm going to move Azazel down to the chamber until she wakes up, and we can figure out what steps to take next."

Natalia nodded. "Once she's locked up, head back to the compound. I'm going to stay here for a while longer to try and salvage what I can of the kingdom."

After the fall, Raziel only had one thing on her mind: love. Every time she finished a cycle on Earth, the idea of *love* intrigued her. She had seen hundreds of plays and movies based on love, read countless books and poems describing the feelings that people have when they are falling for their heart's desire, and it sounded like the next best thing to Heaven, in Raziel's ears. While her sisters were looking for praise and power, Raziel wanted to retire on a plot of land and dive deeper into the world of love.

Nirvana was created when Raziel fell, the compound built on the holiest land in the depths of the Amazon rainforest. For the longest time, it was just Raziel preparing the compound. She sustainably built small cabins, large gardens, and greenhouses. By the time she had completed her work, the compound became an environmentally-sustainable oasis, and when she was pleased, Raziel slept for several weeks after.

Over time, word traveled by mouth that there was a community welcoming anyone looking to break free from societal norms and wanting to embrace their inner flame. People from all over the world came in search of free love. They lived in harmony with the other tribes that lived in the forest's depths, and had a strong relationship with the animals that called the jungle their home. In all her years of existence, Raziel had never felt the type of peace that she felt when the walls of Nirvana were erected.

While the people were free to come and leave as they pleased, once they felt the sense of community and the warm embrace of true freedom, no one wanted to. They lived their days working on the land, singing and dancing in the rain, and engaging in bacchanals that would cause Caligula to blush. There was no hatred, no despair, and no one ever needed to ask for anything because everything was already provided.

Raziel treasured her community and tried to shut off her thoughts before she landed on Earth. Whenever she thought of her sisters, a pang of guilt pulled at her heart; she knew they could only stay apart for so long before the darkness took over them. Over the years, Natalia stopped requesting that Raziel come to help immobilize Azazel, which was ideal for Raziel. Azazel's hunger scared her, and the damage she could cause left some of the deepest trauma that Raziel had ever experienced.

The Nirvana commune had fallen into a comfortable routine, one that Raziel was prepared to live with for the rest of eternity. Everyone was in love with each other and cared about the safety and well-being of the commune, doing their part to keep the balance. Once a week, they gathered together in Raziel's hut to talk about religious theology and discuss how their belief system could change the world for the better. Raziel taught lessons in free love and being one with nature, appreciating everything from the smallest creatures to things that seemed insignificant, like boulders or small pebbles.

While things were mainly foraged from the jungle and their own gardens, there were certain supplies that were needed from town. Once a month, a select few would venture into the closest city to get enough supplies for their pantry.

The city didn't bother them, and they didn't bother the city. While they walked the streets, they would busk to raise more money for their groceries and spread Raziel's message of free love. By the end of their visit, however, people were usually ready for them to go back into the jungle, although after some time, the locals were unable to pinpoint exactly where in the jungle they had come from.

While they were in the city, Raziel wouldn't worry about them and would sleep until they were back within the walls; they had all become so close that when they were gone, she felt like a part of herself was missing, a part she could only find in sleep. The night they returned, a large feast would take place, and they would celebrate the departed members' return for days. The commune was everything that Raziel wanted in life; she felt the most content when she was tangled up with her loves.

The only thing she couldn't ignore was the small and empty feeling in the deepest part of her body, and while she did feel love, Raziel always thought that she experienced it in a different way than the humans in her care did. Angels were created to carry out orders, not feel emotions, and regardless of how much she tried, Raziel couldn't fall in love with anyone. She just didn't feel connected to them.

With each passing year, the feeling became harder to ignore. She eventually reached a point in her leadership where she wanted to enforce rules that would benefit the entire community. Raziel saw how large the group was getting and knew that to maintain order, boundaries were a necessity. When gathered the community together in her cabin and laid the rules out, which included prohibiting violence, negativity, and monogamy.

Raziel came to the conclusion that because access to every person in the community was open, there wasn't a need for monogamy, and Raziel had gone through enough violent situations during her time of being on the front line of Heaven's most loyal defenders.

The Nirvanians were welcoming and open to the rules and had abided by them for centuries. The one thing that Raziel *wasn't* prepared for was the sting she felt when members of the community died. It left holes in her heart, and even when new members came looking for their Nirvana experience, it still wasn't enough to repair the woe that she felt for every lover she'd lost. While Raziel tried for millennia to fall helplessly and deeply in love, regardless of what she did, she could never achieve the exact feeling that she had always dreamed about. Most of the time, she just felt numb.

If she had it her way, she would have been forgotten. Raziel always felt like the responsibility of being an angel was too much, and rarely enjoyed going to Earth with her sisters. It always turned into some sort of battle, and by the time Raziel fell, she was beyond ready to leave Heaven and the tyranny that came with it. And while her sisters needed time to understand and cope with the Creator's decision, Raziel thrived in her exile.

And even when new people coming in to the compound became a rarity, she had grown to appreciate the community she had and realized that they were worth their weight in gold. They had all fallen into a comfortable way of living.

Everyone played their part, and Raziel kept intruders and malicious characters away from the compound with an invisible barrier around the outskirts. It cloaked the community from any sort of scanning devices, satellites, and even signals would be lost if explorers got too close.

It had gotten back to Raziel that locals had started to refer to their corner of the forest as the fauna *Devil's Triangle*. This brought Raziel much relief; it meant that people wouldn't look for a third fallen angel in case her sisters were ever discovered and overpowered. Over the years, Raziel stopped thinking of her sisters and focused on her own world. The longer she was on Earth, the less she cared about a search party coming for her or for her divinity. Eventually, people stopped wanting to leave, and babies started being born within the walls of Nirvana.

It truly *did* take a village to raise a child, and that's exactly what conspired. Raziel cherished every baby as if the infant were her own, and ensured that both the mother and child had everything they needed—plus more—to achieve the highest quality of life in the community.

At first, Raziel had concerns about the men in the community. But then she came to realize that all the men who had journeyed to Nirvana were a different breed of man, more in touch with their feminine side and did the work to close the toxic masculinity wound that so often took over men's lives. Each man cared for the children and allowed the women to heal themselves both physically and mentally. It was better than Heaven; it was a new kind of bliss, and Raziel wished that her sisters could have stayed and enjoyed it with her.

Raziel was brought out of her daydream by the sound of a ringing bell. She looked around and realized that she had been so deeply entrenched in her memories that she had completed the entire potato harvest without even paying it any attention. She smirked, pleased with her work. She turned to the baskets and picked them up to bring them inside. When she got closer, she heard her people singing, singing their praise and gratitude for her bringing them all together, for her choosing Earth over Heaven, and for her wanting Nirvana to rival Heaven in every way.

The people here experienced a love like nothing else, and they were in constant awe of her and what she could offer them in terms of leadership. They had their own beliefs in the commune; they didn't pray to the god that banished Raziel and her sisters. No, after years of restructuring the humans in her care, Raziel taught them to give thanks to the Universe, thanking the cosmos for blessing them with her and guiding them to Nirvana.

Even though she didn't need any kind of nourishment, the prayers revitalized any depleted energy, and Raziel felt ready to face her family, the people who made Nirvana otherworldly and truly a better Heaven. She walked through the large doors and greeted the community. They all erupted into thunderous applause when she walked to the front of the large room, waving at everyone and greeting anyone who ran up to her. The children ran around her in excitement and tried to pull her to where they were sitting. Even though she had never felt the deepness of being helplessly in love with someone, this type of love had its own kind of magic and was something Raziel would be eternally grateful for.

She looked around the room, trying to make eye contact with as many people as she could. Once the parents came to collect their children, she continued to the front of the crowd and held her hands up to signal that she wanted to speak. Raziel began explaining the upcoming harvest for the full moon that was due the following week. She explained that the adults would be partaking in their monthly moon ritual, and that the children were expected to be in bed and asleep long before then. Raziel made sure to wink at the small children, causing them to all start giggling in excitement and call out for her. Once they quieted down, Raziel mentioned that the wall at the south end of the compound looked like it was leaning, and immediately, several members of the group volunteered at once to fix it, making Raziel's heart swell with pride.

2

They all said a final prayer, and Raziel gave her blessing for everyone to begin their meals while she gathered her own plate and filled it before going to sit at one of the tables that had space for her. When she settled in, one of the members at the table—who worked in the kitchen—brought up that the pantry was starting to get low again. Raziel furrowed her brow, trying to remember the last time she had sent a scavenging crew into the city.

Once she had swallowed her food, she asked, "When was the last time we went into town?"

The kitchen hand, Ramona, replied, "Approximately six months ago."

Raziel nodded. "Okay, get a group of five people together

and leave tomorrow afternoon. We will move some things around and ensure that you're prepared."

Ramona nodded and asked, "What about the ritual?"

Raziel paused for a brief moment before she replied with a question of her own. "Do you think you'll be able to get everything we need in five days?"

Ramona looked around the table. "You think we'll be able to get *six months* of rations in five days?"

Raziel kept eating as if she didn't hear Ramona's question. Several minutes later, Raziel calmly said, "Ramona, if you feel like you're going to fail, you will. If you feel like you'll succeed, you will. If you want to get the proper amount of rations in the shortened time to make it back for the ritual, you will." She stood up and looked around the table. "I trust that you'll all be able to sort this out amongst yourselves."

Raziel walked through the aisles between the tables and stopped to talk to those who needed to. When she reached a table where several very pregnant women were eating fresh fruit, she stopped and took a seat.

"Hello, my vessels. How are we feeling today?" Raziel reached out and gently cupped the swollen belly of the woman beside her.

The woman smiled and inched closer to Raziel. "She's strong. She was kicking earlier." The woman moved Raziel's hands to where she felt the flutters earlier, as if the unborn baby sensed her. It wasn't very long before Raziel felt the small kicks of the life growing inside.

This caused Raziel to frown, and she looked up at the woman to say, "You're right, she *is* strong." Raziel continued to ask each woman how they were feeling and if they needed anything. Each one declined her offer until she got to the end of the table, where a blonde woman—who was approaching her due date very quickly—was avoiding eye contact.

Raziel approached her and grabbed her hand as she sat down beside her. "My sweet, beautiful Lily. What's wrong?"

Lily looked embarrassed. "I have been feeling… something. For the past day or so."

"You didn't tell anyone?"

Lily shook her head sheepishly. "I didn't want to worry anyone. I was sure that it was just gas or something, but I'm afraid the closer you came to me, the stronger the feelings have become."

As she finished her sentence, Lily let out a cry of pain, and Raziel recognized it at once. She looked around to find the midwife and instructed her to ready the birthing cabin. The expecting mothers all stood up as Raziel helped Lily from the table. As she stood, there was a wet *whooshing* sound, followed by the sound of it splattering all over the floor. Lily's water broke, and Raziel smiled. Lily looked up in fear. It was her first birth, and Raziel reassured her that she would be just fine as she guided her out of the dining hall.

They slowly walked the path to the birthing cabin that was tucked away in the quietest part of Nirvana. With every contraction, Raziel guided Lily through the pain with breathing exercises, and Lily cried out in pain as the contractions started to become increasingly aggressive. When they reached the cabin, Raziel opened the door to reveal a tranquil space, complete with a birthing pool, a view of the forest with the sun poking through the spaces between the branches, candles everywhere, and the sound of a harp being played from the corner of the cabin, giving a new meaning to serenity.

"Lily, you are about to embark on the most divine journey that any birth-giver can go on." Lily groaned, and Raziel quietly said, "Give yourself over to the pain, Lily. Birth is natural, and your body knows what to do. Stop fighting your body and let go."

Lily bobbed her head, and she asked through gasps, "Will it take long?"

Raziel and the midwife, Lorena, exchanged looks, and

Lorena jumped in. "The first one usually takes the longest, but it's the perfect time to connect with your foremothers and feel what each of them went through to bring each new person into the world. Ride the waves and give thanks to the Universe for providing you the opportunity to experience it."

Lily screamed, "I need drugs!"

Raziel remained calm, and Lorena replied, "It will be a long night if you think like that." She helped Raziel lead Lily over to the sitting area. There were books, toys, and other things to help relieve pain without any kind of pharmacological interference.

Raziel had faith in Lorena. She had over twenty years of midwife experience, and she even worked in the city's emergency department for ten years before that.

It had been several hours of labor contractions when Raziel heard a knock on the door. When she opened it, she was relieved to see that Ramona had brought a platter filled with food, and glasses with a pitcher of ice chips. Raziel graciously thanked her and brought everything inside to cut down on outside contamination until *after* the baby was born.

She brought the tray over and set it on the small table. She then put together a glass full of ice chips for Lily, who was now lying naked on the couch, covered only by a translucent sheet. When Raziel handed Lily the glass, it slipped through Lily's fingers and shattered all over the floor. Raziel looked at Lorena, who had a concerned look on her face and shook her head.

"The baby is breech," Lorena suddenly said when she took a look under the sheet.

Raziel shook her head and asked, "What do we do?"

Lorena ran her hand through her hair and replied, "I need to turn the baby around." She sheepishly looked at Raziel. "We need to sedate her. It's the humane thing to do; it's already too much stress on the baby and on Lily."

"It's your call, Lorena. It's what you're here for. Do your job."

Lorena jumped to action and rushed to the door. "I am going to the infirmary to get what we need. Keep Lily calm; that's the key here."

As she ran out the door, Lily watched her and desperately asked, "Where is she going?"

Raziel rushed to Lily's side, paying no attention to the glass shards all over the floor. She started to pat Lily's forehead to get rid of the sweat starting to form, and she noticed that Lily's breathing was shallow and her eyes were darting around the room.

Raziel started to speak in a soothing voice. "Lily, your baby is breech," she began. This caused Lily to sit up, and before she could panic, Raziel put her hand over Lily's chest, and as her hand started to glow, she looked deep into Lily's eyes and said, "Lily, you're going to be just fine. We are going to sedate you so you don't feel anything, but you need to stay calm. It's important that you control your breathing and focus on having a new baby soon." She raised her hand from Lily's chest, and Lily leaned back, her breaths slowing and her body slumping in relaxation.

When Lorena came back, Lily was almost asleep. Raziel was cleaning up the broken glass and ice, and made sure it was clear for Lorena to walk over. Lorena was able to administer the sedative, and as Lily began to drift off, Lorena quickly turned the baby back around and got Lily back on track, checking every half hour to ensure that the baby didn't turn around again.

Just as the sun was beginning to rise—while the moon was faintly still in the sky—a healthy baby girl came into the world, loudly announcing her arrival. Lily fell back, exhausted, as her body gave one final push. Raziel was the one to cut the umbilical cord and placed the freshly washed baby on her mother's chest.

Once the mother and child were wrapped up in warm blankets, Raziel approached Lily and asked, "What name have you decided on?"

Lily smiled and looked at the perfect new addition she held in her arms. "Oriana."

"It's beautiful; *she* is beautiful."

Raziel slipped out of the cabin, filled with a renewed sense of hope. She always found so much pride in herself watching babies being born, knowing this was all her doing. A new generation of Nirvanians filled Raziel with the love she so desired that she stopped missing Heaven when she figured out how much Earth had to offer her.

As Raziel walked through the field toward her cabin, she braced herself for the morning and what it offered her. The dew drops on the grass glistened, and the birds started to sing through the trees beyond the wall. It was a beautiful day to be born, and Raziel thought that a bouquet of flowers for Lily and Oriana would be the *perfect* way to welcome Oriana to Nirvana. It never brought her much joy. Nothing really ever did, except for true love, but she did it anyway.

She plastered on a straight face as she opened the door to her home. Her cabin. It was just small enough for her and contained a simple sitting area, a place to brew tea, and a large canopy bed at the back of the cabin that was surrounded by several large potted Monstera plants, soaking up the early morning sun. Raziel treasured her simple life and thrived on minimalism, unlike her overindulgent sisters.

Raziel threw her long blonde hair up into a messy bun on top of her head and secured her hair with two sticks that she made from a pair of branches found on the ground. When she looked at the small reflective mirror in front of her, she was pleased with her appearance and became excited to break the news of Oriana's arrival to the rest of the community.

When Raziel left her cabin, she stopped by her personal rose garden and picked the most beautifully-bloomed roses for Lily and Oriana. When she had a large bouquet of flowers, she continued toward the Main Hall, where the community would be waiting for their daily schedule. When Raziel rounded the corner to the front of the building, she was greeted by the sound of people whispering excitedly, and when they saw her, they stopped, and it felt like they were holding their breath as Raziel smiled widely and announced.

"It's a girl!" The community erupted in applause and celebration. "Today, we will be celebrating Oriana's birth with a grand feast... and also the departure of our foraging crew."

She looked to Ramona, who nodded, acknowledging that a crew had been procured. Raziel nodded back and dismissed everyone, looking forward to bringing them all together again and introducing Oriana to them all.

Raziel continued to the kitchen to get a glass vase for the bouquet. When she found one, she filled it with water and placed the flowers inside of it. After fluffing some of the blooms, Raziel made a simple breakfast for Lily, including fresh fruit with lots of chia and hemp seeds. It was the *perfect* meal to replenish Lily after the hard work she did the night before.

She gathered everything she needed, placed them on a platter, and walked out the back door to avoid anyone stopping her and prolonging Lily from eating. When she approached the birthing cabin again, she was overwhelmed with a sense of peace and optimism for the future. Oriana was the future of the compound, and Raziel knew that everyone in the community would work hard to ensure that she had the best possible upbringing.

When Raziel opened the door to the cabin, the inside was saturated with sunshine and peacefulness. Lily and Oriana were snuggling in bed at the back of the cabin. As Raziel approached the pair, she saw that Oriana was sleeping, and she was able to get a better look at the beautiful bundle. Her cheeks were plump, and her little thumb was brought up to her mouth as her eyes squeezed shut.

The look on Lily's face was one of gratitude when she saw what Raziel had in her hands. She mouthed her thanks as Raziel rested the platter near her and backed away again, trying to leave as quietly as possible. Before she left the cabin, she blew them a kiss and took the scene in once more. Raziel had never wanted children more than when she saw new babies being held by their mothers, still fresh to the world.

As she closed the door behind her, she heard her name being called, and she turned around to see a group of people walking toward her. She waved and started to sprint toward them.

When they met halfway across the field, one of the men, Troy, came forward and told her that there was a problem with the garden. Raziel's face darkened as she replied, "I was just there yesterday and saw nothing wrong."

Troy exchanged looks with the other people in the group and continued, "It looks like everything is now frozen. Half of the garden is ruined."

Raziel shook her head in disbelief. "That's impossible. It doesn't frost in Nirvana. I'll take a look, but stop wasting my time with nonsense."

She dismissed the group and turned her attention to the

large garden. When she approached the closest fruit trees and saw that they were indeed in rough shape, Raziel felt a strong shiver shoot up her spine. She paused and closed her eyes, relying on her other senses to weed out the intruder. Whatever it was, it was powerful enough to radiate through the barrier.

When she didn't feel anything, she focused back on the garden, and when she opened her eyes, the garden was back to its original lush and beautiful state. Raziel looked around at the garden and couldn't help but feel a bit uncomfortable. She quickly harvested some peaches to bring to the kitchen. When she walked into the industrial kitchen, it was quiet, and the community members were all circled around the island. Raziel brought the fresh fruit over and placed the basket down on the island.

"There's nothing wrong with the garden," she simply stated.

But then one of the chefs in the compound stepped forward and replied, "Troy told us that there wouldn't be any fruits or vegetables today."

Raziel raised a brow, and she sternly asked, "Is that so?" She tapped her fingernails on the hard surface. "Well, I guess Troy knows better than I do. And if any of you dare to agree with him over your leader, well, you're free to leave at any time."

She left the kitchen, fists clenched and brows furrowed, as she left her humans behind in shock. She rushed to the back part of Nirvana, which housed a large body of water that was home to fresh salmon and other types of crustaceans. As she got closer to the flowing stream, her frustration started to lessen, and with every glimmer of the shiny scales, Raziel returned to her peaceful demeanor.

Once she felt like she was back to normal, she backed away from the water. And when she turned around, she saw several of the community members hanging back. Raziel took a deep breath and realized that she had overreacted, though she still felt no sympathy for those behind her. The group all exchanged nervous looks when she approached them, and one of the members stepped forward.

Raziel stared at her for a minute before reaching out a hand. "What do you want, Sarah?"

Sarah cleared her throat and said, "The foraging team is preparing to leave. Ramona is eager to get everything stocked and back in time before the full moon."

"I'll be there shortly." Raziel strolled away from the group and went to sit down beside the water.

The group backed away from her, and as they walked away, Raziel could hear them mumbling amongst themselves but couldn't make out what they were saying. She focused on the sounds of the rushing water, the frogs in the distance, and the birds flying overhead.

When she finally felt grounded, Raziel let out a slow breath and felt herself finally relaxed. Standing up, she started to slowly walk to the gates, where all the village people had gathered to bid their farewell. She forced a smile on her face and approached them, and the closer she got, the quieter they became. Humans were shifting uncomfortably, and she could feel her agitation start to bubble.

What a bunch of pathetic weaklings…

Raziel tried to keep her emotions in check when she saw Ramona in the center of the group, shaking hands and exchanging departing words. When she spotted Raziel, Ramona broke away from the crowd and dropped to her knees in front of her leader, and she cautiously whispered, "I hope you don't mind. I moved things up because I wanted to ensure that we had enough time. I didn't want to disturb you."

Raziel sighed and crouched down in front of her most faithful follower, cupped her face in her hands, and she quietly whispered back, "Ramona, you have my blessing. Just don't screw it up." She stood up and pressed her hands together in prayer. "Please join me in a silent prayer for our brave foragers. May they return safely and with abundance."

The entire compound turned quiet as they all prayed. Raziel could feel the energy radiating off of the crowd, and she felt the overwhelming vibration of their prayers drifting into the Universe. She took a deep breath, feeling it nourish her entire being. She was lucky that all she needed to sustain her divinity was the energy that humans offered to the Universe when they prayed.

Once she felt like she was ready, she broke the silence. "Now get out of here. We'll all die if you don't." Raziel hollered at the foragers. Nervous chuckles erupted through the crowd, and Raziel watched them leave the large gates. She turned to the rest of the commune and loudly asked, "Shall we have a bonfire tonight? We have a new addition to welcome." She felt like something was off. Typically, the commune would share a last meal with the group before they left. Perhaps Ramona figured that with Raziel's mood, it would be best to leave sooner.

Raziel sighed at the thought of Ramona. She had been a part of the community for twenty years, coming to Nirvana as a bright-eyed teenager after running from an abusive household. Raziel had welcomed her with open arms and stepped into the maternal role that Ramona needed. In return, Ramona had shown nothing but dedication and faith to Raziel and her dreams of Nirvana's evolution. Ramona was the one community member whom Raziel could trust wholeheartedly; she was the only one to lead the excursion into the modern world.

As Raziel crossed the field again, she changed directions to go check on the garden once more. She wanted to be sure that things were indeed healthy, and perhaps, she had just been seeing things from the lack of sleep.

When she reached the garden, she was pleased to see that

everything was overflowing with growth again. She picked up a big, juicy tomato and was surprised by the size of it. But her mind was still confused from the morning's occurrence. She knew what she had seen, and other members of the community had seen the same thing.

4

It didn't make sense to her and was something that Raziel couldn't ignore. The entire time she had been in Nirvana, they never had anything but sunshine and the perfectly-timed rainstorm. She looked around her and noticed that none of the community members were anywhere near her. She then looked up at the sun's position and realized that they were probably all in the dining hall. Putting the tomato in her pocket, Raziel left the garden and walked toward the entrance.

As she got closer, she heard the hum of conversation, and a small smirk crept upon her face. Raziel knew she had some wounds to heal. These people depended on her to remain stable and level-headed; lashing out at them just reiterated that she wasn't above human emotions. She couldn't let them think that she had any sort of humanity in her; she had spent too much time convincing them that she was indeed a fallen angel.

Raziel was thrown back into memories of the early days of Nirvana. To convince the first generation of the commune members to join her, she had to spawn a magnificent rose garden before their very eyes to prove her divinity. She relished in the memory of the shocked smiles on her followers' faces. They had all dropped to their knees, asking for her forgiveness, treating her as if she were the Messiah himself, while she thrived on their love and the energy that they radiated.

But she also knew that she would be struck down if she continued with that narrative. Instead, she told the humans about her time in Heaven, and how she and her sisters wanted the people on Earth to have free will and to advance mankind so they wouldn't rely on the Creator so much. When the humans heard this, they became angry with the god whom they had prayed to, and they immediately renounced their faith in Him and followed Raziel instead. However, right now, she wasn't proving herself to be much better. She needed to make things right again. She *had* to gain their trust back.

When she walked into the hall, it turned silent instantly. Raziel felt her face fall, and she walked to the front of the room, feeling everyone's eyes on her. When she turned around to face them, she felt as if a spotlight was on her. Raziel cleared her throat and forced another smile as she looked around, trying to make eye contact with as many people as possible.

"I feel like I need to be open with all of you." She watched as people looked around. "This morning, I was a lesser form of myself. I had a poor reaction to something that I didn't understand, and truthfully, I *still* don't understand." She saw

Troy in the back of the room perk up as she continued. "The garden that morning really *did* look like it had been overtaken by frost. Troy didn't lie when he said that there wouldn't be any fruits and vegetables. I don't know exactly what happened between his check and mine, but when I had gone to inspect it, everything had returned to normal." She pulled the tomato out of her pocket, and the crowd murmured at the beauty of the fruit.

Raziel looked around and asked, "Will someone sacrifice their knife for a moment?" Several people rushed toward her, and she took a knife from a burly-looking man. She walked over to the closest table and gathered the crowd around her. "See, everything is just fine," she said as she sliced the tomato in half, expecting the plush red flesh to appear before her.

Instead, the inside was black and rotten! There were dozens of maggots pushing their way through the fruit. Raziel recoiled in disgust, and everyone gasped at the scene. Raziel looked around, and then back at the tomato in confusion. She stepped closer to it, and as everyone gathered around to get a better look, she had no answers.

Troy quickly came up to the front and stood beside her. "I don't know how this could've happened. It's like the Garden of Eden here," he said cautiously, and she glared at him.

"Never mention that place here!" she hissed, catching those close enough to hear off-guard.

Troy stared at his leader, and his voice dropped. "I am so sorry. I didn't realize there were prohibited terms." His mouth went into a straight line as he challenged her with his sarcastic words.

Raziel came closer to him. "That place has *nothing* on Nirvana. It's an insult to even begin to compare the two, and you will be sure to remember that." She gripped his arm and dug her nails straight into his skin, piercing just deep enough to get the message across. Troy gasped as Raziel brought him to her face, and she whispered, "Can you come to my cabin tonight? We have some things to discuss, one-on-one."

She smirked at him and released his arm as he nervously sputtered, "Yes, I think it's best if we discuss it privately."

Raziel looked back at the tomato. It had been a while since she'd seen anything like this, and it could only mean a few things—all of which were detrimental to their quiet way of life.

She took a deep breath and bellowed, "Perhaps we just need to move the garden! The soil may be tainted from producing so many wonderful things for us, all of which we should be grateful for. Perhaps we could say a prayer thanking the Earth for doing its work and providing us with the things we need to nourish our bodies properly."

Everyone began to whisper amongst themselves. Raziel could feel her frustration starting to creep up again. She clapped her hands loudly, and everyone's necks instantly snapped to look at her. In a calming voice, she said, "We are all going to carry about our days. We are going to move the garden to the east side of the compound. Thank the Earth for its service, and then we are going to celebrate the birth of Oriana. Is that clear?"

The crowd all nodded at the same time, none of them blinking or moving. Raziel grabbed the tomato and chucked it out of the closest window. She clapped her hands together loudly again and announced, "Let's eat!"

When she walked over to the serving table, she saw Troy staring at the spot where the tomato had been. Raziel could see that he was trying to figure out what had happened. She knew there would be a mental gap for everyone, but as long as they went back to normal and the whispering stopped, that's all she cared about.

Raziel grabbed a plate and made her way down the line to get her vegetarian macaroni. She then went over to a table at the back of the usually empty hall. It had a view of the forest behind the compound. As she sat down, she saw a flock of birds flying out of the trees. She ate in silence as she scanned the area, looking for other signs of what might have happened. Raziel felt her body tense, as if she were expecting something to happen or someone to come crashing through the wall.

Before she realized it, her plate was empty, and she stood up. As she turned around, most of the people had already left. Raziel was relieved that no one had approached her while she was deep in thought. She came to the conclusion that perhaps she needed to take a bit of downtime. Her grounding from earlier hadn't taken, and she realized that it had been more than a day since she had gotten any real sleep.

Walking away from the table, Raziel said to the closest kitchen worker, "Can you ensure that a full plate gets over to the birthing cabin? I bet our new mother needs something to fill her belly."

With a smile, the worker nodded enthusiastically. "Absolutely, I will deliver it myself!"

As Raziel walked to her own cabin, a loud crash got her attention, and she looked in the direction that it came from, pleased to see that the garden was being ripped up, and the surrounding gates and fences were being brought down. She was always impressed with the speed at which things were accomplished in Nirvana. The people who lived here were something remarkable.

When she opened the door to her cabin, she was met with the overwhelming scent of roses, feeling completely relaxed. She looked around at the soft light coming in through the windows and the serene setting, realizing that this was *exactly* what she needed. She walked across the room and threw herself face-first onto the bed.

She was asleep by the time she even hit the bed and fell into a dream that felt incredibly familiar. Raziel roamed the forest after landing on Earth, calling for her sisters with no response. She felt alone and like her search efforts were pointless. She called for God, begging for forgiveness, crying for Him and His light.

As she moved her shoulders, she screamed out in pain. The places where her wings once rested were now ugly, raised scars, but the excruciating agony from having her wings ripped from her was her only companion. Knowing that she could never return to the Kingdom of Heaven left her feeling lost and dark. As the sun fell, Raziel's fear increased with every crackle of leaves and snapping of twigs. She felt like she was being watched as she walked deeper into the forest, hoping to come across her sisters or someone who could help her.

When no one came to save her, and her sisters wouldn't answer, Raziel finally understood that she was all alone. She collapsed to her knees and let out a monstrous cry. Any animals that were around her quickly left the area, knowing that they were in the presence of something otherworldly.

The scene quickly morphed into a dark time. It had been about fifty years since the fall. The land started to rot, and the food tasted like ash. Raziel was summoned to help her sister after years of unanswered calls. They had come to the realization that one of the Creator's cruel punishments was that while they rested and kept each other's divinity in balance, if one slipped and started to take too much from Earth and from the cosmos, the other two would suffer for the shortcomings of the third. The kingdoms would wither, and they would lose their powers until they were able to come together to balance their divinity again.

The image of Azazel's face gushing blood and the countless bodies piled up while her hunger still wanted more was enough to wake Raziel up. She sat up and looked around, expecting to see blood covering both the walls and her own body, with an estranged look on a face standing beside her. When she realized that she was alone, Raziel sighed in relief.

It had been so long since she had dreamt of her sisters, of their fall, and of the newfound punishments they now had to live with. She sat up and rubbed her head, knowing that it was coming. Azazel's hunger would *never* be squashed, and it was almost due for another reset. Raziel let out a groan when she thought of Azazel. In Heaven and in her service, hunger had never been something they had to deal with.

They weren't exactly sure what initiated the insatiable need, but when they finally figured out that she needed to be stopped, Azazel had taken out the majority of her kingdom, only leaving six families, and even then, they were thinned out. The first time, they made her sleep for a hundred years so the kingdom could replenish itself. Raziel and Natalia took turns checking in with the kingdom and made the decisions that needed to be made. Azazel still had no recollection of that ever happening; she thought she only slept for one night, which worked in everyone's favor.

Raziel stood up; she hated thinking of her sisters and the responsibility that came with being divine beings on Earth. Part of her wished that they had just followed orders and stayed in Heaven. She looked around her cabin, aggravated that her dreams had been plagued by Azazel.

She decided that she needed to rest longer that night and look for a medicinal solution, knowing that if another reset was coming, she would need to be as rested as possible. She changed into a flowy bright yellow dress, figuring that the bright color would help brighten her day and help her get into a celebratory mood.

She walked out of the cabin and could see that a giant pyramid of wood was built for the bonfire. Raziel felt her heart start to warm and become overwhelmed with love when she thought of Oriana's entrance into the world. It was so raw and was one of the only times they were able to tap into their divine powers, and she was always so intrigued by it.

As she approached the pyramid, she heard her name being called. She turned around to see Troy coming toward her, and he was walking with quite a bit of speed.

When he got close enough, he roughly asked, "Where have you been?"

Raziel's brow furrowed, and she replied, "None of your business. What do you want, Troy?"

Troy bowed. "I've just noticed that you're rarely around to help with the heavy lifting, and I need to be honest. It's kind of a crappy personality trait to have. Laziness."

Raziel turned her head slowly and titled it, finding the right words. "Laziness? I built this entire compound before your parents were even born, before your family even immigrated here, by myself, getting it ready, perfect!" Her tone became harsh and sharp, causing Troy to look around. She took a step closer and whispered, "Come with me, Troy. I think it's time we solve this issue once and for all. Don't you?"

He anxiously nodded, following her as she turned to go back into the cabin. She led him past the small building and into the rose garden. He looked around. "I have never been back here before."

Raziel smirked. "I tend to keep this place for myself, my own oasis within an oasis." She motioned around her and continued, "I have a secret to getting these magnificent roses. Would you like to know how?" She glared at him.

If he had looked at her instead of inspecting the roses, he would have seen the psychotic look that had taken over her face. When Troy finally looked back at her, Raziel put her hand on his forehead and gripped both sides of his head. She began to absorb his life force, and the more she took, the more his body shrunk down to bones, and eventually, Troy became a shell of what he used to be.

Once the body collapsed to the ground, Raziel shivered as her body was replenished, and she felt as if she was new again. She quickly looked around, and when she realized that she was alone, she promptly dug up several of the rose bushes to reveal numerous dried-out, decomposing bodies inside the hole.

Raziel rolled Troy's husk into the hole and covered it with dirt and the rose bushes again. Once she was satisfied with her work, she quickly watered all of the roses and walked out of her garden. Her hair had become incredibly shiny, and her skin looked supple and youthful. She had forgotten the vitality that the human life force gave her. She hated killing humans; she loved all of them, but some just weren't capable of change and were more valuable as fertilizer for her rose garden instead of being released back into the outside world.

She knew she would need to come up with a story. There were many people who were with Troy up until he came to find her, knew that she was going to be the last to see him, and Raziel knew that questions would be raised.

When she saw the group outside of the dining hall, her worries subsided; they all loved her and would believe whatever she told them. They had also seen Troy challenge her repeatedly and would undoubtedly support her in whatever choice she made. Raziel could simply tell them that Troy opted to leave the commune, and she'd supported his choice, given they had been butting heads the last several days. She knew they would believe her and move on from their grief of never seeing Troy again.

Raziel smirked as she got closer to the crowd, and one of them noticed her approaching. They reached for her and pulled her into the middle of the group. Music began to play from behind them, and they all started dancing, giving their thanks to the Universe for the safe arrival of a new generation at Nirvana. The party went on late into the night, good food had been prepared, and everyone ate their fill, danced until their legs went weak, and laughed until their throats were raw. Raziel always loved these celebrations; it showed how much love humans were capable of, and would erase any knowledge of the horrible things that they were more likely to do if given a chance for a short amount of time.

When the new mother and baby had retired for the evening, the celebration took a deliciously wicked turn. Raziel got lost in the sea of caresses and fevered kisses until the first sun rays crept across the compound. When she opened her eyes, she felt at peace with the world and felt like she was surrounded by an impenetrable wall of love. Just as she'd always wanted.

5

As Raziel lifted arms and legs off of her, she quietly giggled, amused at how deep her lovers always slept afterward. She stood up and quietly walked away from the pile of people cuddling near the bonfire. As she approached the kitchen, the birds started to sing their morning tunes, and a light breeze brushed against her naked body. Raziel felt free. Any lingering regret about Troy had disappeared into the night.

She walked over to her head chef and kicked him hard. "Get up," she hissed. "The people need breakfast."

The chef quickly scurried up off the floor and rushed into the kitchen, throwing together a mountain of fruit and pancakes, which Raziel quickly snatched away from him. As she brought it out to the serving area, people were just starting to trickle in, all of them smiling at her.

"Come, eat!" she shouted to them. "I prepared this all by myself."

One of the men approaching her beamed. "It's hard work satisfying a goddess. Good morning." He took her hand and kissed it gently. Raziel felt her heart warm as she dragged a finger down his beard when he dropped her hand.

In the distance, a loud rumbling could be heard, and it perked Raziel up instantly.

"Shall we dance in the rain?" she exclaimed.

Numerous people eagerly agreed, and as she put her own plate together, her excitement started to creep in. Raziel loved the rain and felt like there was no other natural force that had the same power as a rainstorm. As they all finished their breakfast, the clouds began to open and pour down over the compound.

"Come! Let's go! Now!" she shouted at them.

Many people followed her out and spun around in the falling raindrops. Raziel held her arms out and tilted her head back, allowing herself to succumb to the sheer beauty of the storm. And almost as if it were queued, a bright bolt of lightning lit up the sky over them, causing Raziel to gawk at it.

"You see? The storm wants to dance, too! Keep going!" she bellowed, causing the other members of the group to increase their intensity.

The rain started to get heavier, challenging them to dare to stay outside. Once the thunder sounded like it was outside of the gates, Raziel finally ushered the group back inside, just in time for dinner. They all ran in and were met with plush towels to wrap around themselves. The rain outside looked like a water curtain outside the window; they all watched in awe as it moved the trees outside the walls.

"Have you seen Troy?" one of the kitchen maids asked as

she dropped some potatoes onto Raziel's plate during dinner.

Raziel faked a look of concern and replied, "I haven't seen him since yesterday."

"That's odd. He went to go talk to you. Are you saying he didn't even do that?"

Raziel shook her head. "Nope, I didn't see him at all." She made sure to force a look of concern as she looked around the room, pretending to look for him.

As the other people looked around the room also, and some ran into the kitchen, Raziel felt a pang of nervousness start to creep up in her stomach. There were murmurs floating through the crowd, and Raziel knew she needed to get on top of it.

She stood up and whistled. Everyone's heads turned to her, and she calmly said, "Perhaps Troy left. We hadn't been seeing eye-to-eye for some time, and maybe he thought it would be best for him to leave Nirvana. If that is truly the case, we will wish him nothing but the best for his future endeavors." The humans looked around at each other, and then back to Raziel with concern in their eyes. Raziel looked around and made eye contact with each of them. She could feel her eyes dilating as she said, "We wish Troy nothing but love and happiness outside of these walls."

In monotone voices, the entire room repeated, "We wish Troy nothing but love and happiness outside of these walls," as their pupils dilated twice as large as usual.

Raziel clapped her hands together and yelled, "Yes, exactly!"

The group started to shake their heads slightly before going back to their conversations.

As everyone settled back into their individual spots, Raziel sighed in relief. Now they could move on, Troy would become a distant memory, and no one would look for him until the foraging group came back. Raziel gripped the bridge of her nose. She had almost forgotten about the foraging group and knew they would look for Troy when they came back, or mention that they hadn't seen him in the city. But that was an issue for the future, and she didn't want to ruin the vibe that had taken over.

Raziel quickly wolfed down the rest of her dinner and rushed out into the rain, clasping a blanket over her, and ran toward her cabin. When she walked in, the blanket was thoroughly soaked, so she hung it over the garden fence. She glimpsed at the freshly dug-up rosebush and back up to the sky. She felt a sense of relief. The flowers would be well hydrated, and the compound wouldn't wonder about Troy.

But then she felt uneasy. It was unusually dark, and her senses were on full alert. She scanned the room and quietly said, "Natalia?"

Out of the darkest shadows, her sister stepped out into the limited light coming through the window. She scanned Raziel and raised her brow at her nakedness. Raziel grabbed a dry blanket that was slung over the small chair beside the door and wrapped it around herself.

"Sister, what are you doing here?"

Natalia looked at her nails to admire them and said, "Did you not get my message?"

"Your… message?"

She looked around, and Natalia sneered. "I killed your garden for the better part of a day, Sister. Do you not check your garden daily?"

Raziel rolled her eyes. "That was you?"

Natalia slowly clapped. "Very good, Sister. Well done, you solved the mystery."

Raziel scrunched her face. "You don't need to be like that."

Natalia dramatically sat down on the bed, and she said, "You know what's coming up, don't you?"

Raziel nodded. "Yes, I can feel her hunger."

"We need to make sure that it doesn't get as bad as last

time. I don't think her kingdom could recuperate like it did before. It's already incredibly thinned out."

Raziel listened, cautiously asking, "Has Azazel built her chamber yet?"

Natalia shrugged. "I don't think so. Her festival is taking place, and they are due to choose the sacrifices in the next several days."

Raziel sighed. "But that is what triggers it."

"True, but if we stay ahead of it, perhaps she wouldn't want to build her chamber again."

Raziel looked at her skeptically. "It's Azazel. She will *always* have a want—a need for that death chamber."

Natalia scoffed. "What does it matter to you? They are humans, vermin that can reproduce effortlessly." She looked at Raziel. A wicked smile came over her face. "Sister, don't tell me you've fallen in love with one."

Raziel quickly looked up at Natalia, "No, of course not!"

Natalia laughed. "Right, I almost forgot that you're incapable of love. It's all mimicked." Her cackle filled every corner of the small cabin. "Sister, I must admit, it's been a while since I have laughed like that. The thought of you trying to fall in love will *never* cease to be funny to me."

As she started to laugh again, Raziel stood up, angry. "Natalia, you're on your own this time. I want to be left alone."

Natalia stopped laughing, stood up, and walked over to stand in front of Raziel. She placed her hand on Raziel's shoulder. "Sister, true love is true pain. I promise you that you're not missing anything. You're quite blessed that you can't feel true love. You'd never survive it."

Raziel shrugged her sister's hand off of her and quietly said, "You know nothing. I've seen humans fall in love and can feel the energy that it radiates. It's the only thing that matters." She could feel tears starting to fill her eyes, and she turned her face away.

But Natalia turned Raziel's head back to face her. "Sister, you know we need to do this together. I will keep an eye on Azazel, and when I return, you know it will be dire."

Raziel nodded, and when she looked back, Natalia was gone. She let a sigh out and sat down on the chair nearest to her. She hated how condescending Natalia was, and was always relieved when their interactions were over. Raziel thought of Azazel's kingdom and the people who lived there, knowing that some were about to sacrifice family members to appease her hunger. She felt sick.

She was angry that her sisters could feel love if they wanted to, but instead, they chose to treat their human charges as enslaved people and livestock. Regardless of how many times she brought up her concerns with them, they would brush them aside and tell her that she was crazy to want to live in peace with her humans.

The thought of Troy's withering body slowly crept its way back into her mind, and she felt sick. Was she *really* that much better than her sisters? She looked out the window in the direction of the rose garden, knowing how many bodies were buried underneath those bushes.

Raziel leaned back against the chair and let out a sigh. She *wasn't* better than her sisters, no matter how much she tried to convince herself that she was; the only difference was that she didn't give in to her divine primal needs unless she was angry enough to do so.

She shook her head, frustrated. Whenever Natalia came around, she always ended up questioning herself and what she was doing, even though her sisters literally consumed humans like they needed them in order to breathe. She stood up and walked over to the closet, pulling out a simple pink dress. She slipped it over her head and left the cabin and her insecurities behind.

The further Raziel walked from the cabin, the more at peace she felt, and before she walked into the maternity cabin, she took a deep breath and replaced her furrowed brow with a forced smile. She was ready for baby cuddles. But when she walked into the cabin, she was shocked to see a man standing there, holding the baby. Raziel looked from Lily to him, and realized that he was one of the builders in the community, Brian.

He turned around and drew a wide grin on his face. "She's beautiful, isn't she?" Then he looked back to the sleeping Oriana in his arms. Lily watched the scene, and Raziel could feel the intense emotions radiating from her.

Raziel blurted out, "You're the father?"

Brian and Lily both nodded, and Raziel asked, "With the events that go on around here, how can you be sure?"

Brian and Lily looked at each other nervously, then Lily responded. "We have never been intimate with other people."

Raziel felt her rage starting to bubble from the deepest parts of her body. "There are *no* monogamous relationships in Nirvana!"

Lily held her hand out. "We weren't going to say anything, and we aren't monogamous. We've... just never been intimate, or felt the need to be intimate, with anyone else."

Raziel glared at the two of them, and she seethed. "All three of you are leaving in the morning."

Lily gasped. "You can't be serious! You expect me to trek through the dense forest with a newborn baby?!"

Raziel shrugged and carelessly said, "Sounds like you have everything you need within each other. You no longer need Nirvana. Get out!" And she turned to leave the cabin as quickly as she could.

As Raziel stood outside the door, she felt a strange feeling when her eyes started to overflow with tears filled with betrayal. She had given them *everything* that they could possibly ever want in life; why would they bring *monogamy* into the compound?

She walked away from the cabin, her entire head buzzing with everything that had just transpired. Between Natalia showing up and finding out that members of her commune were keeping themselves from other people, Raziel felt like she was losing control.

Lily's first day at Nirvana ran through Raziel's mind. She remembered how shy the young girl was, and how she used to jump to be the first one to do any task that needed to be done. For a small-framed woman, she was incredibly strong and resilient.

She shook her head and buckled down on her decision. The first rule every newcomer was told was that there was absolutely no monogamy. This was a free-loving community, and everyone was to engage with everyone else. Raziel saw hundreds of fireflies floating out of the forest, and they seemed to light a path for her. It helped her calm herself down by the time she reached her cabin. She was more than ready to sleep all night.

When she reached the front door, she paused before grabbing the doorknob. Half expecting her sister to be waiting for her on the other side, she cautiously opened the door and peeked around it. When she saw that she was alone, Raziel walked inside, slammed the door shut, and threw herself onto the bed. She closed her eyes and summoned sleep to come to her.

Natalia's words floated through her head; Raziel *had* felt like Azazel's reset was approaching. She felt the disturbance deep inside of her, and whenever the hunger was taking over, things in Nirvana became chaotic. Regardless of how many times Natalia and Raziel had tried, they couldn't figure out how Azazel's needs affected their domains. When Azazel was sleeping and was forced to stay still, things flourished, and Raziel thrived.

In her sleep, Raziel fell into a time when Nirvana was lush and full of life and love. Everyone was carefree, and the world seemed light and easy. The reset ritual came next, Natalia and Raziel holding hands, whispering an incantation in a language only angels could understand, and watched as Azazel glowed brighter than a star being birthed. And when the glow subsided, both Natalia and Raziel felt invigorated, as if they had just been touched by the hand of the Creator.

Images of past humans who had been thrown into the rose garden pit started to float around through the images of the reset, asking why they weren't worthy of life outside of Nirvana. Raziel pushed them aside, trying to get back to her good feeling. The faces started to fade and were replaced with a dark shadowy figure. Raziel could barely make out the face in the darkness, but she felt a fluttery feeling in her stomach. She felt safe and truly happy, something she had never really felt before.

When Raziel opened her eyes and saw that she had slept through the entire night, she frowned; she was curious about the figure who wouldn't leave her dreams. Whenever she saw those types of images in her dreams, it was usually an indication of something else to come. Raziel wouldn't know until it was happening, but it was something that she would start to look forward to. Perhaps it was an indication that new people would be called to find themselves in Nirvana, and whatever it was, Raziel was excited at the new prospect.

When she stepped out of the cabin, she was overtaken by the scent of the rose bushes. Raziel closed her eyes and took a deep breath; the scent could calm her down even on the most hectic days. They were her most prized possessions, and there were some that could be traced all the way back to the beginning of Nirvana, still producing the most beautiful blooms she had ever seen.

She walked slowly in the direction of the dining hall. She wasn't even halfway across the field when Sarah came running toward her, a look of horror on her face when she saw Raziel. When she got close enough, she desperately asked, "Lily, Brian, and Oriana left Nirvana this morning; why?"

Raziel looked at her, and she calmly asked, "What is rule number one here, Sarah?"

Sarah's face scrunched up in confusion. "But Lily and Brian weren't in a monogamous relationship, Raziel."

Raziel grabbed Sarah's arm and aggressively pulled her close as she hissed, "They admitted to only being intimate and enjoying each other. No one else was welcome. What does that sound like to you?"

Sarah's eyes started to water. "Why would you let them leave? They won't make it out of the forest alive!"

Raziel tilted her head and replied, "You make it sound like it's my problem when I was explicitly clear about the rules to living in Nirvana. If you don't agree, you're more than welcome to go after them. They may need an extra set of hands."

Raziel let Sarah's arm go, causing Sarah to slowly back away from her. "You're going to regret it," she spat as she pointed at Raziel before running away from her.

The fallen angel watched Sarah run away from her and felt that her morning was already ruined. "I just want one full day of peace and quiet. Why is that so hard?" No one was around to answer her, and she knew she would never get a sign, but she needed to ask it out loud.

Once she calmed herself down, Raziel decided that she no longer wanted to eat or see anyone, so she turned around and started walking toward the new garden location. Working in the soil always made her feel better, and she would be able to ground herself properly.

When she approached the garden, she was relieved to see that she was the only one there, and she grabbed one of the empty baskets, slowly filling it with fresh tomatoes. Raziel had harvested half of the first part of the garden before she stopped, hearing people approaching.

She turned around and called out, "I'm going to handle the garden today. Perhaps there are other jobs that need to be done. Maybe later, you can start pickling some of this harvest." She forced a smile toward them, but none of them returned it; they simply bowed and backed away from the garden.

Raziel continued to fill four more baskets with tomatoes. When she ran out of baskets, she started stacking them beside the garden, intending to get sacks to carry them into the kitchen. Before she knew it, the sun was over top of her, and she was covered in soil. Raziel fell to her knees and started to cry over Lily, Brian, and Oriana, and over the responsibility that she carried for Azazel. For the first time in a very long time, she fully allowed herself to succumb to her sadness. She collapsed onto the ground, tears watering the grass around her face. She gripped the ground, digging her nails in, begging for relief from the overwhelming pressure that she was feeling.

When she felt like she could no longer cry, she raised her head, and in the places where her tears had fallen, light pink flowers were starting to grow. Raziel looked at them, and when she picked one up, it died and fell apart in her fingers. She had never seen anything like it, and she looked around her, wondering if Natalia was behind it.

But instead of seeing her sister, she felt a breeze caress her face and bees buzzing around the flowers. The negative feeling soon subsided, and Raziel stood up, ready to face her community. The tiny flowers withered and retreated back into the ground beneath her as she stood on her feet. Raziel stared at the spot for a few moments, trying to figure out what was happening, until she realized how quiet it was. She looked around and didn't see anyone in the clearing or anywhere near the cabins. Nervousness crept up into her stomach. She grabbed two baskets and started to walk toward the kitchen, unsure of what she would find when she reached it.

6

As Raziel approached the building, she was relieved to hear laughter inside. When she opened the door, the group stopped and looked at her. Raziel could tell that they were bracing themselves for some sort of outburst. Instead, she gently placed the baskets on the island in front of her and smirked at them all.

She took a deep breath and calmly said, "I have harvested the entire garden. I will need some help bringing them all in, but we also have a large task ahead of us, jarring and pickling after the ritual this weekend."

The kitchen staff exchanged looks. Sarah stepped forward to bring one of the baskets closer.

As she got close to Raziel, she quietly asked, "Are you okay? I'm here to listen if you need to talk, you know."

Raziel took Sarah's hand and responded, "That would be appreciated. Let's go sit by the water after lunch. I have so much weighing my heart down."

Sarah bowed. "Sure. Please come find me when you are ready."

Raziel nodded and backed out of the kitchen to retrieve the rest of the harvest, followed by several kitchen workers. They were all buzzing with excitement over the upcoming full moon and the abundance that it was already bringing to Nirvana.

If only her people truly knew how much influence Raziel had on the abundance and well-being of Nirvana, they would change the ritual into a ritual for her and allow her to feed off of the energy that they radiated willingly. Raziel felt her mouth water when she thought of the power that could have been hers if she were just selfish enough to convince her followers to do so.

She sighed quietly and looked back. "This ritual is going to be special; it's the blood moon." Raziel thought of past rituals for the blood moon and felt herself indulging in the anticipation as well. She always looked forward to the full moon. It was the one time she felt truly connected to Earth and the people around her; the energy that radiated from the group was unmatched.

As they reached the garden, Raziel handed each person a basket and started to pile some of the fresh vegetables and fruits on top of it, and sent them on their way. As she grabbed the last basket, the remaining harvest could wait until after they ate their lunch. The group was already ahead of Raziel, and she could hear the low chatter as they returned to the kitchen.

She placed the basket outside and called in, "I'll be taking my lunch at the maternity cabin. Could someone bring me a plate?"

Someone shouted back that they would, and Raziel left the kitchen, her sadness increasing the closer she got to her destination. When she reached the cabin, she opened it and was surprised to see how clean everything was. Lily cared enough to ensure that there wasn't a trace of her before she left, and even made sure to fold up the bedsheets and other blankets that were dropped off for her.

Raziel felt a pit in her stomach, wondering if she had indeed crossed a line by banishing them. She fell to the ground and was bombarded with the memory of welcoming Oriana into the world, how scared Lily was, and the way she looked to Raziel to be her source of comfort. She wiped a tear from her eye as she remembered the first time she saw Oriana and how absolutely perfect she was.

When she looked through the window and saw birds flying across the branches, she thought that perhaps the one way she would be able to feel true love like Lily and Brian was if she allowed monogamy into the compound. Raziel let her head fall back as she closed her eyes; knowing that she wouldn't be having these thoughts if it weren't for a good reason, she stood up and decided that she needed to go find them. She heard a soft knock at the door and got up to answer it. Sarah was standing on the other side of the door with a tray of food.

Raziel looked at her, and in a broken voice, she said, "I need to find Lily."

Sarah bowed and handed her the tray. "I know. We will go find them after you eat." She stepped into the cabin.

Raziel stepped aside so Sarah could fully enter the cabin. Once she was in, she shut the door with a free hand and brought the tray over to the small table off to the side of the large bed. Sitting down and starting to pick at the fruit, Sarah sucked air through her teeth. "Raziel, can I speak candidly?"

"Unburden your mind, Sarah, then I'll do the same."

Sarah took a deep breath before saying, "Brian and Lily aren't the only ones who have chosen to exhibit monogamy in Nirvana. They were just the only ones to have been caught." She watched Raziel's face as she continued, "We all love you, Raziel; whether you believe it or not, we are all incredibly devoted to you and your ideas. We are more than dedicated to enforcing the reality that you want to bring. Monogamy doesn't change any of that. We just want to be able to choose."

"Are there more people who are leaning toward this path?"

"Our feelings don't change for you, and we will do everything in our power to ensure that you never feel a lack of our love."

Raziel let out a long sigh. "I agree, Nirvana is not above change, and maybe it's time that we move forward and embrace free love and the choices that it brings. We will go search for them today, and when we return, we will have a community meeting and take a vote. I want everyone to have their say. I won't fight it, and I will embrace everyone and their choices with open arms."

Sarah stared at Raziel in disbelief; she whispered, "Really?"

"Get a group together. I will meet you at the gates shortly."

Sarah bowed and stood up to rush out of the cabin. Raziel felt as if a weight had been lifted, hoping that it would get rid of the negative fog that had been hovering around as of late. She sighed and pushed the half-eaten meal away from her. When she had first started Nirvana, she made it clear that everyone was to enjoy each other; never did she think that people would eventually want to couple up and move away from that lifestyle.

She felt a pang of jealousy start to boil deep inside of her.

She wanted to feel, truly feel, what the humans felt when they were falling in love with each other, and she wanted it for herself. Raziel was almost brought to tears, knowing that regardless of how hard she tried, she could never *truly* feel love. She sat there for a few moments as countless thoughts ran through her mind, memories of celebrations that she took part in, and the delicious entanglements that Nirvana took part in; she hoped that more people would opt to stay in an open lifestyle.

Standing up, Raziel felt that it was time to search for her beloved Lily and Oriana. She hadn't gotten to know Brian on a more personal level, but the work he did around Nirvana was impeccable, and he seemed incredibly genuine, from what she did know. When she stepped outside, the sun seemed to be shining brighter than before, and even the grass looked greener the longer she stared at it.

When she approached the gates, she was happy to see a group of people waiting for her. When they saw her approaching, they all waved and smiled widely at her. Raziel knew that when they found Lily, she would have an incredible amount of apologizing to do and hoped that Lily would find it in her heart to forgive her.

They opened the gates and walked into the dense rainforest on the beaten path leading out to the world. It had been decades since Raziel walked out of Nirvana, and the beauty the forest held made her regret it.

Monkeys were swinging through the trees above them as colorful birds sung their songs. Raziel took a deep breath in and was comforted by the thick, warm air; it felt like a hug. The group was quiet until they came to a fork in the path. Sarah looked back at Raziel, and she suggested that the group split up; one led into the city, and the other led to a water source deeper within the forest.

The group quickly split, and Raziel took half of them toward the water. As they got closer, they could hear the bugs buzzing and frogs croaking. When they reached the large waterfall, they gasped at the beauty it held; the water was ice blue and surrounded by lush, bright green fauna. Raziel looked around and basked in the beauty, suddenly grateful for the opportunity to come back out into the forest. The others in the group all wanted to cool off, so they all decided to hop into the waterfall's basin. Excited squeals erupted from the group as they realized how cold the water was, but once they adjusted, they shouted gratitude to the Universe for the blessing bestowed upon them.

After some time, the other search party found them, and when Raziel saw Sarah's face, she knew something was wrong. She lifted herself out of the water and ran over to the group, all of their faces white, and half of them looking like they were in shock.

Raziel looked at all of them and asked, "What happened? Did you find them?"

Sarah started sobbing and shook her head. "We found them, but…" She trailed off, and Raziel urged her to continue. Sarah barely got out, "They didn't make it."

Raziel shook her head and looked around at the group. "No, that can't be. They left during the day. They stayed on the path, right?"

One of the men, Kody, came forward, and he quietly said, "It looks like something attacked them. They didn't get close to the city; it was a brutal scene. We dug holes for them; that's why it took us so long to get back here."

Raziel grasped her face and shook her head in disbelief.

Sarah watched her leader, and she whispered, "See what happens when you act on your impulses; we are the ones who pay for it!"

Raziel shook her head. "We will honor them tonight with a funeral pyre."

The group looked at each other again.

Sarah asked in an angry voice, "You think that will

suffice?! Three people are *dead* because of your stupid rules. Take the vote now. Get everyone's opinions on what we talked about in the maternity cabin. Now!"

Raziel looked down at the ground; she quietly said, "Fine."

She motioned for the group to follow her to the waterfall, where the other half of the group was watching, curious as to what happened. When Raziel told them, they cried out, their sorrow deafening.

Raziel cleared her throat, and she loudly said, "Some rules are going to be changed. The first one is that if you want to be with one person only, you're free to. There are no rules when it comes to intimate relationships." This caused the group to gasp in surprise. Raziel continued, "The second new rule is that if someone is going to be banished, we are going to take a vote as a whole to see if anyone can come up with reasons as to why they should stay, and if they are deemed worthy reasons, they will be allowed to stay."

She looked at Sarah, who nodded in approval, and her arms were crossed over her body. When she looked up at Raziel, her eyes were filled with tears. Raziel felt guilty and now understood the weight of her actions. She knew that she may never know true human love, but she was finally starting to understand true human pain and loss. She didn't like it, and she wanted to avoid ever feeling it again.

The entire group silently made their way back to Nirvana, none of them in the mood to continue playing in the water. The air was heavy with sorrow, and Raziel wished she could take all of the pain away. She wasn't sure how she was going to tell the foragers what happened when they returned, just to go through the mourning process all over again.

As they walked through the gates, none of them spoke to Raziel, and she concluded that she would be building the funeral pyre herself. She was okay with it; she wanted to and wanted to put enough care into it so that Lily, Brian, and sweet Oriana felt how sorry she was wherever they were beyond the veil. While the group split off to break the news to the other members of the commune, Raziel went to a secluded shed in the back of the property that contained wood left over from other construction projects.

She single-handedly built a giant pyramid and found sweet grass to put inside of it. She then went to her rose garden and cut the majority of the flowers from the countless bushes, and created a garland long enough to wrap around the entire structure. When she was finished constructing the pyre, she took a step back and was pleased with her work. Raziel was sad that she had let her jealousy and anger make such impulsive decisions. While she constructed the pyre, she thought of the many years she shared with Lily and put the emotion that she knew as love into every bit of it.

She didn't hear the rest of the community approaching her as she was lost in her memories. Sarah gently placed her hand on Raziel's shoulder. She quietly said, "It's beautiful. Lily would have loved it. You took a step in the right direction today, and I'm proud of you for attempting to right your wrongs. You have to remember that we are a bit more fragile than you."

Raziel nodded, knowing she was right. In the grand scheme of things, human lives were always so delicate. She knew that this group of people was her responsibility, her children, and she needed to act accordingly. She looked around at her community as they wrapped their arms around each other, sobbing and calling Lily, Brian, and Oriana's names out.

The fire began to creep up the pyre, engulfing the entire structure in flames. The commune was quiet as they all watched the fire take over the pyramid, smoke billowing up to the blanket of stars watching them mourn their loss. Once the structure had dulled down and crumbled to ashes, the silence that followed was something that Raziel had never experienced before. While there were countless deaths at Nirvana, she had never felt the weight of loss like this. She looked around the group and made sure to take in each of their emotions; Raziel wanted to carry the weight for everyone since these deaths were on her hands.

It wasn't long before someone in the crowd started to sing a hauntingly beautiful song. The group began to hum, and Raziel simply listened, taking in their pain and praying that the small family hadn't suffered for long. Once the singer finished, they all began to slowly disperse from the pyre until it was only Sarah and Raziel left, watching the coals glow. Raziel looked at her, and even in the dull light, she could see how hard Sarah had been crying. She held her breath as she walked the short distance to stand beside her; Raziel grabbed her hand and squeezed it.

Sarah pulled her hand away from Raziel and turned to her. The look on Sarah's face was replaced by anger, and she hissed, "This is all your fault."

She took a step closer to Raziel, causing her leader to step back in surprise and respond, "I know it is, Sarah. I take full responsibility. I feel like I have made that abundantly clear."

Sarah shook her head. "It's not enough."

Raziel looked at her in shock. "What would you like me to do about it?"

Sarah shrugged. "That's your job. Figure it out, Great Leader. Building the funeral pyre wasn't the solution, and you have a lot of hurt to heal."

She quickly turned around and headed toward the cabins for the night, leaving Raziel to stew in her emotions and thoughts.

7

Raziel waited until the fire had completely died down before she turned to go back to her own cabin. It was pitch black as she walked across the clearing, the dew on the grass soaking the bottom of her skirt and feet. By the time she reached her cabin, her skirt was thoroughly soaked, and she had started to develop a chill. She looked up at the moon, and while it wasn't completely full, she figured it would be a perfect night to take a moon bath and shed off some of the guilt that she felt.

Raziel walked through her cabin to the back, where there was a small deck with a large clawfoot bathtub surrounded by candle-filled lanterns. She started to fill the large tub from the water reservoir beside it and pulled a medium-sized fire bowl from under the tub to start the healing process as she lit it and pushed it back underneath the tub. Once the tub was filled with water and beginning to warm, Raziel took a thin piece of wood, gathered some of the fire, and walked around the deck to light all of the candles, casting a soft glow around the deck.

As she undressed, she let her head fall back and felt admiration for the location of her cabin. The opening in the trees allowed her to have a full view of the moon above her, allowing the moonlight to charge her bath and heal her with its magic.

When she placed her hand into the water, she was content to find that the water was as hot as she wanted. She pulled the firepit from under the tub and allowed it to brighten the glow around her. Raziel stepped into the tub and lowered herself into it. Sighing in pleasure, she closed her eyes and placed her arms on either side of the tub.

After a few moments, she opened her eyes again and into the darkness beyond the lanterns. "I attract all of the pain my people feel. I embrace it and release it into the Universe to heal." Raziel waited, challenging the darkness, and when she didn't feel anything come rushing to her, she started to lean back.

All of a sudden, as if she were electrocuted by lightning, her back arched, and all of the pain, frustration, and sorrow rushed into Raziel's body. She started to shake as if it were going to completely consume her until she shot her head back, and a fast stream of black smoke poured out of her mouth and spiraled up to the sky.

Once she felt completely empty, her body collapsed back into the water. Raziel opened her eyes and looked around as if something were to come out of the woods. When nothing jumped, she relaxed her body and sighed. Tomorrow was going to be a new day at Nirvana, and with the negativity that everyone was carrying officially gone, Raziel knew they could genuinely heal. In addition, it was the day that the foragers were supposed to be returning, and they would be spending the day preparing for the ritual the following night.

Raziel was exhausted, but she felt herself smirk. The ritual always brought everyone together, and they rode the waves of love and happiness for weeks afterward. Raziel looked forward to having everyone be happy and together again.

She waited until the water had cooled entirely before she got out of the tub, pulling the plug and allowing the water to run freely. Raziel felt as if she had been renewed, and that the horrible events were draining out of the tub with it. She blew out the candles and snuffed the small fire out. When she went back into the cabin, she felt as if she had walked into a wall of exhaustion. After she dried herself off and rubbed lotion all over her body, she crawled into her bed, grateful that she was able to take her family's pain away, hopeful that they would be able to move past it the next day. When Raziel finally fell asleep, she fell into a deep sleep, dark, with no dreams or nightmares.

When she woke up the following morning, she felt like she had slept for hundreds of years. Completely rejuvenated, she jumped out of bed and quickly got dressed. She then walked out the front door and was taken aback by how bright the sun was.

It felt like a new day at Nirvana, and even the energy outside of her own cabin was light-hearted and felt nothing short of amazing. While she remembered the night before and knew what had happened, Raziel wasn't sure how the people would react when they saw her.

As she walked to get her breakfast, the people she passed offered smiles and morning greetings. Raziel was cautious, but she was thrilled to see that people were in higher spirits. Before she entered the kitchen, Raziel took a deep breath, bracing herself. When she opened the door, the entire kitchen was abuzz with excitement. The chef was cooking up chocolate chip pancakes, and Raziel saw a mountain of strawberries waiting to be devoured. She picked up a fat berry and popped it into her mouth. The juice was sweet, and it was the most perfect strawberry she had ever tasted.

The chef looked at her and sweetly asked, "Would you like me to prepare you a plate?"

Raziel shook her head. "No, I can wait. I just wanted to see how everyone was feeling."

Suddenly, Sarah came rushing in from the dining room and had a large grin on her face. "Raziel! Good morning!" She beamed.

Good, it's working. "Good morning, Sarah. How are you?"

Her eyes twinkled as she replied. "Just awesome! The sun is beautiful, *and* we have a full moon tonight. There is nothing better!"

Raziel chuckled in relief; perhaps her negativity release worked better than she'd intended. She felt her heart swell with ease and happiness. Her community was going to return to normal, and the mourning period was short and sweet.

The chef interrupted her thoughts by announcing, "Breakfast is ready!"

Raziel smirked and ran to the dining room, ready to indulge in one of her favorite breakfasts.

Everyone talked amongst themselves, and Raziel did her rounds to each table before taking a seat. The other pregnant women were ecstatic to see her, and she placed her hands on each of their bellies, silently begging the babies to kick, to acknowledge her. The mothers weren't as far along as Lily was, but she felt like they would be here within the next three full moons.

As she held the last mother's belly, the unborn baby kicked hard. Raziel looked up at the mom "He's a feisty one."

The mother grasped her belly. "He?"

Raziel nodded. "I'm getting very strong male energy from him."

The mother started to cry tears of joy and grasped Raziel's hands in gratitude. Raziel continued to her table and started to eat her breakfast. She felt complete and hopeful as if it were the first several days of Nirvana, and it oozed promise. When she finished her meal, she put the empty dishes in the bins, and when she walked out of the dining room, the group was waiting for her outside.

Raziel took them all in and opened her arms as she declared, "Let's get the firepit set up and tables brought out. The amethyst cathedrals need to be dragged up from the shed as well, while candles and fairy lights need to be placed in their normal spots."

Several people left the group with their tasks while others waited. Raziel looked at them and said, "Let's get enough flowers together to make a path from the gates to the firepit. I want the foragers to feel the immense love we have for them when they return. There are several species that can be found in the forest. Be careful; take weapons with you and the large baskets. Only the most beautiful blooms must be picked and brought back."

The other members of the group left her and headed toward the gates. Raziel was ready for her only task of the day. It was up to her to harness energy from the moon and disperse it across Nirvana; it helped to keep the protective barrier strong for Nirvana to stay the way it was.

Raziel walked down to the water source, and when she reached the riverbank, she didn't stop. She stepped over the surface of the water, and when she reached the middle of the large lake and sat down, she crossed her legs and placed both of her palms on the surface of the water and closed her eyes. She could still feel the moon's energy buzzing around her, and she focused on it, pulling it into her and feeling it shoot out of her fingers and into the water, radiating from her. She felt the entire place buzz with the energy, and she focused on strengthening Nirvana from the core, from *her* core.

Raziel sat on the water's surface for hours until she heard her name being called. She turned her head to see Sarah running and pointing to the gates. The foragers had returned. Raziel stood up and walked back to land. As her foot touched the bank, she started to run across the clearing. She saw countless totes and bags being brought through the gates and more people returning, hugging each other.

When Ramona came through the gates and saw Raziel, they sprinted toward each other. Raziel pulled her into a long hug, gripping the back of her head as she whispered, "I've missed you. There is much to talk about."

Ramona pulled back from her and nodded. "There is."

As she looked back to the gates, the most beautiful man Raziel had ever seen walked through. Ramona looked to Raziel, whose breath was taken entirely. The group welcomed him, and each person hugged him, welcoming him to the compound.

Raziel walked over to him, and it felt as if time had stopped. He smiled warmly at her, revealing perfectly straight white teeth; she looked him up and down. He had shoulder-length shaggy blonde hair, piercing blue eyes, a jawline that wouldn't stop, and broad shoulders. He extended his large hand toward her, and Raziel took it, surprised by how soft it was.

A small gasp escaped her lips, and she stumbled over her words as she said, "Welcome to Nirvana. I am Raziel."

He nodded and shook her hand slowly as he replied in a deep and seductive voice. "I am Angelus, and I am looking for enlightenment."

Raziel placed her other hand on his arm, taken back by how muscular he felt. "You are in the right place, Angelus."

They stared at each other for some time until someone interrupted them by screaming, "You guys got the pink pitaya? Finally!"

Raziel pulled her hands from him and cleared her throat

as she roared, "Can someone please show our newest initiate to the men's cabins, please?"

Several men stepped forward, clapping him on the back. As he walked away from the crowd, he looked back and smiled when he saw Raziel watching him leave. Ramona grabbed Raziel's arm and excitedly asked, "Did I do good?"

Raziel stared at her. "Where did he come from?"

Ramona giggled. "He approached us, but I haven't seen him act like that the entire time we were in the city."

Raziel tilted her head. "I'm intrigued."

Ramona laughed and replied, "I bet you are! He didn't seem to take an interest in any of us, either."

Raziel couldn't help but smile, for real this time. While she knew that she had some sort of an effect on men, it never ceased to amaze her how flirty they could get the first time in her presence.

Ramona coughed and asked, "What is it we need to discuss?"

Raziel took her hand and led her into the garden. She sat down and pulled Ramona down with her. Ramona looked around, and Raziel went on to tell her everything that had happened while they were gone. Ramona broke down in tears and screamed Lily's name; Raziel hugged her tight and placed her palms on the back of Ramona's head. She felt her palm start to tingle as she pulled the sorrow from Ramona's body, dulling her sobs to whimpers, and then finally, nothing. She pulled back from Raziel and wiped her nose.

"Lily is better off. This world is declining, and at least, she is at peace, and she knew true love before she passed."

Raziel nodded, even though the mention of *true love* made her feel like she had been impaled.

Raziel grabbed her hands as she whispered, "I know it's tough, but I promise it will stop hurting."

Ramona bowed. "I trust you. I already feel so much better."

They stared at each other, and Raziel radiated the love she could into Ramona, trying to fix her broken heart. Raziel then pulled back and asked, "What else can you tell me about our newest member?"

Ramona's eyes went wide as a wicked grin crept over her face. "Oh, my goodness, Raziel, wait until you see his body. His voice sounds *otherworldly*, and he seems incredibly hardworking. We barely had to explain things to him, and he was always quick to help us with whatever we needed."

Raziel listened closely, her excitement growing as Ramona spoke higher and higher of him. If he was highly recommended by one of her most favorite people, Raziel knew that he had *some* substance to him and was thrilled that he wanted to be a part of the community.

They stood up, and Raziel kissed Ramona on the cheek before she said, "Thank you. Thank you also for not dying out there."

Ramona blushed slightly, and they both walked to the kitchen to go over what had been brought back to Nirvana. As they entered, they could barely get through the door. Boxes of dry ingredients and supplies took up so much space, and people had begun to start jarring the garden harvest, the smell of cooking vegetables filling the air.

Watching everyone work toward a life of self-sufficiency always brought Raziel so much pride in herself. She knew that while the outside world would suffer shortages eventually, the family within Nirvana's walls would always have full bellies and remain safe. Raziel stayed in the kitchen and helped the jarring and restocking process move quicker.

Under normal circumstances, she would show the newest members around, explain the rules, and learn more about them. But Angelus raised a feeling in Raziel that she had never experienced before; she was nervous, excited, and felt like she was on fire... all at the same time.

8

Once everything was cleaned up, the staff started to prepare lunch in their newly stocked kitchen. When Raziel stepped out of the kitchen, she saw Angelus and several other men constructing a small building; she looked at the group curiously and walked over. None of them acknowledged her until she cleared her throat loudly. They all stopped and looked at her.

One of the best carpenters in the compound, Tyler, stepped forward, and he said, "We are building a stargazing gazebo. We thought it would be the perfect addition to our ritual for tonight."

Raziel nodded, and indeed, it was already an incredibly

beautiful structure. She looked around the crowd and asked, "Who's idea was it?"

Angelus stepped forward, and he looked into her eyes directly. Raziel's breath caught in her throat. He ran his hands through his hair and said, "I wanted to showcase my talents. I heard you enjoy looking at the stars, and this was the best thing I could think of to honor you for allowing me to become part of the community." His expression changed as he jokingly scolded, "You weren't supposed to see it until it was finished; off you go."

Raziel was taken aback by his command, and while she would typically object, she nodded and replied, "I look forward to seeing it complete."

She wasn't sure what just happened, but she didn't want to give Angelus a wrong impression. Instead, Raziel walked around the compound to see how other aspects were going for the ritual. She was pleased to see that the lights were hung up and candles were spread out, while flowers were starting to take over the clearing. Raziel felt a sense of ease and allowed herself to begin to relax.

Walking around the compound, she suddenly heard the sound of a loud cowbell. She wasn't sure what was causing it but walked toward the ringing. When she found the cook signaling that it was time for lunch, Raziel smirked. It was smarter than word of mouth, and it was clearly working as people started to flock from all directions to the sound. Raziel hung back and allowed everyone else to flood into the dining room for their meal. She felt like she was witnessing a change that she didn't even know was needed. Something definitely had clicked into place.

Raziel scanned the room when she went inside and saw that Angelus was nowhere to be found. She waited for a few moments, but when everyone had begun to eat, he still didn't appear.

She walked down to where the new gazebo was with two

full plates and found Angelus hammering nails on top of the roof; his shirt was off, and he was glistening with sweat under the sun. Raziel couldn't take her eyes off of him. It looked like he had been chiseled from stone. He was perfect.

She felt a fluttering feeling in her stomach, and when she got close enough, he yelled, "I was wondering when you'd show up!"

Raziel smirked. "Well, I figured you could use something to eat from all of the hard work."

Angelus put his hammer down and climbed down from the structure. He smiled and took a plate from her. "I also heard you're incredibly involved. I knew it was only a matter of time." He smiled at her and had a mischievous twinkle in his eye.

Raziel put on a fake look of annoyance. "You're talking about me behind my back?"

Angelus quickly responded, "I just wanted to know how to please you, so I asked questions." As he took a bite of fruit and looked up at her, Raziel could feel her cheeks start to flush. She was trying to fight the feeling that was coming up inside of her.

"How did you hear about Nirvana?"

Angelus sat down on the grass and patted the area across from him. Raziel sat down, and he began, "I come from a very small town. There were always whispers of a free-loving commune hidden in the middle of the rainforest, passed down through generations. Many places tried to replicate this." He motioned around him. "But I knew it wasn't the real thing. My parents tried to raise me in one of the copycat societies when I was young, but the rules became so severe over time that I ran away when I was fifteen."

Angelus looked down, and Raziel could feel that he was still upset about it. She quietly asked, "Are they still there?"

He shook his head. "They helped me escape, and I'm sure they were killed afterward as traitors. That was how they evolved over time. The leader became cruel and bloodthirsty. He demanded pure devotion and had a no-questions-asked regime."

Raziel listened to him, intrigued that people had tried to copy her; she had no idea that other communes had popped up. She was pleased that people wanted to embrace free love, but it needed to be peaceful; apparently, humans didn't understand that concept.

She looked at Angelus and asked, "How long have you been looking for Nirvana?"

He smiled. "My entire life."

"I'm glad you're here; we're all glad you're here. You're home, and you're welcome to stay for as long as you need to."

Angelus bowed, and a cloud seemed to cast over his face as he asked, "What kind of rules do you have here?"

Raziel put her plate to the side, and she answered, "While free love is encouraged, if monogamy is more your path, you're free to follow it. We all help raise any children who are born; we care for each other and work toward a better version of humanity as a collective."

Angelus listened and was focused on Raziel's face. He took everything in, and then looked around before. "I feel like I fit in here, like I was always meant to be here."

Raziel grabbed his hand. "I agree wholeheartedly."

They stared at each other for some time, and Raziel felt like Angelus was staring directly into her soul. Her breath caught in her throat, and she pulled her hand away.

Angelus quietly asked, "Did you feel that?"

Raziel quickly stood up. "I, uh, need to go check on the other members. Enjoy your lunch. Everyone will be back to help you shortly."

Angelus stood up as well. "Please don't leave just yet."

Raziel shook her head and replied, "I need to do my rounds. I will see you later." The look on Angelus' face broke her heart, but she needed to get away from what she was feeling. It was new, and she didn't know how to cope with it. "I will find you later."

He nodded and watched her quickly walk away.

Once Raziel was far enough, she realized that she had been holding her breath. She sighed and looked around her. She saw that Angelus was back on top of the gazebo, so she focused her attention back in front of her. Numerous people were starting to file out of the dining room and going off in their opposite directions to continue preparing for the ritual.

Ramona appeared through the crowd, and when she saw Raziel, her face lit up. Raziel saw her eyes shift behind her, and when she nodded, Ramona smiled even wider. They met halfway through the clearing when Raziel said, "We need to talk."

Ramona bowed and followed Raziel to her cabin. Once they were inside and the door was closed, Raziel whipped around to face Ramona. "Where did you find Angelus?"

Ramona's eyebrows furrowed, and she said, "He was in the city."

"*Where* in the city?" She had an urgency in her voice that Ramona had never heard before.

Ramona's face held a look of concern as she said, "He approached us. He seemed to just know that we weren't from the city, and he asked if we knew where he could find Nirvana; he was looking for inner peace and a sense of belonging."

Raziel was silent as she let the information settle. She started to pace around the cabin, and then she stopped. "Something is... magnetic about him; something is pulling me toward him on a divine level. I can't explain it."

Ramona smiled. "Could it be that you're experiencing love at first sight?"

Raziel shook her head. "Impossible. Utterly impossible!"

Ramona chuckled. "Many things have proven to be

possible since I've been here. Lean into it, Raziel. It's okay. It'll do you some good to experience new things."

Raziel got a bit frustrated; humans would *never* understand what she was feeling. It wasn't like the type of love they were used to or could even comprehend.

The last time she'd felt any kind of pull like the one she was experiencing, she was still in service to the Creator. It was with one of the archangels, and it was the only time in her existence where she had ever felt anything *close* to being in love. In Heaven, they didn't call it *love*. It was simply a feeling that pulled angels together and paired them for eternity. What she was feeling with Angelus, felt like the same kind of magnetism that she'd felt right before the fall.

Raziel sighed; she felt uncomfortable and wasn't sure how long she could go before she gave into the feeling. Ramona was studying her and seemed to read her thoughts before she said, "I know it's scary, especially if you've never felt anything like it before, but the attraction you're feeling is so normal, Raziel. It's okay!"

She reached for Raziel, who pulled her hand away from Ramona. "It's fine, Ramona. I don't think you truly understand what I'm conveying, but it's quite alright. I'll figure it out."

Ramona took that as a dismissal, and before she exited the cabin, she looked back and said, "Raziel, sometimes new things set off alarms in our heads because it's an opportunity to grow from our past self. Growth is uncomfortable, but it's entirely worth it for your gain in the long run."

Raziel watched her leave and weighed the words that were spoken to her. While she knew that Ramona had some truth behind them, she also knew that Ramona would never understand the divine spectrum and what feelings comprised of that. She wasn't sure if it was love or not, but she felt something when Angelus looked at her, touched her, and spoke to her.

Raziel went over to her bedside table and pulled out a small teapot and a heating plate. She waited for it to heat up, and she grabbed a large teacup from the shelf below her other supplies. As she poured the hot water over the tea, Raziel tried to calm her nerves; she hoped that the peppermint would do the rest as she let it cool for a few moments before taking the first sip. The tea warmed her from the inside out, and Raziel felt like she was able to think clearly again.

She needed to get Angelus' face out of her head and focus on the ritual. It required her *entire* focus. Suddenly, the shadows from the darkest corners of the cabin stretched over the cabin's floor. She squinted her eyes and sighed as she heard Natalia's voice.

"Sister, hello."

Raziel looked over her shoulder, and Natalia stepped forward from the shadows. She walked to the front of the cabin and turned around. Raziel watched her stroll through her home as if she owned it, trying not to let it bother her. She gripped the cup harder and tried to keep her emotions locked down.

Natalia looked around her and took Raziel in completely. A slight smirk came over her face as she asked, "Is he here?"

Raziel looked up in surprise. "I'm sorry?"

Natalia's face morphed into a large grin. "I felt the ground beneath me shudder with the arrival of a new divine being."

Raziel shook her head. "No, no one is here."

Natalia's face turned downward in disappointment. "Too bad, I was looking forward to a battle royale."

Raziel looked up at her, seeing that Natalia wasn't kidding. She quietly said, "I simply want peace. I don't want to fight."

Natalia nodded. "That's alright. I welcome it and will gladly take on the violence." She looked around and tried to see if she could see any of the community members through the windows. When she couldn't, she turned back to Raziel. "You're telling me you didn't feel anything?"

Raziel shook her head. "No, I didn't."

Natalia's face dropped into a slight pout. "That's too bad. It was powerful. I'm sorry you missed it."

Raziel smiled weakly. "If anything happens, I will be sure to reach out, and we can assess together."

"Oh, Sister, I'm sure I'll feel it before you even see anything. I'll be in touch," and Natalia slipped back into the shadows.

Once she felt like she was truly alone, Raziel started to sip her tea again, going over the information that she was just told. By the time she finished her tea, it had grown dark, and it was time for the ritual to begin. She grabbed a silver circlet and placed it on her head. She then took a deep breath and left the cabin.

When she stepped outside, her breath was taken away. The entire compound was radiating a soft glow from the delicate lights and candles. Raziel walked the path to the large firepit as others came from all directions to surround her. When she saw Angelus standing on the opposite side of the pit, she felt nervous by the intensity of the look that he was giving her.

Raziel broke eye contact with him and looked around at the rest of her family. She opened her arms and loudly exclaimed, "Family, welcome! We are blessed again with this full moon. Let us thank the Universe for our blessings and our newcomer, Angelus. Welcome home."

Angelus smiled and looked around as people clapped quietly and murmured amongst themselves, giving thanks. They all circled around the pit as Raziel lit the flame. It wasn't long before a large fire shot up between them all. They all joined hands and began to chant up to the sky in a language that Raziel had taught them.

None of them would ever know that it was actually an

incantation that would transfer some of their energy to her, and as they sang it, Raziel felt stronger, better, and her beauty was radiant. Once they finished, they hugged each other, and the kitchen staff ran to get food to continue the celebration. The fire was roaring, and someone suggested that they bring out some of the moonshine in honor of the full moon.

Raziel grinned; it *had* been a while since they had taken part in moonshine and agreed that it was a special occasion. She didn't see who ran off to get some, but all of a sudden, glasses were being passed out as the kitchen staff came back with planks filled with meat, cheeses, and pieces of bread. Raziel felt her heart swell, knowing that the night was going to be a good one.

Angelus was suddenly beside her. In a low tone, he said, "That song was beautiful. I apologize for not knowing the words."

Raziel smirked. "You'll learn."

He bowed. "It didn't sound familiar. What language was it?"

This caused Raziel to look at him. "A lost language."

Angelus took a step toward her. "I have learned many ancient languages. That didn't sound like any dialect I have heard before."

"It's a mix of Tamil and Aramaic."

Angelus nodded. "I thought I picked up some ancient Egyptian as well."

"Very good, there was some influence."

Angelus smiled wide. "Can I get you a refreshment? Some food?"

Raziel nodded and watched as he crossed over to the platters, weaving through the crowd.

When he returned, he had two glasses and one plate. He shyly said, "I thought we could share. Would you like to go down by the water?"

Raziel looked around and saw Ramona staring at the

interaction with a grin on her face. Raziel could hear Ramona's voice in her head. "Just go with it!" So, she bobbed her head, and then followed Angelus. She looked back to see the group celebrating and whopping with excitement around the fire.

As they got to the lake, the glow from the fire and the rest of the lights were a dull glow. The only other light sources were the full moon overhead and the thousands of fireflies coming out of the surrounding woods. It was idyllic and romantic.

"It's so beautiful here," Raziel whispered.

Angelus agreed. "It truly is the definition of Nirvana."

Raziel smiled to herself. It was what she had always wanted to achieve. She wasn't sure what had happened over the last few days, but it truly transcended anything that she had ever experienced on Earth. Angelus handed her the plate that he had brought, and she popped some grapes into her mouth. Raziel felt like it was the first time she was eating the sweet fruit. They tasted sweeter than anything she had experienced before.

They sat in silence for several minutes, the sound of frogs and other small creatures filling the air. Angelus cleared his throat and asked, "Did you feel what I felt earlier?"

Raziel started to cough, choking on the bread that she had just taken a bite of. Once she stopped, she looked at him and cautiously said, "I felt *something*. I don't know what, though."

He quietly said, "I was sent here for a reason, Raziel." She felt her heart drop as Natalia's words floated through her head. He continued, "I was drawn to you the second I saw you. I have been looking my entire life for someone to make me feel the way that you have."

Raziel looked at him, and in the faint light, she could see the outline of his features, and she could feel the seriousness of the moment. She had never been confronted in this sense, and while she felt uncomfortable, she felt that perhaps the Universe was rewarding her for her dedication.

She took a deep breath, and she replied, "I have never felt the way that you make me feel, especially given that it has only been a day. I shouldn't feel like this."

Angelus placed a gentle finger over her lips. "Love has no time frame. I will spend every second of my life proving myself to you, if that's what you need."

Raziel was touched by his dedication already, but the moment was interrupted by the sound of people loudly approaching. She could hear the drunk slurring and figured that they were coming to the lake to cool off.

She whispered, "Let's continue this later."

As they stood up, the group of people reached them, only to run past them to jump into the lake. Squeals from the cold water filled the night air, and Raziel smirked in amusement.

Angelus asked, "Are you going to jump in?"

Raziel replied, "No, I'm going to go back to the fire. I'm starting to get cold. If you want to, please join them."

Angelus pulled all his clothes off and jumped into the water as if the moon were his personal spotlight. It seemed to increase in intensity as he came up from the depths, and it highlighted his muscular body. Raziel felt herself staring too long and shook her head to snap out of it. She turned to go to the firepit, her head a chaotic mess from what Angelus had told her.

When she reached the fire, Ramona was waiting and patted the ground beside her. She was holding a glass in her hand, and when Raziel sat down, she snatched the glass from Ramona and took a deep gulp.

Ramona stared at her. "Good talk?"

Raziel shook her head. "I don't know how to feel right now."

Ramona nodded. "Infatuation will do that. It turns you upside down and makes you question everything."

Raziel listened as she looked at the flames. "I don't know what to do, Ramona. I have so much responsibility; I can't lose myself like this."

Ramona grabbed Raziel's arm. "I can understand that, but at some point, it's okay to do something for yourself. It's okay to be happy."

"I know you're right. I know it's okay, but I can't allow myself to feel these things. In case something happens, I don't know *what* would happen if I were to have my heart broken, or if I break *his* heart."

"I can't tell you what to feel or how to feel. I can only tell you that it's *okay* to feel." Ramona pulled Raziel in for a side hug. The two sat in silence, passing the glass between them until the liquid was gone. The fire was starting to die down. Eventually, Ramona whispered, "I'm tired; are you going to stay up a bit longer?"

Raziel shook her head. "No, I am ready to rest."

The two of them stood and hugged each other before parting ways. As Raziel walked to her cabin, she heard silence coming from the lake, happy that people had found their way back to their cabins, and that the compound was dying down for the night. She felt energized and was satisfied with the success of the ritual.

When she opened her cabin door, she was relieved to see that it was empty. Raziel quickly changed into a simple nightgown and crawled into bed, not even bothering to turn any lights on in the process. Her head had barely touched the pillow when she fell asleep.

She was thrust into a dark room, naked, and she felt complete bliss. When she reached her hand out, it was grabbed by a stronger one. It was attached to a muscular arm, and she found Angelus in bed with her.

The two engaged in a passionate affair, engulfing each other with lust. Raziel could feel the strength in his touch. While it was also delicate and soft, it was unlike anything she had ever felt before, on and off Earth.

When she woke up, she found the bottom half of her face covered with saliva, followed by the morning sun around her. She looked around; it felt so real. She touched her lips. Angelus' kiss was soft, yet earnest, and left her wanting more.

She lied back down and closed her eyes, hoping to slip back into the dream. Instead, when she fell back to sleep, she was thrown back into a time when she and her sisters were trying to repair humanity. Natural disasters had killed so many, and the sisters were sent to help rebuild society and help further humanity under the Creator's orders. He wanted them to advance but not enough so that they would ever question Him or His will.

They had been on Earth for months by the time they'd gotten frustrated enough by the slow advancement. Fights broke out between the three angels, and they went back and forth between giving the humans more knowledge and going back to the Creator to ask him to intervene. Eventually, they chose to talk to the Creator, and it led to the fall. Each sister was given a burden that they had to carry to ensure that they would *never* know true happiness.

Years flashed before Raziel's eyes as she watched humans experience true love while she was left empty and wanting more. The images were then replaced by Azazel's blood-covered body and Natalia's lifeless corpse draped over her.

Raziel sat up abruptly and was covered in sweat. She looked down and realized that she was shaking violently. The good feeling that she had was replaced with fear. Her dreams were usually prophetic, and while the first part was promising, she didn't feel hopeful about the entire experience. Raziel wondered if she should contact Natalia to tell her what she saw but chose not to act on it. Instead, she slid out of bed and slowly got dressed before leaving the cabin. The energy in the small home felt strange, and she wanted to get away from it.

When she stepped outside, she could smell something delicious and decided to follow the aroma. Angelus had several people by the firepit, and they were cooking something over a small flame. As Raziel approached the group, she scanned the faces and saw that Ramona wasn't there but continued walking toward them. She looked over to the gazebo, noticing that half of the roof was done. While it wasn't finished, she was impressed with how beautiful it was turning out.

When Angelus saw her approaching, he said something to his companions, and they all made room for her and greeted her warmly. She looked around and asked, "What smells so delicious?"

Angelus smiled. "We are making biscuits and gravy."

"You're a man of many talents."

Angelus smirked. "You have no idea."

He handed her a warm biscuit with a small bowl of gravy. She took it from him, and when she tried it, she was surprised by how delicious it was. While the kitchen staff never failed to supply a delightful meal, this was a different experience and was somehow elevated.

Angelus leaned over and quietly asked, "Did you sleep well last night?"

Raziel stared at him and replied, "I did. How was your first night here?"

He looked over his shoulder and scanned the group in front of them. He then leaned in closer and whispered, "I couldn't get you out of my head. The dreams I had would make the most experienced sinner blush."

Raziel's mouth dropped open, and she felt herself getting hot. "Perhaps we shouldn't discuss such things in front of an audience."

Angelus bowed. "I'd much rather show you."

Raziel looked at him, and she could feel herself getting angry. "I am not just here to please you. I don't know what your idea of free love and a free community is, but I think you need some education."

"I only want you to know my feelings."

"Perhaps it's best you keep such feelings to yourself until you know my stance on things." Raziel shoved the bowl into his hands and said, "You can start proving yourself by ensuring that the community is properly fed." She walked away from the firepit and could feel Angelus' eyes on her as she left.

She didn't even think about where she was going to go. She started to walk toward the large gates and through them, heading toward the city on the beaten path. Raziel eventually hit the fork and kept walking toward the city. She was almost at the point where the foragers would meet someone to take them into the city when she saw the shrine built for Lily, Oriana, and Brian.

It was a large clearing, and two mounds of fresh dirt were surrounded by rocks outlining the graves. Raziel figured that sweet baby Oriana was buried with her mother; it was only fitting, and when she saw the burial spots, she dropped to her knees as tears poured from her eyes. Raziel's sorrow overtook her, and her entire body shook with anger and sadness. If she hadn't banished them, she wouldn't have been forced to change the rules and wouldn't be facing the feelings that she had about Angelus.

She leaned back so she could look directly up at the sky. "Lily, forgive me." Raziel screamed into the air. She felt heavy with emotion, and she threw her fists into the ground as the tears fell from her face. The night Oriana was born felt special; it felt sacred, and it connected them. Without them on Earth, Raziel felt as if a part of her were missing.

Raziel soon heard footsteps approaching, and she called back, "Leave me!"

The footsteps continued and stopped shortly behind her. Raziel looked over her shoulder and saw Angelus standing there.

Raziel groaned and asked, "What do you want?"

He stepped closer and said, "I am truly sorry for any offense that I've caused. I know I'm still new here, and there are rules to be followed. I wanted to apologize for stepping out of line."

"Okay, you've apologized. Now leave me alone." But when he sat down beside her, she rolled her eyes. "You're not a very good listener, are you?"

Angelus chuckled. "Not really, but it wouldn't be a very smart move to leave the compound leader out in the wilderness by herself. I'll stay silent. I'll be ready when you're ready to leave."

Raziel dropped her head in frustration. She didn't feel like she could properly let out her emotions with the newest member around. She groaned again and stood up. "Let's go." She started to walk back to the compound, and Angelus hung back a short distance.

Good.

As they walked through the gates, Angelus called, "Are you going to be alright?"

Raziel curtly said, "Yes."

As she continued to walk away from him, she looked around. There was nowhere she could go without him or anyone else bugging her. Ramona was in her path, and she asked, "Raziel, are you alright?"

Raziel nodded and motioned for her to stay away. This day felt odd, and she didn't want to do anything or say anything that she would come to regret later on. Raziel walked toward her cabin. She knew it would give her the space that she needed, and everyone would get the hint.

As she walked away, Raziel shouted back, "I'm taking my meals inside the cabin!"

She could smell the roses as she approached her oasis. They were starting to bloom, and with the countless bushes, the scent was overwhelming. Raziel stormed into the cabin and threw herself onto her bed.

She let her eyes unleash the true fury and sorrow that she had been holding in. Raziel felt like her emotions were spinning out of control and were bringing her down with them. She wasn't sure how long she'd spent crying into her pillows, but eventually, she stopped, and when she turned her head to look out the window, the sun was already at its highest point in the sky.

Raziel sniffled and knew that she couldn't hide from her community for long, even though she wanted to and was contemplating it. Eventually, a soft knock sounded at the door. Raziel sighed, getting off the bed and going to unlock the door. Ramona was standing on the other side with a tray of food, a concerned look on her face as she whispered, "Raziel, we need to speak."

Raziel rolled her eyes and loudly said, "Fine."

Ramona entered the cabin and placed the platter on the bed while Raziel began to pace around the cabin.

Ramona sat on the bed and watched Raziel for a moment before Raziel abruptly broke the silence. "Do you think I'm stupid? Heartless?"

Ramona stared at Raziel in shock and stuttered out an answer. "N-no!"

Raziel stopped in the middle of the room and looked at Ramona. "Are you sure?"

Ramona bowed and took a deep breath in, as if she were preparing for some kind of backlash. "I've noticed how you've been a bit on edge lately, especially since Angelus—"

Raziel cut her off. "No, I know where you're going with this—"

"Do you, Raziel? Because we've never had an in-depth conversation about love or what you look for in a partner, and now that Lily, Brian, and Oriana are gone, we can tell that something is off."

Raziel took a step closer, and in a hushed tone, she seethed, "Who are *you* to question the will of gods?"

Ramona shook her head and let out a sigh. "Raziel, you're *not* a god. You're here on Earth with us, and while you're still our leader, we still have free will."

Raziel's eyes went wide, and her head fell back. She let out a loud cackle that threatened to shatter every window in the cabin. Ramona watched her and became uncomfortable with where the conversation was headed.

Raziel eventually stopped laughing and rushed toward Ramona. When she was just inches from her face, she whispered, "Don't you find my rose bushes lovely? The blooms are so plump and robust."

Ramona cautiously replied, "Yes, they are quite beautiful this year, but that isn't what I wanted to talk to you about, Raziel. Please, can we stay on topic?"

Raziel's eyes went into slits. "I cannot fall in love, Ramona. It's not possible."

Ramona stared at her in disbelief. "What are you talking about?"

The fallen angel smirked and said, "My curse is that I cannot fall in love. Angelus sparks something inside of me and makes me feel crazy."

"That sounds like love to me."

This caused Raziel to grip Ramona's shoulders and shake them slightly. "Ramona, you have *no idea* what you're talking about. Stop it!" She let Ramona go and started to pace again.

Ramona quietly asked, "Is your guilt so great that you changed the rules because of Lily? You blame yourself for their deaths?"

Raziel stopped walking and looked at her, simply nodding.

"It took you this long and three deaths to change the rules?"

Raziel scowled at her. "Everyone had been happy living in the free love society—"

"It wasn't a *true* free love society if people couldn't choose, though."

Raziel nodded again. "Exactly, which was why I changed it."

Ramona shook her head. "It took people *dying* for you to deem it worthy of changing. How many people have to die for you to change any other rules?"

Raziel's rage started to bubble under the surface. "What *other* rules would you want to change, Ramona?"

"I don't know, Raziel, but I'm saying that it's messed up—"

"You can leave."

Ramona stood up, and she walked across the cabin. As she gripped the door, she looked over her shoulder. "Something is wrong with you. I don't know what happened for you to become erratic like this, but you need to realize a few things before we can see you as our leader again."

Raziel ran over and grabbed Ramona by her hair, and she slammed her onto her back. Ramona let out a grunt as the air was knocked out of her lungs. Raziel climbed on top of Ramona and seethed, "I am *always* going to be your leader. It's because of *me* that all of you have this!"

Ramona turned her face and spat. "Bullshit, Raziel. Look at yourself right now!"

Raziel was beginning to see red as she said, "I would be very careful and watch the words that are coming out of your mouth, Ramona. I can kick you out, and I won't lose a moment of sleep over it."

Ramona looked up at her. "Do it, then. Banish me like all the others who stood up for the commune."

They stared at each other for some time before Raziel sighed and got off of Ramona. She walked over to the tray of food and hissed, "Get out! Someone else will bring me my meals. I don't want to see your face for the rest of the day."

Ramona rushed out of the cabin. Raziel slumped onto the bed, and in a fit of anger, she pushed the platter off. Dishes shattered under her feet, and the food was splattered all over the bed and up the wall.

Raziel sighed and fell back onto her bed. She ran her fingers through her hair and went over the conversation with Ramona. She knew where Ramona was coming from, and while part of her was angry for the insubordination, she knew there was some truth to what Ramona was saying. The rules had been in place since the beginning, and Raziel hadn't changed them for anyone… until Lily.

For the first time in a very long time, she felt like she wanted to end Nirvana. The humans were starting to drain her again, and she felt like her divinity was depleted. Raziel heard a *whooshing* sound, and she looked over to her side to see Natalia coming out of the small shadows in the corner.

Raziel sat up and sighed. "Natalia, I'm not in the mood for a meeting right now."

Natalia tiptoed around the spilled food, and she said, "Unfortunately, you don't have a choice. I got a tiny little nudge that told me I needed to be here. What's wrong with you?"

Raziel sighed and sat up. "I can't do this anymore…"

Natalia looked at her in confusion, and Raziel motioned around them. Natalia giggled and asked, "Oh, Sister, how come? Have the humans finally gotten to you?"

"They just take and take from me, and when I finally give them what they want, it's too late. Or they only focus on the negative situations that caused the changes."

Natalia walked over to the large Monstera plant in the corner, inspecting it. "What do you expect? Humans are overgrown babies. Of course, it's never going to be good enough. Of course, they are just going to continuously take from you and give nothing in return; they are selfish. You should know that by now."

Raziel stared at her feet, and Natalia inspected her nails. "You forget that we never turn our backs on the humans."

She looked up at her sister, and Natalia whispered, "Make them remember what you're capable of, Sister. Get your community back in line. *You* are in charge, not them." Raziel nodded, and Natalia pointed at her. "You're drained, but you know what needs to be done."

10

Natalia walked past her again and faded into the tiny shadows, disappearing from the cabin. Raziel felt something start to rise inside of her, and she stood up, snapped her fingers, and instantly, the dishes were reassembled, and the food was cleaned up. Raziel looked around, and when she was pleased with the clean-up, she changed into a blood red floor-length Grecian gown. It accentuated her curves perfectly and was just thin enough to see her body beneath it without being too revealing. She flipped her head over and fluffed her hair up again, and when she flipped it back, she was pleased with its volume.

Raziel left her cabin and walked to the main hall, where the great horn was located. She saw the chef walking toward her, and she called, "Can you prepare a big batch of your jungle juice?"

When the chef bowed to her request and walked away, Raziel blew the horn, indicating that a community meeting needed to be held. People began to come from all directions and walked toward her. As they approached in large groups, Raziel noticed them talking amongst themselves, and she lifted her head in slight defiance. The more people gathered in front of her, the more Raziel became confident that this was the right thing to do.

The entire commune filled the clearing, and before she began to speak, the kitchen staff brought out several large coolers, liquid sloshing in them as they moved and were set down beside Raziel. She looked out into the crowd and saw Angelus and Ramona's faces. She cleared her throat and looked at Ramona again, who was glaring at her. Raziel felt a pang in her chest, and it felt like her heart was breaking. She knew Ramona was disappointed in her, and Raziel wondered if there was any chance of reconciliation.

The more she looked into the crowd, the more she saw that there were several pairs of couples who had clearly jumped on the monogamous bandwagon. Raziel sighed as she felt the familiar feeling of jealousy start to rise inside of her. She couldn't help but think, *Why should they be happy in pairs? I offer them paradise. Why should they be able to fall in love while I simply get to experience pleasure? It's not fair!* The longer Raziel stared at her community, the angrier she became.

They all stared back at her, and she began to pick up the uneasiness that was spreading through the crowd. Raziel sighed; she was curious as to when they all started turning on her. It didn't seem like that long ago when they were all content just living by the rules.

She cleared her throat, and she loudly asked, "Are you unhappy here?" Her followers all exchanged glances, and she saw them shift uncomfortably. She said even louder, "I'm waiting for an answer. Someone speak up!"

A gentleman stepped forward, Leonard. He was one of the carpenters and had been at Nirvana for over twenty years. Raziel was shocked to see him come forward, and even more surprised when he said, "The rules, Raziel. You have never been one to change them, and now you give in at the smallest mishap."

"You think Lily's death was a small mishap?"

"Did you kill Lily yourself?"

Leonard and Raziel both gaped at each other, and the commune held their breath, waiting for Raziel's response.

Raziel shook her head slightly and said, "I'm the reason they left."

Leonard shrugged. "That might be, but they didn't follow the rules, and you held them accountable. It's not your fault that they couldn't make it into the city, to safety, in time." Raziel felt her eyes start to well up with tears as he continued, "The leader I knew, the one I loved and dedicated my life to, would stand her ground because she knew that the rules she implemented made Nirvana, well, Nirvana."

Raziel nodded, and as she looked around, she saw the couples start to pull away and continue to look at each other nervously. She said loudly, "I will not beat myself up for their deaths. As much as I miss them, it isn't my fault."

Leonard bowed and stepped back into the crowd. Raziel smiled at him, thankful for his support, and she looked out at everyone else and loudly asked, "Does anyone else have anything to say?" The silence was deafening.

Someone from the back cleared their throat, and Raziel shouted, "Speak up!"

Angelus stepped forward. Raziel's breath caught in her throat, and with some disdain, and she said, "You haven't been here long enough to have an opinion."

Angelus shrugged. "That may be, but I still have a right to speak and to be heard."

Raziel shut her mouth, and she went to pour some of the jungle juice into one of the cups that she was handed by one of the kitchen staff. She gripped it with both hands and felt it start to warm up, and she saw the liquid glow slightly. Angelus watched her as she handed him the cup.

She smiled at him and said, "Drink, then speak." She smirked at him as he drank the entire thing in one long gulp and handed the cup back to her before turning to the crowd. "Nirvana isn't supposed to be a dictatorship; it's not even supposed to have a matriarchal system. It's supposed to be free. Free to love whomever, free to be yourself, and free from societal expectations and rules!" He pointed to Raziel. "She's still imposing rules, just under the guise of it being for the greater good."

Raziel was confused. Angelus should have snapped into line with the drink, and she looked out to the crowd, murmuring and agreeing with Angelus. Raziel coughed, and then said, "Well, let's welcome a new dawn in Nirvana with a toast. Everyone line up to get a cup!"

Every time she filled a cup, she transferred some of her divinity into the drink, enchanting every person to become obedient and wanting things to go back to how they were. She didn't know what happened with Angelus, but she was under the impression that she needed to watch him closer; something was *definitely* off about him.

Once everyone, including herself, had a cup in their hands, she raised hers and yelled, "To Nirvana!" And this caused the crowd to echo her. She watched as everyone took their first sip, and they all had the same shudder at the same time, as if they were being reset.

Ramona stepped forward and said, "Rules are in place to ensure that Nirvana runs smoothly!"

Raziel nodded and replied, "Thank you, Ramona. You're

right."

Angelus looked around him, confused, and then turned his attention back to Raziel. He stepped forward again. "What happened to a *new dawn* in Nirvana? You were all so keen about it earlier."

Leonard yelled, "Don't like the rules? Get out of here!"

Angelus looked at Raziel, and there was an odd expression on his face. She avoided his eyes and clapped her hands together. "Well, shall we get everything ready for a meal?"

A sound of approval rippled through the crowd. Raziel was pleased, knowing that things were going to go back to normal. Before they all departed, Angelus tried once more, "Can we get a vote on the rules?"

He was met with disapproving glares, and someone from the back called out, "You're free to leave!"

Angelus looked at Raziel, who shrugged. Everyone broke off into smaller crowds, and the kitchen staff started to make their way back to the kitchen. Angelus approached Raziel, and she couldn't help but notice the misunderstanding on his beautiful face.

When he got close enough to her, he asked, "What just happened?"

Raziel stared at him, and she replied coolly, "The commune has spoken, Angelus."

She put both of her hands behind her back as she began to walk away, and heard him start to run after her.

"But how did that happen?"

Raziel stopped and looked at him as suspicion crept into her tone. "If I didn't know any better, I would think that you were trying to overthrow me, Angelus."

He looked to the ground and quietly said, "I just want to make Nirvana better."

Raziel glared at him. "Better?! Better than the oasis that I have dedicated my entire life to creating?"

Angelus looked up at her and replied, "Yes."

The sky above them began to darken as Raziel became increasingly angry, and she carefully whispered, "I suggest you choose your next words wisely."

Angelus sighed. "You know how I feel about you. I just want you to myself."

Raziel tilted her head slightly and thought for a moment as the sky started to light up above them again. She closed her eyes and whispered, "I am for everyone, Angelus. I am not only for one man or for one woman. That's the beauty of Nirvana, and if you cannot appreciate Nirvana for what it is, then perhaps this isn't the place for you." Raziel smirked at him and left.

He stood in the same spot and watched her walk away from him.

Raziel's heart was beating so fast that she was sure it would give her away. When she got back to her cabin, she slumped to the floor, trying to rationalize her swaying the community again. She knew that no one would truly understand what happened, but they would all be happy once more and go about their everyday lives and routines.

She sighed, and when she stood up again, she couldn't help but wonder why it didn't affect Angelus. She saw him drink from the cup! She wondered if she should contact Natalia about it, but Raziel knew that if she got Natalia involved with the atmosphere of Nirvana, it could ruin everything. She sighed. Maybe if she spent a bit more time with Angelus, she would be able to figure out what his angle really was.

As Raziel looked out the window, she saw that several of the rose bushes were wilting. Her face scrunched up into a scowl. She quickly went outside, and as she walked through the garden, she saw the roses turning black. The smell that was coming from the garden was rancid, and Raziel recognized that it was the smell of rotting flesh.

She looked around. None of the bodies were exposed to the air, but it smelled as if she were right beside them. Raziel felt sick to her stomach; she knew she wouldn't be able to hide this from anyone in the compound. Dropping to her knees, she began to claw at the earth under one of the very first rose bushes that she had planted.

When she reached where she had placed the body, she was relieved to see that he was still there. He was almost reduced to his skeleton, and as she stared at the hand, the flashback of Timothy trying to organize an uprising flooded her mind. Raziel became angry once more, and she stared at the corpse.

"You deserve to rot here," she said out loud.

She stared at it, and for a moment, she thought that it had flinched ever so slightly, causing her to fall back in shock. Raziel looked around her, suddenly realizing how quiet it had become. She couldn't even hear voices in the distance or the birds above her; even the bugs had become silent. Raziel inched closer to the small hole and looked in again, relieved to see that Timothy was still dead, decomposing, and not moving.

She breathed, but she couldn't shake the feeling of doom that had suddenly overwhelmed her. Raziel, all of a sudden, felt like someone was going to find her graveyard. It would unravel everything that she had worked so hard on, and Nirvana would be destroyed. She knew that she needed to take protective measures, so Raziel began to separate the rose bushes and place them at the front of the garden, hoping that the fresh flowers would mask the smell and distract anyone from going closer to investigate.

Raziel spent the entire afternoon transferring rose bushes to other places around the garden, and when she was finished, it hit her that no one had bothered her the entire time. She stood up and looked around at her handiwork. She was pleased with her efforts.

She then looked down at herself, realizing how filthy she had become. Raziel walked around to the back of the cabin and started the water in her tub before placing the heater under it. As she turned on the water spout at the side to wash her hands, the water dripping turned from brown to crimson red, shocking Raziel. She looked at her hands and saw that they were dripping with blood, and the dirt that had covered her dress previously was now red and leaking from the skirt seams.

Raziel stared at her hands in horror. Every time she tried to wash the blood off, more seemed to drip from them. She closed her eyes tight, and when she opened them again, the bathtub was overflowing with red, bloodstained water. She started to slowly back away, and she screamed, "Enough!"

She blinked, and the blood had disappeared. Looking at her hands once more, they were stained brown from the soil, and her dress was almost black from the amount of dirt that it was saturated with.

Raziel looked around, her breathing rapid and her thoughts scattered. The soft bubbling of hot water started to sound as the liquid in her tub began overheating. She ran over and pulled the flame from underneath it and sighed. The water was boiling hot, but she undressed and stepped into the scorching tub anyway. Raziel hoped she could cleanse herself of what she had just witnessed.

She sank down into the water until she was completely submerged. Dunking her head under the surface, she held herself there until her lungs were threatening to burst from a lack of oxygen. When she sat up again, Raziel's skin was as red as if she had been in the sun for too long.

When she got out of the water, her skin was red and sore. She walked in through the back door and quickly braided her hair, and as she looked out the window, she saw that the sun was starting to set, and the smell of food cooking started to waft into her cabin.

As she left for dinner and walked past the garden, Raziel stopped and inhaled deeply. She was met with the sweet floral scent of the rose bushes. She stared at the garden, perplexed; she knew what she had smelled before. She would know the smell of decaying bodies anywhere, and she was confident that she had smelled it earlier. She was confused but continued to walk across the clearing to the dining hall. Raziel watched for any disturbances to indicate that her divinity transfer didn't go well.

When she walked into the eating area, she was greeted by the sounds of happy, carefree conversations running down the hall. No one paid her much attention as she entered the building, but she had the urge to eat alone anyway and wanted to process what she had witnessed at her cabin. As she was about to leave the building, she heard her name called, and she turned around to see Ramona coming toward her.

Raziel held her breath, expecting some kind of backlash, but as Ramona came closer, the look of concern was blatant on her face as she looked at Raziel's skin and asked, "Raziel! What happened?"

Raziel looked down at her very red arms. "I've been in the rose garden all day. The sun got to me."

Ramona bowed and replied, "I will harvest some aloe after dinner and come to apply it for you."

Raziel agreed, and then continued to walk out of the dining hall.

When she reached the lake, she set the plate down on the ground, and when she stood straight again, she closed her eyes, trying to calm her nerves. If things were going to go back to normal, she needed to change her attitude; she needed to be the carefree leader that they saw her as.

These past few weeks had been so chaotic and had affected her on a divine and molecular level. Raziel knew that she was the only one who could balance the community.

While she felt depleted after transferring her intentions to her followers, Raziel knew she needed to focus again.

Leaving her plate on the ground, she walked out to the middle of the lake and sat cross-legged on the surface. She allowed herself to become immersed in the calmness of the water, surrounded by the sound of wings flapping and frogs singing their tunes. She finally felt herself becoming grounded as the nature around her consumed her. She released her stress, concerns, and fear into the Universe.

When she opened her eyes, the area around her was black, as if it had been consumed by a black hole. The water beneath her had turned to tar, and she had lost her focus; she plummeted into the depths of the lake. Raziel tried to reach the surface, but the harder she fought, the further she was pulled into the watery abyss. She felt her body start to resist taking a breath, her lungs beginning to burn, and she finally inhaled, causing everything to turn dark.

Raziel opened her eyes to see Angelus on top of her, breathing into her mouth. Both of them soaking wet, she began coughing, and all of the lake water that she had swallowed exited her body. Raziel sat up, alarmed, and looked around, the dusk providing a beautiful golden glow on the crystal-clear lake.

She shook her head, and she quietly asked, "Did you see that?"

She pointed out to the lake, but Angelus just looked at her. "Raziel, you fell into the lake. I got to you as soon as I could."

Raziel shook her head. "No, everything was black, dark, and the water was…" She trailed off when she saw the look of disbelief on his face.

She cleared her throat and thanked him for saving her. She then shakily stood up and walked over to the plate on the ground to pick it up. Raziel wasn't sure what was happening, but she didn't want Angelus anywhere near her while she figured it out.

11

As Raziel picked up her plate, she fell over. Angelus ran to her as she tried to stand up again.

"Raziel! Sit down, I mean it."

She glared at him and sputtered, "How is it that you always find me in my most vulnerable moments?" He pulled her back down and got her into a comfortable position. He still hadn't answered. Raziel said even more aggressively, "Angelus!" He looked up, and she asked him again, "How is it that you're always there?"

His eyes softened, and he whispered, "Call it a hunch? I just want to be there for you."

She scanned his face, and the image of her drowning in

the tar flashed in her mind. She jumped, and he stared deep into her eyes.

"Maybe we should go to the infirmary."

Raziel shook her head. "I just want to be alone, Angelus. Please leave me alone." He went to object, but she held her hand up. "I said leave, please." He knew better and didn't say another word as he stood up and left her staring out into the lake.

Raziel felt like her entire world was crumbling around her. She had never felt so out of control before, and she didn't know what to do. As her eyes welled up with tears, she knew she needed to contact Natalia.

Once she felt better, she stood up and was relieved to see that no one was near her. Raziel still thought that it was odd how Angelus just happened to be there. Sighing, she was grateful that, this time, he was.

Walking slowly to her cabin, Raziel felt nervous about contacting her sister. She was worried that she wouldn't come; Natalia could be slightly abrasive. As she opened the door, she was surprised to see Natalia sitting on her bed, inspecting her nails. Natalia looked over her hand as Raziel opened the door. She pointed with a finger and motioned up and down.

"What happened?"

Raziel crumbled and told her everything. Initially, Natalia had her legs crossed, but by the time Raziel finished, her older sister was leaning forward, a slight look of interest on her face.

They stared at each other for some time before Raziel finally said, "Natalia, say something!"

She watched as Natalia stood up and motioned for her to stand. When they were at eye level, Natalia reached out and placed her hand on Raziel's chest and quietly whispered, "Breathe."

Raziel took a deep breath in, and Natalia's hand began to

glow a soft pink. They looked at each other, and as her hand grew warm, Raziel felt recharged and at peace.

Natalia pulled her hand back, and Raziel asked, "How did you know?"

Natalia smiled at her and replied, "I can always sense when you're spiraling. Next time, don't leave it for so long."

Raziel's brow furrowed. "This time was different though, Sister."

Natalia nodded. "I told you, there is another force walking this Earth right now. I don't know who they are or what they want, but Azazel is losing her mind, and I felt your shift. Keep your wits, Sister."

Raziel shook her head. "Something isn't right."

Natalia nodded and replied, "Whoever is here has tipped the balance." She pointed at Raziel and said, "Stay sharp. I mean it, Raziel." She turned back toward the darkness of the cabin and disappeared.

Raziel had enough of the day and decided to turn in for the night. Stripping off her soaking dress and placing it over one of the hooks on the wall, she changed into a pink gown and crawled into bed. Once she was covered and comfy, she pulled the sheets over her head and closed her eyes, waiting for sleep to consume her.

It didn't take long for her to fall asleep and back into the days at the garden. It was easy when there were only two humans in the entire world, and they were contained in one place. Raziel had always been convinced that there was more to the story than just the apple. She had kept her theories to herself for millennia, but when she fell back to Earth, she knew *exactly* how she wanted to model Nirvana. It was to be reincarnated in the image of Eden.

She'd worked so hard to keep everyone safe, happy, and satisfied.

Raziel was spinning around in the open space after she had just erected the walls, when suddenly, a large dark cloud floated over the top of the compound, threatening to pour down on her.

She looked up at the sky and screamed, "Smite me if you are so angry! Do it!" She had never defied the Creator in such a way before, but when she figured out how cruel, selfish, and conceited He was, she was willing to do anything to reject and offend Him.

Raziel stared at the sky, repeatedly screaming to be struck down if He were indeed that offended. Eventually, the sky started to brighten, and the clouds began to open. She laughed and said to herself, "That's what I thought!"

As she turned her back, Raziel heard a crack, and when she looked back, a beam of white light was coming straight for her.

She sat straight up, screaming in her bed. Raziel felt all over herself; she began to cry as she realized that she was okay, and it was just a nightmare. She fell back into her pillows and tried to calm herself again. She needed to find out who this influence was. She needed to help Natalia set things right again, and if Azazel really was giving into her hunger, then it was only a matter of time before it got out of control again. If Azazel was spiraling even half as bad as Raziel was, that could mean total annihilation for Azazel's kingdom.

Raziel rolled over onto her side, a million thoughts running through her head.

She stayed awake until she saw the glow of the sun starting to creep into her cabin. She had spent the earliest hours of the morning thinking about the last time that Azazel needed to be reset, and it made her heart ache. As her cabin filled with sunshine, Raziel pulled herself out of bed and decided that she wanted a cold dip in the lake.

When she stepped out of the cabin, her breath was taken by the beauty that Nirvana offered in the morning. Before everyone woke up, the dew glistened on the grass, the birds flew low to get their breakfast, and chipmunks scurried around. Raziel grinned; the simplicity of these things was what made Nirvana so great, in her mind.

She got to the water's edge and was thrilled to see the sun reflecting off the water's surface. It gave the scene a euphoric glow, and it made Raziel excited to start her day. As she undressed, she pushed the images of her drowning the night before out of her mind.

Once Raziel was completely naked, she stepped into the water, which turned out to be a lot colder than she had anticipated. She kept walking into the depths, confident that no one would disturb her this early in the morning. Once the water was up to her shoulders, she dunked her head under, allowing herself to become cleansed by the water.

When she broke the surface once more, she wiped her eyes and saw naked Angelus entering the lake. She glared at him, furious that he had followed her again, and as he approached her, he started to glide through the water.

Once he got close to her, Raziel asked in an irritated tone, "What are you doing?"

Angelus smirked and replied, "Same thing you are, I suppose."

He went under the water and swam further into the lake. Raziel watched him and considered turning back; she hadn't accounted for anyone coming to disturb her peace.

While she wasn't embarrassed to be naked, Angelus made her feel vulnerable and exposed, and she wasn't sure if she liked it or not. She was shaken out of her thoughts when he swam closer to her again.

He quietly said, "I wasn't sure if you'd ever be able to get into the lake again."

Raziel tilted her head. "Water is healing. It cleanses your body and your soul. I'd be silly if I turned my back on it."

Angelus nodded. "I agree."

His eyes were so intoxicating that Raziel had to look away

every few seconds; she feared that they would peek into her soul and see who she really was.

Angelus continued, "I am truly sorry if I offended you before. I feel called to follow you, comfort you, and care for you. I had an inclination that you have never had before."

Raziel's face scrunched up, and she said, "I have an entire community who cares for me."

Angelus shook his head and pulled himself even closer. "Not in the way that I want to take care of you."

Raziel looked at him and felt like her heart would beat out of her chest as he grabbed her gently and pulled her to his chest. He softly tilted her chin up and kissed her lips. It sent a current of electricity through her entire body and made her crumble at the same time. She melted into his embrace and allowed him to wrap his hands around her submerged waist. The two were lost in their passionate affair, lost in time, lost in each other.

When they pulled apart, Angelus whispered, "I know you felt that."

Raziel grinned and coyly whispered, "Shut up before I change my mind."

She pulled him back to her. Raziel's entire body was buzzing, and her mind was racing. She had never experienced these feelings before, and she heard Ramona's voice inside her head, "Lean into it." Raziel had spent her entire existence making sure that humans were taken care of and happy. It was finally her turn, and she refused to apologize for it.

After some time, they began to hear voices in the distance.

Angelus pulled away first and said, "I'll leave first. I'm sure you want to keep this quiet."

Raziel smiled at him and nodded. "Come find me later, though," she said reassuringly.

Angelus smiled back, swam to the edge, and got himself dressed quickly. With a look over his shoulder and a quick wave, he took off running toward the huts. Once he was out of sight, Raziel swam to the shallows and stepped out of the lake; her heart felt full. She knew that this was something special, a gift perhaps for staying on her path.

As she got dressed and walked back to her cabin, she was lost in the feelings of Angelus' mouth on hers. She had never tasted a kiss so sweet. Once she was inside, she shook her hair out, allowing it to flow freely around her body. Raziel felt light, and like she would float away if she allowed herself to lose herself in her feelings.

When she stepped out of her front door, she smelled breakfast and was excited for the food. This day had so much promise already, and Raziel was excited to see what else it had in store for her. When she reached the dining hall, she was greeted with the smell of a full scrambled egg breakfast and fresh fruit bowls. She grabbed a plate with sausage, fruit, eggs, and some toast. Out of nowhere, she became famished.

Raziel then walked over to the table that had all of the pregnant women and asked them how they were doing. She loved being able to feel the growing lives in their bellies. After her blessings, they all began to eat. Raziel was surprised that even the food tasted better. Every time Raziel looked over to his table, she saw Angelus staring at her. She would blush and look away, but she couldn't ignore the hunger that she saw in his eyes.

Raziel kept thinking about their moment at the lake; she kept touching her lips in between bites at the thought of Angelus' lips on hers. She started getting lost in her thoughts, and finally, someone grabbed her arm, and she noticed that the entire table was empty.

She looked up and saw Angelus. She beamed and quietly said, "Hi."

He kissed her cheek and asked, "Would you like to go for a walk?"

He motioned toward the gates, and Raziel enthusiastically

agreed. Once they were outside, Angelus grabbed her hand, and they walked down the path, further into the jungle.

When they were quite a distance away, Angelus looked around and whispered, "This is the perfect place."

Then he turned his attention to Raziel, and she couldn't stop staring at him. When he took a step closer to her, Raziel became nervous.

Angelus tucked some of her hair behind her ear and whispered, "You're beautiful."

Raziel blushed and replied, "You're too kind."

Angelus shook his head and continued, "You are a *goddess*."

Raziel looked at him, unsure if he'd meant to use that term, but then he kissed her, and she forgot any feelings of apprehension that she had before.

Angelus picked Raziel up effortlessly and carried her over to a thick tree so that her back was against the trunk. As he kissed down her neck, he whispered, "I needed to get you deep into the forest so no one would hear you."

He ran his hands up the outside of Raziel's thighs, and a fire ignited inside of her. She kissed him passionately and bit his bottom lip. Angelus let out a low growl, and the two of them gave in to their most primal needs, spending the entire morning deep within the forest, and ultimately, lost in each other.

Eventually, they decided that it was time to go back to Nirvana. They walked back slowly with their fingers entwined with each other.

As they approached the gates, Angelus leaned in for one last kiss and said, "I'll come to you tonight if you want."

Raziel nodded and grinned as she said, "Please."

Angelus smiled one last time and walked through the gates. She watched him walk away, and as he was about to go over the slight hill, he looked over his shoulder and winked at her.

Raziel felt like she could fly. It was the most beautiful, passionate, and intense experience that she had ever had with a human, and it felt like it was just for her.

Suddenly, she heard her name being called, and when she spotted where the voice was coming from, Ramona was running toward her with a giant smile and a plate filled with food.

When Ramona got close enough, she giggled. "Raziel, you are absolutely glowing today! Could it have anything to do with Angelus?" Raziel's eyes went wide, and she went to object, but Ramona shook her head. "I saw the two of you at the lake this morning."

Raziel's mouth dropped, and she felt her face flush. Ramona smiled knowingly and said, "Let's go have lunch inside your cabin. I could use some tea."

The two of them continued walking to Raziel's cabin, and when they were behind the closed door, Ramona set the tray down onto her bed, and Raziel went to grab her kettle and cups.

Ramona sat on the bed, and she looked at Raziel innocently. "Well?"

This caused Raziel to reveal everything that had happened in the jungle. By the time she had poured the tea into the cups, she finished the entire story, causing Ramona to squeal in delight. Raziel was smiling the whole time, and Ramona pointed at her.

"I like this look on you."

Raziel looked down at the teacup as she handed it to her friend, and she nodded. "I like it, too." She sat beside Ramona, and she whispered, "He scares me, though, in a weird but wonderful way."

Ramona popped a tangerine slice into her mouth as she answered, "Love will do that."

Raziel shook her head. "It's not love, Ramona."

"It sure sounds like it! And you've been doing this back

and forth with your feelings about Angelus since he got here. It's okay to give in to them; no one is going to stop you."

Raziel grabbed a grape and ate it thoughtfully. Ramona sighed slightly and asked, "Would you be okay with Angelus taking multiple partners?"

Raziel quickly looked at Ramona, and she felt like she had been stabbed in the heart. It hurt her to think of Angelus touching someone else like he'd touched her, to think of him kissing other people like he'd kissed her. She shook her head. "I don't think I would be."

Raziel felt confused, and she was trying to keep her feelings under the surface but couldn't deny them any longer. Ramona smiled knowingly, and she popped a strawberry into her mouth. After she was finished, she said, "That's love, Raziel."

12

Raziel looked at Ramona in shock and shook her head. "That's impossible, literally impossible!"

Ramona smiled and nodded reassuringly. "That's what we all say."

Raziel sighed and stood up. "No, Ramona; it is absolutely *impossible* for me to fall in love. It's a curse. I can watch others experience it, and I might come close to it, but I will *never* truly experience it."

"Why?"

"It's my punishment for my part in the uprising that caused the fall."

When Raziel looked back at Ramona, she saw Ramona's shocked face. Raziel rarely, if ever, talked about the fall with her community. After the initial explanation when Nirvana opened, the story had been passed down through the followers so that Raziel would never need to retell it.

Ramona had never heard Raziel talk about it firsthand, and the look on her face was full of awe and wonder.

Raziel sighed and said, "You see? There's no way."

Ramona shook her head. "Everything you described is everything that I have felt any time I have ever been in love."

Raziel started to play with her hair, and she felt confused. "Ramona, I felt so connected to him."

Ramona bowed. "As if you were one."

Raziel nodded as Ramona stood up and started to pace around the cabin. She looked at Raziel and said, "If it's not love, then what is it?"

Raziel sighed and answered, "Infatuation that will turn into obsession if I don't cater to it."

Ramona shook her head. "No, I have seen you infatuated with people in the past, and I have never seen you act like this with anyone else for as long as I have been here."

They both stared at each other in silence until Raziel sighed and picked up the tray. "Okay, enough of that. Let's finish this platter." They continued to eat in silence, and Ramona let Raziel eat stress-free.

Once the platter was clean, Ramona cleared her throat and quietly asked, "When are you going to see him again?"

Raziel slowly smirked as she whispered, "He's going to spend the night tonight."

"Raziel, you're going to be spending the night with him, and after today in the jungle and this morning at the lake, you're telling me that it's not some form of love?"

"It could be a very mild form of it, I suppose, but if this is only a mild form of it, I don't know if I would be able to handle full-fledged love."

Ramona nodded. "It can be very intense."

The two women stared at each other intensely, and a deep

cough interrupted them. Raziel looked behind them and saw Angelus approaching them. She smiled as Ramona took her leave. When he got close to Raziel, he kissed her cheek. She pulled away a little as she looked around to see if anyone was near them, and Angelus picked up on her signal.

Taking a step back, he quietly asked, "Are you ready for dinner?"

Raziel nodded, and he motioned toward the opening. "After you."

The two of them walked into the dining hall and saw that everyone was too preoccupied with their own meals to pay any attention to her and Angelus. They each grabbed their dishes and parted ways as Angelus went off to sit with the builders. Raziel sat with Ramona and some of the other women, and they all spoke about the upcoming event, the harvest celebration. Raziel had almost forgotten that it was quickly approaching.

The foragers all went into town at the perfect time, and it was almost time for autumn to come. They spent a whole week giving thanks to the Universe, leading up to the full harvest moon. Raziel smirked, knowing that another full moon celebration was coming.

But she couldn't help but let her mind wander to how she and Angelus would celebrate. After dinner, it was suggested that a bonfire be created, and Raziel couldn't agree more that it would be a perfect way to end the day. Word spread throughout the hall, and once dinner was over, the commune split up, some to get the firepit ready while others went to grab warmer clothes for the fire starters.

Raziel decided on a thicker blanket, and she went to the firepit to oversee the creation. She was pleased to see that there was already a large fire started by the time she reached the pit. Angelus was heading the group and dictating the jobs that needed to be done next. Raziel suddenly felt complete, as if he were truly the piece of her that she had been missing.

He noticed her and smiled. When she smiled back, he motioned for her to come closer, and as she did, Raziel's heart began to race violently once more.

Once she reached his side, Angelus looked around and lowered his voice. "So, when would you like to sneak off."

Raziel smirked and replied, "Let's wait until *after* the campfire."

Angelus bowed, and she noticed a slight look of disappointment on his face but knew that she would make it up to him later. They both watched the flames grow higher, and as more people started to gather around, Raziel pulled away from Angelus and began to mingle with the other members.

After a long night of singing songs, telling stories, and roasting marshmallows, everyone began to disperse for bed. There were still a few members who were watching the flames die down as Raziel decided to take her leave. She made sure to make solid eye contact with Angelus as she left.

Raziel got back to her cabin and started to light candles around her room. It wasn't long before she heard a gentle knock on the door.

"Come in!"

"Wow, this is beautiful!" Angelus exclaimed as he entered the hut.

Raziel looked around, and she felt an overwhelming sense of gratitude. "It really is, isn't it?"

They looked at each other and instantly ran into each other's arms. Their bodies melted into one another, and they spent the entire night giving into lust.

Raziel wasn't sure when they passed out, but eventually, she found herself in a pitch-black forest. She felt like she needed to walk forward, but with every step she took, a growl began to sound off in front of her. She felt the pit of her stomach start to get more intense the closer she got. She couldn't see where the sound was coming from, but it began to come from behind her the further she walked. With her final step, it sounded like it was *right behind her.*

She gasped, and it felt like someone had pushed her over a cliff. She was falling into the abyss, and her arms were flailing in the air around her, reaching for anything that could help her. Raziel felt like she was going to crash into the ground, and the longer she fell, the faster she fell. Just as she was about to crash, she heard Angelus' voice. He was laughing, and it sounded like he was whispering into her ear. He was saying every name of the people whom she had killed and buried in her garden. As she hit the ground, she woke up.

Raziel sat straight up and looked around. Angelus was *gone.* She panicked and rushed out of bed. When she looked out her side window, she was relieved to see that the garden was empty, but she felt slightly vulnerable, waking up alone. It was still dark outside, and she climbed back into bed. She was sad that Angelus would leave after the incredible night they had just had. Raziel rolled over onto her side and closed her eyes, trying to keep her disappointment at bay so she could fall asleep again.

This time, when she fell asleep, she didn't dream once. When she woke up to the sun, Raziel felt like she had been awake all night. It was heavy exhaustion filled with sadness and regret. She got out of bed and got dressed. She then braided her hair and tried to keep her face neutral as she stepped out of the cabin.

People were already walking around with breakfast, and Raziel started to get a little pep in her step as she got closer to the dining hall. As she grabbed her food, she looked around and still saw no sign of Angelus. Even as she ate, Angelus was missing, and Raziel knew that something wasn't right. The builders even came around, saying they were looking for him, and she began to grow concerned.

"How did last night go?" Ramona came over seconds later and asked.

Raziel groaned and quietly told her everything. Ramona stared at her, shocked as she said that he left in the middle of the night.

Raziel finished by bitterly asking, "Still believe it's true love?"

Ramona shook her head in disbelief. "No, there needs to be a reasonable explanation for this. I'm sure it's totally innocent."

Raziel rolled her eyes. "I think we both just got caught up in it, and I thought it was more serious than what it really was."

They sat in silence as Raziel finished her breakfast, and as she stood up, Ramona quietly said, "You're wrong, Raziel. I saw the two of you; I saw how you both looked at each other. You weren't imagining things or overthinking anything. Sometimes, those feelings are overwhelming, especially for men. Give him time. I'm sure he'll be back."

Before Raziel could disagree, Ramona stood up and left Raziel by herself. Raziel felt terrible, and now she felt worse; she hated this part of human emotions. The negative ones were so heavy and felt like they were suffocating.

As she walked out of the dining hall, she heard whispers of people asking where Angelus was, and she tried to ignore them; even the sound of his name left an awful taste in her mouth. She felt betrayed, allowing herself to be his for the day and allowing herself to feel vulnerable while he provided a safe space for her. If he ever came back, he was going to have to face her wrath, and she vowed that she wouldn't go easy on him.

Raziel spent her day overlooking different tasks around the compound. The cabin was coming to a beautiful finish, regardless of not having Angelus around to head their progress. As the lunch bell rang, Raziel started to walk toward the dining hall, and as she walked over the small hill, she saw the entire community surrounding *something*. Curious, Raziel began to run, and the closer she got, she realized that it was Angelus whom they were gathered around.

Her curiosity was instantly replaced with rage, and she stormed toward the group as people began to part for her. When she reached the center of the circle, she was surprised to see Angelus holding the most beautiful bouquet of red roses that she had ever seen. Raziel stopped and looked at him as he approached her to hand them to her.

"What are these for?" she asked.

Angelus smiled and replied, "For being an incredible inspiration to us all. I feel like I can speak for all of us when I say that we all strive to be even half of what you are so effortlessly."

Raziel searched the crowd and found Ramona's eyes, and she wished they could speak telepathically. She turned her attention back to Angelus, and she smirked. "Well, this is very sweet of you. Where did you get them?"

A sneer washed over his face as he said, "From your garden."

A collective gasp sounded, and people began to walk away hurriedly. Ramona was pulled aggressively by other members of the kitchen staff, and Raziel tilted her head as she threatened and asked, "What?"

Angelus bowed and replied, "Yes, I noticed how plump the flowers were, and I figured there was no better gift than the most beautiful flowers for the most beautiful woman."

Panic and anger started to breathe deep inside of Raziel, but she collected herself. "I looked for you all day and didn't see you anywhere."

"I took the flowers early this morning out of Nirvana to fully prepare them. I didn't want anyone to see what I was doing." He smiled at her, and his eyes began to twinkle.

Raziel looked down at the flowers, and the only thing she could smell was decay. Angelus waited for her to say something, but she simply looked at him and said, "Do *not* go into my garden again." She began to walk away from him, but Angelus chased after her.

"Raziel! What did I do?"

She stopped and glared at him. "Don't go into my garden, Angelus."

He tilted his head. "Why?"

"It's private."

They stared at each other for a few moments before he stepped toward her, lowered his voice, and asked, "Because of all the corpses?"

Raziel's eyes grew wide, and she hissed, "Excuse me?"

Angelus smirked. "I said, because of the dead bodies buried beneath the bushes?"

Raziel felt like her stomach fell to her knees, and she tried to deny it. "I have no idea what you're talking about."

But Angelus smiled wider. "No? Shall we go see what I'm talking about? I wouldn't want you to be framed for someone else's murder."

"Who are you?!"

Angelus looked around them, and he snapped his fingers. Everything around them suddenly stopped, and when Raziel looked for the humans around her, they had all frozen in their places.

Angelus stretched his arms out to his sides, and a pair of elegant white wings spread from his shoulder blades. Raziel took a step back and stared at him in horror. Angelus' skin started to glow ever so slightly, and Raziel was almost blinded by his ethereal beauty.

He held his hands up and said, "I'm not going to kill you. I was sent to observe... for now."

Raziel felt sick, and she shook her head. "No, no, this is a dream! It has to be! There's no way you're here!" She screamed, and he took a step forward.

"Do you really think the Creator would be able to forgive you and your sisters' violent tendencies toward His pets?"

Raziel shot him a nasty look with all the hate inside her body. "I don't care what His opinion is," she answered curtly.

Angelus smirked. "He said you would say something like that." He sighed and took another step forward. "Did you enjoy the games we played? Did you think you were going crazy? I know I did." The look on his face made Raziel's skin crawl.

She threw the flowers onto the ground, and she spat at him. "What now?"

Angelus shrugged. "I haven't gotten any further orders yet. Do you think the humans would rise up against you and take over Nirvana if I told them that you killed their family members to nurse your ego?"

Raziel lifted her head slightly. "They love me."

Angelus replied, "Let me guess, they get sick of your rules, mention they want change, and then you influence them back in line, forcing them to surrender to your wants and narcissism."

Raziel finally understood everything. Trying to keep herself as calm as possible, she looked around them and asked, "What do you want, Angelus?"

He innocently answered, "To watch you suffer. You have no idea how horrible it's gotten up there since you and your sisters ruined everything and sent Him on a warpath, taking His anger out on the angels left. I was sent to ensure that you pay for it."

Raziel looked at him skeptically. "Well, looks like you ruined your own plan, now that I know who you are."

Angelus sneered at her wickedly. "Don't you worry your pretty little head about it." He raised his fingers and snapped.

Raziel sat straight up in bed and looked around in the

darkness. Angelus was sleeping soundly beside her. She could feel herself shaking but couldn't figure out why. Leaning back against her pillows, she snuggled into Angelus' back and drifted back to sleep, her dreams foggy and unclear.

When she woke up in the morning, she felt like something was off.

Angelus rolled over and smiled at her. "Good morning."

Raziel gave him a small smile and replied, "It is."

He stretched his arms out and whispered, "Stay here. I'm going to get us some breakfast. Let's stay in today."

Raziel nodded. She felt like she had already lived the day once before, but it was different, like a dream that felt real. Raziel couldn't sort the thoughts out in her head, and she couldn't quite put her finger on it, but she felt different after Angelus had left the cabin.

Angelus soon returned with a large platter of fruit and a cheery disposition. He handed her the platter, and when she took it, he asked, "You alright?"

Raziel looked at him cautiously. "I'm not sure. I feel off."

He nodded. "Sometimes that will happen when you've connected with someone the way we have." He reached forward to tuck a strand of hair behind her ear, and when he touched her, Raziel felt repulsed.

13

Raziel tried to hide her disgust.

"I guess I can't get rid of all your hesitation, but I want to try." Angelus looked down at the platter. "How about you stay here, and I will go oversee how things are going out there? Take your time coming out."

Angelus leaned forward and kissed her on the forehead. Raziel felt like she was going to puke and stepped back slightly, nodding. "Okay, I'll see you out there."

Once he left, Raziel sat on her bed and slowly ate the fruit. She couldn't figure out what she was feeling. When she stood up, something caught the corner of her eye, and when she turned to look, she saw a large group of community members walking toward her cabin. Many of them had torches, and she watched in horror as one of them threw a torch into her garden. The bushes went up in flames, and Raziel ran out the front door to a mob of angry Nirvanians.

A man shouted, "Murderer!" The others echoed him.

Raziel held her hands up, trying to calm them down, but then the unmistakable stench of burning, rotting flesh filled the air around them. Raziel's eyes widened as everyone realized what it was.

Angelus came through the crowd and said, "I told them how you've been fertilizing your beautiful garden."

All of a sudden, Raziel remembered everything, and as she was about to scream, he snapped his fingers, and everyone was silent, still, and time had stopped. He walked around different members, and he called out, "It looks like I was right about their reaction!" He chuckled. "How long do you think it would take for them to kill you?"

Raziel violently shook her head. "Impossible."

Angelus sneered. "Maybe, but they sure would relieve a lot of frustration trying!"

"Enough, Angelus! Enough!"

He had a smug look on his face. "Oh, sweet Raziel, we are just getting started. I'll be in touch." He snapped his fingers again, and Raziel woke up in bed.

She looked around and began to panic. She remembered everything and knew she needed to get ahead of it. As she got out of bed, Raziel realized how much she was shaking. The sun was shining brightly through her windows, and she quickly got dressed.

Raziel ran toward the dining hall, where the kitchen staff was preparing breakfast. Without answering any of their questions, Raziel went over to the large containers of pink juice and placed her hands on them. The only thing that washed over her mind was *death*. The liquid began to bubble and turn into a lime green color. Raziel knew she needed to erase any memory of Angelus. When she took her hands away, she felt better.

She looked back to the staff and asked, "Can you bring these out? I have an announcement to make."

Raziel felt a twinge of guilt for interfering with her humans again, but she needed to protect Nirvana. As she walked out of the kitchen, she began calling everyone to gather around for her announcement.

"Come in close, everyone! I have an important message."

They all looked at each other and murmured amongst themselves. As the kitchen staff brought out the liquid, people began to get excited. Raziel heard whispers of *sour apple* or *limeade*, knowing that it was a group favorite.

"Shouldn't we wait for Angelus?" someone called out.

Hearing his name made Raziel feel ill. She shook her head and replied, "Angelus will have his when he returns." She looked around the compound as far as she could see, and when she didn't see any sign of him, she began talking to her followers.

She took a deep breath and said, "Brothers, sisters." She looked around as people stared back at her. "We are on the verge of something truly amazing here at Nirvana, and all of you are on the precipice of greatness, to go down in history as the *only* true free-loving society. Being a part of Nirvana is more than just being here in body; it's about truly immersing your soul into the essence of Nirvana." She felt the atmosphere start to soften as she motioned to everyone to start drinking from their cups. "Please, everyone. Drink, and then we shall all be merry." She looked around and took one of the cups, handing it to the chef. "I want you to take part as well."

He took it from her and greedily gulped it down. As Raziel attempted to start talking again, she noticed that someone in the back was starting to convulse and foam at the mouth. His eyes rolled into the back of his head, and he collapsed. Soon, everyone in the group began to shake, and they all dropped to the ground.

Raziel shook her head; this wasn't what she'd wanted! She rushed over to Ramona's side. Blood was starting to trickle from Ramona's nose, and she looked up in fear as Raziel held her.

Tears streamed down Raziel's cheeks, and she screamed, "No! No! This wasn't supposed to happen!" Ramona started to gurgle and made an attempt to speak, but Raziel shushed her and whispered, "Save your strength."

The entire compound took exactly seven minutes to succumb to death, and finally, Raziel stood up. She felt a hint of immense sadness when she saw the future mothers clutching onto each other. Raziel fell to her knees and let out a screech that shook the ground beneath her.

She bent over and began to sob into the grass. In the distance, she heard the sound of faint whistling, and when she popped her head up, she saw Angelus walking toward her. Raziel was filled with rage, and she stood up.

But before she could take a step, Angelus was right in front of her, and she screamed, "What did you do?!"

"I didn't do this, Raziel. You did."

He pointed at her, and she quickly shook her head. "No, no! I didn't mean to. I would *never* want to hurt them!"

There was a pleading undertone in her voice, and Angelus sucked the air through his teeth. "Has it crossed your mind that divinely influencing your following would have repercussions at some point? Perhaps humans are just meant to live out their pathetic little lives until it's time for cosmic judgment? Maybe we aren't to interfere because it gets to a point where the weak humans can't take it?"

"I know it's because of you," she denied. "Ever since you landed on Earth, everything has—"

He interrupted her. "Now, now, don't go blaming your

shortcomings on me. There has *always* been something wrong with you and your sisters, trying to get the Creator to go against His own plan for the humans, trying to give the humans free will and further their learning." Angelus started laughing. "I can't believe you killed your entire following!" He looked around them. "Being on Earth really *has* made you lose it, huh? The Creator is going to be absolutely furious, and I can't wait to see what He unleashes on you and your pathetic fallen sisters."

Raziel felt hopeless; she couldn't believe she had just killed all of her beloved community.

She looked up at Angelus. "You can turn back time."

Angelus nodded. "Yes, I can."

Raziel continued, "You can fix this. You can bring them all back to life."

Angelus nodded again. "Yes, I can."

Raziel pleaded, "Please, bring them back. Please." Desperation was seeping from Raziel's entire body, and she felt empty as Angelus shook his head.

"Absolutely not."

Tears began to flow from her eyes again, and she let out a sorrowful howl. Angelus watched her in pure glee, and he looked around the entire compound. "So, what are you going to do with the compound now? You can't cover the ground in rose bushes." He chuckled as he began to walk away from her.

Raziel felt a rage inside her that she had never felt before, and she stood up quickly, chasing after him. But Angelus turned around quickly, grabbed her by the neck, and slammed her to the ground when she got closer.

"You've been on Earth for far too long, and I promise you that your powers aren't even a faint whisper to what mine are. I suggest you stay on the ground."

He let go of her neck, and she asked, "What are you going to do?"

Angelus walked away from her and yelled back, "You'll know when it happens."

He disappeared and left her staring at her fallen family members. All of a sudden, she heard her name being screamed, and she looked back and saw Natalia walking toward her, a look of utter shock on her face.

"Sister, what happened?!"

She looked around, and Raziel answered, "I lost it. I lost control. Angelus, one of our new members. He's an angel."

Natalia looked at Raziel and sarcastically said, "Oh, really? A man named Angelus was an angel? Shocker, Raziel."

Raziel always hated Natalia's sarcasm, but even she couldn't help but agree with her sister. She had let her feelings control the outcome instead of using her head. Raziel looked around, and Natalia sighed. "This is a serious mess; you understand that?"

Raziel nodded. "How do we fix it?"

Natalia started to maneuver through the bodies. "We are going to bury everyone, and you're not going to allow *anyone* into Nirvana for at least a hundred years. That way, we can be absolutely sure that the bodies will be completely dissolved into the earth."

Raziel bobbed her head slowly, and Natalia clapped her hands. "Well, let's do this."

Raziel felt her eyes start to fill with tears again, and Natalia shook her head. "Sister, no. Don't start; they are *just* humans. Pull yourself together!"

Natalia lifted her hands, and the bodies started to sink into the ground. They were underneath the surface in mere seconds, and wildflowers had begun to sprout up in their place. Natalia glanced around, and then confidently said, "See, that's so much better."

Raziel sighed. "I feel so heavy, Sister."

"I know, but you need to pull yourself up out of your sadness. We have bigger issues at hand."

Raziel looked up at her and saw Natalia looking into the distance. She then looked over her shoulder and saw Angelus walking toward them.

Natalia lowered her voice and whispered, "I see why you were so distracted, Sister; he is scrumptious."

Angelus stood before them and said, "Ladies."

Natalia scoffed. "They sent the poster child down here?"

Raziel looked at Natalia in confusion. "You know him?"

Natalia shook her head slightly. "Barely. He was entry-level while we were doing all the hard work."

Angelus smirked. "And then when the three of you had your grace and wings ripped from you, I had the honor of carrying the brunt of the rage that filled Heaven."

Natalia rolled her eyes. "Oh, the tragedy plays that they could write about your sorrowful life."

Angelus glanced at Raziel. "I should have just killed *her* instead of wasting my time with *you*."

Raziel stood up. "Angelus, you're a *yes man*. You won't act until you have orders."

Angelus nodded. "Yes, you're right. But I was able to almost drown you in your own lake. I was able to convince your own followers to almost kill you. And I didn't have orders to do that, so I suggest we all play nicely, or I *will* act accordingly."

Natalia and Raziel exchanged looks, and Natalia spoke, "So, cut the chase. Stop wasting our time. What is it that you want?"

Angelus replied, "The Creator wanted to know if you three had changed and were worthy of getting back into Heaven."

Raziel shook her head. "No, you're mistaken. We were told that there would *never* be a chance of that happening." Natalia nodded in agreement.

Angelus shrugged. "I'm only relaying the information that I have."

Natalia smirked. "Well, I think you got something confused because we were told that there is no way that we could ever come back."

The three of them stared at each other, and Angelus asked, "Where's Azazel?"

Natalia shrugged. "Don't know."

He looked at her skeptically. "You don't know?"

Natalia shook her head. "She has put her own divinity into protecting her kingdom. Azazel doesn't show up until she *wants* to show up."

Angelus smiled widely. "Right, and the divine source for the fallen trio has no idea where one of her dependents is."

Raziel felt nervous, and she could sense that Natalia was reaching her last nerve as she said, "Look, I'm getting bored with you, your empty threats, and watching you harass my sister. Either you leave us be, or you get on with it and try to kill us."

Angelus bowed. "Ladies, I shall be back."

As he left, Natalia looked back at Raziel and said, "He's kind of an asshole, yeah?"

Raziel nodded. "This was nothing. His power is truly something else."

Natalia studied her sister's face, and she solemnly said, "You're going to tell me everything that happened."

Raziel nodded and began telling her everything, from Angelus arriving to the blood dripping off of her like a fountain when she started a bath, from drowning in the lake that had turned to tar to Angelus turning back time. When she finished with the mob coming to get her, Natalia's face was as white as the clouds in the sky.

Natalia was quiet for a moment, and then she said, "We need to hide Nirvana. Blanket it so he can't get back in or find you once I leave."

"What?! You can't leave!"

"I have my own kingdom to look after, and I need to check on Azazel."

Raziel shakily said, "Fine, but promise to come back to check on me regularly. I mean it."

Natalia nodded. "I promise, Raziel. I'll check in constantly." She grabbed Raziel's hands. "I absolutely promise you."

Raziel stood up, and the two of them joined hands. They closed their eyes, and Raziel imagined a dome being lowered over the Kingdom of Nirvana. Once she felt like it had surrounded the entire compound, Natalia dropped her hands and pulled her into an embrace.

"I'm sorry this happened to you, Sister. I'm sorry you were tricked by an awful man."

"I thought it was love, Natalia. I feel so stupid."

Natalia sighed. "They have a tendency to do that." She pulled away from Raziel and said, "You are a fallen angel, a goddess on Earth. Remember who you are, heal yourself, and get him off of our radar." Raziel nodded. "Walk me back to the shadows. I will be back in a few days to see how things are going. I want to observe Azazel." Natalia studied Raziel's face for a few more minutes. "You're going to be okay, Raziel. Everything is going to be alright. Now that we know who we're dealing with, I won't let anything happen to you or to Azazel."

Raziel scoffed. "The fact that you have to observe Azazel just goes to show how unstable we are, Natalia."

Raziel looked around to where the bodies were and felt her sadness swell once more. She still couldn't believe that she had caused the massive death of her people.

Natalia sighed. "Well, Sister, I do believe that you are experiencing true heartbreak. You truly did love everyone here, and the only way to heal is to mourn. Do whatever you need to do so you feel better, Raziel, but *do not* stay in that mindset; it will kill us all."

When they walked back to Raziel's small hut, Natalia turned to her and gripped both of her sister's shoulders. "Sister, it's going to be just fine. In a hundred years, no one will even begin to remember what happened here, and you can start advertising Nirvana as the oasis it is again. Spend time bettering it, even though I doubt it's possible."

Raziel smiled at Natalia weakly. She just wanted her sister to leave so she could be alone.

Natalia picked up on it, so she finally said, "Sister, I'll see you in a few days. You're stronger than you're giving yourself credit for."

Raziel looked into Natalia's eyes and saw that she meant it. She nodded, and she turned to leave the cabin as Natalia disappeared into the faint shadows in the corner.

When Raziel walked out into the open space, she felt how empty the compound now was. Looking around, she was able to hear the birds chirping and the frogs croaking down by the lake. It was serene but incredibly sad. She breathed and decided that she would build the largest funeral pyre in Nirvana's history.

She spent two days and two nights building the large wooden structure, and then went on to carve the name of every member who had perished into it. When she carved Ramona's name, Raziel screamed out in anguish, and her guilt consumed her. She sat on the ground and sobbed until she felt like she had been depleted of any moisture left inside her body.

It started to get dark, and she gathered herself once more and continued to carve Ramona's name and finished everyone else's names. Once darkness fell over the commune, she lit the structure on fire. As the smoke drifted up to the sky, she sent her anger and sorrow with it.

14

Raziel wasn't sure when she fell asleep, but she opened her eyes to the sunshine blinding her. She was covered in dew, and when she looked at the structure, it had been reduced to ash. She stood up and saw the coals glowing, and her sorrow became the tiniest twitch in her heart. Raziel knew that the next one hundred years could either go as slow or as fast as she allowed it to, and if she stayed in her sadness, it would feel like an eternity.

As she continued to immerse herself in her thoughts, she heard a loud bang, and it felt like Nirvana shuddered. Raziel looked around, and she heard the deafening sound once more; it was coming from the gates. She walked over and opened them, and she was surprised to see Angelus on the other side.

Raziel raised a brow and called out, "Something wrong?"

She saw him chuckle, and he replied, "Seems like Nirvana is invite-only now."

"Yeah, and you're not on the list."

Angelus looked up and around him. "Is this powered by Natalia?"

Raziel shrugged. "Not sure. It just appeared."

"You know I can just dismantle it if I wanted to."

Raziel smirked. "So, then why aren't you inside?"

"I'm waiting for the right time."

Raziel rolled her eyes and waved to him as she began to close the gates.

Angelus screamed, "Raziel! Wait!"

She held off on closing them completely and asked, "What?"

She watched as Angelus' wings stretched out. His eyes turned completely white, and he began to subtly glow. She looked above her as she heard a creaking sound, as if the barrier were under immense weight. When she looked back at Angelus, she saw how red his face was from the amount of effort that he was radiating.

"You should stop before you pop a blood vessel or strain a wing."

Angelus seemed to take that as a challenge, and she watched as his entire body started to turn bright red from his efforts. Raziel waved again, and she closed the gates. If he was going to succeed, she needed to give herself a slight head start. As she walked across the clearing, she heard a faint sound, as if someone were tapping the glass.

Her stomach began to twist with anxiety, knowing that Angelus was back and could potentially get to her if he wanted to. As she approached her cabin, she had a thought in her head and ringing in her ears, realizing that it was a download.

"He won't get in."

Raziel hadn't experienced it in so long. It felt so foreign to her, and just as soon as she heard that thought, the anxiety in her body seemed to evaporate, and she began to feel safe once more. She was hesitant, but she wanted nothing more than to have a bath. It was such a warm day that a cool bath sounded like the perfect remedy. When she turned the water on, she was relieved to see that it was running clear and thought of when it looked like blood. She shuddered at Angelus' creativity.

Once the tub was filled, Raziel undressed and climbed in as she lowered herself. The cool water felt more refreshing the higher it climbed her body. Once she was settled, Raziel tilted her head back and let her mind wander as she closed her eyes. It was quiet and felt peaceful.

A quick memory of the bonfire from the night before flash in her mind. She was surprised that instead of feeling the immense sorrow that she'd expected, it was replaced with an overwhelming sense of ease. Raziel smiled. She knew that her beloved family would always be with her, giving Nirvana life and filling the atmosphere with love.

When Raziel opened her eyes, Angelus was standing over her, a crazed look on his face as he pushed her head down under the surface. Raziel struggled against him, but it felt like his strength was increasing the further she was under the water. He took his hand off of her, and she sat up, taking deep breaths and gasping.

Raziel looked at him, panicked, and Angelus sneered. "I told you." He walked around the tub, and then said, "Now, I'm due to have a consultation with the general, and I wanted to tell you that I'm going to ensure that you and your sisters lose every drop of your divinity. You're going to suffer once the humans realize what monsters the three of you are."

Raziel shook her head, and she felt her anger start to rise.

She stood up, water pouring off of her, and she stared him straight in the eyes as she asked, "Angelus, why are you doing this? Why me?"

Angelus' pupils widened as he replied, "Torturing you? It's fun."

Raziel shook her head. "No, why did you connect with me the way you did? Why did you put so much effort into getting my attention?"

Angelus smirked. "You were so desperate to experience anything relatively close to love. I smelled your desperation the second I stepped into the forest."

"Angelus, you felt something. I know you did."

Angelus scanned her entire body and looked back up to her eyes. "You were nothing."

Raziel stepped closer to him, and he was forced off the small deck. He kept denying it, but she continued to walk toward him until he stood firmly and forcibly yelled, "Stop!"

Raziel stopped where she was and whispered, "I can sense your nervous energy, Angelus. Stop trying to deny it."

Angelus shook his head. "You're insane."

Suddenly, Raziel felt eerily calm. "No, I've just had enough. You keep threatening me; you keep saying that you're going to kill me. Do it." They stared at each other in silence, and Raziel could see that he was taking it into consideration. When he didn't move, she said, "Then let's go inside."

She took his hand, and he was a bit hesitant. She looked back and said, "Angelus, indulge me one last time."

The two of them went into the cabin, dropped onto the bed, and got lost in each other once more. Raziel had the upper hand, and while he was focused on her curves, she leaned over to reach behind his head and felt the edge of the mattress until she found the handle. As she rocked her body seductively over his, she looked down and saw that he had his eyes shut, giving himself entirely over to her. Raziel pulled the blade from the mattress and waited until it began to glow white. She sat up straight and started to rotate her hips, sending him into pure ecstasy. Raziel then drove the knife deep into his chest cavity, causing Angelus to gasp loudly and look down at the weapon sticking out of him.

He looked up at her, and silver tears began to fall from his eyes as he sputtered, "Raziel."

However, she held a finger up to his lips and whispered, "I think it's best that we see other people."

Angelus' eyes went wide, and as his last breath escaped his lips, a shockwave radiated from his body, sending Raziel flying back. She landed on the floor and groaned in pain. When the pain eased slightly, she stood up and saw the pile of white ashes where Angelus previously was.

She heard a *whooshing* sound behind her, and she casually said, "Natalia."

"What happened here?"

Raziel smirked and looked over her shoulder. "Our little friend had an accident."

Natalia walked over, and she hissed, "You killed *another* angel?!"

Raziel nodded. "I had to."

"Raziel, if you kill one, more will be sent to enact their revenge!"

Raziel's face dropped; she hadn't thought of the repercussions. She looked at Natalia. "He got through the barrier and tried to drown me."

"But did you forget that you're literally immortal, and even if he succeeded, you would resurrect?"

"He made it seem like I would be dead, dead."

Natalia nodded earnestly. "Yes, Raziel. He was a prick, but mind tricks are only just that, tricks." They both looked at the pile behind them, and Natalia sighed. "Azazel has completely lost it. She's started killing her kingdom, and we need to reset her."

"What do we do about *him*?" She pointed to the pile.

Natalia replied, "If you think humans fertilize Nirvana's grounds beautifully, see what divine remains do for you."

Raziel moved past her and grabbed a dustpan, shaking the ashes into it while Natalia watched. She held the dustpan out her front door and allowed the breeze to carry the particles off across the compound. Raziel gleefully watched as the grass became greener. The air also seemed to smell sweeter, and she saw the flowers glow brighter in color. A comforting, warm, and peaceful feeling washed over Raziel. She felt like she could finally, truly, heal from Angelus and the pain that he had caused Nirvana.

When she turned around to go back inside the cabin, Natalia looked at her and impatiently asked, "Are you done now? Can we leave?"

Raziel scoffed. "Oh, I'm sorry. Did my handling of the nuisance in my world really hold us up that long?"

"Yes, Sister. It could have waited."

Raziel rolled her eyes. Natalia was always so keen to look after Azazel that the youngest sister was often forgotten. It was hard not to feel hurt, but Raziel was satisfied knowing that she had taken care of Angelus, on her own, without her sister's interference.

Raziel snidely asked, "Do you mind if I change first?"

Natalia smiled, and with an underlying venom that only an older sister can manage, she said, "I thought you'd never ask. I'll wait for you outside."

After Natalia left the cabin, Raziel turned her attention to her closet and picked out a dress from the very back. It was pink silk and hung on her curves beautifully; the delicate straps that rested on her shoulders led to the tie-up details on the back of the dress. It was one of her favorite pieces to wear, but she rarely had events where she could wear it. Raziel went on to clip her luscious locks on top of her head and allowed a few strands to fall around her face. Deciding to go barefoot felt right, and she knew that it was the best way to connect with the earth beneath her and allow her to have the freedom to ground herself if needed.

As she stepped out of her home, Natalia turned around, and her expression softened. "Ah, what a perfect outfit. Beautiful!"

Raziel blushed from Natalia's unexpected praise. Natalia slightly cleared her throat and asked, "Sister, how did you manage to kill our little problem?"

Raziel quietly said, "I had a blade secured to my mattress."

"And was this something you've always had so accessible?"

Raziel paused for a moment. "Yes, since I started Nirvana. I was scared we may lose our divinity the longer we were here, and I wanted to be able to defend myself if needed."

"Smart, and it clearly proved its use." Natalia extended her hand to Raziel, who took it, and the two of them started to walk through the clearing.

In the blink of an eye, they were inside of Azazel's kingdom. The streets were empty, and they exchanged looks; the domain felt dark and heavy. Natalia sighed, and Raziel started to storm up to the palace. As she tried to walk through the gates, she was pushed back by a force. She staggered backwards and looked over her shoulder to see Natalia's fuming expression.

Natalia shook her head. "It seems that our sweet sister doesn't want visitors."

Raziel felt a deep rage inside of her also and replied, "That's too bad."

Raziel walked back to Natalia, who grabbed her hand, and Raziel pointed to the Great Hall as they walked toward the castle once more. This time, they entered the Great Hall and were met with a massacre. Raziel dropped Natalia's hand and placed her own hand over her mouth in horror. It looked like someone had painted the entire room blood red!

Natalia glanced around, and Raziel screamed, "Sister, your bloody tyranny is done! That is enough!"

Azazel paused her feeding and smiled wickedly at her sisters. Once Natalia and Raziel finished surveying the damage that Azazel had done, they found her torture chamber and put her in her bed. The sisters waited for her to wake up once more. They had bound Azazel's arms and legs to her bedframe, and while they waited, they sat in the small sitting area in Azazel's grand bedroom.

Raziel whispered, "What do you think happened?"

Natalia shrugged. "The same thing that always happens. She succumbed to her curse, and she lost herself to her hunger."

Raziel shook her head. "It hasn't been this bad since the very beginning."

Natalia nodded. "I know, but I suppose we were due for something of this caliber. It ties in nicely with the mass extinction that took place at Nirvana. You're not in the position to be judgmental, Sister."

Raziel slumped in her seat ever so slightly. "That was different."

She pouted, and Natalia lifted her brows. "Was it? How so? Both of your kingdoms were slaughtered because you both can't keep your divinity in check. So please, Sister, do explain how your situation differs."

Raziel stuttered. She was unable to and knew that Natalia was right. She simply whispered, "It won't happen again."

Natalia nodded. "You're right; it *won't* happen again. It seems that I need to be in full control of our powers."

Raziel's mouth dropped open. "I don't think a transfer needs to take place."

Natalia sighed. "I think it might, Sister. I am tired of

having to watch over the both of you. I am exhausted from having to clean up your messes when they could've been avoided in the first place. There was no reason, besides your own ignorance, why you couldn't pick up on Angelus' energy. For Heaven's sake, I picked up on it before you did!"

Raziel hated to admit that there was some truth to what Natalia was saying, and her entire community was dead because she was so blinded by Angelus. She felt like she was completely insane by the time she gave her family their final drink. When Raziel thought back to placing her hands on the juice containers, she felt sick to her stomach. She still didn't understand why the only thing that crossed her mind was the word *death*.

"Raziel, snap out of it! It's done and over with. No one is going to come looking for them or for you."

"Natalia, I feel awful. It could have been avoided. I know it could've been. I don't really understand or know where my head was. I don't even really understand how the drinks were filled with that intention."

Natalia sucked air through her teeth. "Have you and Angelus been intimate?"

Raziel looked at the floor, and Natalia stood up. "Right, so I'm assuming that is a yes. That is a power exchange; you allowed him to know the deepest parts of you and gave yourself over to him completely. He was able to put a—we'll call it a bug—in your system, and it began to drive you insane, whether you wanted to see it or not. Plummeting into the lake, the blood in the bath, the killer mob, all leading up to you killing your own followers. It may have been because of *him*, but you were most certainly at fault for not having more control over yourself."

Raziel bowed slightly, and Natalia continued, "I don't want to speak of this again, Sister. We have to get Azazel back in control of her own divinity so the two of you can transfer them over to me." Raziel tried to object, but Natalia held her hand up. "I will not argue about this; you clearly cannot handle it, and let's be honest, Azazel has *never* been able to control hers." Natalia walked over to the bed. "I promise that when I am in control, I will ensure that both of you are well taken care of and never wanted for anything, divine or mortal." Raziel felt defeated but knew that, maybe, it was the right thing to do until they could get a grip on themselves. Natalia sighed. "Honestly, you both are immortal beings and seem to lack the knowledge or control to act as such."

Raziel remained silent, and Natalia walked over to her and leaned forward. "You may be angry with me right now, Sister, but we cannot afford to alert more humans about our presence. They always find a way to kill the divine, and I will not allow that to happen to us." Raziel nodded, but Natalia pushed harder. "I want to hear you say that you will transfer your powers over to me when we reset Azazel." Raziel sighed, and Natalia grabbed her arm, digging her nails deeper into her skin. "Sister, I *need* to hear you say it."

Raziel gasped, and she whispered, "Sister, I don't know. There might be some good to it, but that may be too much power for one of us."

Natalia dug her nails in even deeper. "Sister, I want you to say it."

Raziel looked up at her sister's eyes and saw how unhinged she looked at that moment.

Raziel quietly said, "I will transfer my powers to you once we get Azazel reset and healthy once more."

Natalia nodded and released Raziel's arm. "Good."

They heard a commotion coming from the bed and saw Azazel starting to struggle. Raziel stood up, and as they walked over to the bed, Azazel let out a high-pitched scream.

Natalia tapped her fingers on the edge of the bed. "It seems like you have been quite busy, Sister."

Azazel rolled her eyes and replied, "Big deal, they're just

humans. They breed like rats, and my kingdom shall be overpopulated once more in a few years."

Raziel was shocked by how her sisters talked about the humans. It was as if they never took the time to get to know them or find out how wonderful they could be.

15

Azazel had a crazed look in her eyes, and she looked from Natalia to Raziel and motioned to Raziel with her chin. "What'd you do?" Raziel groaned, and Azazel began to cackle. "You killed your followers."

Raziel and Natalia exchanged looks, and Raziel quietly said, "Unintentionally."

Azazel laughed. "You're going to go down in history as one of the worst cult leaders ever, Raziel."

The term made Raziel flinch. "I wouldn't call myself a cult leader."

Azazel radiated with smugness. "No kidding." She looked at Natalia, and she faked a pout. "Big bad Natalia, here to save the day once more."

Natalia exhaled loudly. "Azazel."

"Are you going to beg me to control myself again, Sister?"

Natalia shook her head. "No, the two of you are going to transfer your powers over to me, and I will regulate them, so we don't have to go through this process ever again."

Azazel scoffed and looked between them. "There is *no way* that I will *ever* transfer my powers over to *anyone*, and you're absolutely *insane* if you think there is."

Raziel walked over and sat on the bed next to Azazel. She quietly said, "I think it might be the best thing, Azazel. I think it's the only solution before the humans truly catch on to what's going on."

Azazel slowly looked at Raziel and spat at her. "You're a *pathetic* excuse for a divine being; you always have been!"

Natalia walked over, slapped Azazel across the face, and seethed. "If you would've been able to control your hunger, we wouldn't be here, and you wouldn't be facing a tremendous loss." Azazel gave Natalia a nasty glare. "Raziel killed an angel. Now it's only a matter of time before the divine cavalry is called to enact revenge, and frankly, the two of you are so unstable that if I allow either of you to continue with your powers, you will wipe out the entire human race."

Azazel started to laugh loudly. "Oh, Natalia, you say that like it's a bad thing! Look at everything we have witnessed; look at the death, destruction, the hatred! Sister, would it *really* be so bad if all the humans were wiped out?"

Natalia, Raziel, and Azazel all exchanged looks, and Raziel could see that Natalia was genuinely considering it.

Raziel coughed. "Natalia!"

Natalia looked at her and sighed. "Azazel, the repercussions."

Azazel shook her head and pulled at her binds; she was growing wilder by the second. "Think about it, Natalia. Think about how peaceful the world would be if the humans weren't around anymore. We would have so much fun taking them out one by one, or even by the thousands! Think about how much power we would have, and for how long it would satisfy us."

Natalia stared at her, and Raziel interrupted. "You can't be serious."

Natalia stood up straight. "That's enough!"

Azazel whined, "Come on, Natalia. You used to be fun."

Raziel glared at Azazel. "Enough."

Azazel sneered at her. "Oh, yes. The human lover. You don't get a say, Hippie."

Raziel rolled her eyes, and Natalia coughed. "Okay, we get the point."

Azazel pulled harder at her binds, her bed starting to creak.

Natalia shook her head. "Sister, your hunger brings out your ugliest ideas."

Azazel nodded. "Yes, but they make for interesting goals."

Natalia and Raziel exchanged looks, and Raziel firmly said, "Azazel!"

Natalia held her hand up. "Enough of the back and forth. You don't get to say no."

Natalia walked to the side of the bed and crawled up beside Azazel, who was starting to struggle aggressively, and she began to scream, a panicked look on her face. Natalia looked at her in concern and said, "Azazel, you're never going to be without. You can't sleep for another one hundred years. I won't let it happen."

Azazel had so much hate in her voice as she replied, "I would rather sleep for a *thousand* years."

Natalia nodded and whispered, "Well, your punishment is having to watch your kingdom replenish slowly. By the time it's full once more, your hunger will be overwhelming. You will be in excruciating pain. I'll return, and we will hold the most wonderful feast."

Raziel stared at Natalia in disbelief. She stood up and started to walk toward the door.

Natalia called, "Don't go too far, Raziel! I need you next."

Raziel stopped and turned around. She saw how tender Natalia was being, and it caused her to feel anger and jealousy. She stormed back toward the bed and looked at the both of them, unsure of what to say next. Natalia whispered something to Azazel and placed her hand over top of her chest. Raziel watched as Natalia spoke the ancient language of the angels, and soon, Azazel began to glow, and her eyes turned white. The glowing began to intensify and rise from her body.

Natalia leaned forward and raised her hands. The radiant essence traveled into Natalia's hands, causing her to throw her head back as she began to chant faster. She reached out to Raziel and screamed, "Now!" Raziel grabbed her hand and felt her whole body vibrate.

When Raziel looked at their hands, they were glowing white, and she felt hot, and then everything turned dark. When she opened her eyes, Azazel and Natalia were having tea in the sitting area while Raziel had been placed onto the bed.

When Raziel sat up, it felt like she had fallen down a mountain. She heard, "Ah, finally!" Raziel looked over and saw Natalia's smiling face.

Raziel shook her head. "How long have I been out?"

Natalia quickly replied, "A while; you did beautifully, Sister. Your powers truly brought me to an enlightened state."

When Raziel got out of bed, her legs felt weak, and she leaned back onto the pillows. Azazel stood up and quickly came over. "Sister, let's get some food in you. It'll help."

Raziel looked at Azazel cautiously. "Are you feeling better?"

"Much."

When they reached the sitting area, Natalia had a plate of

food waiting for her, and after Raziel began eating, she felt better.

Natalia waited for a bit before she said, "I think it is safe to say that you will experience human needs. But you won't need to worry about anything. I will ensure that you both *always* have the nourishment that you need."

She smiled at Raziel, who had a mouth full of bread and butter. She nodded and asked, "How are you going to know? Are you going to be popping in randomly to see us while you have your own kingdom to run?"

Natalia shook her head. "No, I am so in tune with the both of you. I feel what each of you needs."

Raziel placed her plate beside her and looked Natalia in the eyes. She started thinking about one of the cookies at the far end of the table, refusing to look at them. Natalia smiled and leaned over to grab a cookie with lemon curd in the middle, the exact one that Raziel was craving. She took it from Natalia and began to greedily eat it.

Natalia grinned and said, "We are going to help Azazel clean up, and then we are going to return to Nirvana."

Raziel nodded and continued to eat off the plate, happily looking from Natalia to Azazel. After they had eaten their fill, they went to clean up the Great Hall.

It took them several months to get the chamber taken apart, clean up the Great Hall, and start to replace the humans in Azazel's care. By the time they were comfortable leaving Azazel's kingdom, a year had passed, and Raziel felt light-hearted and comfortable leaving Azazel.

Over the past year, Azazel had been caring, kind, and a version of herself that Raziel hadn't seen since they were in servitude to Heaven. Raziel loved being able to reconnect with her sisters, and hoped that they would be able to continue down the path that they were starting to forge as they rebuilt Azazel's kingdom.

On the last day, they were all sitting in Azazel's room, and

Raziel noticed that the longer they sat there, the more Azazel's face fell... until Raziel couldn't ignore it any longer. She grabbed Azazel's hand and asked, "Sister, what's wrong?"

Azazel shyly replied, "I miss Mulligan. I truly feel awful for the way that I ended things for him."

Raziel looked at Natalia, and Natalia grinned. "I might be able to do something about that."

Azazel's face lit up. "Really?"

Natalia replied, "Perhaps. I don't want you to get your hopes up, but I do feel an excess of energy, and with all of our powers, I think I might be able to come up with a solution."

Azazel gripped Raziel's hand tighter. "Whatever you can do, Sister. I will be so grateful."

Natalia smiled at her sisters and got up to leave the room. Azazel watched her leave in confusion, and Raziel started to ask her questions about her new plans for the kingdom. Azazel excitedly explained the new gardens that she wanted to plant to honor the kingdom's fallen, and wanted the arena where she held The Cunning to be torn down. Raziel felt optimistic and hopeful that Azazel would be able to control herself, now that Natalia was sole the power source.

They talked about the type of flowers that Azazel was thinking of, but were soon interrupted by the door opening. Natalia walked through and had a triumphant look on her face.

She was completely in the room when she looked back and quietly said, "It's alright."

Suddenly, Mulligan walked through the door, much to Azazel's surprise, who jumped up and screamed, startling him. She rushed over and hugged him tightly. Raziel could hear her sobbing and sniffling from her place on the couch.

When Azazel pulled away from him, she desperately said, "I am so sorry, Mulligan."

He had a shocked expression on his face and looked at Natalia, who nodded encouragingly at him. He looked down at the ground and replied, "It's okay, Goddess. I understand."

Azazel's face turned dark as she insisted, "Mulligan! I want you to be angry with me. I deserve it. I slaughtered the entire kingdom. I want you to be *angry* with me!"

He looked up at her cautiously and shook his head. "There is no point in living with the anger, Goddess. I'd rather we just start over."

Azazel's face broke into a smile, and she hugged him again. "I would love that, Mulligan. Until we have a full kingdom and staff again, I want you to be at my side. I don't want you to lift a finger. We are going to do this together."

Raziel and Natalia exchanged looks, and Mulligan sighed. "I would love that."

Azazel nodded. "Good! Good. Now, you're to call me Azazel, and once we have a full staff again, you will assume your position of power, and I expect you to never lift a finger again in servitude."

Mulligan nodded and replied, "Thank you, Azazel."

The two hugged once more, and Raziel couldn't help but be touched by the interaction. She became hopeful that perhaps Natalia would be able to resurrect Ramona, and she looked forward to returning to Nirvana.

When Natalia and Raziel decided that it was time to leave, Azazel held onto them for a considerable amount of time before she let them go. Natalia grabbed Raziel's hand, and they walked through the barrier.

Once they got to the other side of it, they were in the overgrown clearing of Nirvana. Nature had started to take over the compound, the walls were beginning to grow moss, and the grass was up to their knees. The wildflowers were abundant, and fat bumblebees made their way from one flower to the next. Raziel looked around and felt empty.

Natalia gripped her hand and reassured her, "We are going to get it back to its glory."

Raziel shook her head. "I think it's beautiful."

"Yes, but it's inhabitable for the humans whom you want to take care of."

Raziel couldn't help but agree, and they spent another year returning Nirvana back to its prime. The gardens were overflowing with abundance, the grass was greener, and the wildflowers were free to grow as much as they wanted.

After they had cleaned up the cabins, Natalia looked around the compound and said, "This really is a beautiful place, Sister. I see why you love it so much."

"It's even better when it is full of laughter."

Natalia smiled at her. "Ninety-eight more years, Sister. It will fly by. I promise."

Raziel nodded. "Maybe, or it might drag on frightfully slow."

"What can I do for you, Sister?"

Raziel sighed and knew that the moment had come. "You brought Mulligan back for Azazel. I miss Ramona." She trailed off, and a sad look overcame Natalia.

"It was easier to bring Mulligan back because he was still so fresh, Sister. It has been years since Ramona was buried beneath the earth. It's impossible at this point."

Raziel shivered and felt the hot tears threatening to overflow her eyes.

Natalia softly said, "Perhaps you can use this time to reflect on how you want to change things. Maybe instead of trying to interfere with their free-thinking, listen to them."

Raziel grinned. It made sense, and she knew that her leadership skills would need to be evaluated. She looked at Natalia and said, "I like this version of you, Sister."

"I feel a lot better; your energy gave me a new sense of gratitude that I'd never felt before. I felt hollow before, almost empty." Natalia hugged her sister and whispered, "I'll see you soon."

Raziel watched her leave, and when she turned back to Nirvana, she felt hope for the first time in a long time.

16

Ninety-Eight Years Later…

aziel rushed to the gates. She heard the thunderous chatter on the other side of them and was more than ready to welcome her newest family members. As the gates opened, Raziel smoothed her hair and looked around to ensure that everything was perfect. The crowd poured in and circled around her, speaking out their affirmations of love and gratitude.

As everyone entered and stopped around her, waiting for her to speak, Raziel knew precisely where she wanted to start. She looked around at the new faces and loudly said, "Welcome, everyone. I am so glad that you have all found your way to Nirvana. May we all find peace, love, and true ascension." The group burst into applause, and Raziel continued, "Now, before we all get settled in, there are rules that we all must follow in order to keep Nirvana healthy. The first rule is that everyone must pull their weight. Whatever skills you have, we will find a position for you. The second is that this is a free-loving environment; monogamy, polyamory, or any kind of love is strongly encouraged." Murmurs traveled through the crowd, and Raziel smiled radiantly as she tried to make eye contact with everyone whom she possibly could.

Three years ago, she put out a rumor that the rainforest community was opening up. The old Nirvana had died, and with it, the negativity. Raziel had spent the last years growing and becoming the best version of herself. She had reached her highest level of ascension and was eager to put her newfound skills to use.

As she crossed the clearing, watching people go off into the cabins, she was approached by a small-framed man with shaggy brown hair and wild eyes. Raziel felt an odd feeling as he got closer, and he held his hand out and introduced himself as Charlie. Raziel smiled and asked him what he was looking for in Nirvana, to which he replied, "Inspiration."

"I think you will find plenty of that here."

Charlie bowed and held his hands up in prayer, thanking her.

As the days went on, more people came in from the outside world. Raziel felt excitement and spent her days happier than she had been in years. As people tried to get close to her, she had to keep them at arm's length. Raziel came to the conclusion that she couldn't let anyone into her inner sanctum. She needed to have boundaries, but also be approachable.

Raziel kept the gates open for a week to allow anyone who wanted to enter to come in. She was particularly taken by a man who was a talented Gospel speaker and went by the name of Jim. He didn't stay long, but while he was at Nirvana, he made a significant impact. And after his appearance, several people left with him.

Raziel was sad to see people leave so quickly, but she couldn't deny that he was persuasive and confident in his abilities. Charlie and a small group of girls left the compound about a year after the gates opened, and while Raziel was sad to see more of her followers leave, she was happy that the weird energy that both Charlie and Jim gave off went with them.

After some time, Nirvana fell into a comfortable routine. Everyone knew their place in the community, they respected each other and her as their leader, and for a while, Raziel forgot about her sisters and what had happened.

After a lust-filled full moon ritual, Raziel walked to her cabin and was surprised to see Natalia sitting on her bed. She gasped and ran to Natalia's open arms.

"Natalia! It's so nice to see you."

"Sister, Nirvana is thriving!"

Raziel nodded. "It's become everything I ever wanted." Natalia beamed, and Raziel saw how radiant she appeared, but she could sense that something was off. She asked, "What's going on?"

Natalia sighed. "I felt a shift last week. I wasn't sure if it was anything serious, but I felt it again today, intensely."

"Well, it's nothing you can't handle, right? You have all the powers you could ever need."

Natalia sighed again. "I haven't felt as connected to the powers in years, almost eighty years at this point."

"You went eighty years with mine and Azazel's powers dormant?"

Natalia nodded, and Raziel started to panic. She knew that the powers needed to be used consistently, or they could die out, and it would cause the user to divinely implode.

Natalia picked up on Raziel's thoughts, and she continued, "Which brings me to why I am here. I need to offload some of your powers back to you."

Raziel shook her head. "Sister, I can't. I am so scared of what could happen."

"Raziel, I know you can handle them. They are *your* powers. They were *made* for you, and you're the only one who can bring out their full potential if something goes wrong."

Raziel was quiet for a moment, and then she asked, "Have you seen Azazel yet?"

Natalia went silent, and tension formed between them.

Raziel cautiously asked, "What?"

Natalia cleared her throat. "Azazel's hunger has returned."

"What happened?!"

Natalia looked down. "Azazel killed Mulligan again."

"How is that possible?"

Natalia looked up and quietly answered, "I'm not sure, but she only lasted twenty years." Raziel was shocked. Natalia whispered, "I'm proud of you, Sister. Truly. Nirvana is beautiful, and you seem to be doing well."

She held out her hand. As Raziel touched her fingers, their hands began to glow. Raziel felt warm, and the emptiness inside of her was filled.

Raziel pulled her hand away, and Natalia said, "There is just one thing. You still won't be able to feel the love that you want so badly."

Raziel nodded. "I understand."

"I am going to hold on to Azazel's powers for a while longer. I have lulled her into a deep slumber and will awaken her when I deem her ready."

Raziel observed her feet, and Natalia said loudly, "Speak."

Raziel sighed. "I don't think she should *ever* get her

powers back, Sister. How many times do we need to go through this?"

Natalia's expression hardened. "Eventually, I will have to, correct?"

Raziel agreed and continued, "How many times do we have to paint over blood, tear down a torture chamber, and babysit her?"

Natalia said harshly, "I need to put her powers *somewhere*."

Raziel looked up. "I can host them until you are ready to wake her."

Natalia studied her face. "I will leave them with you tonight, if you are ready." Raziel had a look of surprise, and Natalia explained, "I don't know if what I felt was another angel, but if it was, you are the most exposed. I want you to be as protected as possible."

Raziel felt a wave of excitement wash over her, and she held her hand out to Natalia once more. When Natalia grabbed it, her fingers were ice cold, and it spread through Raziel's entire body. She shuddered, and finally, Natalia let go of her hand. Raziel felt electric; she shuddered, and Natalia had a serious look on her face.

"You will eventually feel her hunger. It is quite intoxicating and painful. You *must* resist it, Sister."

Raziel nodded. "How long are you going to keep her asleep?"

Natalia sighed. "Five hundred years."

Raziel couldn't believe what she was hearing. "That long?"

Natalia nodded. "She is a danger to everyone."

Raziel couldn't help but agree; Azazel *had* always been a liability.

Natalia exhaled. "I feel much better. I will come back to check on you soon. Keep a lookout for anything out of the ordinary."

Natalia quickly turned and melted into the shadows. Raziel felt delicious. A tingle went up her spine, she was covered in goosebumps, and she felt like she was buzzing. She walked over to her bed and threw herself onto it. It wasn't long before Raziel drifted off to sleep, where she dreamt of broken scenes, absorbing different human life essences. She went through countless humans before she got the wicked idea to drink from them, and the next humans she killed, she bit deep into their necks, drinking the warm, coppery blood that flowed freely from their bodies.

Raziel opened her eyes as the sun washed over her. She felt a deep hunger, thinking that she was just feeling the effects of the ritual from the night before and the power exchange with Natalia. She figured that her body finally caught up.

Raziel quickly got dressed and ran to the dining hall, where they were dishing out thick pancakes. She requested double servings, and they happily obliged. Raziel sat at the table closest to the door and began to tuck in, every bite satisfying her for a second before she became famished once more.

Once the hall cleared, Raziel walked up and asked for all of the leftovers to be brought to her table. The kitchen crew brought trays over one by one and set them down in front of her. Raziel began shoveling food into her mouth as if she hadn't eaten in months.

She emptied all the trays, and when she took the last bite, the hunger seemed to only deepen. Raziel tapped her fingers on the table and looked around. A sweet smell swept through the dining hall, and she got up to follow it.

When she got to the kitchen, she saw the staff baking cookies. They greeted her excitedly, and the chef, John, asked if she wanted to taste what they were making. She agreed and took an entire tray from them, causing the staff to exchange concerned looks. Raziel thanked them and carried the tray out the door.

She walked down to her cabin, and when she was behind the closed door, she shoved three cookies at once into her mouth until she finished the entire tray. Raziel looked at the tray until it went fuzzy. She didn't think she would feel Azazel's hunger so quickly; she didn't know how her sister had dealt with it for so long.

She called out, "Natalia!" Hoping that her sister would hear her, Raziel waited for several minutes, and when her sister didn't appear, she called out to her again.

Raziel felt like her stomach was going to rip itself apart. She screamed for her sister, and finally, heard the familiar *whooshing* sound.

Natalia asked, "Already?"

Raziel nodded. Natalia sighed and looked out the window. "Sister, which member irritates you the most?"

Raziel shook her head. "None of them. I love them all."

Natalia smirked. "Impossible! Humans can be so irritating. It's okay to sacrifice one. It's not the same level that Azazel did; it's one. I will condone it."

Raziel groaned. "Pick one of the men."

Natalia sneered. "Sister, I like your choice."

Natalia left the cabin and returned a short while later with one of the cabin builders. Raziel knew that he agitated most people in the compound; he was smug and slightly ignorant. He wouldn't be missed in the grand scheme of things.

When he was brought in, Raziel tilted her head in interest, and without looking away from him, she said, "Leave us."

Natalia bowed and backed out of the cabin. Raziel smirked at him and asked, "Your name is Kurtis, right?" He nodded, and she took a step closer to him. "Have you been enjoying your time here in Nirvana, Kurtis?"

She cooed his name, and he smiled wide. "Yeah, it's been super awesome, but I've been told that I make it better."

Raziel scoffed. "Ah, there it is."

Kurtis looked confused, and before he could object, Raziel placed her hands on his chest, pushing him to the ground; he was shocked by her strength. Raziel crawled on top of him, her hands beginning to glow. She watched as a tiny glowing faint ball came up between Kurtis' lips. She leaned down and inhaled the ball, her entire body feeling replenished, and her hunger subsided ever so slightly. Kurtis' body began to wither beneath her, his cheeks sunken in, his eyes became dark sockets, and his bones began to protrude from his skin.

Natalia opened the door and looked at the corpse beneath Raziel, and asked, "Feel better?"

Raziel looked up and said, "One more."

Natalia nodded and repeated, "One more."

Raziel turned her attention back to Kurtis. She knew he would make beautiful compost and would bury him later. She stood up and walked over to her bed. Flashes of her dream from the previous night popped into her head, and a wicked grin came across her face as the door opened to another builder.

The first thing he did was look at Kurtis on the floor. He viciously shook his head and yelled, "No!" as Raziel rushed toward him, and Natalia pulled the door shut behind him.

Raziel was feral. She grabbed him by the throat and started to dig her nails in until they began to draw blood. Her mouth watered, and she whispered, "Now, now, builder. That's enough out of you."

Raziel threw him onto the floor, and he tried to claw himself away, but Raziel pulled his legs, flipped him over, and sat on his chest. She placed both hands on his chest. "Now, you're going to cooperate, or I promise I will make it as painful as possible for you."

The builder nodded, and as Raziel leaned down to lick the blood off of his neck, he groaned in pain. He tasted sweet, and she couldn't help what happened next. Raziel bit into his neck, causing him to cry out. She bit in deeper as his blood flowed out around her mouth. Raziel saw the faint glow out of the corner of her eye. She felt the blood rush out of her mouth as she sat up to absorb the glow. She bent down and surrounded her mouth around the orb, and similar to what happened to Kurtis, the man withered away to nothing.

Natalia came back into the cabin, and Raziel smiled at her. "I'm full."

Natalia nodded and asked, "What are we going to do with them?"

Raziel wiped her mouth with her arm. "Rose garden."

Natalia scoffed. "You're so predictable."

This caused Raziel to shrug. "Maybe, but my flowers always look the best when they are being nourished by humans."

They picked up the corpses and walked out the back of the cabin, dropped them onto the ground, and began to separate one of the most enormous rose bushes.

Once they had dug a big enough hole, they pushed the two bodies in and placed the flowers over top of them. When the bodies were covered up, Natalia looked around the garden and whispered, "They really *are* immaculate, Sister." Raziel nodded. They locked eyes, and a concerned Natalia asked, "Are you going to be okay if I leave?"

Raziel paused. "I think so. I didn't think it would overtake me so quickly." Natalia agreed, and Raziel continued, "I think I will be satisfied for some time now."

Natalia replied, "I hope so. I can't authorize you to kill any more humans. You're trying to rebrand Nirvana."

Raziel sighed; she still had to think of a story to tell the rest of the commune when they realized that Kurtis and the other man were missing. Raziel's eyes went wide as she remembered that she didn't even get to know the other man's name.

She groaned. "Natalia, that was awful. I wasn't... divine; I was some horrific monster."

Natalia smiled and replied, "It's such a wicked thing, isn't it?" Raziel nodded, and Natalia added, "But the rush?"

Raziel looked up at her quickly. "It's something I have never experienced before."

"It makes sense why Azazel was willing to risk her entire kingdom for the feeling." Natalia pointed at Raziel. "You need to fight it longer, figure out how to hone it until it is transferred back to Azazel. No more deaths, Raziel. I mean it."

Raziel's face fell into a pout as she whispered, "Fine."

As Natalia walked past her, she asked, "Have you noticed anything?"

Raziel shook her head. "Nothing besides my new feelings."

"Keep your eyes open."

Raziel gripped her sister's hand and squeezed it. "Thank you for helping me."

Natalia smiled and pulled her hand away as she walked back into the smallest shadows of the cabin. Raziel waited until the coast was clear and walked through her cabin. As she caught a glimpse of herself in the mirror, she saw that she was still covered in blood. It set something primal off in her brain. Raziel walked out the front door and up to the dining hall, requesting that the kitchen staff make a large batch of jungle juice.

The kitchen staff rushed to her, asking if she was okay. In a monotone voice, Raziel told them she had just injured herself doing some gardening but was alright. She told them in a commanding tone to make the juice quickly.

When she walked out of the dining hall, Raziel walked over and rang the bell to signal a community meeting. People started to fill out the space in front of her. Raziel held her arms up and loudly said, "Everyone, circle around me. Don't be shy. Get close."

The members all stepped close to her, and the kitchen staff brought out a large pitcher of jungle juice. Raziel smirked and loudly said, "Would you be able to find me a chalice in the kitchen?"

One of the women ran back and returned a second later with a large silver chalice. She handed it over to Raziel, along with the jungle juice pitcher. Raziel poured some of the juice into the chalice, and as the liquid flowed into the cup, she thought about absorbing the other members and how good it would feel.

She then noticed that the liquid turned a bright yellow before returning to the usual dark color that it initially was. Raziel lifted the cup above her head and yelled, "Brothers! Sisters! We are on the verge of making history. I have decided that I want you all to be ingrained into Nirvana's very essence for the rest of time."

There were murmurs of appreciation throughout the crowd. Raziel welcomed them all to begin to drink from the cup. As each person sipped, Raziel made sure to whisper words of encouragement to each and every member. With each person who passed, Raziel grew colder, *hungrier*. As the last family member took a sip, the first few started to foam at the mouth. One by one, they all began to drop to the ground, and eventually, the glowing orbs raised from their mouths, and Raziel held her hands open and summoned them into her.

Raziel felt powerful, and she smirked as the last few orbs made their way into her. She stepped over the bodies, leaving them there to fertilize the ground. She went back to her cabin and washed the blood from her face and neck, then braided her hair into a thick braid that draped over her shoulder.

She then left her cabin and calmly walked over the bodies toward the gates of Nirvana. The gates opened, and the only thing that Raziel wanted was to go into the city. She coolly walked the path through the forest; the animals were quiet, and the breeze had stopped entirely. As she approached the city, Raziel was overwhelmed with *hunger*. She continued to walk into the city, soon realizing that the streets were bare. Raziel was starting to feel a sense of desperation without any humans in sight.

She stopped in front of a building that had hundreds of windows. She walked inside and saw a woman behind a desk. Raziel smirked as the woman welcomed her and said that she was at one of the city's hotels. Raziel didn't catch the name of the hotel. She was too focused on the sound of blood flowing through the woman's arteries. It made Raziel's mouth water, and she felt the hunger starting to take over her entire body once more.

She asked the woman to grab a map of the city. As the woman turned around, Raziel jumped over the desk, dragging the woman to the ground. When Raziel bit into her, she started to cough and retch in disgust.

Raziel backed away from the woman and screamed, "What's wrong with you?!"

The woman whimpered, "I'm sick."

Raziel spat at her and roared, "You are vile!"

She went over and snapped the woman's neck. When the orb flew out of her mouth, Raziel allowed it to float up into the air until it disappeared. She got up and left the hotel, and she started to run down the street.

Raziel felt like a wild animal on the hunt. Her latest victim wasn't worthy of being absorbed, and she *hated* it. Her ears began to ring, causing her to stop, and she looked around. There was no one around her, but she felt like she wasn't alone. Raziel continued walking down the street and smelled the sweet scent of baked goods.

She followed it until she came to a small bakery. The shop was filled with several bakers and customers, and Raziel felt herself salivating. When she walked in, she locked the door behind her, bringing attention to herself.

Raziel held her hands up and calmly said, "You are all so lucky that I am here to relieve you of your humanity."

The humans all exchanged looks, and a woman with a piece of cake in her hands chuckled, "I don't know what you've been smoking, but you've got to give me the number!"

Raziel stared at her and sneered. "You're first."

She walked over to the woman and grabbed her by the neck. The sheer force of her grip crushed the woman's throat, and the glowing orb instantly flew out of her mouth. Raziel inhaled it, and it caused the other people inside the bakery to panic.

Raziel looked around and loudly stated, "There is no need for fear. Come to me, my children. You shall be blessed for all of eternity." The humans began to cry as they cowered in the corner. Raziel walked over to them and said, "Be not afraid. You're going to be a part of history, of something so much bigger than you could ever begin to imagine. Die with dignity, and I will ensure that you'll never be forgotten." She stared at all of them and motioned. "Who's next?"

A large man stood up and lifted his head slightly. Raziel smirked and whispered, "Brother, welcome home." The man grabbed her hands, and Raziel said, "Please, lie down."

He did so, and she climbed on top of his chest. She absorbed him, followed by the others, until there was only a small pile of corpses left on the floor.

Raziel went through every single building in the city until she had absorbed every human. After the last, Raziel started to slowly walk back to Nirvana. She allowed her fingers to run through the fauna, and the sun was peeking through the trees, casting beams through the branches. It was beautiful. Raziel felt like she was on top of the world.

As she walked through the gates of Nirvana, she felt

comfortable and relieved to be home. Walking past the pile of her followers, Raziel smirked, knowing that they would be a part of her for the rest of eternity. When the lake came into view, she decided that a refreshing dip would be the *perfect* way to end her day.

She stripped down and slowly walked into the lake. The water was refreshing, and she felt tingles all over her body. Dipping her head under the surface of the water, Raziel had flashbacks of the absorptions that she had just completed, and her heart felt elated. She finally understood why Azazel was always angry and wanted to keep humans as livestock.

When she came back up, something felt off. She looked around and felt like something had changed; she felt like she was being watched. Raziel wiped her eyes and felt exposed all of a sudden. She slowly swam over to leave the lake. With every step she took, a feeling of dread became increasingly overwhelming, and she felt like her lungs were being squeezed. Raziel dropped to her knees, and as the water dripped off her body, it felt as if she were being licked by the hottest flames.

As quickly as the feelings started, they stopped, and Raziel glanced around. Nirvana was utterly empty. She stood up and walked toward her cabin. As she opened the door, a very disheveled Natalia was crawling across her floor. Raziel gasped and ran over to her.

Natalia looked up and weakly whispered, "They're here."

Raziel shook her head, not understanding.

Natalia gasped, "The high council. They found Azazel."

Raziel's eyes grew wide. The high council was the highest tier of angels in Heaven, and they doled out punishment and justice; they were right below the Creator himself.

A sense of nervousness overcame Raziel, and she desperately asked, "Natalia, what happened?" She helped her sister up onto the bed.

Natalia continued to tell Raziel that she had been at

Azazel's kingdom, checking on her. She had been in Azazel's bedroom when the doors flew open, and six white-robed angels came flying in. They tried to grab Natalia, but she had shrunk into the shadows as they circled Azazel's body.

"They are coming for us," Natalia warned.

Raziel paced in front of Natalia. She cursed under her breath and said, "Sister, if they come here—"

Natalia shook her head. "Not if. It's *when* they get here."

"Sister, I have done something."

Natalia tilted her head and quietly said, "Oh, Raziel. No."

Raziel nodded. "I couldn't help it, Natalia. The hunger was excruciating."

Natalia became livid, and when she tried to stand up, she felt weak and had to sit back down. She glared at Raziel. "How many?"

Raziel refused to look her in the eyes, and Natalia screamed, "Raziel! How many humans did you kill?"

Raziel looked up and said, "The entire commune, and the whole city."

Natalia whispered, "The entire city, Raziel?" She nodded, and Natalia gripped the bridge of her nose. "Raziel, how could you?"

Raziel became angry and hissed, "It is the *worst* pain that I have ever felt. I needed to satisfy it. I felt like it was going to destroy me."

Natalia seethed. "You speak as if I have never felt it, experienced it." Raziel stared at her. "I'm aware of how awful it is, Raziel. I'm aware, yet I didn't go on a massive killing spree because of it. Do you realize that because of you and Azazel not being able to control your basic primal needs, you have both alerted them to where we are?" Raziel remained silent, and Natalia screamed, "They are going to capture us, and we are going to be brought in front of the Creator. Judgment will be dished out, and we will have *nowhere* else to go."

As Natalia finished her sentence, the door of the cabin flew open, and six white-robed figures were standing in the doorway. Raziel stared in shock and screamed with such force that the windows in the cabin shattered.

Natalia faintly whispered, "Raziel, stop. We need to go."

Desperately, Raziel pleaded, "I need to get dressed first."

The angels stared at her, their eyes milky white, and they all opened their mouths at the same time. A deep voice sounded, "You have been summoned."

Raziel started to panic, and before she could say anything else or reach Natalia, they were transported to an all-black circular room with the six angels surrounding them, sitting on oversized chairs that towered over Raziel, Azazel, and Natalia. When Raziel tried to speak, nothing came out. She patted her throat and tried to scream, but again, silence.

Azazel had been brought out of her slumber and was starting to fully become aware once more. When she tried to speak, it came out as raspy squeaks. Natalia was the only one who was focused and staring forward.

The high council opened their mouths and said as one, "The fallen have been accused of using mankind as their personal food source. Millions of humans have been slaughtered, precious lives stolen, and they have done *nothing* but be detrimental to the delicate mankind ecosystem."

Raziel and Azazel glanced at each other, and Raziel saw the fear in her eyes as the council continued, "The fallen shall be condemned to the lowest level of the pit. They will be bound for all of eternity, lose their ability to speak and their powers, and the being who houses the hunger shall only know starvation until she withers away to dust."

Raziel started to shake. The pit was in the darkest place of Heaven, and when prisoners were sent there, they were forgotten and perished in the cells. Once the sentence had been issued, Raziel was pulled out of the court, away from

Azazel and Natalia. Azazel was the only one who looked at Raziel as she was dragged away.

Raziel was brought to a room with a mattress on the floor, black walls, and no windows. She was to sit in darkness for all of eternity, to be forgotten, and eventually, die. Raziel slumped against the wall and fell to the floor. Her stomach started to grumble. She smirked as she thought of every absorption, every death, and every scream of desperation. Raziel finally agreed with Azazel wholeheartedly. Humans deserved it, and she would *never* feel remorse. Raziel was relieved that there was finally no pressure on her. Eventually, she could slip into the darkness and become nothing more than a legend.

The End

ABOUT THE AUTHOR

Viola Tempest is a dystopian fantasy and paranormal romance author who yearns to expose the truth of those in the modern world: the good, the bad, and the ugly. Her inspiration primarily stems from life experiences, those who annoy her, ex-boyfriends, and the crazy dreams that pop into her head every once in a while.